"*Muddled Cherries* is a love letter to the ephemeral yet trans-formative power of summer, a time ripe with exploration, discovery and ultimately, change. Through Emily's eyes, Collins deftly transports readers to the tourism industry of northern Wisconsin, where a summer job, new friendships, budding romances, and second chances unlock the door to Emily's autonomy, self-awareness, and sense of agency. This is coming-of-age at its finest."

—Amy Gail Hansen, author of *The Butterfly Sister*

"Author Sally Collins writes with wit and clarity, telling a coming-of-age story that is both important and entertaining in *Muddled Cherries*. . . . Collins writes with a sharp eye for de-tails and quick ear for realistic, amusing dialogue. . . . *Muddled Cherries* is a pleasure to read and a story to savor."

—IndieReader (4.6/5 rating)

"Reading *Muddled Cherries* brings back deep-rooted memo-ries of the heady, sun-soaked days of my early twenties, but Sally Collins's story goes far beyond a hot, sticky summer spent on the water. Her heroine, Emily Schmidt, is a complex young woman who must face the loss and trauma of her dif-ficult childhood. She will have readers cheering out loud as she finds her way toward wholeness, healing, and self-sufficiency."

—Laura Anne Bird, Wisconsin-based author of *Crossing the Pressure Line* and *Marvelous Jackson*

"Sally Collins captures the essence of coming of age, wrapping the pains and pleasures of youth in a fresh and compelling narrative in *Muddled Cherries*. . . . This novel not only charts a young woman's journey to independence but also explores the deep cuts of trauma and the healing that follows.

"*Muddled Cherries* is a poignant, uplifting tale of self-discovery and redemption. It's a must-read for those who appreciate stories that delve into the complexity of human emotions and the beautiful messiness of life's journey."

—Independent Book Review

"*Muddled Cherries* captures the confusion, self-doubt, fears, anger, and joys encountered along the tumultuous passage to self-agency. Sally Collins reminds us that although we each carry our past experiences and emotional baggage with us, the journey also provides the potential to learn, accept, and address them. *Muddled Cherries* is an insightful, fast-paced, debut novel by a perceptive and talented young writer."

—Dan Powers, author of *How Long a Shadow* and *Edenton*

"*Muddled Cherries* is a beautiful novel, more than a coming-of-age story, one of growing comfortable in your own skin, trying to find your way on this beautiful, often messy, journey that we call life. There is truth and hope within the writing that feels necessary in the times we are living in, with a relatable main character who is not without flaws and that both men and women will recognize within themselves. There are important themes that are revealed to us with the turn of each page, and for me, one of the most important is resilience."

—Chuck Murphree, author of the novels *Everything That Makes Us Feel* and *Somewhere Between the Trees and Clouds*

"A diverse group of friends and fractured families come alive in this debut novel that finds twenty-year-old Emily at a crossroads. As she grapples with her own traumatic past and uncertain future, she helps more than one friend do the same as they navigate complex issues such as alcoholism and sexism along with the age-old challenges of romance and shucking parental control. With the keen eye of the librarian and newspaper writer that she is, Sally Collins captures the significant details that put readers smack-dab in the middle of Door County bars, restaurants, and beaches right along with Emily. She also immerses them in other parts of Wisconsin with equal authenticity. The realistic scenes and dialogue in *Muddled Cherries* make readers feel like they're eavesdropping on the characters' most personal and intimate experiences. Collins shows what it's like to *be* Emily, from the sour taste in her dry mouth to her loneliness and conflicting emotions to the taut skin of her sunburned face. This can't-put-down book grabs readers from the first page and holds them captive to the last."

—Patricia Obermeier Neuman, coauthor of *The Val & Kit Mystery Series* and *Dressing Myself*

MUDDLED CHERRIES

SALLY COLLINS

Sally Collins

www.ten16press.com - Waukesha, WI

Muddled Cherries
Copyright © 2024 by Sally Collins
ISBN PB: 9781645387541
ISBN EBook: 9781645386636
First Edition

Muddled Cherries
by Sally Collins

For information, please contact:

www.ten16press.com
Waukesha, WI

Editor: Shannon Booth
Cover Designer: Kaeley Dunteman

TO GRETA

when we are loved we are afraid
love will vanish
when we are alone we are afraid
love will never return
and when we speak we are afraid
our words will not be heard
nor welcomed
but when we are silent
we are still afraid

From "A Litany for Survival"
by Audre Lorde

CHAPTER ONE
- MAY 2009 -

Emily grips a tattered rag, wiping the chipped walnut bar long worn of varnish. Dull burgundy stains the wood grain like a giant fingerprint. Twenty years' worth of Angostura aromatic bitters embedded in there, as old as her, spilled over the edge of countless old-fashioneds. They're never coming out. But she drags the damp cloth over them anyhow, with more vigor than usual. Anxiety riddles her bones and tickles her muscles.

She's prepped. The maraschino cherries and stuffed olives stocked. Her chipped nails smell like Lysol from the lemons, limes, and oranges she sliced. The citrusy scent might waft over the whole joint if not for the cigarette smoke exhaled by regulars seated at their usual stools, drinking their usual drinks. She'd open a window, but manure spreaders rumble back and forth on the farm fields surrounding The Honky Tonk. The digital clock with a faded PBR logo reads 3:47. In 43 minutes she can set out the cheddar cheese spread and salted crackers.

Until then, she listens and waits. She listens to Larry describe replacing the timing gears on his Harley, Doug whine about the Chippewa tribe spearing all the walleye, and Fred gripe about the money lost on a garage full of Mary Kay products his wife struggles to sell. Tammy can't stop the damn squirrels and deer from eating up her birdseed, and Margaret can't believe her son's latest DUI wasn't a misunderstanding, the result of a defective breathalyzer.

Emily listens to Webb Pierce singing "There Stands the Glass" from the tinny jukebox speakers.

Her ears ache from listening. And her throat itches to confess, an itch she can't swallow away. It's a feeling somewhere between suppressing a giggle and stifling a cry. She's ready to blurt the news to the vintage posters of Ernest Tubb and Hank Williams grinning in crisp Western shirts on the wall. *Holy shit, you guys. I did it. It's happening.*

Gladys hunches over her Bombay and tonic with two limes. Donning her blue nursing scrubs, she rests a wrinkled cheek in her palm while swirling the skinny straw around clear bubbles. Her husband, Jack, presses a red button on the digital "for amusement only" slot machine.

Emily likes listening to Gladys. She works at St. Joe's and talks about feet purple and swollen from hearts unable to keep up, ovaries riddled with cysts, genital warts, and ingrown toenails. What it's like to clean the blood and saliva from a dog bite, the difficulty of inserting a catheter, the satisfaction that comes from draining an abscess. Emily longs to tell her what she's done: submitted transcripts, secured reference letters, filled out forms, and handed over a big fat check to cover the first semester of tuition. She's going to start classes at Westwood Technical College in the fall. She's going to be a nurse as well.

"God dammit," Jack mutters, gripping the bill of his Packers baseball cap. He feeds another five-dollar bill into the machine.

Emily picks a maraschino cherry from the pile out of habit or boredom and pops it in her mouth. The burst of sweetness so familiar there's hardly a taste anymore. The corner TV blinks and flashes. The Lakers beat the Nuggets by two points. Dust floats in the air and layers a row of antique whiskey bottles lined on a high shelf like dirty snow. Emily sings along to Webb with that slight twang, the ire of her choir teacher: "You're not even from the South!" She can't help it. It's what she grew up with.

While she waits, she hopes. She hopes tonight's shift zips by in that meditative rush that clears her brain. Something happens when she scribbles orders for cheese curds, gabs and gossips with folks she's known her whole life while balancing the plastic baskets of bread-battered cod and walleye shimmering and sizzling with hot grease in the crooks of her elbows, the wad of cash in her apron growing thicker as the night wears on. But that hasn't happened in a while.

Webb Pierce fades. The regulars talk about the weather— spring wobbling up after the long winter like a newborn calf. They talk about Brett Favre officially retiring from the

NFL after a season with the Jets and the Brewers' 2-2 game series against the Diamondbacks. Emily continues wiping, listening, waiting.

Dad is upstairs, likely sorting through the mail, bills, invoices, accounts, spreadsheets—whatever he does. He intends to teach her once they climb over this "financial hump," as he calls it. But numbers and money were never her thing. C in algebra, C- in accounting. He intends to pass The Honky Tonk on to her "and whoever's desperate enough to marry you," he often jokes.

But she's waiting for the right moment to admit that her aspirations of becoming a nurse weren't a fleeting dream brought on by too many episodes of *ER*, *Scrubs*, and *Grey's Anatomy* like he said it was. She's waiting to break her promise.

Emily swept her tassel from right to left at high school graduation with every intention to stay at The Honky Tonk, her future secure, her destiny predetermined, like a royal, most of the farm kids, or her classmate Jared, a third-generation plumber. But once that first post-high school summer faded to fall, her friends and classmates scattered like grain in the wind. She hadn't realized so much could change so fast.

She joined Facebook at the L.E. Phillips Memorial Library, accepted and requested friends, scrolled through picture after picture of their arms draped around strangers. Beer pong and bonfires and concerts and apple-picking at the orchard mere miles from The Honky Tonk, and she wasn't invited. Hardly anyone asked her to supply them at-cost Goldschläger or Jägermeister anymore. Loneliness bit her like a mosquito, again and again and again. Left behind. Abandoned. Forgotten.

Maybe that's the moment she realized she didn't want to stay, or didn't have to stay—tears sliding down her cheeks at the library while the fifty-something man beside her watched a grainy video of two big-breasted blondes tonguing. Or maybe it's when she ran into Mr. Anderson, her old high school basketball coach, at Walmart a few months ago. "It's never too late. I'll write you a recommendation letter anytime," he said. "I hate to see you waste your potential." She thanked him and went on with her day. But the remark left her defensive, angry. There's nothing wrong with working behind a bar, making people happy. The Honky Tonk's home, family.

The anger dissolved, but she couldn't get that voice out of her head. Maybe the moment came with Todd in that post-sex haze of honesty. Something about lying horizontal, side by side, and naked throws off the equilibrium. Things spill like a tipped beer bottle.

"I was thinking maybe I wanted to try something else. Be a nurse? I don't know," she said every sentence like a question.

"Yeah," Todd said, yawning. "You don't want to be at The Honky Tonk your whole life, end up like your dad."

She cautiously mentioned the idea to Dad. "I'll be mad at myself if I don't at least try something else." Live on her own. Cut down on hours. The Honky Tonk would always be a part of her life. No matter what.

Dad shook his head. "Don't you do this to me right now. The Honky Tonk needs you more than all the obese diabetics around here. I need you. You're all I got."

But she hardly had anyone. Her best friend, Ashley, moved to Madison to pursue an art education degree and took longer and longer to return calls. And Todd, her non-boyfriend, boyfriend situation left her confused and wanting.

"Join a bowling league or something," Dad suggested. "Make some more friends, and you'll be fine."

But one morning she found herself walking through the doors of Westwood Technical College like her feet had a mind of their own. The woman behind the counter gave her an enthusiastic smile, brochures, a to-do list. Emily checked the items off, one by one, step by step. The last item on her to-do list: tell Dad.

He shuffles behind the bar with invoices in one hand, a sweaty tumbler clinking with ice tinted brown from whiskey and Coke in the other. A slight paunch protrudes from his lean, bony frame. His face is puffy and deflated all at once, like a party balloon days after the party.

"That stupid interstate," he mutters, gesturing out the window, beyond the gravel parking lot, an unkempt baseball diamond, and sparse line of maple trees, to the far away flashes of cars, trucks, and semis whizzing by. For a few years now, Interstate 29 has rerouted the locals and potential customers from the doorstep of The Honky Tonk to a rest stop complete with a McDonald's, Country Kitchen, and Kwik Trip just six miles east.

"This year is shaping up to be a doozy, I tell ya." He pours Maker's Mark in his glass. "Recession. Hussein what's-his-name in the White House."

"Now he's pulling troops out of Iraq, did you hear?" says Fred, slapping a meaty hand on the bar for emphasis. "Bring 'em home, then, no, 'Let's put more in Afghanistan,' he decides. A real mess."

"Don't start, guys," Emily says. But they don't listen. They go on.

She doesn't know much about money, the war, or Barack Obama other than she'd guess he's a better tipper than George W. Bush and John McCain. But she knows too well how worked-up patrons get when they talk about things they can't control. Dad will get worked up when she tells him her plan. She feels like she's tiptoeing around a motion-activated bomb, waiting for the moment she can break into song and dance without losing a limb, but that doesn't seem to be coming anytime soon. She retreats to the kitchen.

Bernie, the only other employee of The Honky Tonk, portions tartar sauce in four-ounce cups. Emily snacks on a packet of oyster crackers and pulls her flip phone from her back pocket. Still no reply from Todd. She rereads the text she sent hours ago: "Hey! Want me over tonite? I can bring walleye. Yum." Breezy. Sweet. He's probably busy in the barn.

"How is your summer looking, Em?" Bernie's tattooed arm flexes as he pours the goopy cream riddled with relish.

"Oh, not sure," she answers and tucks the phone away. "Ashley will be up this weekend, so that'll be nice. And her brother, Ryan. Finally back."

"He's back? Real good. Hope he wasn't in the worst, ya know. My cousin over there in Rice Lake, well, 'Nam was pretty ugly for him, and he didn't never get back to himself."

"Oh, jeez. Yeah, I don't know," says Emily.

She doesn't know much of anyone anymore. And they don't know much of her.

To distract the patrons from Fred and Dad's ongoing political tirade, Emily opens the till with a bang and slides quarters from the change drawer.

"Pick a few songs," she says, dividing the quarters between them.

"Goodie! Thanks, hon." Larry winks and Tammy hands him her quarters. "B19 and G5." Doug drops the dull metal coins from one palm to the other, waiting his turn.

"You need some real live music in here," says Gladys. A sore subject between Emily and Dad. This does nothing to help her case. Because there's no one lined up, and he won't let Emily book bands after the last time.

A few high school friends called themselves Erik Jones and the Rebels. She arranged for them to play their first official gig at The Honky Tonk. But after Erik cracked and screeched his way through three Journey covers, Dad unplugged their amps and told Emily she wasn't booking a band again. Humiliating. They sounded good at Carrie Ludwig's party. Maybe she was drunk. Regardless, there weren't many options that suited Dad. Bands either disbanded, grew too expensive, or had a falling out with him.

"That stage has been empty too long," says Gladys. Emily wishes she'd go back to talking about dislocated bones and burst appendixes. Dad adds more whiskey to his glass.

"Baseball league starts up soon," Emily says to change the subject. Doug presses in his jukebox selections.

"Make those cheap bastards pay for their own music," Dad says before climbing back up the creaky steps. She wipes the rings of condensation he left behind.

A claustrophobia coils tightly around her, tighter and tighter, like the pine snake she and Dad once witnessed constricting a mouse. They used to take hikes together. They used to go on snowmobile and motorcycle rides. On random weekdays, they'd keep the "Closed" sign up and ride through the surrounding countryside. She would lean against the backrest, humming and singing to herself, taking in the scenery. Sometimes she relaxed against the curve of Dad's back and wrapped her arms around his torso, pressing her fingertips against the thick leather of his jacket, the fraying thread on his patches, her helmeted head bobbing and knocking between his shoulder blades.

They ate at roadside taverns and talked to patrons. "Research," Dad called it. They compared menus and beer selections, played cribbage and bar dice. Dad asked around until they found live music that made him smile and softly stomp his worn black boots.

Every summer they'd spend a day or two zipping north across the woodlands and sprouting farm fields to see the cargo ships pass between Superior and Duluth or journey south to ride between the towering beige-brown bluffs and wide Mississippi River. Then there was the epic two-week ride to South Dakota, a real family vacation. They saw a palace made entirely of corn, a mountain carved with the faces of long-gone presidents, Sturgis and Deadwood, motorcycle museums, the chair where Bill Hickok was shot, mammoth bones, and the jagged striped rocks of the Badlands.

Their next planned venture was to Nashville for Emily's twenty-first birthday. They would fly commercial. Visit the Grand Ole Opry, the Country Music Hall of Fame and Museum, stop by as many honky-tonk bars as they could before borrowing a motorcycle from an old friend of Dad's and riding to the Smoky Mountains. Emily turns twenty-one in a few months. They haven't talked about that trip in a while.

He's changed. Or maybe she's changed? Either way, she aches with guilt standing behind the bar, listening, dreaming of something other than the life he planned for her. Tammy and Margaret compare potato salad recipes. Fred complains about the freeloaders living off his taxes. Larry analyzes the Brewers' chances of winning the World

Series this season. They don't realize how much she doesn't want to listen anymore.

But The Honky Tonk is home. Family. She remembers navigating between the regulars' vehicles from the school bus, dropping her backpack to the welcome of five or six half-drunk adults. She set up games of Duck, Duck, Gray Duck, marching down the scuffed wooden floor littered with hardened dirt and manure, patting the patrons square on the back—usually Gladys and Jack, Larry and Doug, Steve before he died of a heart attack, and Bert before he went to jail for cooking meth in his basement.

"Gray duck!" she would squeal and race around the eight dining tables, pop up on an empty bar stool, and go again. Tina, an old girlfriend of Dad's, set up games of musical chairs. With a wild tangle of bleached hair and fire-red lipstick, she held the volume dial of the jukebox between her press-on fingernails while grown men with cigarettes dangling from their lips would feign slowness, so Emily won. Tina didn't last long, or Sherry, or Barb, or Lori.

The slam of the screen door stops her memories there and jolts her whole body like a seizure. She drops the rag. "Shit." Sunshine silhouettes a figure like a beaming spotlight, someone who doesn't patronize the place often; regulars know to shut the screen door slowly.

"I'd like some alcohol."

Emily giggles, intrigued, as the figure approaches the bar and comes into focus. He's tall, scrawny, in his early twenties, with brown wispy curls he shakes from his eyes.

"Well, have a seat," says Larry.

"You came to the right place," adds Doug.

Emily doesn't recognize him.

"Hello," he says, scooting his stool toward the bar. "Hello. Hello." He nods to Doug and Larry. Emily sets down a cocktail napkin.

"Can you be more specific?" she asks.

The newcomer takes in the scene, anxiously bobbing his clean-shaven, freckled face with an open-mouth smile like he's stepped into a foreign country. He studies the taps lined up like soldiers in formation, the rainbow of liquor bottles reflecting against the mirrored back of the bar.

"I don't even know where to begin," he laughs. "Jeez. Overwhelmed. Help me out."

"Well, it's Friday, and usually folks have an old-fashioned on Fridays, but it's not five o'clock yet, so I don't know if you'd rather start with a beer?"

"I've never had an old-fashioned."

"Never?" asks Emily.

"Sacrilegious," mutters Fred.

"I'm not proud of it. So yeah, that, please."

"Good choice," says Doug. "She makes the damn best old-fashioned you've ever had."

"Not true," she responds, blushing. She drops cherries and an orange slice in a glass. "I think ginger ale is good, instead of sweet, sour, or press, but it's up to you." She adds a sugar cube and a couple dashes of bitters. She muddles.

"I have no idea what you just said. So, the ginger ale." He unzips his Packers hoodie and pulls a wallet from his back pocket. "Want to see my ID?" He unsheathes the plastic from the creased leather before she can answer. She leans over. He smells like spring and Old Spice and fresh laundry.

"Umm," she struggles to find the birthday, catching his name and address instead.

"I'm twenty-two," he says. "Just graduated."

"Congratulations," Larry says, raising his pint. "You know what, make me one too, sweetie."

"Thank you, sir."

Emily retrieves another tumbler. "Jacob Larson from Prescott. Where's that?"

"By the mighty Mississippi. And you are?"

"Emily."

Jacob offers a hand across the bar. He grips her hand quickly and firmly. His eyes are brown, like coffee with cream. He's cute with the potential to be handsome, like George Clooney.

She worries she looks like a country bumpkin with her French-braided pigtails and smells like a deep-fried manure cigarette. She wishes she had chosen a Honky Tonk t-shirt with fewer grease stains.

"This is a real nice place. Real welcoming."

Emily can't help smiling as she pours the brandy and ginger ale, stabs a couple of cherries, and sets them on the cracking ice. She perches an orange slice on each rim, adds the straws, and slides the cocktails over.

Jacob takes his in hand, still glancing around. "I like all this," he says, studying the vintage concert posters of Lefty Frizzell, Kitty Wells, and Merle Haggard that Dad collected over the years.

He takes a drink. "Yeah, that's good." He lifts the glass and winks at Emily.

"Prescott is a nice area," says Larry. "Great for a motorcycle ride."

"Real pretty," answers Jacob. "Big bluffs and rivers, of course, and the eagles." He focuses on the small stage at the end of the dining room. "You guys have bands here too?"

"Not much anymore," Emily admits, sorry to disappoint him, relieved of Dad's absence.

"Oh, bummer. Bet that'd be a cool stage to play on."

"You play?" asks Emily.

"A bit of guitar, not the best, but I played for a group in college, for bands here and there. You own this place?"

She's weighing how to respond—no, technically not, but yes, Dad has called her his business partner since she was eight years old and wants her to take over one day. *He's going to be so pissed.*

"My dad does," she goes with.

"Nice. My family owns a small grocery store. Not nearly as cool. My brother's taking over. This place seems way more interesting than the IGA."

"I'm sure the IGA is great," she says. A brightly lit grocery store with neat rows of produce and cereal boxes and employees in clean shirts. She thinks of how nice and ordinary Jacob's family must be. How fortunate to have siblings who wish to take on the family business.

"It's okay," he says. "But, like, this is so sweet. You got a stage. You've played on the stage, haven't you? You've totally been up there."

"Maybe a time or two. When I was little," she admits shyly. She's studying his freckled forearms and cheeks, a nose too big for his face, like he's not done growing. He's so unabashedly light, like a bird flying through the sky for the first time and finding everything—even The Honky Tonk—beautiful. His reaction to the place compounds the guilt she feels for wanting to leave. No. Not leave. Take a break. Try something new.

"Let's do a shot," says Larry.

"No, sir. No, thank you." Jacob raises a hand. "I still got a drive ahead of me."

"Where you going?" asks Emily.

"Door County. The thumb." He holds up his hand.

"Good fishing there," says Doug.

"Lots of little touristy towns, right? I hear it's cute," says Emily. "Never been."

"I'm gonna be a kayak guide," Jacob tells them. He's going to lead tourists along the caves of Lake Michigan and hopefully make enough money to spend the winter in New Zealand. "That's the dream," he says. "And figure out what I'm supposed to do with my life."

Emily wishes Dad was present to hear that. "Sounds so great," she says.

She wants to know more, but Doug interrupts for a refill and a round of bar dice. They introduce Jacob to the game and recommend the fish. He orders walleye. He meanders to the jukebox when a few more customers walk in, and Emily retrieves menus, trying to hurry the pleasantries so she can return to him. He flips through the artists: Porter Wagoner, Dave Dudley, George Jones, Loretta Lynn. Emily opens the register and slides out a couple of quarters.

"Here you go." She offers the coins, ignoring Dad's earlier demand.

"Oh, wow. Thank you. I'm ashamed to admit I hardly recognize any of these guys. But I like their sparkly Western shirts."

"Very sparkly cowboys." She laughs.

"What's your favorite? I want to hear your favorite."

She presses F12 without hesitation. He smiles at her, and she smiles back as the familiar, friendly tune embraces her. It starts out with a piano ditty, some fiddle, and then Charline Arthur's brassy voice. She still likes listening to this song. "I'm Having a Party All by Myself."

"You've heard this one?"

"No, not this one," he admits. He sucks thoughtfully on his straw. "I like it."

"Yeah, she's great, isn't she?"

"It's so cool you grew up on this stuff. So cool. Like, I don't know who this lady is."

"What'd you grow up listening to?"

"Contemporary music, I guess. Easy listening. Pretty sheltered, not like you."

Living her whole life in this bar and still here, she's the sheltered one.

"Will you go back to Prescott?" she asks.

"It's a nice area, but time to see what else is out there, you know."

Emily bites her lower lip. She does know. And she's bursting. The secret at the edge of her lips.

"What?" he asks, with a playful smile, taking in her expression.

"You can't tell my dad this," she says. "Pinky promise right now." They link pinkies.

"I'm starting school this fall. I want to be a nurse."

"Heck, yeah," he says. "Good for you. What made you want to be a nurse?"

She tells him. She tells him about the shows that gave her goosebumps. She tells him about her fascination with the human body—its resilience and fragility, all it can endure, and all that can go wrong. "I can sit there and stare at my foot or elbow, you know, and be like, 'whoa.' It's amazing, everything that's happening in there." He nods along. He's listening. "And I want to help people." She begins to describe that nurse, the one who held her hand, but patrons at the bar crane their necks and jingle ice cubes in empty glasses like a call bell. She didn't notice the Bronson family arrive.

"Oh, shit. Sorry," she says to him. "Pick another song. Your walleye's probably getting cold."

She refills pints and tumblers while Jacob eats his fish. She takes food orders and grins her way through small talk, aware of Jacob's presence.

The sunlight filtering through the dusty windows transitions from hazy white to soft orange as Jacob and Emily continue talking in bits and pieces. Nothing deep. Nothing personal. They talk about cricket and rugby, popular sports in New Zealand. They talk about the best strategy to break in tennis shoes. They talk about unlikely animal friends, including a giraffe and an ostrich, an elephant and a sheep, something Emily saw on the feel-good portion of the news. An invisible string, like a spider's thread, keeps pulling her back between serving the other customers. But tables fill. The fryer overflows with fish and French fries. Dad's slow to take his post behind the bar, even after she tapped the wall with a fist, her signal for help.

Finally, Jacob says with a half-hearted smile, "You're busy. And I better get on my way."

She doesn't disagree, but her chest tightens. She doesn't want him to leave. Being with him feels cozy and light, like slipping on a spring coat, and she doesn't want to take it off.

Emily prints his check.

"This has been a great first stop for me. I'm glad I came here."

"Me too."

He leans in with a conspiratorial expression and whispers, "Good luck, you know. I'll stop by on my way back. Maybe we'll meet again?"

"Maybe," she says.

He opens his wallet. "But, hey, if things don't work out. If you ever need a change of scenery, there's plenty of jobs in Door County, lots of money to be made, and it's pretty epic."

Emily's contemplating how tempting that sounds when he hands her cash, their fingers brushing. But something thin and shiny and dollar-sized catches her eyes between the stack of bills.

"Some Things Are Better Than Money," she reads.

"Oh crap," he says.

Emily continues out loud. "Like your eternal salvation, that was bought and paid for by Jesus going to the cross."

"My mom," Jacob says. "My mom put those in there. We're—she's religious. Shoot. I'm sorry."

Now the kindness makes sense, the attention, the listening. He's trying to save her soul.

"So, am I like a bad person or a sinner 'cause I work at a bar?" Emily avoids his eyes. Her stomach roils with disappointment. Sweat crawls down her back like a wood tick.

"No, not at all. You got a garbage back there?"

She gestures to the plastic bin near her knees. He leans over the bar and tosses a small stack of pamphlets.

"Well, nice to meet you," she says curtly.

"Hey. I blew it there at the end." His brows furrow in apology. He reaches out a hand as if to touch her and shakes his head. "That's not who I am anymore."

"Yeah, well. Okay." She moves on to the other patrons and fills their empty glasses. But that string still tugs at her when the screen door slams shut, and Jacob disappears.

A text from Todd: "Walleye."

CHAPTER TWO

Emily showers after the meager dinner rush, scrubbing off the scent of cigarettes and fish, thinking about Jacob, his kindness, lightness, those damn pamphlets. She scrubs harder, thinking about God, Jesus, the Virgin Mary, and devils. These abstract images make her feel uneasy, exposed, judged.

She didn't realize growing up above The Honky Tonk was strange until a classmate told her in first grade. "I seen where you live. That's not a real house," Michael Berg said in the lunch line. "It's a bar. There's devils in there." Her chin quivered. She told Doris, the lunch lady, who told Mrs. Eagan, the first-grade teacher, who told the whole class that there are many kinds of homes.

Emily didn't go to church like most of her classmates. On Sunday mornings, she prepared yellow and green Jell-O shots for Packers games with Bernie, learning the stories of his blurry tattoos instead of stories about Jesus. Dad didn't believe in any of that crap. But his parents did and took Emily to their small Catholic parish when Dad used to drop her off for a week or two every summer. She felt anxious by the stained-glass figures lining the walls with sorrowful expressions, the priest's monotone humming, the hard pews like a rock pressing against her bony butt, the rows of candles burning blood red, and the statues everywhere— Jesus towering over them all in agony, front and center, half naked and nailed to a cross with a crown of thorns.

But she enjoyed watching Grandpa Carl go down the rows with that fishing net, collecting money like he owned the place, and she liked the hymns, listening to Grandma Bev's strong, husky voice like Tammy Wynette. She could pull off "Stand by Your Man" no problem. But Emily left each service in a haze of fear and confusion, with so many questions: sin and penance and hell and Eucharistic Prayer and what kind of name is Virgin?

"Her name is Mary," Grandma said with a grin. "A virgin ... a virgin is someone who says no to men."

Emily sprays a generous spritz of Victoria's Secret body spray. The word *devil* buzzes around like a bee she can't swat away. She takes in the sheer yellow curtains of her room, stained with orange swirls from rainwater; the promotional horse calendar Todd gave her thumb-tacked above her bed; and the teal dresser Ashley's family passed on after they remodeled a guest room. The giant, clunky deadbolt Dad installed on her door last fall.

Maybe her classmate Michael was on to something. There were songs about devils in the jukebox. Dad called Emily's mom—who left when Emily was three—a devil woman. Phil, a longtime regular and great tipper, blamed the devil and God for what he did. Religion never quite fit in the equation of Emily's life until that night. It was up there with Santa Claus and the Easter Bunny, which she learned were hoaxes far sooner than most.

"Hazards of the trade," Dad called the incident—Emily waking to Phil perched on the edge of her bed, roughly stroking her hair, mumbling her name. Then coiling his fingers around thick plaits. Emily stops the memory there, remembering Dad passed out downstairs. Patsy Cline spilling a sad song from the jukebox. Maybe that's the moment she realized she had to get out.

She clears Dad's cocktail glasses from the surfaces of their home—the rickety coffee table she built in shop class; the office desk strewn with spreadsheets, torn envelopes, and promotional posters from Budweiser and Leinenkugel's; Dad's nightstand beside the framed photo of them, his arm wrapped snug around her narrow shoulders, on the precipice of the Badlands.

When is she going to tell him? Not tonight. Tonight, she's relieved for the refuge of Todd.

Cranking Miranda Lambert, she drives her white Ford F-150, Dad's old truck, toward Todd's. Nine miles to clear her head, to focus on Todd. He's twenty-seven. He owns his grandparents' old farmhouse. He cares for horses, cows, and chickens and grows corn and soybeans with his dad and brothers. He's a grown-up. He's solid. He's safe.

Their first interaction took place when Emily was fourteen, sitting at the bar with algebra homework while Todd celebrated his twenty-first with Jäger bombs. He slid onto the stool beside her.

"Whoa!" he hollered, bumping against her with an exaggeration that nearly sent her to the floor. "Turbulence." She laughed nervously. He skimmed the fractions, letters, and numbers in her textbook, reading aloud, "Complete the equations."

"Dude. Darts, Todd. It's your turn," Bobby Moore called.

"I remember this. Um, if you—huh, the x is y, I think? How the fuck did this go?" He shook his head. Emily giggled and assured him she understood what to do. Though she didn't have a clue.

"You'll be so glad when you're done with that shit," he said, giving her shoulders a slight squeeze and resting his cowboy hat over her braids. "Hang on to this for me while I beat these guys in darts." She remembers that moment as some kind of promise, a peek at destiny.

As the years passed, he always gave her a lingering smile, a nice tip. She poured him and his teammates countless pitchers of Bud during the summer baseball league. She brought him and his family deep-fried fish and cheese curds on Friday nights. She served him and his girlfriend, Nicole, burgers and cocktails every few weeks. Nicole's gorgeous. The ideal employee for Fiona's Fine Cuts with that voluminous hair the color of Hershey's Kisses. Streaks of her beige foundation and burgundy lipstick colored the paper napkins crumpled in her basket.

"I just want to give you a makeover," she'd say to Emily. "You should come to the salon."

Emily opted for the haircuts the local Babski's Barber gave her in exchange for cocktails. Greg Babski cut her thick, straw-colored hair since she could remember. No gels, sprays, mousses, or blow-drying. Just a shampoo, blunt cut, and heavy wet hair an inch shorter.

"Yeah, I should," she'd respond to Nicole.

Mid-December, Todd came to The Honky Tonk three, four times a week on his own.

"Nicole broke his heart," Gladys reported.

Sullen and soft-spoken, Todd watched ESPN until a couple of Fireball whiskeys warmed him up. Then he'd join conversations about the Packers' weak defensive strategies, the eight-point buck Doug gunned down, the mailboxes mauled by the snowplows. "Looks like a war zone driving here." His smiles lingered longer on Emily.

"How old are you now?" he asked one night.

"Twenty," she answered, pulling on the hem of her faded black Honky Tonk t-shirt, shrunk from too many washes.

"Emmy. Can I call you Emmy?"

She liked the way that sounded. "Sure." She examined his bushy, unkempt beard. She wanted to touch it, tug on it. He never grew a beard when he and Nicole dated.

"Emmy, want to do a shot?"

"Don't let my dad see." She discreetly poured the shots. Drinking on the clock was not allowed unless she recognized everyone in the joint. But she was clocking out soon. She knew almost everyone, and she wanted to please Todd. His attention made her giddy.

Todd winked before tossing his head back. The whiskey spread through her body like liquid sunshine. Fifteen minutes later, they did another. Dad shuffled down the bar. Emily tried to behave normally, walk in a straight line, and enunciate every word so she wouldn't betray herself by slurring. Todd set a fifty on the bar.

"Keep it." He smiled, holding her gaze, tilting his head toward the front door.

She pulled a basketball hoodie over her head and crept out the fire exit. Fresh December snow blew up her flared jeans as she jogged to his truck. The buzz of alcohol lifted as she shivered in the cold cab. He slid a heater vent toward her and turned down Kenny Chesney. He wrapped a long arm around her shoulder, pinching one of her braids between two fingers. The slight smell of horse manure and exhaust, the hum of the engine, and the light of the dashboard casting a soft glow on him exhilarated her. She reminded herself to breathe.

"How do you train a horse?" she asked nervously, delaying the inevitable.

Todd smiled. He gripped one of Emily's wrists with a calloused hand.

"Horses learn by pulling on 'em tight, stringing 'em along, and making 'em uncomfortable." He bent her wrist back slowly. Slight tremors of pain reverberated in her arm. She pretended to laugh, pushing through the discomfort, the way the sensation brought back images of what occurred mere weeks ago with Phil, like a hazy View-Master reel. She tried to squirm her arm away.

"And when they do what you want, you ease up the pressure." He let go. She exhaled. He kissed her. The frightening images faded. This she liked. This felt good. He tasted like warm cinnamon.

He placed her hand on his crotch, and his penis hardened beneath her fingers like a magic trick. She unbuttoned and unzipped his jeans like she knew he wanted her to. She gripped him and decided she liked this too. The power, how he surrendered to her, closing his eyes, sinking his head against the seat.

"Yeah, a little harder, faster," he instructed. He moaned. His mouth opened like he was drinking up something sweet. "Yeah, like that, Emmy. Like that."

After he came, he kissed the corner of her mouth. She wanted more, but he leaned into the backrest. "That felt awesome. Thanks."

"You're welcome." She didn't know what else to say.

"It's been a while since I got one of those. I'm sorry. I'm so relaxed. That felt so good. I'll get you next time. I promise."

She didn't want to return to her room that December night. She wanted Todd to fulfill his promise. She wanted escape.

He came back a few days later and a few days after that. And she kept following him to his truck.

Emily kicks her Skechers beside Todd's cowboy boots and sets her purse among the belt buckles, leather work gloves, and horse bridles on the dining room table. Todd clicks his cell phone shut and takes a swig of Miller Lite. Rocket leaps from the couch and wags his tail at her feet.

"Hey," Todd says.

"Hi." Emily smiles. "Thanks for having me over."

"Thanks for the free food."

They watch *Sons of Anarchy* while they eat. Emily tosses the to-go containers. Todd stretches out on the tan couch, designed to camouflage stains. Emily returns, maneuvering, adjusting herself to fit in Todd's nooks. A litany of topics run through her brain, things she wants to say, to ask. Dad and Phil and school. Them. Are they a couple? Is he her boyfriend? Jacob.

"A guy came in with those religious pamphlets today," she says to a stray white whisker in his beard.

"Huh," Todd replies to a text and closes his phone.

"Like my age too. Isn't that weird? And he was really nice. It felt like the whole thing was an act. I was annoyed. He could tell I was annoyed."

"People get nuts about that stuff."

Emily thinks of Phil. The morning after he snuck into her room, he returned to The Honky Tonk with a black Bible in hand. She wondered what that had to do with anything as he dropped the book on the bar with a heavy thud. She crossed her arms and leaned against liquor bottles and pint glasses lining the counter, clinking like a creepy tune. Dad sat at a barstool. He shook Phil's hand. Their eyelids drooped heavily from hangovers.

"Emily. I didn't know what I was doing last night or where I was," Phil began. He didn't look at her.

She studied a zit on his receding hairline, irritated and red like he'd been picking at it. He gripped the Bible with both hands.

"I had too much to drink. It was a wake-up call for me—a sign from God. I gotta do better. I thought I was home. I thought you were my wife. A misunderstanding."

She couldn't keep up with the explanation. "But you were saying *my* name," Emily said, shuddering like she was naked in a snowstorm.

"The devil made me do it." He shook his head apologetically, like he had no choice.

Dad nodded. "Well, we'll make sure it won't happen again, right?"

"I swear to God. Never again," Phil said. "And we can keep this between us."

"What do you think of that kind of stuff?" Emily asks the whisker.

"Like God?"

"Yeah."

"I don't know." Todd blows a raspberry in thought. "Do

onto others as you want them to do to you. I think that's all, right? That's enough."

He's never given her an orgasm. That's her first thought. She's given him plenty. But that's not what he means, of course. "Yeah. I like that," she says.

He rises from the couch, takes her hands, and leads her to the bedroom. He's done talking.

The ceiling fan's breeze sends goosebumps down her back as she wrestles off her shirt. She thinks of Phil at her bedside, rubbing her face, mumbling her name. Todd takes off his jeans and Brewers t-shirt. He kisses her neck, reaches behind to unhook her bra, struggles, and laughs. "Just take this damn thing off next time for me too, will you?"

She laughs as well. He smells like fish and alcohol, sour and sharp. His phone buzzes.

Emily's thoughts drift. *How long was Phil watching me?*

Rocket whines at the foot of the bed. Todd pulls off his boxers, and she peels off her underwear. *How long was he in my room?* She trembles as Todd pushes inside of her. She moves to his rhythm, struggling to ward away images of Phil.

Todd presses down on her, the plain of his belly tight against hers, no space between, and she can hardly breathe. She won't come this time either, but when it's over, he'll hold her, pull her from these plaguing pangs of loneliness and confusion and fear. Safe. He comes.

"I love you," she says. The words fall like slippery minnows from her mouth before she can catch them. They feel foreign and strange. But it's what people say after sex, right? After they've been sleeping together semi-regularly for months. Shadows cling to his face. He says the same.

CHAPTER THREE

Emily and Ashley meet for hoagies and iced coffees at their favorite café. Abstract paintings with squares of dull reds and yellows and purples hang on the walls.

"Looks like a Mark Rothko knock-off," says Ashley. Emily agrees for fear of sounding ignorant and budges the conversation along, complimenting Ashley's streaky highlights and clear skin. After two years of college, she even looks smarter.

"Thank you! My roommate introduced me to Proactiv. Jessica Simpson uses it. Changed my life."

"The roommate I met?"

"No, one of my new roommates—Amber. You met Trish. She'll be living with us too." Ashley slurps up a saucy tomato spilling from her sandwich. "I missed these. The bread, so soft. And that barista, so cute."

Emily laughs and peeks at the rangy man with a five o'clock shadow and navy scarf wound tightly around his neck. "You should give him your number. See if he's free for the bonfire tonight."

"Yeah, right. You know he has a smoking hot girlfriend who writes poetry or is a tattoo artist or something way cooler than an art ed major." Ashley rolls her eyes. She was never the brave one of the two and didn't date in high school like Emily. Not date per se, but hang out, make out, have sex with Zach Lehnardt in the janitor's closet a few times, Mark Nygard in his two-door Pontiac a few times after that.

"I know them too well. It's gross," Ashley would say. But Emily knew she crushed hard on Blake Warren, an upperclassman who practically lived in the art room, playing Pink Floyd and painting naked bodies curled in the fetal position.

And Ashley didn't want a crowd at the bonfire, no high school friends—just her family and Emily.

"It would feel weird," says Ashley. "I've changed."

"Me too," says Emily. Though she's not sure that's true, not yet anyway. "Like, I'm so excited to be pursuing my own thing finally."

"You tell your dad yet?"

"No."

"You should get on that—it's gonna rock his little world."

Emily's aware.

"What made you finally decide?" Ashley asks. "Just bored as hell?"

"Lots of things. Yeah. I mentioned it to Todd, and he was like, 'Go for it.'"

Ashley rolls her eyes once more and scoffs.

"What?" Emily smirks.

"I told you to move to Madison with me after high school, and you were all, 'No. Got to stay with Dad.' Then Todd tells you to be a nurse, and you're all in. You only do something if you have a man's permission." Emily assumes these are echoes of Ashley's Women's Studies class.

"That's not true. I can't afford to live in Madison. And I had to help Dad after the interstate screwed everything up ... and this recession," Emily says. Ashley doesn't look convinced.

"You could afford Madison. You've been working your whole life. How much do you have in your bank account?"

"Umm ... well, I don't know," Emily admits, cringing, calculating. "Dad handles all that—the deposits and mail."

"Emily! Oh, my God. Seriously?"

"Okay. Stop. I hear myself. I know I have thousands in there, enough to cover tuition. I just got to tell Dad what's coming, and then I'll be better at that stuff." She's done defending herself, explaining herself. She's wondering why Ashley can't be happy for her. She's wondering when they'll fall into the easy banter and consuming laughter that defined their friendship. Being together always felt like a simple puzzle. The pieces fit even as they grew and became their own distinct selves. But since Ashley left for college, the puzzle felt more complicated, the pieces wonky and trickier to put into place each time they spoke or saw each other.

"I don't know how you live with your dad," says Ashley. "I'm so excited not to be moving back with my parents this summer. And now, with Ryan home and his shit. All about him, as always." She takes a long sip from her straw.

Ryan partied. He was a wild card with a tough exterior who cared more about having fun and causing harmless mischief, like smoking weed behind the bleachers and stealing gnomes from people's yards, than his grades. The Army was meant to straighten him out, give his life direction. He agreed. He signed up.

"Is he okay?" asks Emily. She pictures the pre-Army version of Ryan with a flame of red hair he gelled in lopsided spikes and jeans that slipped off his ass. She teased him about his taste in music—heavy metal or some variation. "It sounds like people hurling while screaming."

"Better than hicks who get hard singing about trucks," he teased back. She remembers him launching her sky-high on the trampoline as kids. He dunked her in Lake Wissota and the Deer Valley High School pool. She remembers he liked Jameson whiskey and hooked him up from The Honky Tonk cellar until he was twenty-one. He squashed spiders creeping in Ashley's room, annihilated Emily in Mario Kart, and introduced them to Wes Craven and John Carpenter before Ashley was allowed to watch PG-13 movies. He called Emily "Ems," and the house felt emptier when he went away. She's not sure what to anticipate after his tour in Iraq.

Ashley shakes her head. "The one time I tried to ask, he said I'd never understand and made a crack about my major. 'Must be nice to learn how to finger paint with kids,' he said," Ashley says, putting on a deep voice. "He sleeps and plays video games and works a few shifts at Blockbuster. It's lame."

"That sucks. Maybe he just needs time. My grandpa's brother didn't talk about World War II until he saw *Saving Private Ryan*, and then he bawled."

"Great, so in like fifty years." Ashley blows between her lips. "I know he lost a friend or friends. I know he saw bad things." The floor vibrates from Ashley's bouncing heel. "But I don't know. It's best I get out of there, and Mom and Dad can deal with it. I didn't even want to come this weekend."

"Why?" Emily feels stung. Wasn't she worth visiting?

"No offense." Ashley puts her hands up in surrender. "I want to get my internship started and settled in my new place. I feel like I'm wasting time."

After lunch they take Dilly Bars to Carson Park like they used to, perch on the swings, and kick at woodchips while gnawing at the cold chocolate coating. Everything feels off-kilter. There's a tension Emily can't crack.

"What's Todd up to tonight?" asks Ashley.

"I don't know. Watching baseball." Emily doesn't feel like tackling this topic with Ashley either.

"I don't think you're mature enough for him, or whatever you think is going on with him." Ashley licks the vanilla ice cream center.

"I'm mature." Emily shakes her head, realizing as she struggles to connect with Ashley that Todd's currently her best friend, all she's got. Maybe that's why she said, "I love you."

"You totally cheated on Todd when you were in Madison."

Emily winces. She doesn't remember much but laughing with that guy—Dustin was his name—who Ashley invited to the house party they stumbled upon when Emily visited in March. Lounging on a stranger's futon, Dustin offered Emily a weed brownie. A DJ bobbed his head while scrubbing Kanye West in a corner. Christmas lights dangled around the wide-open room. Two girls in bright lipstick made out, smearing red and pink all over each other's faces.

Dustin tried convincing her that *The Big Lebowski* was the greatest film—he used the word *film*—ever made. Emily found it hilarious to disagree with him, tossing out other movie titles. "No. *Titanic. Clueless.*"

He pinched and tickled her. "*Big Lebowski!*" Soon they were kissing, a pleasant, relaxing rush, a thick taste of chocolate in her mouth. She's not sure Todd even crossed her mind.

After twenty minutes of making out, Ashley's roommate pulled Emily into the rust-lined bathroom. "FYI. Ashley likes Dustin. She like really, really likes him." The roommate's disapproving tone turned Emily's insides.

"I was high. Didn't mean anything. I bet Todd would think it's funny." Emily tries to play it off. "Who was that guy even?"

"Dustin," Ashley spits out quickly. "Are you and Todd even official? I bet he's just happy having someone to screw. Like, has he even taken you out on a date?"

There'd been no conversation, no DTR, or define the relationship, as the girls in school called it. She purposefully avoided the topic because Todd's twenty-seven, and maybe you didn't need to talk about these things as you got older, and she didn't want to scare him off.

Emily turns around and around, twisting the chains of her swing like a double helix. As for a date ... no, not really. He had her over for leftover chili once. He called her when a calf was being born so she could watch. "I know you like that medical stuff," he said. He confessed that he secretly loathes deer hunting. "It's cold and boring." He grew up longing to be a rodeo cowboy. "A dumb dream." That's something.

"We said 'I love you' last night." Emily lifts her legs and spins like a tornado as the chains unwind, pleased with that response, hopeful it's enough to shut Ashley up.

"Who said it first?"

...

John and Diane set glistening brats, steaming brown beans, potato salad, and a pile of Cool Ranch Doritos on the counter. "Buffet style," says Diane. "And put two paper plates together. I bought the flimsy kind."

Ryan playfully shoves Emily in the line. "Come on, Ems. I'm hungry." The anxiety she felt about seeing Ryan, about enduring more of Ashley's beratements, faded as she pulled in the driveway, wrapped in the familiarity of the Carrs' home like a beloved blankie.

"So, what's the plan, Em?" asks John as they settle in canvas lawn chairs circling a fire pit in the middle of a manicured lawn. Emily likes John, who's got the candor of a game show host. Interested but detached. Funny but polite. "Still sticking it out at The Honky Tonk? You know, I think you'd make a great dental hygienist."

"You think everyone would make a great dental hygienist," says Ryan, biting into his brat. "Don't fall for it, Ems. Dad's trying to pull the same shit—"

"Language," interrupts Diane.

"Stuff with me." Ryan smirks, his cheek puffed out like a chipmunk as he chews.

"Well, you have your G.I. Bill, and I hate to see it go to waste," says John. "We've had this talk."

"Military was not my first choice," says Diane as the fire cracks and pops.

"You wouldn't think it from all the swag you put in the house," says Ryan. "It's like you were preparing a shrine for my death. Did you see it, Ems?"

Emily witnessed the transition. Before Ryan joined the Army, the Carr home maintained an aesthetics influenced by Diane's two favorite things: antiques and plants. Emily and Ashley called Diane a classy grandma when she was deciding between which floral-patterned plate to display above the kitchen cabinet.

"You just wait, girls. One day you'll care about these

things," she'd say. Eighteenth-century floral illustrations and family photos adorned the walls. Potted plants sat on shelves, hung from the ceiling, and hugged either side of the TV.

Once Ryan passed basic training and prepared to deploy, Diane popped American flags in the plants' soil and replaced decorative plates and family pictures with portraits of Ryan in uniform.

"I want to hear about Emily," says John.

Ryan takes a swig of Leinenkugel's. Emily's surprised Ashley hadn't mentioned the news.

"I registered for classes at Westwood," she says. "I think I want to try nursing, maybe."

"There you go," says John, nodding with approval.

"Oh, Emily," says Diane. "Such happy news! Good for you. You girls going after things." She sets her plate on her knees and claps. "You'll be a great nurse, Emily."

"Nurse Schmidt," says Ryan. "Sounds cool."

Emily smiles. "Thanks, guys."

Diane squeezes Emily's knee before turning to Ryan. "Did you ask your sister about her internship?"

"Yeah." Ryan looks at Ashley. "I did, right? Working with kids? Art? Children's museum or something?"

"A children's program at the art museum, so yeah, close enough," says Ashley.

While the siblings have a conversation prompted by their mother, Diane leans toward Emily and whispers, "Keeping up on your checkups?" Emily can feel her cheeks dialing a shade darker, but dusk is settling. Diane scheduled Emily's first physical at the free women's clinic in Eau Claire when she was sixteen. "It's none of my business, but you gotta keep an eye on things," she said one morning while Ashley showered. She taught Emily the proper techniques for shaving. "Against the grain and use shaving cream. You don't want razor burn." She discreetly tucked boxes of tampons, and later condoms, in Emily's overnight bag throughout middle and high school. "We have extra," she'd whisper.

"I am," Emily says. "Thank you."

"Good girl." Diane pats her knee. Emily longs to hug her again. How she missed her. But she forgot how Diane's caring, attentive presence awakened this deep-seated ache for a mother of her own.

Very young, Emily realized dads are the absent ones, not moms. Moms accompanied their children to the library; Dad dropped her off. Moms heaved their children in the cart at Festival Foods; Dad always opted for a basket and strolled purposefully a few paces ahead. Moms took classmates back-to-school shopping at the Oakwood Mall for light-up tennis shoes, backpacks with Disney princesses, and jeans embroidered with flowers; Dad took her to Fleet Farm.

Diane's such a mom. She wears tapered jeans, has crispy permed hair, a purse as big and mysterious as Mary Poppins' carpet bag. What was in there? Everything a child could need or want. Ashley and Ryan never knew how good they had it.

Ryan pulls another beer from the red Igloo cooler.

"If you girls want one, go ahead," says John. "I know you do it anyway, and you're almost twenty-one."

Ryan snaps the bottle caps off two more beers. Diane and John prattle about the deer they leave apples for and the new dock they plan to install at their cabin in Rhinelander. They talk until the moon shines bright and a whip-poor-will sings. Then they call it a night.

Ryan stares at the flames with glazed eyes, a bottle of beer resting on his thigh while Ashley describes a painting she's planning. "I want it to represent Mother Earth, but like a Wisconsin one. It'll have this beautiful, ethereal woman, but she's composed of Wisconsin trees and animals and nature."

"I like that idea. And like, you could put barns by her feet or something," says Emily, trying. "So people know it's Wisconsin."

Ryan grins.

"No," says Ashley gently. "The title should be enough, and the animals. I think people will get it."

"She could have a badger head," says Ryan, rising from his chair, eyes wide, a gleeful expression. "Or a cow's head. She could be holding cheese in one hand, a beer in the other."

"Shut up, Ryan." Ashley crosses her arms.

"No, seriously. She could wear a Packers jersey. Get a brat somewhere in there."

Emily snickers. She can't help herself.

"You guys don't get it," says Ashley.

"I'm Ashley and I'm an artist," says Ryan mockingly.

"Go to bed, Ryan."

"Go to bed, Ashley."

Emily has been at the center of their sibling spats before. It's familiar, but this exchange feels sharper than she remembers. "I think it sounds cool," she says, treading carefully, resting a hand on the point of Ashley's elbow. Ashley stares ahead. Ryan walks toward the woods.

"Where are you going?" calls Ashley.

"Taking a piss!"

"I feel like his babysitter right now."

"He seems fine," says Emily. "What can happen?"

"Well, he went out with friends last week and ended up chipping David Gonski's tooth over a pool game. So, a lot."

"Holy crap. Seriously?"

"Tori, his ex, brought him home. He'd vomited in her car, then passed out. And Mom lets him sit at home and play video games all day because she read somewhere that video games help rewire trauma in the brain or something stupid. It's like, get him a therapist, Mom and Dad."

Ryan walks back like he can't find his center of gravity, wobbling this way and that. "We should see how big we can make the fire," he says.

"No," says Ashley.

"I'm not talking to you. Ems, what do you say?"

"Let's go inside, Emily," says Ashley.

"You two are no fun." He tosses a beer bottle into the fire.

"I'm not gonna sit here and make sure you don't burn the house down."

For a moment, Emily feels ageless in the twin bed that pulls out from beneath Ashley's. Nine? Twelve? Sixteen? Now twenty. Her thighs tingle from the buzz of alcohol. The plastic stars on the ceiling emit a faint green glow. How many nights has she stared at these, slept beneath them? How many laughs and tears and made-up games and conversations have she and Ashley shared in this room? But they're off. Something has shifted.

Ashley runs through her Target shopping list: bedsheets, a lamp, dishes, cleaning supplies. "So much to do tomorrow," she says before turning on her side, a clear signal since Emily can remember that Ashley's done talking, ready for sleep.

Emily wills sleep to come, but a gnawing sensation chews her insides, but it's not about The Honky Tonk, Dad, Todd, Phil, or school. She feels, for the first time in her friendship with Ashley, that she isn't welcome. She's an imposition.

It's 1:23 a.m. The sleeplessness sends Emily to the bathroom. Maybe if she skims through the Newsweek on the back of the toilet, she'll replace the cluttered mess of thoughts in her brain. She reads about Star Trek inspiring exploration and Bernie Madoff running the largest Ponzi scheme in history until the hallway light flicks on. Shoot.

She opens the door to Ryan, wearing plaid boxers and a white t-shirt.

"Feeling okay?" he asks.

"Can't sleep. I was reading. Did I wake you?"

He shakes his head. "No. Wanna smoke?" He holds up a joint.

She nods. Yes, that will help.

She slips into his room, always mysterious and foreign to her as an only child—an older boy's bedroom. A Black Sabbath poster hangs above his bed, an AC/DC poster over his dresser. Video game cases lay like fallen dominos on the carpeted floor in front of the TV, amongst socks, boxers, and bright blue Blockbuster polos. Rain falling ... and harps?

"What are you listening to?" she asks, slowly shutting the door.

He sits on the edge of the bed, opens the window, and lights the joint.

"Helps me sleep sometimes. I missed the rain. I just wanted rain. Too much dust over there. There were these sandstorms. Walls of sand. You'd disappear." A chilly gust wraps around Emily's bare legs. Ryan pats the space beside him, takes a hit, and hands off the joint. "My mom got me these CDs—rain and guitars, rain and pianos, rain and violins."

She's tempted to tease him, but he seems so vulnerable in his boxers, without the pointy spikes of hair that once dotted his skull. Smoke floods her chest. She holds in the fumes and exhales with a cough.

"Dusty and hot?" she asks, handing back the joint.

"Yeah, southern Iraq is fucking hot. Especially with all our shit on."

"Was there a pool?"

"No." He laughs and takes a hit.

She wonders if he wants to talk about it, if she should brave other questions: Did you meet locals? What's the food like? Does every woman wear a burka? Do they have birthday parties? What does it smell like? What's it like to be shot at? What's it like to shoot at other people?

"What does it feel like over there?" A loaded question she knows, but intentionally vague, one he can interpret however he wants.

"Umm ... fucking stressful." He exhales and hands the joint back. "I'm infantry, right? So expendable. We're the bait. Ambush after fucking ambush." He tugs his faded black duvet over Emily. "Your legs are all goosebumps."

Ryan runs his hand over his head. He's not okay.

"Ashley thinks I'm a jackass, doesn't she?"

"I mean, she's your sister. So, yeah."

He laughs, handing Emily the joint.

"I think she's annoyed with me too," says Emily. "Or something's changed big time."

"Yeah. Fuck her."

"She's a big college girl now." A cold anger sends shivers down Emily's arms. "Has her new friends and new apartment. I'm not good enough anymore, I guess."

"Yeah. I fought for that. I fought so she could be all stuck up, paint her stupid fucking Mother Wisconsin painting."

Emily laughs, the marijuana smoothing rough corners inside her.

"There you go." Ryan laughs too. "You're welcome! Freedom isn't free."

Emily's brain skitters gently, like she's gliding. There's the patter of rain, the itchiness in her lungs, the dark, swirly lines of Ryan's arm hair against his pale skin. She takes another hit and hands back the joint.

"You know what's fucked up?" he says, studying the gray carpet. "I feel more messed up here than I did over there. When I was there, I was like, 'I'm fine. I got this.' But now, being here and like, seeing everyone go about their days when my fucking friend was blown away right next to me and guys ... guys with wives and kids are killed by some fucking psycho zealots." The floor vibrates from his heel bouncing up and down. He takes a long drag. "That's fucked up." The gliding stops.

Tears prick Emily's eyes. She rests a hand on his spine, this boy she's known so long, so well.

He lets out a weak laugh and gazes up at the ceiling. "Sorry," he says. "Sorry. Here, take another hit." She does, trying to find words, something comforting and reassuring to say. She's got nothing.

"Tell me what's wrong with you now," he says.

"Ryan, I don't have anything like what you went—" she starts.

"Come on. Come on. Anything. Make me feel more normal." She considers Phil in her room, his hands—but how can that compare? She was told that's not a big deal. He's not a bad guy.

"Your mom leaving?" Ryan offers. "That fucked you up, right?"

A punch in the gut. "Probably."

"You ever heard from her? Know where she is?"

"She went to a relative's funeral in Oregon and never came back," Emily says matter-of-factly. "Apparently, she met up with an old boyfriend, and they ran off together. That's what Dad says, anyway. I don't know. Guess I wasn't enough for her either."

"Yeah. That's messed up."

Emily has a vague image of her mother, a photo Bernie discovered sweeping beneath the dishwasher years ago. She didn't look like a mom, almost a woman, but really a girl. A girl with an unmaintained perm, shiny dots of acne on her chin, eyes red from the flash, teeth hidden behind a tight-lipped smile. Her dad, so young too, vibrant and handsome, with his arm wrapped around her collarbone.

As for her mom's presence, Emily is sure she remembers someone sweet and calm who helped her dress and sang her lullabies. Someone safe. Though maybe that was a few of Dad's old girlfriends, Grandma Bev, and Diane combined. Wishful thinking.

"Dad calls her a whore, a witch, a she-devil," says Emily, putting out a finger for each. "But Bernie says she was nice, a kid. She was eighteen when she had me. He says she panicked. But still. Moms don't leave. Dads leave. Why did she leave me, you know?"

"Fuck her." Ryan turns up the CD player. "This is my favorite part." The harp and the rain continue.

"You're a dork." Emily bumps into him and lets out a laugh. She has more to say, but he lies on his back and again pats the space beside him. She hesitates but doesn't want to return to Ashley's room and feel unwelcome or unwanted anymore. She lies beside him. *This isn't cheating*, she thinks as he draws her closer to him. He smells like campfire, like sweat and marijuana and dryer sheets. She drapes an arm across his chest and clings.

"What are we still doing in this stupid town?" he asks.

Dad. The Honky Tonk. Todd. School. But in this state, warm and mellow and sad in Ryan's bed, they don't feel that important or worth living for. In fact, she doesn't want to return to them. That's not right. What *is* she doing?

"I heard Door County's nice in the summer."

"Let's go there." He holds on tighter. And her body aches with wanting. Wanting more conversations like this, wanting to feel seen and heard.

"You think I'm all fucked up now?" Ryan's voice cracks.

"No," whispers Emily. "I think you're real."

CHAPTER FOUR

Dad slides a faded blue Rubbermaid tub behind the sparsely filled barstools. He opens the lid to reveal a jumble of red, white, and blue buntings, banners, and mini-American flags. Memorial Day is approaching. An episode of *Grey's Anatomy* preoccupies Emily. Even Larry and Doug watch the drama unfold: a doctor with a slew of doe-eyed residents in their powder blue scrubs surveying the scene of a ferry accident. "What do we do?" asks one. "Help people!" yells the doctor before rushing into the chaos.

Gladys chuckles. "This is so ridiculous. It's worse than a soap opera. I love it."

Emily has seen the episode before. She's borrowed this season's DVDs from the library many times. She loves it too. Her brain buzzes with emotions as the residents spread out among the victims, the corpses, toward the CGI ferry, with smoke rising from the wrecked hull. So heroic, so important.

Since she crept from Ryan's arms to Ashley's pull-out bed at dawn, she's wanted nothing more than to watch *Grey's Anatomy*, to distract her brain from reality, to escape. Ashley left after Diane cleared floral plates smeared with syrup and whipped cream. So much to do, and she didn't ask Emily to tag along. At the table, Ryan teased Emily about cutting her waffles in even rows, her bedhead, Todd.

"Suppose he's tending to the cows, writing you a country song, waiting for his Emily to walk through the barn doors."

Nothing happened, she told herself. *Nothing to feel guilty about anyway.*

She texted Todd on the way home: "Wanna hang out?"

"Sorry. Busy."

She deadbolted the door and crawled into bed. The walls closed in on her. She felt squished flat with hurt and embarrassment over Ashley's bristliness and Todd's vagueness. She had to remind herself what she was living for. Hence, *Grey's Anatomy*. But what about Dad? What about duty and loyalty and family? Who would wipe the whiskers from the bathroom sink if she left? Who would keep the bar banter on the lighter side? *You will*, she told herself. She wasn't abandoning him. The Honky Tonk would always be a part of her life. She would work there through school and keep an eye on Dad.

"There's no way they'd send second-year residents to just have at it," says Gladys. "And what was with the drive over? Like they had no idea what was coming."

"No?" Emily looked at Gladys.

"No. There are protocols and procedures for mass casualty events. Even here in Dunn County, I'd be better prepared for a ferry accident than they seem to be."

"Would they send nurses?"

"ER nurses, yeah."

That's what Emily is meant for, tending to breaking or broken bodies, learning more about the intricate systems that work together like gears in a clock to keep someone ticking. She reveled in her Human Biology class, scored a B-. Might have made a B, but Mr. Orvis focused more on his football players' grades so they'd be eligible to play than answering Emily's questions about lymph nodes, pulmonary circulation, and fallopian tubes.

"But how does it know to release the egg?"

"Don't tell me you want to have babies now, Miss Schmidt." He joked. "Wait a couple years, promise me. You girls. Is that all you think about?"

"She must be ovulating," said Lucas Murry, leaning back in his plastic chair with a satisfied grin. Half the class erupted in laughter.

"Mr. Murry, I'm impressed you know the correct terminology," said Mr. Orvis. Emily laughed, too, but left the class with unanswered questions.

"Can you turn the TV down, Emily?" Dad asks. "I'd like a little help with this."

Emily rolls her eyes at Gladys. But Gladys studies her drink and swirls her straw around and around.

"Why are we even decorating for Memorial Day?" asks Emily, approaching Dad, elbow-deep in bunting. "It's not like a party holiday, right? We put these up for Fourth of July."

"Well, let's show some respect, and vets might stop in after the parade," he answers.

The screen door creaks open. Phil Karlsen enters with a steady gait, brazen even, the key ring jingling at his hip as if to signal he's a trustworthy, powerful guy. Look at all the doors he can open. Emily doesn't understand why he continues to return after what happened. Doesn't he feel as ashamed and uncomfortable as she does? She told Dad she didn't want him in the bar, not ever again, even after Phil apologized. "That was terrifying, Dad. Creepy. He's a creep."

"He's harmless," said Dad, pouring coffee. "He didn't rape you, right?"

"No," said Emily quicker than her brain could process or care to recall. But he was touching her. He entered her room with intention. He violated her.

"You know, religious people don't handle their booze well. They act out sometimes. They're so repressed like. He's not a bad guy. And come on, we can't kick him out. He spends a lot of money here. He's on town council."

"Dad," she pleaded, "that was scary."

He suggested the deadbolt, and Emily acquiesced. She was too confounded to continue arguing, too baffled. If Dad didn't consider it consequential, maybe it wasn't.

Emily unravels a tangled nest of bunting. "Will you get Phil his drink?" she whispers to Dad. He exhales with annoyance. She texts Todd: "Free tonite?"

"You know what you should do? What would really boost business?" says Larry from the bar, half turning in his stool. "Have Emily wear an American flag bikini. You know, stars on one boob, stripes on the other," he grabs each side of his stout chest, "and hand out ice cold Buds in the parade. People would love that."

Emily shakes her head. "No, thank you." Her skin burns hot with the comment, the way it had when her sixth-grade history teacher told her she was becoming a "shapely woman. Just need a bit of mascara."

Or when Hannah Lund's dad grazed his fingertips on her lower back when she went into the dark kitchen for more popcorn during a sleepover. "Let me help you with that," he said, reaching one hand into the cupboard for a bowl, resting the other on Emily's ass.

Or when a group of men at The Honky Tonk asked how far she'd gone with a guy: "Second base? Third base? Give a BJ yet? Wanna practice?"

And now Phil is here. Fight or flight tugs at each nerve. And he seemed so decent, pious with his gold cross necklace and constant Amens. Phil never asked those kinds of questions or made those kind of remarks. She'd have never guessed what he was capable of.

"You are unbelievable, Larry." Gladys laughs. "Memorial

Day is about people who died. Not you boys getting your ogles in. And it could be fifty-five degrees."

"Just an idea," says Larry, raising his hands defensively. "You go ahead and do that for the Fourth, then."

Dad slides Phil his Stella.

"I won't be in the parade this year," announces Emily, deciding that moment. No. She's participated in the small-town affair for years, with Ashley and a few other girls who giddily threw fruit-flavored tootsie rolls at shuffling toddlers and over-eager kids scrambling for the candy like a pack of hungry wolves. They applied temporary tattoos to their cheeks and showered one another in glitter hair spray. Now the girls were scattered: Kelsey at home with her baby, Tessa coaching at a basketball camp in Milwaukee, Brittany touring London for a summer study abroad program.

"Yes. Yes, you are," says Dad.

"No. No, I'm not." Emily surprises herself. "'Cause I'm an adult, and I don't want to throw candy out the back of a truck anymore." She unfurls the string of flags and lets them drop and drag on the floor.

"You see that sunset tonight?" Phil says to Larry. "Isn't God the most beautiful painter?" Dad returns to Emily, sweeping a hand over his thinning hair. Stress seems to be seeping from him like steam rises off the pint glasses after a wash.

"I don't think you get it," he whispers. "This place needs to make some money."

"I get it, Dad. Okay. See? I'm putting up the bunting. Why don't you let me book a band again? I know we could get some people in here. Or an open mic night. I got like three friends who play music who would handle it."

"I don't want punk-yelly music in here. We're a honky-tonk bar. Your friends don't even know who Hank Williams is, do they? We play old country. Good music."

"What music? This jukebox?" she gestures to the tired-looking machine against the wall. The volume of her voice rises. "No one knows who these dead guys are anymore. No one cares."

"Whoa. She's a spitfire, that one," says Doug.

Dad takes the bunting from her and the chipped coffee mug with used tacks and nails from a nearby dining table and stomps to the front window with red, white, and blue spilling from the crook of his elbow.

"She'll make a man very happy one day," says Phil. Emily seethes in the center of the restaurant, pretending not to hear, her body trembling while the bar patrons return to their drinks and conversations. Doug bought new crankbait at Scheels, Margaret's allergies are vicious this year, and Phil's daughters went on a mission trip to build homes in Louisiana. On the TV, Meredith Grey drowns in a mass of dark water, kicking and clawing for the surface in slow motion. When her head emerges, she doesn't scream for help. Why wouldn't she scream for help? She lets herself sink.

"I'm so sick of this place," Emily whispers. But no one is listening. She yanks her phone from her back pocket. A text from Todd: "Busy."

"Get behind the bar, Emily," says Dad, struggling to hang the bunting, "and switch ESPN back on."

CHAPTER FIVE

A figure hovers over Emily—a blurry haze of gray with shining, piercing, unblinking eyes, a ghostly specter. A hand strokes her cheek, following the line of her jaw to the hollow space beneath her chin. Another hand kneads her left breast. Another massages her belly. Another grips a fistful of her hair. She tries to call out, but another clamps over her mouth. An invisible weight presses down like a vise. She can't move.

The specter swells like a storm cloud, occupying the entire room. Another hand moves up her thigh. Another intertwines its fingers with hers. Another clutches her ankle. She finds enough strength to tap a knuckle against the wall—her signal to Dad. Help.

But he's seated in the old dining room chair by her mirror. His eyes are open, and his arms hang limply at his sides, legs splayed out, resting on his heels. He's pissed himself.

The hands continue searching her, exploring her—rough and eager, pinching and prodding. The screen door slams shut and creaks open over and over again.

The tube of cherry ChapStick shudders and falls. Her phone vibrates on the rickety wooden nightstand and wakes her. The door's shut and deadbolted. She shivers over the awful, lingering sensations of the dream. These fucking dreams.

She reaches for her phone. A number she doesn't recognize lights up the screen. They can leave a message. Once the call clears, she notices a text from Todd: "Can u come over?"

Foreboding floods her veins. She hasn't seen him since the I love yous, since she shared a bed with Ryan. Did he find out? Is he upset? She'll explain: "Ryan's having a rough time. We smoked some weed. He started talking about Iraq. What was I supposed to do? He's like a brother." All true. She felt no physical desire for him. What happened felt right and okay, needed. Todd will understand. He'll forgive her and hold her and evaporate the icky wet weight of her dream. Or is this a morning booty call? She buries her face in her pillow. Whatever it is, she'll explain, they'll have sex. This will be good for them. He's the only thing she has right now, until school starts anyway.

Emily texts back: "4 sure! BRT!" She ties her sneakers, unbolts the door, and notices a voicemail from the unfamiliar number.

"Hi, Emily. Cindy here from Westwood College. Sorry to kick off your Memorial weekend this way, but needed to let you know that the check you gave us for fall tuition bounced, and it's probably not a big deal. This sort of thing happens sometimes. Maybe the amount was too much, so your bank flagged it. Contact them, and I'm sure we can get it sorted out quickly. Have a great day! Bye now." Shit.

Emily rakes her fingers through her hair. First things first. Todd. Then bank. Everything will be fine. Everything's fine.

...

Rocket dashes from the open barn door to Emily's truck, wagging his tail, tongue dangling from his open mouth. Emily anxiously exhales, studying the statue of the Virgin Mary standing sentry over a miniature wishing well beside the other lawn ornaments left behind by Todd's grandparents—a family of deer, a smiling frog, kissing gnomes, and an array of moss-eaten birdbaths. She feels the virgin scrutinizing, judging as she rubs Rocket's back.

Todd waves from the barn door. His beard is gone.

"Hey." She waves back and blows out a breath as she rises away from the yellow dandelions.

"Feeding the horses," Todd says as she steps into the warm barn.

"Your beard." She rubs his cheek, like sandpaper against her palm.

He leans away and grips his chin. "Yep. Feels weird." He turns toward Robin, Prince, and Braun as they grunt and snort, stomping their hooves and waving their coarse, wispy tails from side to side in a vain attempt to ward away flies. She presses the back of her fingers against Robin's velvety muzzle.

"You need some kitties in here," Emily says.

"You've said that before." He lets out a weak laugh and fills the trough.

When Emily stayed with her grandparents, she spent the days with Grandma Bev, sewing and embroidering and mending Grandpa's shirts; weeding the garden, growing tomatoes and squash and carrots; kneading dough and baking fruit pies, lemon bars, and hot dishes topped with tater-tots.

Then Grandma turned on *Wheel of Fortune*, lit up a cigarette, and sent Emily to the barn where Grandpa was feeding the cows, sweeping out manure, or checking the milk tank. He wore a tweed cap and black-framed glasses that slipped down the narrow bridge of his nose. He never said much, mostly led her to the stall where a litter of fuzzy kittens wrestled and snuggled and let out squeaky meows. She settled among them until dinner, naming them, petting them, playing with them, letting them claw up her thighs and shoulders, leaving vivid red marks all over her pale skin. She loved those kitties.

"So, Emily, I was gonna text you, but I don't want to be a dick," says Todd.

She grimaces and grips her elbows. "Yeah. I think I know what this is about."

"You do? I'm sorry." He shakes his head. "I—it just happened. We started talking again and—"

A cold sweat releases from her pores. "What?"

"Nicole."

A thick, hard hurt like a jagged rock forms in her throat. She can't breathe.

Todd stands stiff, calm. "Nicole and I are gonna try again."

Emily tries to blink away the words. "You're back with Nicole?"

This must be what a heart attack feels like. This shooting pain radiating from the center of her chest. Embarrassed. Confused. Disbelieving. Tears tumble down her cheeks.

"Emily. You're young," he says gently.

She finds no sadness in his eyes.

"It was fun, wasn't it? Really fun," he goes on.

She wipes her nose with the sleeve of her flannel shirt. "But you're like all I have. Like, I have no one now."

Todd rests a hand on her shoulder. He furrows his brows and bites his bottom lip. He pities her. "You have your dad. The Honky Tonk crowd."

"Oh, great. Yeah. A bunch of middle-aged drunks."

"We'll still be friends. I'll come to The Honky Tonk now and then, you know," he says. "I'm sorry. I didn't mean to lead you on. I thought we were just having fun."

She feels small. Ridiculous. "Are you gonna come in with Nicole?"

"I don't know."

"Well, please don't," Emily says. "I'm so stupid." She wipes her nose again. The tears won't stop. She wants him to wrap her in his warmth and safety, but he studies his scuffed boots and bites his thumbnail. "Like, is there something wrong with me? Am I a shit person or something?"

Rocket rolls on his back at Emily's feet, whining for a belly rub.

"No. Emily. You're great."

"You said you loved me." Like that might convince him to choose her. Pathetic. She can't stand herself as she pleads.

"I'm sorry," he says again, shaking his head.

CHAPTER SIX

Emily numbly glides the screen door of The Honky Tonk open, then stops at the threshold.

Dad lowers a barstool. The jukebox cranked up, he half speaks, half sings along with Merle Haggard. "Mama Tried." The place smells like pickle juice.

"There you are," he says. "Come on. Let's get to work. Friday."

"Dad," she says. Her throat aches. A lightbulb flickers. Cloudy cobwebs fill corners like smoke.

"Yeah?" He tugs a threadbare rag from the loop of his jeans and wipes the bar, his back to her.

"I went to the bank." Breath empties from her lungs. Her body aches like one big bruise. Maybe it's a mistake. Maybe he used the wrong account. "My money is gone." Dad stops wiping and stands straight.

"Dad," she says again, a plea, letting the door slam behind her.

He faces her, his expression a wary scowl. She holds up

the list of transactions, withdrawal after withdrawal. He runs the bar rag through his fingers, seemingly calculating what to say as he bites the tip of his tongue. "I told you we needed money."

The words feel like a shove that's set her off balance. "But that's *my* money."

"We're a team, Emily."

"That's *my* money," she says again, desperate like she said to the bank teller—a young man with a collared polo shirt. He alerted a manager, a man with a chin that rested over the knot of his necktie. The chin stretched and sagged as he gazed from the transactions to a computer screen to Emily. $410.56. That's all.

"I didn't make these withdrawals," she'd told the manager, tears welling though she'd cried the entire drive from Todd's to the bank. How could there be any tears left? "It's a mistake. Or someone has my account number? Identity theft?"

"Do you check your bank statements? These are mailed out every month."

"My dad handles the mail."

"This is a joint account."

The $410.56 is tucked in her wallet. She's waiting for Dad to apologize, assure her that he plans to pay her back. But he presses his palms over his eyes.

"I ... what do you need that money for anyway?"

"It's *my* money."

"If you're living under this roof, it's my business. You know, this place made that money? I used it to invest in the place. You know how much it costs to keep it up? Heating and licenses and food and liquor, marketing. You know how much an ad in the paper costs? You know how much raising you cost?" He shrugs his lean shoulders.

"But that was *my* account." Her eyes ache, her brain aches, her heart aches.

"We're business partners, Emily. You agreed to that."

"When I was eight!" She struggles to swallow bile down.

"Look, I thought you were sticking by me."

"I am. I stayed. I've put aside everything I wanted for you and this stupid bar."

The disc changes. Emily drops the papers as a steel guitar begins a mournful tune. She doesn't want to hear a single word of it.

"Fuck this place." She leans behind the jukebox and presses the "off" button with such force she winces, wondering if she's jammed her finger. "Fuck."

"Shut your mouth."

"No." Emily straightens and shakes her throbbing finger. "Fuck this fucking bar. What am I supposed to do now?"

"What you said you would. You stand by your dad, and we'll figure it out."

"No. You figure it out. I'm done." Emily stomps past him, up the stairs, and to her room, searching for air as she goes, hyperventilating as she sits on the edge of her bed.

The jukebox switches back on. "Fuck him," she whispers, rubbing her eyes until she sees fuzzy stars.

She rips the horse calendar from the tack and tears each month's image to bits—an Appaloosa resting in a field of bluebonnets, a Clydesdale kicking up snow. "Stupid. Stupid," she says as the pieces fall to the floor like tainted snowflakes. "I'm so stupid."

She bolts the door but can't stand to remain in this room or this bar another minute. There's nothing left for her. She stuffs a duffle bag with jeans, t-shirts, hoodies, shorts, bras, underwear, socks, mascara, lip gloss, a toothbrush, and her hairbrush. She climbs out the window into the sunlight.

"Shit, shit, shit," she says as her truck kicks up gravel. She turns east on Interstate 29.

CHAPTER SEVEN

Emily drives down the interstate her dad hates so much, passing Amish buggies and John Deere tractors, behind semi-trucks, pickup trucks, motorcycles, and those cars that barely clear the pavement. Calls to Ashley go unanswered. She pounds her palms on the steering wheel.

"Shit, shit," she cries, before opening her phone, frantically pressing the tiny buttons: "Quit Honky Tonk. Coming 2 u."

She exhales and presses a shaking hand to her heaving chest. She feels charged, like she chugged a pot of boiling coffee, but there's nothing in her stomach. She struggles to slide her warped and smudged Target sunglasses on, temper the glare of the sunlight. She should stop for a bottle of water and a granola bar.

The phone rings and vibrates. "Dad" appears on the screen. She tosses it to the passenger seat.

She'll go to Madison. She'll stay with Ashley, like Ashley

wanted. They'll reconnect. Their friendship will be stronger. Everything will be fine. She'll find a job and figure it out.

She tries to focus on the banjo of a Taylor Swift song until her phone rings once more. "Ashley."

"What's going on?" asks Ashley. She's walking. Wind whooshes through the speakers.

"My dad. He took all my money." The phone nearly slides from Emily's slick, sweaty palm.

"What?"

"Like, it's gone." Emily's other hand grips the steering wheel so tight her fingers ache. "I went to the bank, and there's nothing in there."

"Oh, God. That's terrible." Ashley says breathlessly. The wind rustles and whistles in Emily's ear. "Can you call the police or something?"

"It was a joint account." Emily's voice cracks. "He says it was for the bar, and we're partners."

"That's messed up, Emily."

"I don't know what to do. I'm done. I'm so mad. And like, so done with Dad and that place."

"Yeah. I can't believe you've stayed as long as you did." Ashley inhales, exhales. Can't she stop walking for a moment?

"I know. What was I doing? He just wanted the free labor. And Todd broke it off with me this morning."

"Jeez."

"I know. So awful. So, I'm probably like two hours away."

"Emily," Ashley says.

Emily's throat tightens at the gentle, apologetic tone—like Todd's.

"This isn't a good time. I'm sorry. I'm sorry your dad is a jerk, and you're in this position."

Emily swallows down bile. "Seriously? You're being serious right now?"

A pause. The wind stops. "Did you sleep with Ryan?"

"What?"

"I saw you, Emily. I saw you in bed with Ryan. Like, do you have any morals? Is that why Todd broke up with you?"

Emily can't feign ignorance. She can't lie her way out of this. "Nothing happened."

They were clinging to each other all night. She slept peacefully and woke with her forehead pressed against Ryan's warm neck.

"I swear. Nothing happened," she says again.

"Okay. Well. Whatever. But I want my own thing for once, and it feels like you just come in, and it's all about you."

All about her? Nothing's ever about her.

"Look, nothing happened with Ryan. He's sad," she tries to explain. "He couldn't sleep, so we smoked some pot and talked."

"God. I don't even want to know. You're both so pathetic and needy."

The cracked pavement. The semi passing on her left. The billboards and farm fields on her right. They blur into one giant mass, a monster, swallowing Emily whole. She's so small. So alone. Pathetic? Needy? She has to swallow down bile before words can come; they're as acrid as the taste in her mouth.

"Well you've become a stuck-up bitch. I can't believe you! I'm your best friend." How could Ashley abandon her like this?

"I can't with you right now, okay? I have two roommates and a new job, and I just can't. Me and my family have done so much for you our whole lives, and I'm done being used."

"Used? How can you say that?"

"Hi, Ellie! Hey, Connor," Ashley says away from the speaker in a sing-song voice. Then her voice returns clear and close. "Why don't you call my mom? I'm sure she'll take you in. You can have my room or sleep with Ryan. I don't care anymore."

Bile comes. Emily can't swallow it down. She lurches to the passenger side, and a yellow-green liquid splashes on the plastic Walmart bag Todd handed her containing a hoodie, CDs, and some socks and underwear. A horn blares. She's drifted to the other lane.

"Fuck!" She tugs the wheel to the side of the road and stomps the brakes.

Ashley has hung up. Emily wipes her mouth, suffused with a sharp, bitter taste. She rests her head on the steering wheel and cries. Somehow her body found more tears. She needs water. Traffic whizzes past. She doesn't know where to go. She clutches her stomach and turns the AC full blast and aims a vent at her face.

She can't turn around; she won't turn around. She looks to the tilled fields lined with trees sprouting young leaves, the silver tops of silos glinting in the sunshine like lighthouses beckoning her every which way. She needs a job, a place to live.

"Lots of jobs," she remembers Jacob said. "Lots of money."

Door County.

CHAPTER EIGHT

one! You're hired. What are you, some kind of angel?"
Chris stands tall, coarse whiskers as black as ink. If he
wore a captain's hat and wool pea coat dotted with brass
buttons, he'd appear right at home on the ships sailing along
in the old photographs adorning The Schooner's walls. But
he wears a navy polo, as do the other employees congregat-
ing by the end of the nearly full bar and the register across
the large dining area. One's filling salt and pepper shakers,
another is marrying ketchup bottles, and the rest chat or sip
from clear plastic soda glasses or brown coffee mugs.

"Introductions later." Chris claps his hands together so
forcefully Emily jolts. "Let's get you a shirt and on the floor.
We're about to get slammed."

She follows, dizzy and disoriented. The carpeted dining
room looks like the belly of some Great Lakes whale that
swallowed all the nautical paraphernalia it could find:
fishing nets, lanterns, compasses, helms, portholes, a couple
wooden figures of bare-breasted women. Chris opens an

office door and points to a pile of polos spilling from a cardboard box.

"Find your size. You can get ready in here. I'll have you follow Ingrid for a while. She's been here forever," he says. "Then give you a small section, like four or five tables." He sets an apron, a couple of pens, and a notepad on the desk strewn with paperwork, receipts, menus, and a laminated OSHA poster—"Job Safety and Health. It's the Law!"

"Ingrid'll tell you everything. God, you're an angel."

Emily swaps her flannel for the polo. She should retrieve a sports bra from her truck, switch the ballet flats for her tennis shoes, maybe tour the cabin she's agreed to live in. But Chris's urgency keeps her in place. And if she opens her truck door, she might climb in and retreat to The Honky Tonk.

Emily feels like a traitor tucking in the new polo, wondering how Dad and Bernie are handling the shift and what Dad will tell Gladys, Larry, Doug, the regular fish fry crowd. "Emily isn't feeling well." "Emily took the day off." Or "Emily went and left me like her no-good mother." She hasn't checked her phone since passing the "Welcome to Door County" sign an hour ago.

"Where r u?!??!!" Dad texted. Twelve missed calls. She powered the phone off and kept her foot on the gas, driving between blocky beige bluffs and the water of Green Bay, reflecting the bright sunshine like a mirror. The radio often turned to static. Unsure where to go or stop, Emily drove up Highway 57, past neat rows of cherry and apple trees with a few blossoms remaining, farms and tilled fields that made her feel she hadn't gone very far from home until she turned a corner and was met with a wide expanse of blue, nothing but horizon. Then a sign staked on the side of the road: "Hiring! The Schooner. Waitstaff. Housing Available!"

Emily adjusts the collar around her neck. She's never been anywhere she didn't know anyone, she realizes, as she knots the apron around her waist and grips the stiff pad of paper. She retrieves the ChapStick at the bottom of her purse and notices her phone. *Maybe I should text Dad*, she thinks, rubbing her cherry-flavored lips together, *let him know I'm okay*. A knock on the door. "Coming!" she says.

Ingrid's hand is up her shirt, fiddling with a bra strap. She's thirty-something with hair so blonde it's almost white. "I'm sorry. These stupid maternity bras," she says while Emily bites a thumbnail, hoping her eyes aren't puffy from all the crying she's done today.

"You're fine."

"I just. Ugh. Like, were these designed by women? I know I'm gonna leak tonight, and this frickin pad won't stay." She does a bit more adjusting, her elbow going up and down like a lever. "Okay. So, training. You've served before?"

"Yeah. My ... family owns a little tavern," Emily answers, struggling over the word *family*.

"Thank God. Because I'm so out of it." Ingrid rubs her

hands over her face. "My four-month-old refuses to sleep for longer than twenty minutes at a time, so I'm struggling." Her red-tinged eyes make Emily less conscious of her own.

"That's fine. I've been serving since I was a kid. I should be fine."

"You *are* a kid. But awesome. Okay."

Ingrid leads her to the soda machine. A woman who looks done up for a night out— shimmery cheeks, lip liner, and afro puffs on either side of her head—chats to another woman who nods along in sympathy, the mole on her left cheek like a fishing bobber going up and down.

"'Am I just your arm candy?' That's what I said to him. I'm more than that."

"Yes. Yes, you are." Both women appear to be about Emily's age.

"This is Emily," interrupts Ingrid. "Emily, this is the soda machine." Ingrid gestures to the machine before them, bulky and boxy, the bright labels of each soda flavor layered in glossy film. "I assume you know how to use one."

"And I'm Molly," the woman with the mole says, putting a hand on Emily's forearm. She has a toothy smile, her chin-length hair pushed aside with a single bobby pin. Emily smiles back, the place where Molly touches her like an ember, glowing and warm.

"And this is Alicia."

"Hey," Alicia says, studying Emily. "Oh, my God. I wish I had your cheekbones. I feel like I can't find mine. I'm all baby fat, and yours jut out like a model's."

"Oh, thank you," says Emily, bringing her hand to her cheeks, sure they're flushed from the emotions of the day.

A young man in a white chef shirt emerges from a pair of swinging doors by the soda machine, breaking up the group of women. "Move it, Chicago." He nudges playfully into Alicia.

"Doesn't she have the best cheekbones, Shawn?" Alicia says.

"This is Emily," says Molly.

"They're nice," Shawn says with a dimpled smirk.

"Okay, moving on," Ingrid says. "So, some people will get all crabby that we don't have Coke or Pepsi. We have RC. They can get over it or go to the gas station."

"Which some people have." Molly laughs.

"Tourists are so entitled," says Shawn, filling a tall plastic cup with ice, the tentacles of an octopus tattoo wrap around his bare calf, the head somewhere behind baggy gym shorts.

"*Some* tourists," Molly corrects him. "Calm down."

"All those rich cocksuckers from Chicago." Shawn nudges Alicia again.

"Who pay for your weird lifestyle," Alicia answers back, laughing. "Don't listen to him, Emily. We're not all bad."

"Anyway, moving on, please." Ingrid strolls toward the register, hunching over a screen smudged with a hundred fingerprints. "It's easy once you get the hang of it," she says. Her unpolished nails click against the surface as she points to each flickering word. "Burgers here, fish here, specials here, salads here. Pick what you want and follow the prompts—how they want it done: lettuce, tomato, or onion, and their side. Drinks here. All the cocktails and liquor are listed alphabetically. Again, follow the prompts. Done. Easy."

"Are you my new roommate?"

Emily turns to a young woman with hair the color of an orange Skittle, the most freckles she's ever seen on anybody.

"I think so?" Emily says like a question. She can hardly think past the present moment. What did she agree to? "Chris said a cabin?"

"Yep. Oh, good. I'm Bridget. You look normal. I was worried. Chris will hire frickin' anybody," she says with a raspy voice like a crackling fire. "I've already claimed bottom bunk. Hope that's okay. I'm scared of heights."

"That's fine." Emily feels scared of everything right now. What is she doing here?

Ingrid passes through the swinging doors, around a corner to a prep room lined with deep sinks and tall refrigerators, everything silver, everything bigger, newer, nicer than The Honky Tonk.

"The only reason you'd need to come in here is to get more salads from this fridge." Ingrid rests a palm on one of the imposing, glinting surfaces. "Or you need a minute. The freezer is good for that too." Maybe Ingrid notices Emily's overwhelmed. No, probably not. She's already flying past her toward the heat of the kitchen, toward the sounds of a blaring trumpet and wails from a seemingly overemotional man singing mariachi music more modern than any played at the Mexican restaurant Dad likes in Eau Claire.

More metal surfaces reflect the fluorescent lights as bright as spotlights, more refrigerators and prep surfaces. A countertop at Emily's eye level glows with hanging heat lamps. Ingrid raises her voice over the music coming from a stereo on top of a microwave. Both appear graffitied by a spray can of chili and cheese.

"The kitchen will buzz you when your food is up. They'll put your ticket out with the food, so make sure it's all there and throw away the ticket so there's no confusion," instructs Ingrid.

"Okay."

Ingrid opens the glass door of a refrigerator stacked with side salads, each one a small pile of iceberg lettuce, a couple of cucumbers and cherry tomatoes, and bits of red onion.

"Here's all this." Ingrid gestures to the portioned tartar sauces and ranch dressings. She moves on to the soup warmer. "Chili, seafood chowder—no, none of it has local ingredients—and the soup of the day." Ingrid points out the soup bowls and extra napkins. Everything feels out of order, out of place. Even the fryer smells off. But Emily nods and notices a man in a backward baseball cap on the other side of the heat lamps scraping the grill. He's looking toward a woman biting into a hard-boiled egg. Delicate earrings dotted with multicolored stones dangle from her ears.

"You want to keep it? Why you gotta be so sweet, chica? That thing probably has lice."

"No. Not keep. Become friends with." The woman covers her mouth as she chews. "She'll kill the mice."

"Javier," Ingrid calls.

He turns. "Yeah?"

"What does Emily need to know about the kitchen?"

"Uh. Don't ask when something will be ready."

"Okay," Emily replies.

"And I'm in charge of the kitchen, girl. Don't touch anything. I'm the king," he continues.

She's used to feeling total control and freedom over everything when it comes to The Honky Tonk's kitchen. She nods, intimidated, until the woman next to Javier gives him a weak push in the arm. "I'm Nora and he's joking. You can ask him whatever you want and touch whatever you want."

Javier winks at Emily.

"Hey. I've been here the longest. If anyone's in charge, it's me," says Ingrid, tossing a few wayward French fries into a garbage can.

"No respect in this place. I'm telling Chris about the feral cat," Javier jokes.

"No, you're not," Nora replies, another gentle shove.

"Are you having a cat in the cabin?" asks Ingrid. "You should check with Emily too."

"You're gonna live with us? You like cats, right?"

"Yeah," Emily says as brightly as she can muster. She does. And she wishes she could hold one this minute.

"Oh, you'll love Luna." Nora pouts her lips and adds, "Sweet little stray."

Ingrid walks off, and Emily follows her past a petite woman with furrowed pencil-thin eyebrows flattening a chicken breast with a metal hammer and a teenage boy loading a dishwasher pallet, his baggy jeans dragging on wet rubber mats. Emily avoids their eyes. She doesn't want to meet anyone else. She wants to start serving or go home.

Following Ingrid behind the bar feels a bit like being home. The setup is familiar. Bottles of liquor line shelves next to an ice tub and soda gun, with tumblers and pint glasses close by. A counter against the mirrored wall features top-shelf liquors and a long line-up of beer handles. The mostly male patrons rest their elbows or forearms on a dark green cushion wrapped around the edge of the bar, gripping sweaty beer bottles or tumblers. A young man in black-framed glasses stocks Coors Light, a folded paperback peeking out from his jeans pocket. A few watch Emily and Ingrid, others watch the baseball game on a giant screen TV above them, and a couple are in conversation.

"So, drink tickets come here." Ingrid points to a receipt printer beside a dented and worn wooden sculpture of a lighthouse. "If they are swamped, get the drinks yourself. But don't forget to pull your ticket so they don't make 'em." She shows Emily where the Stella chalices are, the frozen mugs, and margarita, wine, and shot glasses. "We don't have a beer menu, so write them down if you need to. This is Brandon." Ingrid points to the spectacled man, glancing up from his open book like a raccoon in headlights. "Umm, what else?" Ingrid looks around. "Honestly. I think that's it."

"Thanks," says Emily.

"Yeah. I wish I could have a drink right now."

"Me too."

"You'll get one after work. Don't worry. I have to feed a human from my body, so I better not." Ingrid peers down her shirt and adjusts her bra. "I gotta pump around seven. You're all gonna have to watch my tables for me. It's the worst time, but I don't want mastitis again. It was the most awful thing ever. Like the sickest I've ever felt and the weirdest pain in my boob."

"Pain don't bother me none," chimes a man with a graying combover and bushy beard. He takes a swig from his bottle of Miller High Life.

"Is that right?" says Ingrid, folding her arms across her chest.

"I go to the dentist and say, 'Don't put me on the gas. I don't want nothing.' He cracked a tooth right in my mouth to get it out. And I drove myself home," the man continues. Ingrid shakes her head. "Brett Favre's like that. He don't feel no pain. That's why he can play so long." Ingrid elbows Emily and rolls her eyes.

"You don't believe me? It's true," says the man.

"You comparing yourself to Brett there, Joe?" asks Chris, stocking the green olives.

"Try having a baby, Joe," Ingrid says wryly. "No. First try creating one in your own body—all the bones and eyeballs and organs." Ingrid talks slowly, matter-of-factly, enunciating every word like she's teaching a child to read.

"You do that first, then you push the eight-pound thing out of your body. Then you feed the thing with your body. I bet even Brett Favre would wince."

Ingrid's dry humor surprises Emily. She's not so bad. Customers along the bar chuckle. Chris laughs, stocking the cherries now. Emily smiles.

"I'm not sure I feel pain much either," says another patron with a wide face and white untamed eyebrows. "Hell, I got a penicillin shot when I was a kid, and the needle broke off in my butt. I was in the parking lot, and the doc stuck his head out the window and hollered, 'Get back in here!'"

Emily laughs for the first time today. She covers her mouth, the laugh tickling her palm.

"You didn't know it was in you?" Ingrid asks.

"No, not 'til he told me. Then I started screaming."

"How old were you?" asks Chris.

"Second grade."

"I'd have fainted," says Emily, the ease of the comment pleasing her. *Here I am*, she thinks. *I can do this.*

"He put me back in the room and said, 'Drop your drawers,' laid me on my stomach, and one-two-three, he pulled her out. Sure as shit."

Emily laughs again. Her reflex tells her to find a bar rag and start wiping, stock the pint glasses, see who needs another drink. Everything right and wrong at once.

Emily holds her own at the start of dinner, confident even as she delivers beers and old-fashioneds, cheese curds and onion rings with hot grease still popping off the breading. She serves a vacationing family, a young couple, an old couple, and a small table of fishermen. But the menu stretches longer than The Honky Tonk's. Questions trip her up.

"How would you describe the whitefish? Does it taste real fishy?" "Are salmon native to Lake Michigan?" "Are the nachos gluten-free?"

She mixes ranch dressing with blue cheese dressing, can't find the to-go containers, takes another server's medium-rare burger to an elderly woman who asked for well-done.

"Does this look well to you?" asks the woman, forcefully extending her arm, the burger with a single bite mere inches from Emily's eyes. The interior of the patty pink as bubblegum.

"I'm new. I'm sorry," she says, she hears herself keep saying. She doesn't realize lettuce, tomato, and onion cost extra, which has upset an older man who calls it "criminal to charge seventy-five cents for roughage."

"Sorry. I'm new," she says again. Javier makes her another burger. Bridget teaches Emily to void a charge and remove the seventy-five cents off the man's bill.

Emily navigates drink orders fine and makes a few herself, but her hands reach for where the brandy and vodka are at The Honky Tonk, which she doesn't notice until she begins pouring the liquor. So, she starts the drinks again, then forgets to pull her ticket.

"Just fine," says Chris when she finds sweaty tumblers waiting for her at the end of the bar a few minutes later. Brandon takes the extra cocktails and sets them in front of bar patrons who whoop and holler.

"I'm so sorry," she says.

A vibration in her back pocket—food is up. When she enters the kitchen, she collides with a wall of heat and Mexican music so urgent, so consuming, that she wonders what they are singing about. Love, probably. The cooks glisten with sweat. Shawn drops frozen fries in a fryer basket, and another flips burgers. The woman, once pounding chicken, pours melted butter over baby red potatoes with deft precision. Javier stands in the center, sliding prepared plates on the aluminum counter. They talk in Spanglish.

Emily peeks at the burgers beneath the heat lamp, then her notepad. She sees all but one.

"Are these mine?" she interrupts. Javier's frantic brown eyes rise from the fried perch he's arranging to Emily. "I think one was supposed to have barbeque sauce on it. Did I type it in wrong?"

Javier glances from the tickets to the burgers, the grill, and then back to the tickets.

"Girl, wait 'til we buzz you." She's too embarrassed to tell him she felt a buzz. She leans against the salad bar and studies her notepad. The flats pinch her toes. She should have worn her tennis shoes. A clock on the wall reads 6:48 p.m. When does the kitchen close?

Nora steps in, calm and composed, a few strands of her upswept hair caught in her earrings. "God, I'm starving." She takes a salad from the refrigerator, pours some ranch or blue cheese—Emily isn't sure—over the lettuce, and pops a slice of cucumber in her mouth.

Emily realizes how hungry she feels too. "Can we eat those?"

"Yeah, help yourself."

"Thanks. I haven't eaten all day." Her stomach feels hard and heavy, like she's swallowed a stone.

"Eat. Soup. Fries. Ask Shawn to make you some tenders or something. Go for it."

"Now you're up," says Javier, glancing at Emily.

"Thank you." She rests a plate in the crook of her arm, grabbing the other two. She delivers the food and returns to the register. Table Eight wants split checks.

A woman approaches. "Excuse me. How long is the wait?"

Emily spots the hostess, Madge, a sixty-something with silver hair and sneakers so clean it's obvious she doesn't deliver drinks or food. She talks to a seated couple who appear beyond eighty, walkers beside their chairs like guard dogs.

"Put some butter on it when you put it back in the fridge, then it don't get hard or moldy," Madge says, the couple seemingly engrossed in whatever she's talking about.

"You'll need to talk to her." Emily points, turning back to

the screen. Her body flashes hot and cold. How do you split the checks? She needs help, but the servers are scattered. Ingrid must be pumping. Customers peer at her expectantly, and a man waves his arm frenetically like there's a medical emergency. "Miss. Miss!"

"Yes?"

"Can I get a refill?" He holds up an empty pint glass.

"In a sec." Eyes back to the screen. Panic and urgency twist around every bone in Emily's body. Was she supposed to highlight something somehow, move it over, create a new check? She's still searching, waiting for someone to intercede, and makes eye contact with the fourteen-year-old busser carrying a tub of dirty dishes to the kitchen. Toby? Travis? What was his name?

"Can you get that guy a Spotted Cow?" She points to the man still holding out his empty glass.

"I'm too young to bring beer," he answers, pushing the swinging doors open with the tub and disappearing into the kitchen.

"What do you need?" asks Molly, coming from nowhere, sure and steady. She puts a hand between Emily's shoulder blades.

"I can't figure out how to split these checks." Emily wants to cry.

Molly navigates the computer with ease. "I'll explain that again when we're not so busy."

"Thank you. Yes." Emily could hug her. "'Cause I don't know how to add garnish to the drink orders on here either.

I've had to keep telling the bartenders, and I think the guy with glasses is annoyed with me."

"Brandon? No. He's high. He's high all the time." Molly laughs. "He just looks annoyed. Don't worry."

Emily exhales and asks Toby or Travis or whatever his name is to clear a couple of tables and deliver checks. "You can do that, right?"

"Yes." He sighs.

Emily finds her footing for a time, buoyed by Molly's kindness, until she delivers a check, and the customers wonder what's for dessert.

"I'm new," she says. "Let me check the menu."

She grabs one from a stack on the unmanned podium while Madge chats with another table. "They waited until she was eighteen months for her baptism. The kid was wailing. Too old. It's best when they're teeny. Asleep. Dead to the world."

Emily scans the menu: "Ask your server for dessert options." Shit. She finds Alicia stuffing bills into her apron pocket.

"Just cherry pie," says Alicia. "I'll show you." She leads Emily to a corner of the prep room Ingrid skipped over. "Ingrid didn't show me either. I started last week. I feel bad this is your first night."

Alicia opens a refrigerator full of tubs of coleslaw and mayonnaise, open containers of tomatoes, lemons, limes, oranges, rows of whipped cream, and stacks of white pie-sized boxes. "It comes off the truck, but Chris says if they ask, tell 'em it's got Door County cherries in it. Nuke 'em for twenty seconds. There's vanilla ice cream in that freezer if they want it à la mode."

Emily thanks Alicia and watches her go. She stands in the empty space, drops her head in her hands, and cries for the third or fourth time that day. She's lost count.

CHAPTER NINE

Emily wants nothing more than to slip on her faded gray cotton shorts and a high school t-shirt, wash her face of the sweat and makeup and tears, and brush the chicken tenders and vodka from her teeth. She wants nothing more than to climb into bed and pull a blanket over her head and end this day.

But Nora has other plans. "We need to do some smudging," she says as Emily passes through the screened-in porch and enters the small boxy cabin a quarter mile from The Schooner. "I got weird energy tonight, and we need to do this. Set some intentions."

Emily expected a musty, dusty, rusty scene in disarray. And though the loveseat and armchair are dated, the brown pile of the carpet matted and worn, the framed pictures of a sunset, lighthouse, and bucket of cherries faded almost beyond recognition, the place has clean surfaces, a petite kitchen and bathroom with stain-free sinks, and the space smells like patchouli, like the stores that sell incense and crystals and glass tobacco pipes.

Bridget rotates her wrists and ankles. "My muscles aren't in server mode yet."

Nora calls for Luna from the screened-in porch. "Here, kitty, kitty, kitty." The distant crash of Lake Michigan's waves responds. Tree branches slap in the black breeze. "I want her to be a part of this."

Bridget makes an exasperated expression at Emily, pantomimes pointing to a watch on her wrist.

"Looks like she got the fish I put out for her," says Nora.

"Not sure you should be putting food out like that," says Bridget, now rolling her eyes. "I feel like that could attract other things we don't want around here."

Emily leans against the doorframe of her new bedroom. She clutches her phone; it feels like a dumbbell gathering weight, tugging her down. No response since she texted Dad an hour ago while sitting at a table surrounded by the servers and bussers rolling silverware. It felt safe to do so then. Safety in numbers, in their ignorance, in the lightness of the conversation happening around her—pickle spears sliding off plates, Javier's secret Harry Potter obsession, that customer at the bar whose hairy butt-crack was on full display most of the night. Their unawareness comforting, reassuring as she powered on her phone and scanned the multiple texts from Dad: "Where the hell r u?" "Thought we're partners." "R u alive?!"

"Alive. Need 2 figure stuff out. Want money back," she typed, shut her phone, and took a long drink of her post-shift vodka cranberry.

"Texting a boyfriend?" asked Alicia.

"No," she said, imagining Todd and Nicole reunited. She took another long drink.

"Good. Boys are stupid," Alicia said, clinking her glass against Emily's.

"Hear! Hear!" said Bridget, joining the cheers.

Nora returns to the living room with a bundle of cedar leaves wound tightly in twine. "Dammit. I really wanted Luna here."

"She'll come back," says Bridget. "Let's do this. I think Emily's about to pass out."

Emily feels the tiredness and disinterest radiating off her like stink off a dead skunk. If she knew Nora better, she'd ask if they could do whatever this is tomorrow or the next day or never because it sounds ridiculous. But Nora seems unfazed as she sets the cedar in a ceramic bowl stained with ash and pulls a lighter from her linen shorts.

"Okay. Thank you for doing this with me," Nora says. "I need this."

"No worries," says Bridget, rising from the armchair.

"I forgot about the questions, you know. Multiple tables tonight with the, 'Are you a student? You from here? Married? Children?' One guy was literally like, 'So, what do you do?'" Nora's eyes go wide. Bridget snorts.

"Like, I'm holding a tray of drinks. 'What do you think I do? You think I do this for fun?'"

"What did you tell him?" asks Bridget.

"I told him I spent last winter in Seville, drinking cheap-ass wine and learning flamenco. The winter before that, I was in Belize, snorkeling and doing yoga. And I'm looking at him like, 'Isn't that great? Aren't I lucky?' And I tell him this kind of work pays for that and makes it feasible. He looked at me like I was crazy, and it just diminished everything. I felt so small. And like pissed, 'cause it's also just a job that pays the bills."

Emily couldn't point to Belize on a map and isn't sure if Nora said "flamingo" or not. "You went by yourself?" she asks.

"Yeah," says Nora. "And both experiences were amazing and life-altering, and I feel like I have to defend myself, my choices to strangers all summer long."

"That's annoying. They usually stop after I say I'm a student in Green Bay," says Bridget. "Then it's about the Packers."

Emily got the questions, too, but not many. Maybe customers could sense her panic and newness. When they asked if she grew up in Door County, if she was a student, she simply said, "No," and then pretended the kitchen buzzed her. When her coworkers asked questions, she delivered the basics: Deer Valley, not far from Eau Claire, no.

Nora closes her eyes and asks Bridget and Emily to do the same.

"Let's think about our intentions," says Nora softly. Emily keeps her eyes open, wondering what that means, what's taking place exactly. Is this witchcraft?

During middle school sleepovers, Emily and her friends took turns lying flat on basement floors while others sat around her in a circle with candles lit, the smell of popcorn and damp laundry heavy in the air. They drummed their fingertips lightly beneath the subject's arms, legs, and skull, whispering, "Light as a feather. Stiff as a board. Light as a feather. Stiff as a board." No one levitated. And the image of a corpse never appeared when they turned off the bathroom lights and repeated "Bloody Mary" thirteen times. And though they tried to communicate with spirits on Kendra Zimmerman's Ouija board, Lindsay Mathers cried and threatened to tell her parents.

Is this something along those lines?

Nora lights the end of the cedar stick. The flame catches with a blossom of orange, then shrinks to a laser red line creeping down the green leaves while gray wisps of smoke gracefully drift and swirl toward the low ceiling. Emily closes her eyes as well.

"Thank you for this space," begins Nora, speaking low, soft. "We acknowledge this land is a gift and ask you to purify the space. Fill it with positivity. Take away all the negative energy. We command any malevolent beings to leave. You are not welcome here."

Emily nods. Not sure who the "you" refers to, but this feels different than the rehearsed prayers of her grandparents' mass. This "you" feels less intimidating and more intimate. Feels different than the God Phil blames for what he did.

She's not sure what *malevolent* means, but the word reminds her of a quiet, secret hurt, like Dad taking her money, Ashley drifting away, Todd letting her go for someone else, Phil.

"Yes. Leave," she whispers.

"We state our intention to create a home here," says Nora.

Shivers ripple through Emily's skin. Home.

"To live in reciprocity with one another and with the spirits present."

Emily opens her eyes. Nora holds the ceramic bowl beneath the burning cedar as she moves through the cabin, guiding the stick over the furniture in the bedrooms and in the living room, over the small dining table and appliances in the kitchen, even the bathroom.

Nora's voice comforts Emily, and the scent of burning cedar wraps around her like a hug.

They reform the circle.

"Let's each state our intention for the summer," says Nora.

Emily is still not sure what Nora means by intention. "Can I go last?"

"Sure. Switch places with Bridget. We need to go clockwise."

Nora closes her eyes. "My intention is to focus on the good this summer. To be kind to myself. To know that I am not responsible for anyone's reaction to me or my choices."

She passes the stick to Bridget, who blows a breath from between her lips. "My intention is to not be afraid of who I am." She passes the stick to Emily.

"Emily?" Nora prompts.

"To make money and figure out what to do with my life?" Emily says like a question.

Nora bites her lower lip in a polite cringe. "Focus on you. Simple. Positive."

Emily feels it's a test, and she doesn't have the right answer; there's no multiple choice. To not trust? To be less pathetic and needy like Ashley said? To be worthy of love? To stop living for someone else? She knows the answer now. It appears like a pheasant flying up from the brush in a flash of song and color, then rises steadily into the sky.

"To start living *my* life," she says. "For me."

"Yes," whispers Nora. "Your life is yours. It belongs to you."

Nora smiles, satisfied. "Group hug." She pulls them together, arms around one another's backs and shoulders and necks. Bridget's and Nora's flyaways tickle Emily's forehead.

"I am honored to share this space with you," Nora whispers.

"You're such a hippie," says Bridget, laughing. "Can we go to bed now?"

CHAPTER TEN

Emily wakes to the smell of coffee, gratefully realizing that even on a thin mattress, uncomfortably close to the ceiling, she has slept dreamlessly these last few nights. A soft acoustic tune plays from Nora's room. The air stirs from an oscillating fan on the dresser she shares with Bridget. Emily had already piled eight hundred dollars in that dresser, hefty stacks of bills hiding beneath her socks and underwear.

But like walking into a glass door, her racing thoughts shatter the reprieve of sleep. She's off work today and has a long list of errands: open a bank account, find a washing machine, buy food for her allotted shelves in the refrigerator and cupboard, call Dad. She promised him via text she would after she woke that first morning to more texts and missed calls and voicemails, angry, all caps, which she deleted.

"Call u Tuesday. Need space."

She navigates her way down the bunk and enters the living room. Bridget, perched on the edge of the couch, laces her running shoes.

"Good morning," Emily says with an ease that surprises her. She's falling into a rhythm.

"Hey, sleepyhead," Bridget says. She rises and smooths her hair in a ponytail.

"How can you go for a run after this weekend? Do you start every day this way?" Emily asks, her feet tender and wrists sore, her stomach queasy after eating nothing but ranch-drenched side salads, deep-fried fish, and mistake pizzas the last few days.

"If I don't start the day with a run, I feel so lazy."

Nora appears in her doorframe, holding a blue mug with a white trillium, the same flower that carpets the ground surrounding their cabin.

"I don't get it either," Nora says. "I like some yoga and long walks, but running for more than three miles sounds awful."

"No, really, it's like a high," says Bridget. She stretches her left arm over her head. "It's addicting. I read that it's like taking cocaine."

"I'd rather do cocaine," jokes Emily.

"Have you seriously done cocaine?" asks Bridget. She stretches her right arm over her head.

"A couple times," says Emily. She doubted the effectiveness of the drug the first time she snorted the white powder off a classmate's car key.

"I don't feel any different," she said in a barn full of teenagers, until she sang Carrie Underwood karaoke, finally aware of the euphoric energy bouncing off her blood cells. Then she played ping pong. Swung from the rope swing in the hay loft. Took another hit. Made out with Blake Warren, Ashley's crush, beneath a row of taxidermized bucks.

Why did she do that? Because she wanted to. Because she could. Because Ashley wasn't there and would have been too chicken to do it anyway. Maybe because eight days prior, her grandparents were killed in a car accident, switching lanes on an icy road. Maybe because Ashley had two nice, normal parents; a beautiful, quiet room; no job so she could focus on school; a credit card; six months of counseling for her "severe anxiety" sophomore year; and four grandparents. Maybe because Blake's bleak artist eyes were what Emily needed that night. Him biting her bottom lip. A release. A way of coping.

Emily *is* a shit friend.

"Well, you two sit here and listen to Nora's sad bastard music," says Bridget, laughing. The sound of a mournful, mumbling man singing wafts from Nora's room. "Just boo-hoo, I don't have a girlfriend anymore. Boo-hoo." Bridget touches her toes and falls back to the couch when Nora gives her a playful shove.

"Hey! It's relaxing, bully."

Emily laughs. She likes Bridget and Nora, that they accepted her into the tiny cabin without question. She likes the clean slate and makes a mental note to avoid making out with anyone they might be attracted to.

And she's beginning to get the hang of The Schooner—the nuances of the menu, the flow of the kitchen, the navigation of the computer, and where everything is located, like the to-go containers, napkins, side plates, crackers, crayons and paper, even the ingredient list for the black bean burger.

And while one half of Emily's brain felt saturated with the heaviness of Friday, looping through questions: How had her life unraveled so quickly? When did Dad start taking her money? When did Todd and Nicole start talking again? When did Ashley decide Emily wasn't worth it anymore?

The other half of her brain felt comforted by the busyness of the restaurant and the banality of the conversations around her. When she collected or mixed drinks at the bar, she caught bits of the patrons' conversations about the Brewers' winning streak against the Reds, jigging they used to catch trout, and their home remodeling projects. The kitchen staff bobbed their heads to their energetic music, comparing tattoos, planning frisbee golf tournaments, and debating whether 9/11 was an inside job, while the servers and bussers shared brief moments around the register and soda machine talking about *Twilight*, ketchup stains, and Alicia's terrible luck buying swimsuits online.

No one knew her like they did at The Honky Tonk. A fresh start.

She didn't mind the customers either, the ones who smiled back, didn't demand too much, gave her a twenty percent tip, and went on their way.

She thought she'd done right by a family of four until she dropped off the bill. The man sighed. "You know, you aren't very friendly."

Emily flushed with embarrassment. "Sorry."

"Honey, stop," said the woman. The school-age children gazed down at their remaining French fries, cold and bent out of shape.

"No. We're here on vacation, and it would be nice to be asked where we're from or something."

"I'm new." Emily walked away. She told Molly about the exchange while waiting for Javier to finish plating a burger. "So awkward."

"Ha." Molly shook her head, a narrow bobby pin keeping her thin hair in place. "His poor family. Yuck."

"You got a bitch face, girl," said Javier, peering over the counter with a grin.

"No, I don't." Emily couldn't help laughing.

"You do," said Shawn, dropping a handful of cheese curds in the fryer. "You can tell there's something else going on in there."

"A dark streak," Javier added. "Hope I get to see it one day."

It felt like a compliment, a dare. Empowering. She wanted to see it too.

"Your face is fine," said Molly. "Some people think they're so important."

"Next time, start crying," said Shawn. "Tell him the shit in your life and make him feel real bad."

All the shit. How would she put it? "Well, my dad stole all my money, the man I was screwing broke up with me for his ex, my best friend thinks I'm a needy slut, and I have this nagging fear ever since a man I've known my whole life crept in my room and felt me up one night. I'm not on vacation. I'm here because a random guy told me there was lots of money to be made, and I'm very poor. So please leave me a tip and then leave me alone."

But she wants to hide all those details of her life. She wants to control the narrative.

When Ingrid asked Emily why she wasn't working at her family's restaurant this summer, Emily said she needed a break to see what else was out there.

"Yeah, working with family is tough. My mom wanted me to be a receptionist at the hotel she manages, and I'm like, 'No. We'd fricking kill each other.'"

Then Emily tapped into her bartender instincts and derailed the focus from her to Ingrid, asking Ingrid about that hotel and her mother. Ingrid talked until one of her tables needed a refill: people *do* like to talk about themselves.

Emily decided then to stop trying to avoid the questions and conversations; she'll turn the tables on them and listen. She's a great listener. She grew up behind a bar.

Brandon explained the sheer brilliance of Allen Ginsberg. Nora listed the crystals she keeps in her pockets for positive energy. Maria mentioned the baby booties she knits in her free time. Alicia bragged about Michelle Obama participating in the same book club as her mom years ago. Chris reported on the name, cargo, and cause of the sunken shipwreck just a mile out in the lake from Emily's cabin. "Careful of ghosts," he warned jokingly.

Emily met Terry, the prep cook who spends winters on Sanibel Island making necklaces and jewelry boxes out of seashells that he sells online, Iona, the Romanian busser who misses her dog more than anything, and Chang, the Chinese cook who wants to learn the ukulele. Colin, a part-time server who works at the nearby Shakespeare theater, recited the entire prologue from *Romeo and Juliet* when Emily said she had read the tragedy in high school. She politely nodded as he went on and on.

"What are you guys working today?" asks Bridget, unwinding the headphones around her silver iPod.

"Lunch and dinner," says Nora, sticking out her tongue as if gagging.

"Then you're not invited."

"I'm off," says Emily. "But I need to find a bank and a grocery store and a laundromat. My shirts reek."

"I'll make you a map," says Nora.

"And grab a few more shirts from the office," says Bridget. "If you're full-time, you need more than two. And after you do that boring stuff, want to hang out? Go mini-golfing or something?"

"Yeah," says Emily, the day ahead less daunting and lonely. "I'm in."

CHAPTER ELEVEN

Emily drives north on Highway 57 between towering cedar and pine trees. She passes farm fields and woodlands, a small bar with unlit neon signs cluttering the windows, and an art gallery with painted flowers on the windowsills. It's her first time being truly alone since arriving at The Schooner. It's disorienting, like she's stepped off a merry-go-round going a hundred miles an hour and can't find her footing. She turns down a Reba McEntire hit and glances at Nora's hand-drawn map, the destinations marked by wonky stars. She passes a petite church with a plain cross atop the steeple and a few modest homes with one or two lilac bushes bursting with purple blossoms. She rehearses.

"Dad. That was not okay to take that money. You knew it was mine," she says calmly, clearly, evenly. Chickens scurry into a dilapidated barn. The petals of apple tree blossoms blow like confetti across the road. "I said I would stay, and I'm sorry, but I get to do what *I* want now. I want you to give me that money back, and I'm not coming back until you do." Done. She means to reach for her phone, but her fingertips feel glued to the steering wheel. She'll hold off on the call a little longer.

She parks outside the cinderblock laundromat, across the street from the bank, kitty-corner to the Piggly Wiggly grocery store.

"Everything you need," said Nora, "a hop, skip, and a jump in Sister Bay."

The thick scent of detergent wafts in the laundromat. Clumps of lint litter the worn and scuffed linoleum floor like fearless mice. Unattended washing machines and dryers thrum and moan as they do their work. Emily slides her quarters in for a pack of the cheap off-brand detergent. She throws everything in a single load—polos, jeans, underwear, bras, socks, pajamas—and coughs on the taste of the citrus-scented gravel she sprinkles over the heap.

She sits on the edge of a plastic chair, a fluorescent light blinking with a crackling hum above her. *Get it over with*, she thinks.

Dad picks up on the first ring. "Where are you? What the hell, Emily? What in the actual hell?" The words come out fast and wet, like he's spitting in anger or answering mid-drink. Her stomach twists like a wrung-out rag. He's not supposed to be angry; he's supposed to be sorry.

"Umm," she starts. She won't disclose where she is. Not yet. That's not the plan. "I'm not coming back until you give me my money."

"I want you to get your ass back in here, and we'll figure this out," Dad says. He's rarely this angry with her—with the vendor who messed up their liquor order, yes; the drunk who called The Honky Tonk, The Hick Tonk, yes; and Mark Walsh when he sold his home to the government to make way for the interstate, sure. But he hasn't been this mad at *her* since he found her with that photo of her mom, the one Bernie discovered in the kitchen.

He tore it up. Emily grabbed his forearms and wrists, trying to pull them apart, like trying to pull apart fighting dogs.

"No, no, no," he said, one palm straight and hard to her chest, sending her to the floor. He continued ripping. He ripped it to shreds. "I do not want this bitch in my house. She was never a mother to you."

"Gladys and Doug and Larry and Jack—everyone's worried. They wondered if you died." His booming voice grows louder. "You ruined everyone's weekend; you know that?"

"I know. I'm sorry. It's just—"

"And you not only left me hanging this weekend, you left Bernie too."

Emily feels like she's in a dryer herself, spinning and spinning and spinning. "Dad. You know why I left."

"Taking a page out of your mother's book, I guess."

"Shut up about Mom." Emily rocks back and forth in the chair, gripping her elbow tight against her ribs. "You took my money, Dad."

"*Our* money. I used it to invest in *our* business."

"No, Dad. You know what you did. Don't do that."

"You know, you could have shown more interest in the place, been more involved with the day-to-day, the behind-the-scenes. You could have helped me keep an eye on the books," he says like he's running out of breath, probably pacing around the empty bar. "But you just worked your shifts and then off with your boyfriends living the good life."

"Dad. That's not what happened." She's desperate and confused. How could he turn this around on her?

"You at Todd's?"

"No. He broke up with me, Dad." The door of the laundromat opens with a whine. Emily maintains her gaze on a crack in the linoleum. Tears blur her vision. This is not how it was supposed to go.

"I'm not at Todd's." She blinks away the tears, watching a pair of pale feet in purple plastic flip-flops pass by. "I'm doing my own thing now."

"Not yet, Emily." His voice loses an edge. "Not yet."

"Do you even feel bad?" Emily whispers. The woman opens a dryer of jeans mid-spin. "You know that was mine, right?"

The woman yanks the pants from the dryer, dropping them in a laundry basket.

"Come home," he says like a plea. "Come home, and we'll talk about it. We'll figure it out."

"I'm not coming home until *you* figure it out," she mumbles. "Can't you just say you're sorry?"

Silence. Emily meets the woman's sharp blue, curious eyes as she folds her jeans on the counter.

"I gotta go." Emily shuts her phone.

"That sounded serious," the woman says.

"Yeah." Emily nods, annoyed.

"Boyfriend?" the woman asks, folds another pair. She appears to be Emily's age, with hair a shade of black that could only come from a box.

"Dad," Emily answers, the annoyance fading as she says the word. "Fuck him," she adds, feeling even better.

The woman laughs. "I got daddy issues too. Don't we all?"

"Did your dad take your life savings?" Emily asks, crossing her arms.

"Whoa. No. That's a new one."

"Well, mine did," Emily says curtly.

But the angry inflection seems lost on this woman. She's indifferent. Objective. "Wait. I take that back. I met this girl, and her dad somehow got ahold of her money and her siblings' money, too, everyone's money, and gambled it away or something." The woman piles her jeans in a leaning stack. "They were all in therapy, I think."

"Nice they could still afford therapy."

"Yeah." The woman laughs, opens another dryer, and tugs out a faded floral bedsheet. "You ever want free therapy, go to Al-Anon. You talk about your shit and listen to other people's shit. Just say your dad is an alcoholic. Can you help me with this?"

Emily pinches two ends of the woman's thin bedsheet, hot between her fingers. But he's not an alcoholic. They fold it lengthwise and come together. He drinks. Everyone does.

"I'm Cecelia."

"I'm Emily."

"You keep a journal? Write poetry or music?"

"No."

"That'd help you too if you don't like the idea of hanging out with codependents."

"Thanks." Emily's amused and calmed by this woman's lack of emotion.

"You know you don't have to hang out in here. No one's gonna steal your stuff. People don't even lock their doors up here."

"Oh, good to know. I need groceries and was gonna go to the bank too."

"Yeah, go. Get your money in there before your dad steals it."

Grateful for the joke, for the hint of sympathy behind Cecelia's smile, Emily laughs. "See you around."

"Yeah. You will," says Cecelia, pulling clothes from the final dryer. "You can't hide from anybody up here."

CHAPTER TWELVE

Emily drinks a gin and tonic from one of Bridget's Nalgene bottles layered in stickers— Running is Life, Obama '08, Dunder Mifflin Paper Company, a cartoon taco, a cartoon rainbow, and a Smokey the Bear. The drink goes down easy; it's her second. She had the first in the cabin while Bridget decided whether to wear denim shorts or pants. "There's still that spring chill, but I want summer so bad." She finally opted for the shorts.

They're in Bridget's pollen-dusted maroon Saturn. She talks about the difference between Montessori and Waldorf education methods while Emily swallows one gulp after another—the alcohol sending a cool, pleasant tickle down her thighs.

"I feel like Montessori is more my jam," Bridget says. "If I ever opened my own daycare, I'd lean toward that."

"Yeah. Good idea." Emily nods like she's interested. A fly bounces off the windshield with a buzzy bump that makes her cringe. She's replaying the conversation with

Dad. Maybe she should have shown interest in the books. Maybe she shouldn't have run off like she did. She replays the conversation with Cecelia too: "You can't hide from anyone up here."

She thinks of Jacob. She wants to see him. She doesn't. She wants another conversation with him. She doesn't. That smile. Those pamphlets. His kindness. Those pamphlets.

"But I do love the emphasis on imaginative play with the Waldorf," Bridget says as they pull into the parking lot.

"Kids are cute." Emily doesn't know what else to say. She doesn't interact with little kids much. She's thinking about Jacob, trying to conjure his image, but it's fuzzy and out of focus. She remembers how he made her feel light and seen. She scans the course, searching for him among the fiberglass animals and bearded gnomes. But what if they meet again, and he treats her with indifference? What if that Jacob she met was an act? What if he thinks she's a stalker? That's the last thing she needs. She's raw and vulnerable and can't stomach more rejection and hurt.

"Okay. Let's do this," says Bridget. "I'm gonna dominate."

Emily exhales in disappointment and relief, seeing no twenty-something boys who might be Jacob. She takes a drink. The cocktail cleanses her mind like cough syrup over an itchy throat.

"Well met, my sweet ladies," says Colin, approaching from behind. He bends in an awkward bow, his gel haired glistening in the mid-day sunlight. Bridget chooses an orange golf ball from a shallow basket. Emily chooses purple. Colin peers down at the selection, his fingers twitching as he decides.

"Green." He thrusts the ball into the air in a tight fist. "Let our bloody colors wave! And either victory or else a grave."

Bridget rolls her eyes at Emily, who snickers as she takes another drink.

"That's not water in there, is it?" Colin asks as he prepares his putt. "A pot of ale for your companion?"

"If you stop talking like that, anything," says Bridget, passing off her bottle.

"We have to share?" asks Colin.

"BYOB, Colin," says Bridget, laughing. "I'm not your mother."

"Fine," he takes a drink. "Wow. That's strong." He putts and misses by a wide margin. "Dammit."

Emily sets her ball on the weathered, worn turf. "I suck at this game," she says as she gives the ball a whack. A miss. Bridget lines up her shot. She's taking this seriously. Emily can tell from the tiny pencil and scorecard peeking out of her back pocket, the way she bites her tongue and teeters in her Converse sneakers. Her putt grazes the edge of the hole.

"Shit," Bridget says.

Colin passes the bottle back to Bridget.

"How old are you, Colin?" asks Emily.

"Who's asking?"

"I'm curious 'cause I've drank in front of Chris. I've had drinks after my shifts, like everybody else. He knows I'm not twenty-one, right?"

113

Bridget taps in her ball. "Two," she calls, retrieving the scorecard from her back pocket.

"It's kind of a look-the-other-way situation," says Colin.

"Don't ask, don't tell," says Bridget.

"Screw the military," says Colin. "They don't deserve us."

Bridget heads toward the next hole. Emily takes another drink.

"Has Javier been over yet?" asks Colin, reaching for Emily's Nalgene.

Bridget putts, and the ball glides smoothly and slowly beneath an angry badger, past the hole. "Shoot, I want a hole-in-one," she says.

"No," answers Emily confused.

"It's gonna happen," says Bridget. She turns to Emily and explains: "Javier and Nora started hooking up last summer. He was so into her, like so sweet, and she couldn't handle it. She flew off to Spain and broke his heart, I think. Either way, I don't think it ended the best, but it's gonna happen."

"She's always in the kitchen." Colin putts and misses. "Total flirt mode. All smiles and boobs out."

"They give you a speaking role this year, Colin?" asks Bridget.

"You are looking at MacBeth's messenger." Colin's expression turns to one of dramatic seriousness. "'Gracious my lord, I should report that which I say I saw, but I know not how to do it.' Then he says, 'Well, say, sir.' And I say, 'As I did stand my watch upon the hill,'" he points into the distance at a tiny metal windmill. "'I looked toward Birnam, and anon, methought, the wood began to move.'" Bridget claps. Colin bows his head slightly. "There's more."

"That's enough," Bridget says, laughing. Emily claps and laughs too.

"I read other parts in rehearsal, so that's something." They tap in their balls: a two for Bridget, a five for Emily, a three for Colin. "And they have me painting sets, working the box office. I'm on parking duty Friday, so—look out—I'm a multi-talented guy."

"You're funny," says Emily.

"Don't encourage him," says Bridget, moving on, her red hair swinging back and forth like a metronome, but Emily and Colin aren't trying to keep up, keep rhythm. Emily's enjoying strolling in the sunshine, socializing with people who don't know her dad or Ashley or Todd or Phil, who've never been to The Honky Tonk.

When Colin asks Emily more about the life she left behind, she keeps it simple. "My dad owns a bar on Interstate 29 near Eau Claire. It's got a jukebox that only plays old, old country."

"Oh, cool," he says. And that's that. Emily's satisfied and aims her putt. A slew of rocks strewn across the green reveal a small passageway to the hole. Her arms and legs are loose from gin.

"After this, do you guys want to go on Shawn's boat?" Bridget asks, looking at her phone. "Alicia texted. We can meet them at the dock around four."

"Shawn's kind of a tool," says Colin.

"He's immature, yeah. But he's got a boat."

"I'm in." Emily taps the ball, which rolls steadily down the path. "Oh, my God. Oh, my God!" The ball clips the edge of a rock, spins, and bounces from one to the next.

"Well, that didn't go as planned," says Colin.

...

Shawn's t-shirt billows in the breeze as he steers toward the concrete dock. The tawny boat with a maroon stripe stands out among the stark white and blue yachts and sailboats floating in the nearby marina. Alicia waves from the passenger seat wearing a faded pink sweatshirt that falls over a bare shoulder, her hair in a high bun, her lips shimmering. "Hey guys!"

Emily, Colin, and Bridget wait with deli sandwiches, an assortment of chips, and a twenty-four-pack of Bud Light.

"This is awesome. Thanks," says Emily, climbing in with Alicia's help. She's excited and nervous. She's been on a pontoon boat before with Ashley's family on a small lake in the Northwoods. They jumped on and off, on and off. And she's been on Doug's fishing boat many times before that, snacking on beef jerky and red licorice while Doug and Dad impaled squirming worms on a Snoopy fishing pole for her. But she's never boarded a boat like this one or been on a seemingly endless stretch of water.

"Welcome aboard," says Shawn. He grins as he points to the cushioned V in the front of the boat. "Lifejackets under there." He points to the red cooler against the back cushion. "Beer in there. It's no yacht like Alicia is used to, but it does the job."

"Oh, shut up," says Alicia. "You make me sound like such a snob."

Colin removes his shoes, so Emily does the same. She's tipsy from the booze and the boat, but with her bare feet on the damp maroon carpet, she feels strangely steady and grounded.

Emily and Bridget settle on either side of the V cushions up front. Colin takes the back. "I get nauseous up front."

"Course you do," says Shawn, putting the boat in reverse.

"Beer me!" shouts Bridget. Colin tosses her a Bud Light.

"Me too," says Emily. He tosses another. The women open their cans—a grind of aluminum, a click, and a satisfying hiss.

"Sounds like summer," says Bridget. "Cheers." They clink their cans together.

Emily tucks her legs under her, taking in the vastness of the lake as Shawn approaches the end of the no-wake zone. The water glitters in the white sunshine like the back of a flying blue jay—swaths of cobalt undulating with stripes of an electric blue.

"Ready?" asks Shawn. Synthesizer notes of Van Halen's "Jump" sound from the speakers. Shawn turns up the sound, and the passengers whoop and holler as the motor growls and roars.

Emily's lifted like she's in the palm of a giant hand, speeding toward the thin green thread of the horizon. The wind against her face feels like a million little numbing kisses. The women squeal and cheer. Emily can't suppress her smile. She can't suppress the way the feeling reminds her of riding on Dad's motorcycle. But she doesn't want to think about him now. No. She chugs the Bud Light and looks at Bridget, who's gripping her hair with one hand, her beer in the other, her freckled lips stretched in a wide smile.

They pass the bluffs topped with trees and mansions. They pass pontoons, sailboats, and jet skis. Eventually, Shawn slows up and idles toward an island. Emily can make out a jagged puzzle of wheat-colored rocks beneath the rippling surface of the water, stringy seaweed swaying between them. Shawn tosses anchor. "I'll pay someone a hundred dollars to jump in."

But there are no takers. They open bags of chips instead, peel the clingwrap off their ham and turkey sandwiches, sprawl on the cushions, and soak up the first rays of summer.

"We should hike the island," says Bridget, chewing on her sandwich.

"Sit still for a second, Bridget. Relax," says Colin, who shares a bag of Cheetos with Emily. "We've been on our feet all weekend."

"And I don't want ticks," says Alicia.

"My great-grandma used to tell us this island was haunted," says Shawn. "We'd see lights. Campfires. She told us they were the dead Moravians out here, pissed at how the county was turning out, taken over by a bunch of sinners."

"That's so creepy," says Alicia. "I can't believe your great-grandma told you that."

He chuckles. "Other times, she said it was Indians who were angry we stole their land. She was nuts."

"I'd have probably come out here and tried to find them," says Bridget. "I wanted to be Pocahontas so bad when I was little."

"Eric from *The Little Mermaid*." Colin raises his hand. They all laugh.

"I'd run barefoot in the woods in our backyard," Bridget continues, "talk to willow trees and try to lure raccoons to me to be my friends."

"That's cute," says Emily, her cheeks ache from smiling. She sucks the orange Cheeto dust from her fingertips, one after the other.

"I wanted to be a mountain climber when I was little," says Alicia. "My friend's mom climbed Everest, and I was like, done, happening. But then my older brother told me about all the dead, frozen bodies up there."

"What?" asks Emily. "Dead bodies?"

"Yeah," says Alicia. "There's like a bunch of 'em that died right on the path, and people use them for frickin' markers now."

Shawn chuckles, taking a drink of Bud Light.

"Can't they take them down?" asks Bridget.

"No. It's too much energy or work or something," Alicia says. "I don't even know how my brother knew about that. Stupid jerk."

"I wanted to be in the National Dog Show," admits Colin. They all laugh again. "I don't really remember this, but my mom loves to tell everyone about me trying to leash up our old cat and parade him around. He was having none of it, so I'd pretend with stuffed animals."

"I could see that about you," says Bridget. "You got a graceful walk."

Colin smiles, licking the Cheeto dust off his fingers now. "Thanks, Bridget."

"That's how I knew you were gay," says Shawn. "Your fancy walk."

The comment catches Emily off guard. Abrupt. Personal.

"Whoa. That's not nice," says Alicia.

"Not in a mean way. No offense, man." Shawn holds up his arms in surrender.

Colin shakes his head with a tight smile. "None taken."

"My gaydar is pretty strong."

"Oh, my God. Shut up, Shawn," says Bridget. "You don't even know what you're talking about."

"What? I didn't mean to be a dick," says Shawn.

"I think *you* should jump in," says Alicia.

"Moving on," says Colin. "Let's move on. Emily, what did you want to be?"

Emily bites her lower lip. They're counting on her to pull them out of this awkwardness. She considers for a moment, inspired by everyone's honesty.

"Dolly Parton."

"Love her," says Bridget.

"I'd basically do karaoke to the jukebox in my dad's bar and was convinced someone would walk in and discover me, and I'd be super famous." Then Dad would be so happy and proud. Her mom would come out of hiding and claim her. Everyone would stop and listen.

"That's so sweet," says Alicia. "Were you singing in front of people?"

"So embarrassing to think about now." Emily covers her face with her hands. "But, yeah, all the regulars."

"And I wanted to be a ninja," interjects Shawn. "A Teenage Mutant Ninja Turtle."

Emily feels a vibration at her side, and a tight panic grips her throat. *Not now*, she thinks. But it's Colin's phone. He opens it.

"You guys want to go to a bonfire after this?" he asks.

...

Emily and Bridget approach the glow of the bonfire arm in arm. Silhouettes of at least two dozen people surround tall flames, spitting sparks into a black sky. Some sit on logs, others on lawn chairs, and some stand with a can or bottle in hand. There is laughter and conversation, accents she's only ever heard on TV, a small dog barking, a few guitars strumming. Two men toss a frisbee across the fire.

They stopped at the cabin for jeans, hoodies, and tennis shoes. They calmed their windblown hair and emptied their full bladders. "I'm not gonna know anyone," said Emily. "You can't ditch me."

"You'll be fine," said Bridget. She filled their Nalgene bottles with water this time "to hydrate" and piled the remaining cans of Bud Light in a small cooler. Emily pocketed her phone, noticing a few missed calls and text messages. She could check those later.

The heat of the fire intensifies as they come closer, giving Emily goosebumps. She's still tipsy from the alcohol and the boat ride. She's so tired, she realizes, as Bridget unwinds her arm from the crook of Emily's elbow. She yawns as Bridget taps a woman's shoulder.

The woman rises, and Emily can see her eyes squint in a smile as she hugs Bridget. "Hey!"

The two women are catching up, and Emily lingers for a moment before Alicia waves her over to the log she's using as a bench. Nora is in the middle of a story, and she smiles at Emily mid-sentence.

"The guide was like, 'Clap at the grouper, and they'll come closer.' So we're down there, and I clap my hands at these giant monster fish. Three slo-mo turn and swim toward me." Nora laughs. Javier laughs, too, his hand on Nora's knee. "So, then I'm trying to swim away as fast I can, like batting at them with my flippers. These fish were probably like, 'What the hell, lady? You clapped. What did you expect?'"

"I'd have freaked too," says Alicia. Emily isn't sure if she'd be afraid in that scenario. She's never snorkeled before. But she's afraid to look up, to truly take in the crowd, worried Jacob will be among the twenty-somethings surrounding her. She's not ready for their reunion tonight. She's tired and anxious and puts up her hood.

"Gringos," says Javier, "my uncle snorkels. He reaches under the coral and in rock walls to see what he can find. He snorkels in his jeans. Total badass. One time, my brother and I were with him, and he reached in and pulled out an eel. Waved it around at us."

Alicia tells them about swimming with sea turtles in Hawaii, and Emily's wondering if she's meant to go next, but she has nothing to offer. She's only ever seen tropical fish at the Mall of America aquarium, though she did touch a stingray's rubbery fin and poked a leathery starfish with the tip of her finger while Ashley watched with her hands over her mouth in awe and disgust. "I can't believe you did that!"

But they don't ask her to contribute to the conversation. Nora and Javier bump knees, and Alicia scans the crowd. "There are quite a few hotties here," she says.

"Thank you," says Javier, with a crooked grin.

"Oh, shut up," says Alicia. "You're taken." Nora bites her lower lip and winds a length of hair around a finger.

"You need a man, Emily?" Javier asks.

"No, thank you." Emily tightens the strings of her hoodie.

"You want me to introduce you to anyone, Alicia?" asks Nora.

"Not yet. Still looking."

"Where's Shawn?" asks Javier.

"Parking the boat at his parents, I think," says Alicia.

"Who is Bridget talking to?" asks Emily.

"Courtney," says Nora. "She's a kayak guide."

Emily's stomach turns. She feels light-headed. Kayak guide? Jacob must be here. She studies the unopened can of beer in her hand. She's had too much to drink. She wishes she'd decided to stay at the cabin, call it a night, end on a good note. But she didn't want to be alone. She's had enough of being alone.

"How was the shift, Nora?" asks Alicia.

"Slow. Easy," Nora answers. "It'll be chill now until kids get out of school."

Emily braves a look.

There he is. She sees him. She recognizes him immediately.

He's hunched over a guitar. Of course he is. He's strumming while a woman next to him sings softly. Of course. Emily can't make out the words but hears a clear, strong voice. Jacob watches the woman sing. He's nodding along with a half-smile.

Emily turns her knees toward Alicia. She's talking to Nora and Javier about the empty house she's living in and her parents' plans to visit now and then. "I totally want to have people over sometime."

Emily's phone vibrates. She should have turned it off. A message from Ryan: "U ok? Ur dad came looking 4 u."

Oh, no. She imagines Dad stumbling to the Carrs' front door, knocking, probably reeking of whiskey. She imagines John talking to him like he's a patient at the dental office, putting a hand on his shoulder, "We'll figure this out," while Diane assumes the worst, and Ryan overhears the whole thing.

She checks her missed calls: five from Dad, two from Ashley, and one from Carr Home. Shit.

"Im ok," she texts back, her fingers working frantically: "Sorry. Tell ur parents sorry. In Door County. Dad doesnt know. Need a change."

She types a text message to Ashley: "Sorry about dad."

"Hey. Daddy issues!" a woman calls. Cecelia, the woman from the laundromat, the woman next to Jacob, the woman who was singing. "I told you it was a small county."

"Yeah," Emily nods, looking at Jacob. He examines her with half a grin. There's no hiding now. She offers a small wave and an apologetic smile.

"Emily?"

"Hey," she says, lowering her hood, clicking her phone shut.

Holding the neck of his guitar, Jacob circles the edge of the fire toward her. He pulls her into a hug. She's queasy from so much alcohol, disoriented, and overwhelmed by Dad showing up at the Carrs. The embrace feels safe, familiar even.

"Holy crap," he says. "What are you doing here?"

"I'm not a stalker," Emily says, aware of the eyes watching, the ears listening. "He came into my dad's bar on his way here," she says as a way of explanation. Her coworkers' expressions convey curiosity and intrigue.

"The coolest bar," Jacob adds. She pulls him away from the heat of the fire, from the watching eyes and listening ears.

"Holy crap," he says again. He props the bottom of the guitar on the top of his shoe. Curly wisps of hair swirl over his forehead. Even in the darkness, she can see he's slightly sunburned.

"It was a real last-minute decision," Emily says. "I need some money. I hope you don't think I'm creepy."

"No. It's crazy. Where you working?"

"The Schooner."

"You like it?"

"Umm, it's only been a few days. The money is amazing so far. Everyone is really nice," she gestures to her new friends on the log, back to their conversations, no longer watching, perhaps accustomed to the randomness of life and unexpected meetings living in a place like this.

"How's the kayak going?" Emily asks. Her phone vibrates in her hand.

"So great. It's everything I wanted," Jacob says. His smile bright, his ease so tangible, like they are old friends. "I'm like so surprised to see you. You know, I felt bad how it ended that day. I didn't want you thinking I was trying to convert you that whole time. I really had fun and liked talking to you."

"That's okay." Her heart wallops in her chest. "I liked talking to you too. And now, here I am."

Cecelia approaches and stands beside Jacob. Of course, a girl already follows him around, the only person who knows what Emily's dad did. Daddy issues. Shit. Why did she say anything to her?

"You gotta come kayak sometime," Jacob says. "We do trips all over the county. I'll show you Cave Point. Epic."

"Crazy you two know each other," says Cecelia.

"Yeah, I stopped at her family's bar on my way here. The Honky Tonk. You'd like it. There's a stage and old jukebox, all this country music memorabilia everywhere."

A bittersweet sensation rolls over Emily. She wishes she could go back to that afternoon, knowing what she knows now, trying everything again.

"Cool," says Cecelia, appearing mildly interested.

"Cecelia's a musician."

"Yeah, I heard you singing. You're really good," says Emily. Her phone vibrates again.

"Thanks," Cecelia smiles.

"She's *so* good," says Jacob. "Blew me away the first time I heard her. And you two met?"

"At the laundromat today," says Emily. "Random." The vibration doesn't stop. She glances at the phone in her hand. Ashley is calling. "I gotta take this. Sorry."

"Oh, yeah. No problem," says Jacob.

"We should go," Cecelia says to Jacob. "I gotta open tomorrow."

"Yeah. Okay. I'll see you around?" he asks Emily.

"Looks like it." She smiles and opens her phone and walks toward a few pine trees towering like black giants.

"What's going on?" asks Ashley, her voice quick and clipped. "Your dad showed up at my parents' house looking for you. Ryan texted you're in Door County?"

"Yeah."

"God, I thought you were dead. Mom called crying."

"Oh, shit. I'm sorry. Sorry about my dad. I'm embarrassed."

"Well, my parents know him." Unpredictable, unreliable, prone to humiliating drunken escapades. John and Diane know this and probably remember signing Emily's permission slips, taking her to and from school events and activities when her dad failed to show up or was too drunk to drive.

"It's fine," Ashley continues. But impatience and annoyance ring in Emily's ear. "Your dad was really scared. Mom said he was freaking out. I can't believe you didn't tell him where you were."

"Sorry." Emily bites her pinky until there's a jolt of pain. "Maybe I wanted him to be scared. He knows what he did." Her voice cracks. Cecelia slides into the passenger seat of a car, and Jacob sets the guitar in the backseat. Jealousy sinks down her throat. "It's so messed up."

"Well, are you okay?" Ashley asks, raising her voice, exasperated.

"Yeah. I'm fine."

"Okay. I'll call Mom and tell her."

"I'm sorry. Really. I didn't mean to make this all about me."

"Yeah. I get it."

"And nothing happened with Ryan."

"Okay. Bye."

Emily shivers as she studies the glowing screen of her phone. "Call Ended." She texts her dad without reading his previous messages: "In Door County. Im fine."

Then opens an unread message from Ryan. "Fucking awesome! Good 4 u."

A small laugh escapes her lips, and a few tears skim down her cheeks. She kneels and exhales, trying to process this new course in her life. She rests her hands flat on the ground to steady herself. Pine needles prick like a thousand stings. Catharsis, an avenue for the pain and confusion to escape. She presses harder.

She feels small and lonely, even after a day of new friends and experiences. Maybe it's the alcohol. Maybe it's everything.

CHAPTER THIRTEEN

Emily wakes with a sour taste in her dry mouth. Her skull feels stuffed with cobwebs. The skin of her face pulls taut with sunburn. A damp breeze blows in from a cracked window. Lake Michigan is steady this morning, a slow, rhythmic crash of waves. She grips the blanket tighter around her shoulders. She misses Todd.

She misses the chill, midwinter mornings in his bedroom, his alarm waking them. Cows to be milked, horses to be fed. He would groan, turn it off, then pull her tight against his body, his whiskers scratching her neck. She felt such comfort in his bare arms. Rocket would stir, realize no one was rising, then settle over their blanketed legs and ankles with a sigh. She'd run her fingertips over Todd's thick and muscular forearms. Sometimes they talked, or he drifted back to sleep, or they had sex. His kisses stale from sleep, but after he'd come, he'd hold her tight once more and say, "That's the best way to start any day."

Emily was so close to coming a few times but worried it was taking too long, or he'd change the rhythm and pressure. She could have said, "Keep doing what you were doing," but she'd fake. She'd come on her own later, thinking of them or Ryan Gosling or Clint Eastwood in the old Western movies Dad liked.

Maybe that would clear the cobwebs. Cast aside the thoughts creeping in her head like spiders. Dad crying. Ashley upset. What is Cecelia going to tell Jacob about her? How does Jacob already have a girlfriend? Yes. An orgasm would help.

Emily peeks over her bunk. Bridget's bed is empty, a crumpled blanket over striped sheets. She must be on a run. Emily smells coffee. Nora must be awake in her room.

She turns toward the wall and reaches under her shirt, softly grazing her fingertips over her ribs, her belly, her breasts. Inhales and exhales. She thinks of Todd touching her. No. Not him. He's with Nicole. She's taking up the space Emily once occupied. He was using her. She shouldn't miss him. She shouldn't touch herself to him.

She squeezes her eyes shut and grazes her fingertips over her skin. Ryan Gosling in *The Notebook*. He kisses her on a dock in the rain, passionately, fiercely. Raindrops run down their faces into their mouths as they kiss. He's so beautiful and strong.

She reaches under the waistband of her shorts and underwear, between her legs.

Ryan Gosling carries her into the house he built her. She's straddling him, and he's so into her he can't stop kissing her. He can't see where he's going, and they bump into a wall on their way to the bedroom.

Todd would carry her to his bed. He's so strong. He can pick her up like nothing, no straining. No. Stop. Ryan Gosling.

Ryan Gosling lowers her onto his bed and takes off his shirt. His body glistens from the rain. She grips the rungs of the metal bedframe while Ryan Gosling lifts the skirt of the baby blue dress she's wearing.

Emily rubs herself gently, softly. Ryan Gosling. He's looking at her while he undresses her. His eyes are light brown, like coffee with cream. Like Jacob's. No. Ryan Gosling. His eyes are blue, and he's looking down on her. There is thunder.

Phil is over her, touching her face, whispering her name.

"God dammit." Emily yanks her arm from under the covers and pounds her fist on the thin mattress. She pounds again and again.

The door opens. Emily sits up. Bridget enters slick and shiny with sweat, flushed and breathless. "Good morning, sunshine."

A shower and clean clothes help. Nora leaves to do yoga and hunt for lake glass on the beach. "That hippie," Bridget says as Nora calls for the cat that has yet to return.

While Bridget eats cereal, Emily braids her hair, deciding how to handle her dad today, her phone already blowing up with calls and texts.

"What do you think about Colin being gay?" asks Bridget, scrutinizing the back of the cereal box.

"I don't know," Emily says, unsure. "Kinda weird, I guess. He's my first gay friend."

"Probably not." Bridget slurps up a milky spoonful.

When Emily was ten or eleven, Doug told the regulars at The Honky Tonk he was sure one of his new hires was a "fagot."

Larry stood up, sending his barstool back with a loud scrape. His face red, voice booming. "Shut the hell up." Emily nearly dropped a glass of Sprite. "My nephew is a homosexual, and he's a decent boy." Doug's eyes went wide.

"Okay. Okay," said Dad, putting his hands up between them like he was breaking up a fight. But there was no fight.

Doug nodded. "Sorry. Sorry."

"Shouldn't matter who he likes," said Larry, sitting back on his barstool.

Later that day, Emily asked Dad what he thought of gay people.

"I don't get it. But Larry's a good friend, and I decided it's no one's business what anyone does in the bedroom. There're worse problems in the world. Live and let live."

A few boys in Emily's class were rumored to be gay, and a few other boys encouraged Emily and her female friends to kiss at parties. "Lesbians are so hot," they'd say. She watched *Brokeback Mountain* with Ashley, feeling equally intrigued and turned-on and disbelieving and heartbroken with how it all ended. *Cowboys can be gay*, she kept thinking—a revelation.

"Live and let live," Emily says to Bridget, winding a hair tie around the bottom of a braid.

"Isn't that an AA saying?" asks Bridget with a hint of a smile, rinsing her bowl in the sink.

"I don't know. It's what my dad said about gay people," says Emily. "Does it bother *you* that he's gay?"

"No. I think it's awesome he's honest."

A couple of hours later, the women wander down a trail of woodchips toward the back of the restaurant. Seagulls squawk and shuffle away as they pass the dumpster bin, the recycling bin, a wooden picnic table scarred with names and initials and swear words. Javier leans against the back door smoking a cigarette. "Good morning, chicas. How you feeling today?"

"Blah," says Emily.

"I'll be okay until about one," says Bridget. "Then I'm gonna fade."

Nora smiles. "Fine."

Emily drinks hot black coffee before flipping the dining chairs down from the tabletops. Bridget follows with a rag, wiping the surfaces while Molly sets out the ketchup and mustard bottles and the salt and pepper shakers. Chris stocks beer bottles behind the bar. Nora writes the specials on a whiteboard: California Burger w/ Fries + Slaw. $9.99.

"Did you guys have fun yesterday?" asks Molly. "I was so bummed to miss out. Mom was all excited about family time. I envy you all living away from your families sometimes."

"It was fun," says Bridget. "Emily was all giggly on the boat yesterday."

"That was fun," Emily agrees, remembering the rush of the wind and the sunshine bouncing off the water.

"And she sucks at mini-golf," adds Bridget.

"Hey!" Emily laughs.

"Alicia was on the prowl last night," says Nora, capping the marker. "I saw her talking to some Coast Guard guys when I left. Wonder what happened. And Emily … you were talking to that guy. He seemed excited to see you."

"Now's the time you all start pairing off," says Chris, wiping the bar with a rag.

"Do tell," says Molly, clapping her hands, looking at Emily expectantly.

"Yeah. So random," Emily says, deciding how to handle this. Jacob did seem excited. She was too. But she doesn't want them to know. She wants to appear aloof, uninterested. "He came into my dad's restaurant on his way here."

"Crazy," says Bridget.

"He hung out, and we talked for like a few hours. I honestly think it was the first bar he's ever been in," she says, lowering the last chair to the floor. "I think I served him the first alcohol of his life."

"What makes you think that?" asks Molly.

"He was way too thrilled about it. I think he grew up real religious. Or he is religious," she says, pleased with the distance she creates between herself and Jacob with these statements. "He had those pamphlets in his wallet that people give servers instead of money that talk about God." Maybe she should tell them that he threw the leaflets away.

"No. Really?" says Bridget, wincing. "Yuck."

"I'm all about believing what you want to believe," says Nora, shaking a pointer finger. "But don't thrust it on other people."

Customers, mostly old and young couples, enter the restaurant in a steady stream.

"The newlyweds and nearly deads," Chris says when Emily retrieves a couple of Leinenkugel's from the bar. He winks. She laughs.

Lunch shifts go smoother than dinner shifts. No one orders cocktails or side salads or cherry pies, mostly iced teas, burgers, and BLTs, so she feels more confident, even with her phone vibrating on and off in her pocket. But questions come that she can't answer: "When do they pick the cherries up here?" "What's your hoppiest beer?" "How do you get to Cana Island Lighthouse?"

On her way to ask Nora and Chris for the answers, she alternates between drinking coffee and iced water, snacking on French fries dipped in ranch, and skimming through a few of Dad's messages: 9:32 p.m.: "Made a fool of myself with ur 2nd family! Happy?" 11:05 p.m.: "Rich snobs r better company than people who care about u?" 1:12 a.m.: "Like mother, like daughter." 7:22 a.m.: "Come home now.

Enough. Need u Friday." 12:04 p.m.: "We'll do better by each other. I'll do better." No sorry.

She wants to throw her phone in the lake. She wants to take a nap. She wants to find a library and borrow some *Grey's Anatomy* or *ER*. But there's no DVD player in the cabin.

"What's the name of the Scandinavian church near here?" asks an older woman, sliding a half-eaten chef's salad toward Emily.

"Oh, gosh. I don't know. Let me find out," Emily says, feigning cheerfulness. She approaches Chris at the bar and repeats the customer's question.

"Didn't know you were signing up to be a tour guide, did you?" he laughs. "Boynton Chapel." She likes Chris. She likes his calm patience.

"I wish I cared about Scandinavian churches right now," says Emily, sitting on a barstool. "How nice would that be?"

"You will one day, don't worry," says Chris. "Or something. My mom is into the Amish now. She lives in Arizona, but she's obsessed with Amish furniture and quilts."

"I used to live by some Amish," says Emily. "They're nice. The ones I know. Normal people."

"Oh man, Mom would be jealous," he says, smiling. "But, no. That might ruin it for her. She reads that Amish porn."

"What?" Emily laughs, and it feels good.

"Yeah. Me and my wife skimmed through one of 'em on our last visit," he says. "Very PG. Like, Ruth and Josiah

137

watched the sunset over the farm field, and God blessed their union. Real chaste."

"I guess whatever makes her happy," says Emily.

"Yeah. I'm almost forty, and I'm into Great Lakes maritime history now, like a seventy-year-old," he says. "This place did that to me. I think marriage does too. You stop worrying about your next lay. Frees up a lot of time."

"You're so funny. Do you guys have any kids?"

"Working on it."

An arm comes around Emily's shoulder. "Hey, roomie," says Bridget. "So that religious boy wants your number."

"What?"

"Courtney texted. They work together," Bridget explains with a grin. "He found out we work together and asked if Courtney could ask me for your number. That's a lot of steps for a guy."

Chris laughs and shakes his head. "See, you're all a bunch of horny bunnies."

CHAPTER FOURTEEN

Emily is early and wishes she wasn't. She waits at a table outside the coffee shop Jacob chose. Branches umbrella her from the bright rays of the sun, but she keeps her sunglasses on and takes inventory of the contents of her purse. ChapStick. Four pens. She's nervous. Her wallet. Her new checkbook. Her phone.

A man in his seventies wearing socks and sandals reads a thick book with the painted portrait of a dead president on the cover. She isn't sure of his name, but she knows he's on Mount Rushmore. A couple drinks iced coffees, the man complaining about the blisters forming on his heels.

"I should have broken them in before we came," he says, exasperated. "I can't hike the rest of the trip."

"Oh, you'll be fine," the woman says dismissively. "We'll get some cream."

Emily opens her phone. She hasn't had any new texts or calls for a few days now. Not since she and Jacob arranged to meet between kayak tours for him and before the dinner shift for her. Not since she texted Dad: "U need to cool off. 3 weeks. Talk then." She expected pushback, more calls or texts. But nothing. Silence. That's another side of Dad she remembers—the silent treatment. And though it's what she wanted and asked for, the silence feels strange and eerie, like a storm cloud on the horizon. Something's coming. Or maybe not. Maybe it will dissipate, and everything will be fine.

"Emily. Hey!" Jacob approaches with that constant smile. They hug. He smells like sunscreen.

"Thanks for meeting me," he says. "Still so crazy to see you here."

"I hope a good crazy. Not a creepy crazy." The nervousness seeps from every pore of her body. She grips her elbow and bites her lower lip in an attempt to steady herself.

"No. No way. It's beautiful up here, right?" He gestures around him to the vast harbor of calm slate-blue water bordered by tall bluffs on one side and flat shoreland on the other. A few clouds feather the sky. Picturesque, like a postcard. But she's not admiring the scenery; she's taking in the constellation of freckles on Jacob's cheeks, the pronounced ridge of his nose. "Wasn't I right?"

"You were right," she says, smiling, resting her sunglasses on the top of her head.

They order iced teas and Italian paninis. Jacob talks about kayaking, how his body ached after the first few tours, and how ill-prepared he was to answer the tourists' off-book questions about local history, geography, and wildlife. "I'm making things up about the first settlers and Native Americans," he says, laughing. "I'm paddling along, trying to make it interesting, and one guy is like, 'Tell us about the bat population up here.' So, I make stuff up about bats. 'It's robust,' I say."

"Good word," Emily teases, laughing mid-bite, a sundried tomato slipping from her sandwich to her plate.

"I thought so."

"I didn't know we could make stuff up. I've been running back and forth from the bartender. I'll remember that."

He laughs. The sound gives Emily a light rush, like a little breeze in her belly.

They swap stories about coworkers and customers. Emily tells about Alicia bedazzling her server apron, Molly spouting self-help advice to everyone like an Oprah-wannabe, and the cat Nora is desperate to lure back to their cabin. "I think it's a ghost, actually."

Jacob tells about a group of women convinced there were water snakes beneath their kayaks and an elderly couple with binoculars and a bird checklist, big grins on their faces as they paddled by herons, pelicans, and geese. "They were so pumped to tell me all about the birds up here. It was great."

"Still planning on New Zealand?" Emily asks, her nerves calmed.

"Yes. Still the plan," he swallows and wipes a bit of pesto from his lips with a paper napkin. "But also trying to enjoy now, you know. I found some people to play music with, and we're playing at this outdoor bar on Wednesday. You should come. You should come and bring your Schooner friends."

"Yeah. Sounds fun."

"Great. Yeah, so. I'm trying to be present while I'm here," he continues. "There's so much focus on the future at our age, isn't there? Every decision feels so momentous."

She agrees with a nod. Everything feels momentous lately.

"You going back home for nursing then, after the summer?" he asks. But he's mimicking her expression, pained and grave.

"Did your girlfriend tell you what I told her?" asks Emily. "I was embarrassed she called me 'daddy issues' at the campfire."

Jacob runs a finger down his sweating glass of iced tea. "I'm learning Cecelia has no filter. I'm sorry. And … she's not my girlfriend. I don't know. We're hanging out. But yeah, she did tell me something about your dad taking money."

"Pretty stupid."

"Will he pay you back, you think?"

She's not ready to give up on that thought or that he'll at least apologize. "I don't know. He seems to think it was okay. He keeps saying we're business partners, and he used it for the business. He's complicated. I'm starting to remember all these falling-outs he had with friends and customers. He's just never been this mad at me. I've always been able to make him happy, I guess."

Jacob's eyebrows furrow. He's listening, taking in every word. Emily feels exposed, like she stepped out in a blizzard without a coat and wants to go back inside.

"Parents suck, right?" She tries to make a joke. She takes the last bite of her sandwich. He puts a hand on her shoulder.

"What about your mom?" he asks. She struggles to chew her food, aware of him waiting for a response.

"She's gone," she says with a mouthful. "She's been gone my whole life."

"I'm sorry, Emily." She assumes his expression is one of pity, but she doesn't want to look. She takes a drink of iced tea.

"No. Don't worry about it. I sound so messed up, don't I?" She needs to change the subject. "Let's go for a walk."

A slew of bicyclists zip by on the paved road like a swarm of bright, buzzing insects. A young couple meanders along the sidewalk, the man pushing a stroller. A middle-aged woman waits while her terrier pees on a sign that reads "Private Beach."

"You're not the only one with messed up parents," says Jacob. Emily lowers her sunglasses when she looks at him. "My parents were really against me coming here, especially Mom."

"Why?"

He blows out a breath, rubs his hand on the back of his neck, and keeps his gaze straight ahead. "Half my college friends got jobs at churches around the country, or they are

143

starting ministries and getting married. Some are building homes in Haiti. One is in China doing this underground church thing. That's what was expected of me from everybody. And I wanted a break from it all."

Most of Emily's classmates attended church, and a few went to youth group on Wednesday nights, but only a handful seemed really wrapped up in it all, with parents who wanted to visit classrooms and discuss creation theory when evolution came up in the curriculum, who didn't want their children reading *The Catcher in the Rye* or participating in sex-ed.

"Want to hang out with sinners for a while?" Emily asks, trying to lighten the mood. "We're bad news."

"Something like that," he says with a small smile, wringing his hands. "My whole life has been church and Sunday school and youth group and worship band and Bible study, and it got screwed up and too much at the end there."

She wonders if she should ask what happened. What got screwed up? But they make way for a jogger, then a woman carrying a toddler wrapped in a beach towel.

Emily decides to keep it light. "Did I serve you your first drink, Jacob?"

He laughs. "My fourth."

"Four?" She asks, letting out a laugh and shaking her head. "Seriously? Four?"

He holds up four fingers. "And with each one, I have these Bible verses playing through my head. 'Wine is a mocker, beer a brawler; whoever is led astray by them is not wise,'" he recites. "Proverbs 20:1."

"Impressive."

"I feel bad about those pamphlets." He shakes his head.

"It's fine. Your mom put them there."

"I said that. But no. *I* put them in there," Jacob admits. "There was this part of me that was like, 'I'm gonna be a witness for the Lord and save some people and bring 'em to Jesus while I'm here.' And then I saw your face and felt so stupid. Don't tell anyone that."

She was right about him, and she was wrong about him. They both remove their shoes before stepping on the small public beach. Emily's feet burn in the gritty sand before they submerge in the cool water.

"So, you were going to leave me one?" Emily asks. "Thought I needed saving?"

Children play with plastic boats in the shallow water. Three women float on a giant pink inner tube with Koozies in hand, laughter spilling from their mouths. A few men toss a football in thigh-deep water.

"No. I met you and was like, 'What am I doing? Stop. She's fine the way she is.'" He sits on dry sand and pats the space beside him. Emily isn't sure what to say. She's relieved by the comment; her tender ego laps it up like a thirsty dog. But she doesn't feel fine, not then, not now.

"Last year, my college sent a bunch of us down to Myrtle Beach over spring break," he continues. "We'd start the day praying on the beach, asking God to guide us and help us do His work. Then we'd go up to people and try to share our testimonials and the word of God. It was humiliating. They were playing volleyball and swimming and having fun, eating ice cream and reading and dancing, and we're coming up to them like, 'You're on a path to hell.' I hated it."

Prickles run down Emily's spine. She thinks of Phil then. She remembers how he managed to insert God in nearly every conversation: "God blessed us with this weather." "God must be a Badgers fan." "God is looking over me." When others spoke, he'd interject, "Praise God." "Thank you, God." "Amen." Emily hadn't minded it before she woke to him over her that night. She felt envious of his assuredness and trust in a God, envious of his children and the normal life they led with him as their dad.

She pulls her knees to her chest and wraps her arms around her legs, remembering him over her, remembering the Bible he set on the bar the next day. "And we'll keep this between us," Phil said. Anger bubbles in her chest like boiling water.

"You know what I don't understand about it all," she says, clenching her teeth, trying to control the bitter steam of her anger. "There was this holy guy that came in all the time. I knew him most of my life, and then he … he did something not okay. But he said God was teaching him a lesson, and the devil made him do it. So, do the two work together?" She hears the snark in her question, but she truly wants to know.

Jacob's face grows somber. She feels herself glaring, the bitchy face the kitchen guys tease her for on full display.

"You don't have to tell me if you don't want to," says Jacob. "But did this something happen to you?"

"No," Emily says immediately, looking back to the water. "No. But he did something, and I guess I'm wondering if religious people get to do what they want and then blame it on invisible things. Because how are you supposed to argue with that?"

"Stuff like that," Jacob says softly, almost like a whisper. "That's why I needed to step away."

Emily sinks her toes beneath the sand. "I did tell a few of my coworkers about the pamphlets," she admits. "I won't tell anyone else." She pulls her knees even tighter to her chest. In the distance, a dozen little sailboats manned by children dart to and fro like frantic fish near the marina. A few topple sideways now and then. A motorboat with instructors in neon green buzzes from one fallen sailboat to the next, righting them one by one.

"Here." Jacob hands Emily a white earbud. There's the crackle of an old recording, some piano, a little fiddle, Charline Arthur singing the blues. "I downloaded a bunch of her stuff after I met you. Made me smile."

She loosens the grip around her knees and bumps her shoulder into his.

CHAPTER FIFTEEN

Schools close, the lake warms, busy shifts become more consistent, and the customers more diverse. Honeymooners and retirees, windblown and sunburned fishermen and women; bicyclists in bright spandex and clickity clacking shoes; golfers in their polos and visors; campers reeking of smoke and pine; damp beachgoers tracking sand; perfumed theatergoers wearing collared shirts and casual dresses; motorcyclists outfitted in squeaky leather head to toe. Families—small and large, immediate and extended—some boisterous with conversation and laughter, others with glazed expressions and tension so palpable Emily interacts with them as little as possible. Groups celebrating a birthday or anniversary; bachelorette parties with women dressed almost identically, ordering cocktails, and talking over each other, one donning a sash and tiara. There are bachelor parties with men who order round after round of beer, with usually one or two who ask Emily for her number, ask if she'll join them later.

There are the locals too: the farmers, the librarian, the town constable, the dump truck driver, the plumber, the employees of the gas station and hardware store, and the crew of the charter fishing company. They order their usuals, chat about the weather and local gossip, and complain about the tourists who drive ten under the speed limit or hike with unleashed dogs.

Emily is scolded for cold perch, wilted lettuce, foamy beer, and the price of cheese curds, then praised for the homemade ranch dressing, the crispy bacon on the burgers and BLTs, the friendly service, and the best fish fry in the county. Some customers seem to look upon her with disdain, like she's a nuisance, and others smile and nod when she introduces herself and reads the specials from her notepad. She's warming up to the kind customers and answers their questions as best she can before pointing them toward Chris or recommending the local visitor bureau.

"This is my first summer. I'm still learning about the county," she'll say apologetically when they ask about the boutiques and galleries, wineries and orchards, or lighthouses and state parks. And inevitably, customers ask what she plans to do with her life.

"Nursing," she says, surprising herself the first time. But it feels right to say, better than "I'm not sure" or "Still figuring that out." Nursing.

"What kind of nursing?" some ask. "Clinic, emergency, surgery, NICU, hospice?"

"We'll see," she says with a smile.

But mostly, Emily loses herself in the repetition, exchanging pleasantries, finding herself spouting out the same cliches and jokes as she drops off drinks and food, the bill. "Thanks for coming in. Enjoy the county." She relishes the crinkle of cash and credit card receipts in her palm, the slight resistance as she stuffs them in her apron pocket—a wad that grows bulgier as shifts wane on.

Emily misses bartending, with its banter, less running around, and customers who are more often relaxed and patient. At The Honky Tonk, she excelled at the mindless chatter, playing games of bar dice and keeping up with the Brewers, Packers, Bucks, and Badgers.

But she's realizing the pleasure of leaving the patrons behind, pushing open those swinging doors, exiting the softly lit, air-conditioned dining room, the ambient music and din of eating and conversation, and entering the steamy fluorescent-lit kitchen with all its scents and accents and fast-paced music with beats that thump in her throat.

Emily likes spending time in the kitchen, learning more about her coworkers while they prep for their shift, wait for their orders, and clean up when it's all done. Maria tells Emily about her plans to open a bakery one day and promises to make her a tres leches cake for her birthday. Terry gifts her one of his seashell necklaces, Iona teaches her how to swear in Romanian, and Chang offers a brief overview of Buddhism. Shawn talks about offering a karate class one day and plans to visit Japan eventually. Javier lets Emily hold and study the bracelet he wears with a depiction of the Virgin Mary on each black rectangular bead. "Little miss virgin," she scoffs warily.

"She's not a virgin," Javier says, laughing, shaking his head. "She's a mamá."

Brandon pulls a paperback from his pocket and reads verses of *Howl* to her. "To hell with social constraints. Am I right? War, politics, capitalism."

Molly tells Emily about the farm her family owns and the pictures her parents display of their prized cows. "It's literally us standing by the cow's ass so you can see their huge udders," she says. "They are all over the house—one of me by a cow's ass, one of my brother by a cow's ass, one of my mom, one of my dad, one of all of us, or two of us, or three of us. It's so embarrassing."

Nora explains Emily's astrology sign to her in greater depth than any issue of *Cosmo* ever did, and Colin insists she is familiar with Shakespeare's work even if she doesn't realize it. "If you saw one of his plays, just one, you'd recognize something, you'd be like, 'Oh, that's where that saying comes from.'"

Chris prompts Travis to tell her about rescuing a tourist from a riptide last summer. "This guy is a hero!" says Chris, waiting on some onion rings while Travis portions tartar sauce.

"I could see him getting pulled out and fighting it," Travis says shyly, humbly, looking down at his work. "You got to swim parallel to shore."

"A news crew came up and interviewed him and everything. It was a big deal," says Chris on his way out of the kitchen.

Bridget wants Emily to teach her how to French braid her own hair, and Alicia tells Emily about her dreams of becoming an interior designer or wedding planner. "I got a good eye for that kind of stuff," Alicia says. "I can make things special."

Ingrid points to a coarse black hair on her chin. "This is what having a baby does to you," she says. "Does anyone have a tweezers?"

When Emily's section clears at the end of each shift, she realizes how much her feet ache, feels the dampness in her armpits and on her lower back, notices her parched mouth and full bladder, sees the grease stains smudged near her ribcage where she props up plates. The staff takes turns pouring themselves drinks behind the bar, sucking them down while they roll silverware and count tips.

Deer Valley feels farther away, her phone silent for a week now from Dad's pleas and accusations. It buzzes instead with invitations from her new friends: "Beach?" "Mini-golf?" "Hike?" "Drive-In?"

"I'm in!" she texts back.

"Coming 2 show Wed? Sunny Seagull. 9ish."

"I'll be there," she texts Jacob.

...

"Isn't that the religious guy?" asks Nora. "The one from the campfire?" She and Emily walk along the foggy shore of Lake Michigan, their heels creating a little song as they sink into the soft, fine sand. The breeze is cool, and white slivers appear and disappear over the water as waves roll along.

"Yeah," admits Emily, regretting how she portrayed him. "But he's taking a break from that. He apologized for the pamphlets."

"When?"

"We had lunch last week." Emily smiles.

"You sneaky girl," says Nora with a grin. "I was wondering why you were so about The Sunny Seagull tonight."

"He's gonna play some music," Emily says as casually as she can. "He's nice."

The women step over smooth driftwood the color of bone and clear crowds of seagulls pecking at washed-up salmon and trout, squawking and ruffling their gray and white feathers. A few walkers and a couple of families with small children at play are scattered on the shore.

"I'm glad he apologized." Nora gives Emily a playful glance and gentle shove. "You got a little crush on him, don't you?"

"No!" says Emily immediately. A lie. She does. And Nora's expression suggests she knows the truth. "I don't know. I just broke up with someone, and Jacob already has this Cecelia girl following him around."

"I noticed that at the bonfire. She's a bit of a hot mess," says Nora. "Reminds me of myself a few years ago. You're a way bigger catch."

"Thanks. But I have a lot of shit, you know?"

"I get it. I have shit too."

Emily doesn't ask. She's not sure Nora wants her to. So, she chooses something safe. "When did you get into yoga?"

"A couple winters ago. This woman in Belize had a class on her front porch every morning, a Canadian who married a local guy there. They had a couple kids."

"I don't even know where Belize is," admits Emily, covering her face with her hands.

"Don't be embarrassed." Nora tells her about the small country in Central America with sandy islands, Mayan ruins, reefs teeming with sea life, and a hostel full of people from around the world. She tells Emily about days filled with sunbathing and hiking and snorkeling, rum punch and jerk chicken, dancing in rustic rooftop bars, and spending five blissful days with an Argentinian flight attendant, Ignacio. She didn't notice the long rattail braid down his back until their first kiss. She wound it around her finger.

"It was lovely, Emily," Nora says, blushing. "I needed it. He was fun and interesting and like up for anything: snorkeling, ziplining. We took a beachside watercolor class together." He quoted *Dumb and Dumber* and started each day with a set of sit-ups and push-ups. He whistled Bob Dylan tunes and called her "Girl from the North Country." He gave her orgasms.

"He really wanted to do it in the ocean, but there were these sharp conch shells everywhere, not to mention stingrays and jellyfish and barracudas and sharks," Nora says, laughing. "I was like, 'No. I'm gonna end up being the stupid American that gets wrapped up in a jellyfish while having sex and dies naked on a beach.'"

Emily laughs. "Think you'll ever see him again?"

"No. He said he'd send me some rhodochrosite jewelry, that I should come visit, but neither of those things has happened, which is fine. It's this sweet, sexy memory I get to keep forever. And with where I was in my life, I needed that."

"I can't believe you went by yourself," Emily says. The thought of a solo, foreign excursion fills her with apprehension. "Was it safe?"

"Totally safe. I'm careful, of course. Stuck to touristy areas. There was this guy—I kid you not—in a Door County t-shirt trying to climb a frickin' palm tree and get a coconut. I was like, 'Really, dude?'"

Nora presses her palms together at her chest. She takes in a long breath with her eyes closed and tells Emily to do the same. Exhale. Nora walks her through a few yoga poses, including downward dog, warrior one, warrior two, cat-cow, and child's pose. Emily feels silly and unsteady at the start. She can't touch her toes, balance without shaking, or move gracefully between poses like Nora, whose willowy figure reminds Emily of the plastic ballerina that spun in Ashley's jewelry box. She wanted one so bad. But Nora's seriousness and gentle, guiding hands stave off the laughter and embarrassment. Soon, Emily surrenders to the experience. Her muscles, tendons, and joints awaken and stretch and vibrate.

"Doesn't that feel good?" Nora asks.

"It does," Emily says, brushing the sand off her palms and kneecaps, feeling cleansed and rejuvenated, her spine a bit longer and straighter.

"I've been hearing you tell tables that you want to be a nurse," Nora says as they walk back toward their cabin. "You've been vague, so I wasn't sure if you were saying it to shut them up."

Emily calculates how much to share and how open and vulnerable to be. But talking about nursing feels safe, true, exciting.

"I do." Emily picks up a pebble and tosses it into the water, and it breaks the surface with a satisfying plop. "I've wanted to for a long time, but my dad really wanted me to focus on our bar." She doesn't mean to mention him. Too personal. "But I've always liked medical stuff. I don't get grossed out easy. When my friend sliced her hand washing dishes, I was so into it. I went along to the ER and watched them stitch it up. My poor friend's crying and traumatized, and I'm trying to get a better look."

"To be able to handle stuff like that is a skill right there," says Nora, stepping over a dead minnow. "Is that what made you want to be a nurse?"

Emily considers this. She recalls a memory, one of the moments in her life when someone did something for her that, to her knowledge, moms usually do.

"Well, lots of things. But a few years ago, I had a couple irregular exams. You know what I mean? And they wanted to do a biopsy. I didn't tell my dad 'cause when I told him I got my period, he said, 'I don't want to hear about that stuff.'"

Nora makes an *ugh* sound, and Emily berates herself for mentioning him again. Focus. "And the doctor made it sound routine," she continues. "They told me it was probably nothing. So, I didn't tell anyone. I didn't think it would be that bad. Then I'm sitting there in that gown, my legs in those stirrups, and this nurse knew I didn't know what was coming. And she no-nonsense sat on the edge of the bed and held my hand without asking."

"That's nice."

"Yeah. Because it really hurt, like this weird inside pinching bite feeling," Emily keeps going, surprising herself. "I had tears rolling down my cheeks, and through the whole thing, this nurse held my hand and said, 'Almost done. You're doing great.' She didn't have to do that, you know."

Nora nods with a smile, then exhales audibly before adding, "I had one of those too. Cervical biopsy."

"Aren't they awful?" asks Emily, recalling that sharp pain below her belly, the bloody instruments whisked away, and the red smears on the stiff paper beneath her. When she sat in her truck, it felt like needles deep in her vagina. She writhed as she drove through Eau Claire, down the interstate, shifting her weight from one hip to the other, biting her lip. She took an ibuprofen. The shooting pain gave way to cramps, and she worked her dinner shift.

"Big time," says Nora. "I had my mom with, so that helped with the handholding. But the worst part was afterward. I was with this guy, now my ex-husband—"

"You were married?" Emily interrupts.

"Yeah. I don't like to talk about it. It didn't last long. But we had just started dating, and I didn't tell him about it either. He wanted to hang out, and I didn't want him to not like me anymore, so I went over to his place, and … remember that weird gravelly shit they put inside you to stop the bleeding?"

"Yeah."

"Well, it also blocks penises from entering you." Nora lets out a laugh. "And I remember the doctor saying not to have sex, but again, I didn't want him to not like me anymore. So, he's like trying to push himself inside me, and it hurt like hell, and I was finally like, 'Oh, yeah, I forgot. I had a check-up today. That must be what's wrong.' Then I gave him a blow job." Nora laughs again, but Emily recognizes it comes from a place of regret, pain.

"I should have had him rub my back," continues Nora, her pace quickening. "Should have sat on the couch with a heating pad and watched a movie. I should have told him how scared I was they were going to find cancer or something."

Emily rubs her fingertips against her temple. Even when the results came back clear, she had no one to share in the relief. She told Ashley after the fact. Dad knew nothing.

"I should have told my dad too," she realizes aloud, mentioning him again. She can't help it. He's clinging to the edge of her mind, always.

"Like, what were we doing?" Nora says, fired up, angry. "Trying to protect them, be perfect for them, not inconvenience them? Or did we not trust them to really understand and take care of us like an actual human being?"

Emily considers this, then decides as they step off the beach and onto a woodchip trail, that it's likely a combination of all those things, and the thought fans flames of indignation flickering in her chest.

"My ex thought he'd married this uncomplaining, sweet girl," says Nora. "Like, I made him the center of my world. In so many ways it's not his fault it all fell apart. I couldn't play that role anymore and had to get the hell out. He was so caught off guard and so angry. My parents were angry. I think Mom felt betrayed because that's how she raised me: make your man happy; put yourself on the back burner."

"I know it's not the same," Emily says. Meeting Nora's honesty feels right and fair. "But my dad is really angry, too, that I left."

"Course he is," says Nora, her face flushed, chin quivering. "Because we're supposed to be their little submissive women and make them happy and not have personalities or ambitions or anything that doesn't revolve around them."

Emily loses her breath. She never saw it that way, but that sounds about right. And her mind spins back the wheels of time while she silently scolds herself for being so blind. *I shouldn't have stayed at The Honky Tonk for him. I should have kept a better eye on my money. I shouldn't have trusted him. I should have been more myself with Todd, demanded dates and transparency. I should have called the police that night. I should have thrown that stupid Bible in Phil's stupid fucking face.*

"What does your mom think about you being here?" Nora asks. "Is she mad too?"

"My mom left when I was three." The words are heavy in Emily's mouth. She doesn't like to say it. She always lived in a world where everyone knew.

"That's tough," Nora says. "But, I'm starting to realize that we make our own families, you know. All these people I met traveling and here know me better than my ex ever did, and my parents. Or maybe I feel safer with them, freer to figure out who I am."

Nora opens the screen door to their cabin. Emily doesn't want the conversation to end. She feels cracked open, a little safer herself, and known. And she likes this feeling.

CHAPTER SIXTEEN

A couple of hours remain of Emily's shift, but she wants to begin tidying up, stowing away the ketchup and mustard bottles, emptying the iced tea machine, and rolling silverware. She can't help glancing at the red digital clock in the bar, the round clock with Roman numerals beside the hostess stand, and the clock with a sticker of a panda in sunglasses in the kitchen. She wants to drink, to dance, to see Jacob's smile. Most of the staff agreed to join her at The Sunny Seagull tonight. Carpools have been arranged, and Javier and Molly volunteered to be designated drivers.

Alicia tries to coordinate outfits. "I'm gonna look like a slut if you guys wear jeans and t-shirts, so can we agree to wear cute tops at least?"

Ingrid wishes she could go. "I miss being single and childless. I want to get drunk and make out with a rando too," she says in a pouty voice.

Bridget promises to be Emily's drink runner. "I'll keep you hydrated." She winks.

161

Almost done, Emily tells herself, running a customer's credit card.

Since her conversation with Nora this morning, her brain has felt like a pinball machine, those heavy silver balls bouncing from one thought to the next. *Did Dad ever really care about me? Todd never knew me, really. How could Phil even walk back into The Honky Tonk after that night? Why did Mom never come back for me?*

She misses Ashley. She wants to process all these ruminations with someone who knows about her life up until a few weeks ago. But Ashley wants her own life. A mental ball in her brain smacks into a bitter thought: *Ashley thinks you're a pathetic, clingy, needy slut who uses people, who cheated on Todd, slept with her brother. You're a shit person.*

She tears the receipt cleanly from the printer and strolls toward the table to drop it off when she realizes Madge has sat a couple in her section. Emily narrows her eyes. There is something familiar about the back of that man—the swirl of his hairline on the top right of his skull; those shoulders, thick and broad; that white undershirt peeking out of the neckline of a Brewers t-shirt. She makes eye contact with Nicole, sitting opposite Todd.

"Emily?" Nicole asks, wide-eyed, smiling. "What the heck? Oh, my God."

"Hi," says Emily. She's collided with an invisible wall, winded and dizzy as Todd's eyes meet hers.

"Whoa," he says. He looks younger without his beard. She reads his expressions more clearly. Surprise. Discomfort.

"Hi," Emily says again. She fights the reflex to touch him, hug him.

"I heard something about you taking off," says Nicole, smelling of perfume and hairspray. "A couple of my clients were talking about it. One said you were in Wisconsin Dells. I was so confused."

"Needed a change." Emily nods, wondering what Todd heard. Was he worried or curious about her at all? He glances between Emily and the menu in hand. His ears burn bright red.

"I don't blame you," says Nicole. "I bet you make way more money here."

"I do," Emily says. It comes out as an apology.

"Good for you," Nicole continues. Her tone isn't insincere or snarky; it's so genuine Emily feels small and ridiculous. Did she even know Emily and Todd were hanging out, sleeping together for months? "You like it here?"

Todd tips the ketchup bottle back and forth like a bored child.

"It's really fun," Emily says quickly, breathlessly. *Look at me*, she thinks. *Look at me*. He starts spinning the ketchup bottle, and she's determined to prove she doesn't care about him either. "I'm loving it. I—I've been boating and golfing and to a bonfire and made lots of friends. I even did yoga on the beach this morning." Todd studies the ketchup bottle.

"And had a date last week," Emily adds, wanting to melt into the threadbare carpet and disappear among the grime and stains.

"Yes. Love it. How awesome," says Nicole, resting her chin on her palm, skinny gold bracelets sliding down her forearm. "It's so beautiful up here, isn't it?"

Emily agrees.

"My grandparents love it," Nicole continues. "I've been a bunch of times. Grandpa loves this place. He's all into the maritime history up here, the shipwrecks and lighthouses. But Todd's never seen it. I was like, 'We gotta go!' He was saying how giant the lake is, weren't you?"

"Yeah." He glances from the ketchup bottle to Nicole to Emily. "Like an ocean."

"Yeah. It's big." Emily fixes her eyes on Todd's, spitting out while she seemingly has his attention. "And I'm gonna be a nurse."

"Good for you," Nicole says again, politely.

"That's great," says Todd.

She wants to evaporate.

"Miss? Miss?" A man waves from the next table. "Is that ours? We got a play to get to." He points at the crinkled, sweaty receipt in her hand.

"Oh, yeah. Sorry," says Emily. She nods to Nicole, "Amaretto sour," and a nod to Todd, "Whiskey Coke?"

"No, it's crazy to see you," says Nicole. "Make us one of those old-fashioneds like you did at The Honky Tonk, with the ginger ale. So yummy."

"Oh, sure. Will do," says Emily. "Coming right up."

She drops off the receipt with an apology, clears plates from Table Four, asks Table Three if they'd like refills. She's flustered, frantic, and feels like she might vomit on a string of questions lodged in her throat, questions she might have asked if Todd had sincerely acknowledged her: How is Rocket? How are the horses? Any rodeos coming up?

She asks Iona to bring refills of 7UP and RC to Table Three, then scoots behind Chris and Brandon in the bar, sets two tumblers on the rubber bar mat, a sugar cube in each, and a couple dashes of bitters.

"I didn't see your ticket come up," says Brandon, stuffing a book in his back pocket. "I can handle that. You know we have pre-made old-fashioned mix, right?"

"I know the way they like it," Emily says, dropping in some cherries and an orange slice. "They're from my hometown." She muddles, focusing on the cherries splitting open, the orange vesicles bursting, smushed to a pulp. A scoop of ice, shot of brandy. Brandon watches. Chris watches. A row of bar patrons watches.

"You're like a goddamn machine," says Bob.

"That's it. Brandon, you're fired," jokes Chris.

"Now, that's an old-fashioned," says a man seated at the bar directly across from Emily. He's in his seventies or eighties, a wide face etched with wrinkles that suggest he's spent much of his lifetime smiling. A gray-haired woman sits beside him with similar wrinkles around her mouth. She's wearing a denim jacket with rhinestone roses on the collar.

"We just went on a trip to Nashville, see," he tells Emily. "Stopped at this bourbon place."

"Real fancy place," adds the woman.

"Yeah, they got all the stuff, big silver barrels and whatnot," says the man. "And we goes and says, 'Make us an old-fashioned.'"

The woman shakes her head in disapproval. "It was not an old-fashioned."

"It was not an old-fashioned," repeats the man.

Emily can't help smiling. Their friendliness, their obliviousness to her current situation is comforting, a refuge.

"No?" Emily encourages them on, pouring in the brandy.

"All's they did was put a big block of ice in a glass with some bourbon, and I don't know, not much else, and they called it an old-fashioned," the man says, his faded blue eyes wide, incredulous.

"Boy, they were strong," adds the woman. "Holy buckets."

"Did you like Nashville?" Emily asks, stalling her return to Todd and Nicole.

"Real nice," says the man.

The woman nods. "We saw all the stuff. Went on a tour bus. That's the way to do it."

"You get your meals taken care of," says the man.

"Yep, they get you all set up at different restaurants."

"Good portions."

The woman nods in agreement once more. "They took care of us. We saw, let me think, the Opry, a couple museums, that mansion with the horses."

"Jack Daniel's factory."

"They taught us line dancing," the woman says, laughing. "Oh, we were terrible. Couldn't figure it out. I can two-step all day, but that was too confusing."

"I gave up," says the man. "I got a bad back, see. So, I watched her try. It was entertaining." The woman gives him a gentle backhanded smack on his arm.

"My dad really wants to go. He loves old country music," Emily hears herself say. Maybe it's seeing Todd. Maybe it's hearing the word *Nashville*. Maybe she wants to sound normal and forget for a moment the hurt, the estrangement. Maybe she misses him too. "He wants to fly down there, well we do, then motorcycle through the Smoky and Blue Ridge Mountains." She hooks an orange slice on the rim of each glass.

"Your poor heinie," says the woman with a joking smile. "Well, when you go, you gotta stop at the castle there. By the Blue Ridge Mountains."

"Castle?" Emily asks, stabbing a couple of cherries on a plastic pick. She should get back on the floor.

"A mansion or estate, I guess it'd be called," corrects the man. "What cracked me up is you're walking around like you're in England or something, and everyone there has these southern accents. 'Y'all.' They're saying 'y'all' at this fancy place."

"That didn't feel right," agrees the woman.

Emily laughs, picking up the drinks and smiling at the couple. "I'll remember that. Thanks."

They nod and hold up their cocktails. "Yeah, you enjoy, sweetie," says the woman.

"Lots of luck to ya," says the man.

She feels lighter from the conversation, smiling to herself, scooting behind Brandon, passing Chris, nearly out of the bar, when she hears a wolf whistle.

"I like the way you carry those cocktails," says the whistler, a man at the end of the bar with an empty shot glass and a bottle of Coors Light. His face is shadowed by the bill of his camouflage baseball cap. Emily feels she's been doused in filth but smiles politely.

"Pretty smile too," he adds. "Hey, have a shot on me, babe." He pulls a few bills from the open wallet resting on the bar.

"I'm not twenty-one," she answers, feigning disappointment.

"Well, how am I supposed to take advantage of you later?"

Emily's stomach lurches. Visions of Phil spring up behind her eyes, and she loses her breath.

"Hey! Nah-uh, dude," says Chris. "No-creep policy in this joint."

Emily's insides are hot with embarrassment and anger and getting hotter. She might combust. She might toss the cocktails in the man's face or start crying if she doesn't keep walking.

The man raises his hands in surrender. "Just a compliment."

MUDDLED CHERRIES

Chris follows behind Emily, a hand on her shoulder. "You want me to ask him to leave?"

She shakes her head. "No. It's fine. No big deal."

"Okay," he says. "Your call." His eyes meet hers, and she feels off-center.

"It's fine," she says again, turning back toward her section. *He would kick someone out for that?* she thinks. *Risk causing a scene over a comment?*

"Bathroom?" a woman asks, halting Emily's thoughts.

"Oh, that way." Emily nods her head to the left. "Past the old scuba diving suit." She's studying Todd's back, trying to find her breath, her balance. She recalls running her fingertips over the swirl of Todd's hairline, pressing her cheek between those shoulders as she drifted to sleep, wearing his white undershirts to bed. She woke in his bed a few weeks ago. She told him she loved him.

"Here you go," she sets the drinks down. They hit the table with a crack. She forgot the coasters.

"Yay! Thanks," says Nicole. Todd goes in for a drink.

"So, you decided on anything for dinner?" Emily asks as lightly as she can, the sting of incoming tears behind her eyes.

Nicole orders a chicken breast sandwich, and Todd orders a burger. Her buzzer goes off in her back pocket. Food's up.

"Thanks," Todd says, passing Emily his menu.

"Sure," she replies, looking down. She drops a bill to another table and punches in Todd and Nicole's order before retreating to the kitchen.

Bridget pulls salads from the fridge. Alicia snacks on French fries. Emily stops between them, stares at her hands, pulls out her notepad, and shakes her head.

"Shit," she says. She forgot what she meant to do.

"What's wrong?" asks Alicia.

Emily thinks of the creep at the bar. Her dad wouldn't bat an eye at what happened, would he? And Todd's here and unable to acknowledge her. She feels so insignificant.

"Of all the places, of all the restaurants," Emily says, clenching her teeth to hold back the tears. "Of course, they pick this one."

"What's going on?" asks Bridget.

She doesn't have the energy to hide this humiliation. She needs to share the crushing burden of this hurt. She won't be able to breathe until she does. "My ex-boyfriend or fling, or whatever, is out there with the girl he broke it off with me for."

"Are you serious?" asks Alicia, swallowing a French fry and wiping her hands on her apron. Concern circles her eyes, along with a glow of intrigue. "Where? What table?"

Bridget rests a hand on Emily's forearm. "Oh, shoot. How awkward."

"Table Five." Emily sniffles. "His girlfriend is gorgeous."

"You want me to take the table for you?" asks Bridget.

"No. That would be weird," says Emily. "It's too late."

Her buzzer goes off again. Javier peeks between the heat lamp and counter filled with baskets of cheese curds and chicken wings, plates of fried fish, and burgers. "Girl, get your food out of here."

"Sorry." Emily pulls a plate of perch from the counter.

"I'm gonna look," Alicia says, breezing through the swinging doors before Emily can stop her. Bridget exudes sympathy.

"Why did they have to come here?" Emily asks, pouting her lips, tears pooling. "He won't look at me, talk to me. You'd never know we slept together all winter. I feel so stupid." She balances the fried perch on the crook of her elbow and grabs the bacon cheeseburger, the BBQ cheeseburger.

"Asshole," Bridget says. "Listen, if you want me to run their food or bill, let me know. And soon, soon you'll be dancing with a drink in your hand and screw him."

Emily takes a deep breath. No longer alone in this. She takes a step toward the swinging doors when Alicia enters.

"You're way too good for him," Alicia says. "He wears cowboy boots with a tucked-in t-shirt."

Emily can't help but laugh. "But I like cowboy boots," she says, sniffling again, the tears dissipating.

"We all do," says Alicia. "But not with t-shirts. No. Not okay."

"Emily!" yells Javier. "Get that food out of here!"

Soon the entire waitstaff is aware of Emily's ex sitting at Table Five. Nora takes it upon herself to deliver their food, Bridget clears their empty cocktail glasses and replaces them with Miller Lites, and Alicia takes their plates when they finish eating. Grateful, Emily tries to focus on rolling silverware in the corner of the dining room but hears the deep, mumbling pattern of Todd's voice, his laughter. It begins with a loud "ha" that catches and echoes in his throat. She relished making him laugh. Now the sound adds layers of hurt—heavy but no longer invisible. Her friends swooped in like superheroes, saving her from as much pain as they could.

Finally, Emily sets the bill between Nicole and Todd.

"It was nuts seeing you, Emily," says Nicole as Todd reaches for his wallet. "Now I can set the record straight at the salon."

Todd rests a fifty on the receipt. "Keep the change."

"Thanks," says Emily, giving him a brief glance. A hint of apology, or is it pity, behind his eyes?

Emily sits between Molly and Alicia, picks up a knife and fork, and rolls a napkin around them. Nora and Bridget count their tips.

"That was embarrassing," says Emily. Everyone looks at her with varying degrees of sympathy and concern.

Emily drops the rolled silverware on the table. She can't contain her emotions anymore and spills her rambling thoughts. "I'm such an idiot. Like, we'd have never worked, right? He didn't take me to dinner. Not once. We basically just had sex, but I'm so stupid I thought it was special." She searches one pair of open, focused eyes after the other. They listen. And she keeps going. "But I made out with this guy in Madison, and I slept in a bed with my friend's brother, right? Like, what was that? And I never really felt seen by him. I thought it was so magical when I told him I wanted to be a nurse, like so intimate. And I told him I loved him because I'm so desperate and stupid."

"Oh, you're not an idiot," says Nora. All the women nod their heads in agreement. Emily rests a hand on her sternum to steady her breathing, soaking in their empathetic expressions.

"You are totally normal. Even if it wasn't great, you still go through a grieving process," says Molly. Emily doesn't understand what Molly means. Is she supposed to cry more about it? Think more about it? She doesn't want to do either of those things. Bridget discreetly rolls her eyes.

"I want to run and hide," Emily says, aware of Todd and Nicole finishing their Miller Lites.

"Is he the reason you came here?" asks Alicia.

They look at her expectantly, patient and quiet, rolling their silverware, stacking their bills. She can't stop now. This feels too safe and soothing.

"No. My dad took all my money. Put it into the restaurant without telling me." It feels like chewing on a thistle to say it out loud again. It's excruciating. "He said we're business partners. So, yeah. I don't know about nursing school."

The women pause the rolling, the counting. A chorus of dismay rings out: "Oh, my God." "Seriously?" "That's awful." "I'm so sorry."

"And he's angry at *you*?" asks Nora, an echo from their conversation this morning.

Emily nods. "I stayed after high school. I'm supposed to take over one day. And the bar's not doing good. They put up an interstate. My dad's complicated. But yeah, very angry."

"That's bullshit," says Bridget. "He doesn't get to do that. No. It's your life."

"Wow," says Molly. "So that's super complicated."

Emily nods again.

"Like, I'm sure you love him, right? So how do you process that?" Molly bites her bottom lip, deep in thought, like she's searching for something to give Emily comfort and can't find it.

"I'm getting us drinks," says Bridget, her way of offering comfort.

"Yes, please," says Emily. "Gin and tonic."

"All around," says Nora, spinning her pointer finger.

"I know this isn't the same, Emily. But if it makes you feel any better, my parents cut me off after this last semester," says Alicia. "My grades weren't the best, and I went on a bit of a spending spree. So, they sent me up here to," she makes air quotes, "learn the value of a dollar."

"Toil with the peasants?" Nora asks jokingly.

"I know. It sounds dumb because I know I'm really lucky, blah, blah, blah. But they helped my brother get this internship and are all proud of him, and my dad takes him golfing and on these adventure trips. And they think it's lame I want to do interior design or plan weddings. They don't take me seriously. Does that help, Emily?"

174

"That helps," Emily assures her. It does. She craves the reassurance and solidarity.

"Tonight, forget your ex and your dad, and let's have fun," says Nora.

Bridget returns with a tray of gin and tonics and passes them out as Shawn and Javier enter the dining room. Bridget raises her glass.

Shawn grips the back of Alicia's chair with his palms. "Are we gonna get weird tonight?" he asks.

"Let's get weird, ladies," says Bridget, a smirk on her freckled face. They clink glasses. Emily catches the corner of Todd's eye as he leaves the restaurant. She doesn't return his weak smile. She turns her gaze to the women surrounding her.

CHAPTER SEVENTEEN

Emily dances barefoot on a hard patch of mud surrounded by twenty-somethings kissed with summer sun. A trio of bearded musicians, The Midnight Campers, plays a Tommy Tutone cover: "867-5309." The bodies around her smell like sweat, patchouli, deep-fried food, citrus-scented perfume, marijuana, and cigarettes. Some dancers clutch beer bottles, others plastic cups with brown or clear or pink liquid. Some wear hoodies or t-shirts with the logos of local hotels, restaurants, and orchards; others wear collared shirts or lacy tank tops. Golden twinkle lights hanging from canvas tents pitched above the band and a rustic bar reflect off the inky black water of Green Bay, a pebble beach away.

Shawn bobs his head and shoulders to the beat. Javier rests a hand on Nora's side, struggling to sing along. Alicia and Bridget jump up and down, a few spins and shimmies here and there, shouting the lyrics enthusiastically.

"I'm way too sober," Molly says to Emily when the song ends.

"I'm not," says Emily, grinning. She had already tossed back a shot of tequila with Maria, then a shot of bitters with Shawn.

"When in Rome," he said. The combination left a warm, raw sensation down her throat.

She feels lighter, an effect of the alcohol, she's sure, but also from sharing the hurt over Todd and Dad, like saying it out loud chipped off something heavy clinging to her joints and bones and brain like zebra mussels cling to a dock post.

Nora, Bridget, Alicia, Molly, and Emily convened in the cabin before they all climbed in Molly's mom's minivan and Javier's car. Shawn and Javier waited outside, smoking cigarettes while the women changed clothes, applied fresh makeup, fixed their hair, spritzed themselves with body spray, dabbed perfume on their jaws and wrists, and talked about ex-boyfriends, ex-crushes, ex-lovers.

The scene reminded Emily of high school, preparing for basketball games, the boys' football games, homecoming, and prom with Ashley and a rotating crowd of others. They dusted glitter on each other's cheeks and eyelids, wore matching shoelaces or garters, ate chips or Rice Krispie bars, gossiped, talked, and sang "We Are the Champions" by Queen or "Breakaway" by Kelly Clarkson.

Alicia pulled the French braids from Emily's hair, tousled the waves, and said, "This is sexy." She added a few more curls with a curling iron while Nora shared that her first love was a skinny skateboarder who wore a sideways cap. She bought a skateboard to impress him and be closer to him.

"I was fifteen and listening to a lot of Avril Lavigne. But I sucked at skateboarding and hated it," she admitted, swapping one set of dangling earrings with multicolored crystals for another. "We saw an *Austin Powers* movie and made out. But then he didn't answer my calls and ignored me at the skatepark and finally told me on MSN Chat that he liked someone else. Devastating."

Alicia penciled a thick streak of eyeliner over Emily's top eyelid. "Don't ever put thick eyeliner on both your bottom and top lids, or your eyes will look small and beady," she advised while Bridget shared that when she broke up with her first boyfriend, a hockey jock in her school, he audibly exhaled into the receiver for about ten minutes while she assured him over and over, "It's not you. It's me."

"It was so awkward," Bridget said, slipping a blue paisley tank top over her pale, freckled skin. "He gave me a letter the next day saying he'd always love me and made me a hemp necklace."

Emily felt cared for and pampered as she looked into Alicia's focused eyes, noticing the gold flecks scattered throughout her irises. Alicia slid a wand of lip gloss over Emily's lips as Molly shared that the boy she lost her virginity to, a *Star Wars* fan who played the movies every time they hung out, made out with another girl in front of her.

"I felt like a hammer hit me in the chest. When I cornered him and was like, 'What the heck? I just had sex with you?'

he looked at me like I was crazy," she said, peeling her socks off and slipping on black plastic flip-flops. "He gave me this smirk. It was awful. I'll never watch *Star Wars* again."

Alicia gave Emily a once over and nodded with approval while sharing that her first boyfriend, a boy who dreamed of being a jazz musician, was obsessed with her.

"And not in a good way," she said. "Like constant calling and wanting to know where I was. He would call my friends if I didn't get back to him immediately and would drive by my house randomly to make sure I was there. My parents got involved and called his parents. It was bad."

Emily cringed at the story. "Asshole," she said, and it felt satisfying to say.

Emily brings the straw of her second vodka lemonade to her lips and tells Molly, "This was needed."

"Good! I'm glad you're feeling better."

Emily scans the crowd as the band begins "Brown Eyed Girl," the guitar riff met with hollers of approval.

"Hi-yah!" Shawn karate kicks and punches along to the beat while Javier and Nora laugh. Bridget and Alicia move toward Emily and Molly with sultry expressions—eyes narrowed, lips pursed—their shoulders rocking up and down like teeter-totters as they sing along. They all dance. They all sing.

"Hey!"

Emily keeps her shoulders moving to the music as she turns around. Jacob. He's smiling. "You came," he says, embracing her. "I'm so glad you came."

"Yeah, we're excited to see you play." She gestures to her friends. Molly and Alicia offer a small wave. Shawn continues kicking and punching the air. Nora rotates Javier's bracelet around his wrist, whispering in his ear.

Courtney, the woman from the bonfire, hugs Bridget from behind. "Yay! You're here."

"You're the only one who knows about my background," Jacob half-whispers in Emily's ear. She breaks out in shivers when his warm breath tickles her neck. "So, I need you to understand what a big deal it is for me to be playing secular music tonight." She laughs, maybe too loudly, and puts her hand on his shoulder.

"A big deal," she repeats sarcastically.

"I still don't think you understand." One corner of his mouth is pulled up in a smile. "For a guy who wasn't allowed to watch MTV growing up or listen to anything other than the Christian radio station, this is huge."

"You need a drink." Emily grips his empty hands. Any excuse to touch him.

"Oh, yeah. You want another one?" he asks.

They meander toward the bar. "I gotta hang back. I'm not twenty-one." She presses her pointer finger over her lips and shushes.

"Stay here. I got you," he says. "What are you drinking?"

While he walks toward the bar, Emily catches her breath. She's dizzy with drunkenness, with the realization that she does like this guy. His attention and presence are like a balm over dry, chapped skin—a sting at first, followed by a soothing sensation.

He returns with two vodka lemonades. They tap the plastic cups. "Cheers."

"So, is this drink number ten or eleven for you now?" Emily teases.

He smiles as he sips from his straw. "I've lost count. I'm a wild guy now."

"Look at you."

"These are good." He examines the drink in his hand.

"You're so innocent."

"Door County is stealing my innocence." He winks. "I even smoked marijuana the other night. Coughed for twenty minutes."

"You're going for it, aren't you?"

"I am. My mom would faint if she saw me now."

Emily has sampled alcohol since she was twelve and smoked her first joint at fourteen. Nothing about this scene would shock Dad in the least.

"So, do you have a checklist of all the sinful things? Alcohol? Check. Drugs? Check. Sex?" She stops there. Even in the soft light, she can see he's turning red.

"Uh," he begins, rocking back on his heels.

"I'm sorry. I'm drunk." But she's wondering if he's a virgin.

"Been making up any more history for the tourists?" she asks, changing the subject.

"Ever heard of Camp Meenahga?"

"No."

"Neither had I until some guy in a tour started asking about it. I gathered from what he knew that it was an old girls' camp, and I took it from there. I used *Parent Trap* for reference."

"You're terrible. That's lying. That's a sin. Another checkmark."

His laughter sends a thrill of pleasure down her spine.

"Hey. I tell them all about the limestone and the Moravians and Al Capone and the German POWs working the orchards. I say Niagara Escarpment a lot."

"I don't know what that is."

"You gotta go on a kayak tour."

"I do." Emily sips her drink, aware of Nora smiling at her from the edge of the dancing crowd, raising her hand and rippling her fingers in a discrete wave.

"People ask about the shipwrecks?" she asks.

"Another very popular topic."

"With us too." So many customers want to know what artifacts came from nearby shipwrecks. They want to know why they sank and how many died.

"Name some," he says. "Go!"

"Uh … there's like two hundred," she says, eyes wide, shaking her head.

"No excuses."

Her brain scrambles, trying to recall the names listed in a book about Door County shipwrecks Chris keeps behind the bar: "The *Australasia*? The *Christina Nelson* or something. *Emeline*. I know that one for sure. *Frank O'Malley, O'Brien*? I give up."

Jacob feigns disappointment, wincing and shaking his head. "Shameful," he says. "And you work at The Schooner?"

Emily gives him a gentle backhanded slap. "Bully."

"I'm going to tell my shipwreck enthusiasts to go to The Schooner, ask for Emily, and bombard her with very specific questions about Door County when she appears very busy," he teases. "And she likes verbal tips instead of money."

"You're terrible."

"No, seriously. I'll tell them to go there and order an old-fashioned," he says. "I've tried a couple since I've been up here, and none were as good as yours."

"What a compliment. It's a gift."

The song ends. Jacob cranes his neck toward the band. "I better get plugged in. I think we're up. Promise you'll dance."

Emily gathers her friends once the band returns to the tent with Cecelia and Jacob, once she's downed another shot of bitters. The band sets half-full beers and cocktails on stumps and guitar cases, steps barefoot on a threadbare oriental rug, and takes up their instruments. Cecelia appears confident and comfortable, squaring up to the microphone stand. She wears a purple dress with black hibiscus flowers. Jacob's posture is rigid. He bites his lower lip, looks to Cecelia, who smiles at him and says something Emily can't make out. The drummer smacks his sticks together.

"One two, one two three four." The thud of drums, crash of cymbals. Jacob plays a ditty on his guitar.

"Come on, come on, come on," Cecelia sings.

Nora intertwines an arm with Emily. "He is cute," Nora says. Emily doesn't disagree. The bodies around her move to the music and sing along to "Take Another Little Piece of My Heart." Emily dances, too, though she struggles to lose herself in the music. She's considering, strategizing whether she should give in to her attraction to Jacob. She's wondering if she's too tainted, too dirty, too messed up for this sweet, sincere man. She's wondering if he's looking for an easy lay to conquer another of his secular goals, and she meets the criteria.

He looks at Cecelia and gives her his smile. Emily can't compete with her, that confidence, that voice. She doesn't want to serve these two old-fashioneds one day, Jacob unable to meet her eyes.

"He's too nice," Emily decides.

"You don't have to like anyone right now," Nora says. "You can focus on you."

"That's probably a good idea."

Javier steps between the women, resting an arm on their shoulders. "Let's go swimming," he says.

"Yes!" says Nora.

"I told Jacob I'd watch," says Emily. "You guys go ahead."

"Nora?" Javier drops his arm around Emily and leaves one around Nora.

"You only live once," she says.

Emily scans the crowd. Shawn sings to Alicia, holding her hand. She laughs, tugging her arm away. Molly sits at a picnic table with Maria, deep in conversation. Bridget and Courtney dance, leaning toward one another with dreamy smiles, limp wrists resting on each other's hips. Cecelia sways as she sings, veins visible on her neck as she belts out the lyrics. Jacob gazes at Cecelia like he's in a trance.

Emily stops dancing. The world spins. Her eyelids are heavy. She needs water. She needs to pee. She sucks down more of her drink. Her head feels like fifty pounds—too much strength and effort required to keep it from bobbing. She searches for a toilet.

Emily plops down on the uneven pebbles of the beach, hidden away beneath a leaning cedar tree. She inhales the cool lake breeze moving over her like silk. She's drunk and isn't sure how she managed to pee in the porta-potty without falling asleep. Maybe it was mumbling along to "Go Your Own Way" while resting her head in her hands, or the toxic smell. Now Cecelia sings "Hit Me with Your Best Shot." Nora and Javier sit farther down the beach, their wet hair and skin shining in the moonlight. Nora stacks pebbles between them.

"There you are," says Molly. "I was looking for you."

"Hey," answers Emily.

Molly sits beside her and sets her hand on Emily's knee. "So, I have an idea. You are going to be a nurse, okay?"

"Okay." Emily grips a smooth pebble in each palm, wondering how long they've been on this beach: a thousand years, a million years?

"Sturgeon Bay has a tech school, and we can head down one morning, tomorrow even, and you can apply, check things out."

"Okay."

"Yeah?"

"Why not," Emily says. "I mean. Yeah. Why the hell not? I can't go back to Dad, right?" Her tongue trips over the words, but they keep coming. "He's awful. He's like so screwed up, and what he did is so terrible, right?"

"I wouldn't go back."

"Yeah. I'm way better off here." Emily takes in the hazy glow of the moon, the Milky Way, the brief brightness of a shooting star. She burps up the taste of vodka and bitters. Her head bobs. She wants to go to bed. The music stops.

"Oh, shit." Emily struggles to her feet, dropping the pebbles. "I told Jacob I'd watch the whole thing. I'd dance."

Molly helps Emily navigate over the pebbles, through the tree trunks toward the dispersing crowd, toward Alicia, who's talking to a tall, clean-shaven man in a Coast Guard t-shirt. His fingers interlock over the top of hers.

"I'm learning CPR," Alicia says, grinning. "Don't interrupt me. This is very serious." Shawn sits at the bar.

"Where's Bridget?" Emily asks.

"Off with Courtney somewhere in the woods," Alicia says without looking away from her CPR lesson. The man moves her hand to his chest.

Emily pieces the scene together, the situation clicking into place like a puzzle. "Bridget is gay," she whispers.

"Emily!" Molly scolds. "Shhhh."

"Why didn't she tell me? I don't care. Nobody cares. Like seriously, nobody cares about anybody but themselves, really."

"People care," says Molly.

Shawn returns holding a couple of shots, little squares of maroon liquid. "Emily?"

"I think she's had enough," says Molly, a hand on Emily's shoulder.

"Well, it was supposed to be for Alicia, but she's with douchebag over there." Shawn runs his tongue over his top teeth.

"Give it here." Emily holds out her hand. "Don't want to waste it."

"I'm getting you two some water." Molly strolls toward the bar. "One of you is DD next time."

Emily struggles to swallow the shot. Her esophagus constricts, refusing to accept more, but she forces the pungent liquid down. "This shit again? Yuck." She pretends to gag. "Why do you guys like bitters so much?"

"Something about prohibition," Shawn says, swatting at the air. He steps closer to Emily, the heat radiating from his tall, bulky body. His eyes are hazy, unfocused, pleading. He brings his hands to her face and leans in with his mouth tight and puckered like a sphincter, but she pushes her palm against his chest.

"What are you doing?" She wants to sit down.

"Please," he says like a whiney child who wants their parent to order them soda or French fries. "To make Alicia jealous?"

Emily shakes her head. "No. I'm not a whore, you know," she says, annoyed, glancing toward Alicia and the Coast Guard man. They are kissing now. Alicia's raking her fingers through his hair as he grips her ass. "And I don't think they'd care."

"Fine," says Shawn. "Whatever. Fuck you." He turns back toward the bar.

"What the hell?"

"Hey. I didn't see you out there," Jacob says, approaching Emily. The alcohol courses through her so intensely that she might fall over. Where is Molly?

"Sorry," she hears herself say. "I was listening. Really good. Had to take a break. But great. You did good." She gives a thumbs up.

"Thanks."

"And, fun fact." Her filter, her inhibition gone. "I found out my roommate is a lesbian. And your coworker, Courtney! So, what would your mom think of that, you working with gays?" What would she think of Emily? Temptress? Drunk? Motherless sinner? Jacob rubs his hand on the back of his neck.

"And Shawn, the cook, just tried to kiss me." Emily points in the direction Shawn went. "So, I guess guys look at me and think, 'Slut. She'll do whatever I want her to.'" She isn't sure what's coming out of her mouth anymore. She has no control. And she doesn't care. He's too good for her.

Jacob looks concerned. His mouth opens like he's about to say something when Cecelia approaches with a couple of drinks.

"You forgot this, Jacob." She hands a half-full pint of beer to him.

"Thanks," he says, taking the beer.

Cecelia looks at Emily.

"It's me," Emily says, raising a hand. "Daddy issues."

"Hey," Cecelia answers, laughing. "Jacob told me not to call you that. But hey, daddy issues. You start journaling like I told you?"

"Not yet," Emily shakes her head. Feels their eyes on her. Their arms touch. "You guys sound good together. What's your band name?"

Cecelia and Jacob look at each other with quick smiles.

"I told you people would ask," says Cecelia, resting a hand on Jacob's shoulder.

"Haven't agreed on that," says Jacob. "I mean. I'm leaving, and it's just for fun."

"I told him," says Cecelia, smiling, shaking her head. "I suggested something with 'honeydew' in it. Jacob loves honeydew. Isn't that weird?"

"It's not weird." Jacob smiles, his eyes cast downward.

"Who likes honeydew?" Cecelia laughs. "It's like the filler of the fruit salad."

Emily wonders if Cecelia is staking claim, gently saying, "He's mine." Emily isn't up for the challenge.

"You two should date," she says. "I mean, you're perfect together."

Cecelia covers her smile with a hand. Jacob rocks on his heels. He's half-smiling at Emily, but there's something behind his eyes, a question.

"So date," Emily continues. "You obviously like each other. What are you waiting for?"

Molly returns and hands Emily a water. She holds it for a moment before it slips from her grasp and splashes to the ground. Jacob bends to retrieve the cup.

"Oh, shit. Well, at least it's just dirt," says Emily. Cecelia nods politely.

Jacob rises. "I'll get you another one," he volunteers.

"No," says Emily. "I'm fine. And don't worry about it, you know. The spill. It's just water and dirt. Nobody cares. Don't worry about it."

"Oh, goodness," says Molly, placing a hand on Emily's lower back. "I think it's time for me to take someone home."

CHAPTER EIGHTEEN

Emily pours brandy in multiple old-fashioneds lined up along The Schooner bar. Dad stands beside her, watching, nodding with approval. Emily takes up the soda gun and fills the tumblers with fizzy liquid. She looks up, searching for the couple. She wants to talk about that castle, the mountains. But there's no one at the bar, no one in the restaurant. No conversation or music. Just her and Dad and the relics of a bygone era.

No, there is someone—a figure seated at the end of the bar in her peripheral.

"Get her a shot," it says calmly, evenly. She knows the voice, the silhouette. Phil.

Emily tries to shake her head, to say no, but can't do anything but make the cocktails like an automated robot. While she places orange slices on the edge of a drink, Dad tugs her hair back. Neck bent, jaw opened, he pours liquor into her mouth. The taste like spice and tree bark, cloves and dirt. She swallows and goes back to the cocktails, an orange slice on each.

"Get her another!" says Phil.

Dad interrupts her stabbing cherries with a plastic pick. He yanks her hair and pours. But she can't swallow. The liquid spills from the corners of her mouth.

Her stomach is full and burning.

Her esophagus is full.

Her throat is full.

Emily leaps from the top bunk, her hand clamped over her mouth. She breaks out in a cold sweat as she rushes through the living room toward the bathroom, but she can't make it. She opts for the kitchen sink instead. She hunches over the silver basin and heaves. Tea-colored vomit streaked with bile splashes into a cereal bowl and two coffee mugs. She heaves again, a guttural noise echoing in the sink as she grips the counter and closes her watering eyes. She gags on the pungent, bitter taste. She spits and tries to catch her breath, but her stomach contracts, warmth rises in her chest, and she heaves again.

A hand presses flat on her spine, then calloused fingers brush against her cheeks, gathering strands of hair dripping with vomit.

She spits then belches and moans.

"Fuck," she whispers, spitting again. "Fuck."

"You okay, girl?" asks a deep voice.

"Fuck," she says again, loudly this time, spinning around too quickly. Her head throbs. Her brain is like a wrung-out bar rag. Javier steps back. He's shirtless. In the silver moonlight, she makes out the tattoos of crosses and cursive letters and the Virgin Mary in prayer covering his chest and belly. His eyes are heavy with sleep.

"Just me," he says. He retrieves a water glass from the cupboard and turns on the faucet. "You okay?" He hands her the glass. She sips and spits again. The dream floods back into her brain. Lightheaded, she searches for air.

"I didn't realize you stayed."

"Yeah. I heard you crashing through the house. Had a bit too much?"

Emily nods, wipes the tears from her eyes, and rests a hand on her chest.

"I didn't get all your hair in time," Javier says apologetically.

"That's okay." She touches the wet ends. Her stomach roils. She burps in her closed mouth. "Did I wake Nora?"

He shakes his head. "She's a heavy sleeper. Sure you're okay?"

She struggles to decipher his expression in the weak light but recognizes the gentle sincerity in his tone.

"I had too much to drink. And I have bad dreams sometimes," Emily admits.

"What about?" His dark eyebrows furrow closer. He leans against the refrigerator, scratching his side.

She considers what to say. About a misunderstanding? About something she's been told isn't a big deal? She wants to tell someone.

"This creepy guy," she decides. She fills her mouth with water, swishes, and spits. She should brush her teeth.

"Yeah? Someone you know?" Javier treads carefully. She can tell and appreciates his caution and interest but hasn't decided if it's worth the trouble, the drama. So she nods.

"Someone I know?"

"No. God, no," Emily says quickly. "This guy from my hometown. It's nothing. Just, men can be creepy."

"But we're not all bad," Javier says, shifting his weight. "Right?"

"No," she exhales, managing a small smile. She wants to share more, to feel validated. But she doesn't want to be that vulnerable, especially with a man. "If you ever have a daughter and someone does something that makes her uncomfortable or scares her," she's finding the words as she goes, "and she doesn't like it. Maybe people brush it off, but she's like not okay. What will you do?"

"Fucking kill him," he says, seemingly without a thought. "Or cut his balls off, at least."

Emily takes another drink of water. "Do that."

Emily climbs to her bunk, noticing Bridget's empty bed. She clutches her sore belly as she adjusts herself into a comfortable position, her breath a combination of mint and bile. As her head sinks into the pillow, she remembers feeling this ill before, but not from alcohol. In elementary school, she had the flu or a stomach bug.

She remembers Dad offering Sprite and packets of oyster crackers and placing a dull metal pot on the floor beside the couch. He turned on VHS tapes of Westerns—

MUDDLED CHERRIES

Shane, *Rio Bravo*, and *The Good, the Bad, and the Ugly*—
while she rested her head on his thigh, falling in and out
of sleep to the sound of mumbling, arguing men, ragtime
piano tunes, the *bang* of revolvers, and the *boom* of rifles.
He held her hair back when she vomited.

"There you go," he said as she retched. "I got you."

CHAPTER NINETEEN

Alicia drives her black Lexus down the highway. The car smells new, with a hint of blossoms and vanilla, an expensive perfume that's probably something French and difficult to pronounce. Emily sits in the front seat, searching for a decent radio station with a strong signal while Molly, Colin, and Bridget go over their shopping lists in the backseat.

"Tampons, shampoo, socks," Bridget says.

"Oh, yeah. Tampons," says Molly. "Good call."

They're on their way to Sturgeon Bay to shop in wider aisles for essentials that cost less than the stores up north. They plan to visit the technical college as well.

"I feel like a mom bringing my girl to college," said Alicia when Emily buckled her seatbelt and leaned against the creamy leather, feeling nervous and guilty. Maybe she should talk to Dad first. Maybe she should hold off.

For days, after her brain cleared of Thursday's massive hangover with the aid of hot coffee and salty French fries, she's considered whether to apply. Molly spread the word while The Schooner was abuzz with gossip from the eventful night at The Sunny Seagull: Alicia made out with a Coast Guardsman; Javier and Nora went skinny dipping ("Not true. I'm sure they had their underwear on," corrected Emily) and spent the night together ("True," she confirmed); Bridget disappeared in the woods and went off with the kayak crew; Shawn was hammered; and Emily decided to stay in Door County and become a nurse.

"Whoa, slow down," Emily said when Chris offered to find her a winter residence.

"Well, the cabin isn't insulated. There's lots of options," he said, running one hand over his beard, the other holding the remote and tuning the bar's TVs to ESPN. "And you can work whatever you want. Tips aren't as great, but you'll have a job."

"I might do a semester and then transfer," Emily said, lowering the barstools, "or quit if I hate it. I don't know yet."

According to Nora, word also spread that Emily got wasted and made a scene in front of Jacob and Cecelia.

"Did Molly tell you?" Emily asked, marrying the mustard bottles, cringing at the thought of the bits and pieces she remembered of their last interaction. Even in the haze of her hangover, she recalled telling Cecelia and Jacob they should date; they were perfect together.

Nora nodded, filling the saltshakers.

"I was a mess," Emily said. She considered texting Jacob, apologizing, sending something like: "OMG. So drunk last nite. Sorry if I said something stupid." But what's the point? Now he knows who she really is. "But whatever. I'm gonna focus on me, like you said."

So, she does. She focuses on what's next.

While Terry chopped cucumbers, telling Emily the difference between cat's paw shells and lion's paw shells: "Cat's paw shells are from clams. Lion's paws are from scallops," she was contemplating whether she was smart enough to be a nurse. *I'm gonna have to memorize all the muscles and bones, aren't I? Can I?* she wondered.

While a customer complained to Emily about the pits she discovered in the cherry pie filling she purchased from Halverson's Orchard last summer: "I had to throw the pie away. I don't want no one breaking their teeth," she was strategizing how she would tell Dad. How to avoid the conversation divulging into a fight. *I'll stay calm and stick to facts*, she thought while the woman continued. "I got grandkids! They could choke on those pits."

I'll call in the morning. Less chance of him being drunk, she decided while nodding sympathetically at the woman.

When her phone vibrated with a text from Jacob: "Hey! Want 2 go kayaking?" her breath caught, and a rush of relief and excitement pricked her skin. But she hasn't responded.

"I think he feels sorry for me," Emily said while braiding her hair, "like obligated to hang out with me."

"Why do you think that?" asked Bridget, stretching after her morning run.

He's the reason I'm even here, Emily thought, but didn't say, asking instead, "Did you see him with Cecelia at the kayak house?"

"They were on a couch together for a while," Bridget said. "That's all I saw. He had his guitar. I was playing Jenga."

"Yeah, right. Playing Jenga," Nora said sarcastically, entering the room with her mug of coffee, steam rising in wavy tendrils.

"And what were you and Javier up too, missy?" asked Bridget with a wide grin.

Nora laughed and shook her head.

"He's nice," Emily announced, securing the end of her braid. "I like him."

"I thought you two ended it last fall," said Bridget, stretching her arms upward, her fingertips brushing the low ceiling.

"We did. We're friends," Nora explained, hovering an open palm over her mug. Emily and Bridget remained silent, seemingly unconvinced.

"It was going to happen," Nora said, taking a sip of coffee. "Just needed to get it out of the way."

"Uh-huh. Was it good?" Bridget teased.

"Yeah," Nora said quickly, blushing. "I don't know. Familiar. Like riding a bike."

Laughter exploded from Emily and Bridget.

"Ahh, that's not what I meant," Nora said, unable to suppress her smile, the shade on her cheeks deepening in color. "Bad word choice."

"I bet you rode him," said Bridget.

Emily presses the search button: talk radio, classical music, Christian music, oldies, a commercial, country—finally.

"We're going on a hike tomorrow. Tim and I," says Alicia, adjusting her oversized sunglasses. "He's super naturey. There's some dragonfly he wants to see. Wants to show me some lady's slippers he found. What guy does that?"

"A cool guy," says Colin. "An interesting guy."

"Shawn called him a douche," says Emily, watching neat, tidy rows of cherry trees whiz by.

"Shawn is a douche," says Colin.

"He'll get over it," says Molly. "There's a lot of girls up here."

"Yeah. I know he likes me. He's not my type," says Alicia. "So, I was thinking I'd have everyone over at my house soon. A game night or something?"

"Fun," says Bridget.

"You should invite Ingrid," says Molly.

"Of course, she's invited. Everyone is," says Alicia. "Why?"

"She's having a tough time lately," answers Molly.

"I walked in on her crying in the walk-in freezer," adds Colin.

"Oh, no," says Alicia. "Why?"

"I don't really know. She was wiping her eyes and, I'm proud of this one, I said, 'To weep is to make less the depth of grief.' But she told me to shut up and walked out. So, can't say I was helpful."

"I could tell she'd been crying," says Molly, "so I asked her if she was okay."

"That's an idea, Colin," says Bridget sarcastically.

"I can't help it!" Colin defends himself. Emily laughs, watching corn fields, wheat fields, a faded red barn, silo, outbuildings, and a once-white home with baskets of purple petunias on the porch pass by.

"She told me she hasn't slept since the baby's been born, and Karin, her three-year-old, is a handful. She didn't want to go home, so she feels like a terrible mother," explains Molly. "I told her she probably has postpartum depression."

"Or she's just overwhelmed," says Bridget, sounding annoyed. "I don't know if everything has to be a diagnosis."

"Well, it's a legit thing," says Molly. "And her husband invited some distant relative or friend of a relative to come stay with them for a month this summer, and she's super stressed about that."

"That's sweet she talked to you," says Alicia. "She kind of scares me." They make sounds of agreement. Emily adjusts an AC vent to blow on her face. A gas station comes into view, a supper club, a stop light. Almost there.

"Can we go right to the college," Emily asks. "Get it over with?"

"Sure," says Alicia. "Molly, you gotta tell me the way."

Emily exhales, bracing herself for a question or comment, but Colin says, "Wasn't I right about Javier and Nora? I called it."

"I really like Javier," says Emily, relieved. "He held my hair back when I puked the other night. So, I'm a fan."

"I love how we were talking about how awful boys are," says Molly, "and then everyone starts pairing off."

"Do you like anyone?" Alicia asks Molly.

"No. Turn left up here and then right after the grocery store," Molly says. "You know what sucks about being a psych major? It feels like everything is predictable or explainable. When I get a crush on someone and feel good, I'm like, 'This is the dopamine pouring in,' and if it stresses me out, I'm like, 'Here comes the cortisol,' and if we make out I'm like, 'oxytocin!'" They all laugh.

The sign for Wisconsin Lakeside Technical College comes into view. A bubble forms in Emily's throat. "I'll be quick," she says.

The scene and interaction are eerily, comfortingly, an echo of Emily's experience at Westwood Technical College weeks ago. A woman behind a counter ceases her typing to help Emily, who collects the same pile of brochures and pamphlets, applications and forms for financial aid and scholarships in quick succession. But there is a greater sense of urgency.

"Classes start in six, seven weeks now," says the woman, her thin eyebrows arching up in emphasis. "We can probably sneak you into some generals. If you want to do nursing, let's see, anat and phys, microbiology, chem. Well, first, get all this back to me as soon as you can, and we'll line you up with an advisor and get the ball rolling."

MUDDLED CHERRIES

The woman smiles. Emily smiles back, clutches the pile to her chest, and says, "Thank you."

CHAPTER TWENTY

U and Ashley ok?"

A text from Ryan. Emily shuts her phone. Humidity saturates the mid-morning air. She sits at a picnic table, her sandaled feet wet from the dew still clinging to shadowed grass. Seagulls squawk. Gentle waves slap the giant rocks hedging a bayside marina packed with white and royal blue sailboats and yachts with names like *A Wave from It All* and *Sail La Vie*. She splays the forms and pamphlets and applications before her—so many blanks to fill in. She's waited two days, too long. Today's her day off. No excuses.

She opens her phone: "Not really," she types, biting her lip, deciding on the right words: "She thinks something happened with us that nite." Shuts her phone. A tight knot forms in her chest. She doesn't want to think about Ashley right now, about the distance and silence between them. Fourth of July is right around the corner. She needs to talk to Dad. She needs to fill these forms out.

204

Emily clicks her pen and starts writing.

Name: Emily Jean Schmidt. Date of birth: 09/02/88. Address: She texts Chris: "Can I use schooner address for mail?" Entry term: Fall 2009. Academic Interests: Nursing. Do you intend to apply for financial aid? Yes. Do you intend to apply for scholarships? Yes.

Her phone vibrates: "Shit. sorry. I'll talk 2 her. Mom's worried bout u."

A small smile creeps up Emily's lips at the thought of Diane's worry. *At least someone back home cares*, she thinks, watching an elderly couple in matching olive-green sunhats holding leashes led by flouncy Shih Tzus. She misses Diane too. She misses her inquiries about Emily's health, "You taking any vitamins?"; about The Honky Tonk, "What are those barflies on about these days?"; about her hobbies, friends, favorite music, and movies. She misses the hot dishes, the freezer stocked with pizza rolls and pints of Ben & Jerry's, the Tupperware containers of puppy chow and peanut butter cookies. She misses the clean sheets with blue morning glories or yellow sunflowers. She misses the thick toilet paper.

She misses Ashley.

"Tell her Im good. How r u?" Emily texts back. A young couple holding the hands of two children in matching summer dresses walk by, the littlest with a tiny pink purse shaped like a butterfly swinging from her shoulder. Emily clicks her pen again and again and rolls her neck.

The next item on the form: "Write a short essay about yourself and why you should be accepted."

A family of ducks paddle along. A sailboat leaves the marina. Clouds cover the sun. Maybe she should bring this to work. Maybe Molly or Nora should help. She removes her sunglasses. No. She needs to get these done and turned in.

"My name is Emily Schmidt, and I would like to take classes at your college," she writes. "I was a very good student in high school and got good grades." She pauses and clicks her pen once more.

Emily's phone buzzes: "I will. Not great. Feelin stuck." Emily shuts her phone, thinking of Ryan in his childhood room, playing video games and listening to rain. She isn't sure what to say, so she decides to respond later and goes back to writing. "I took a break from my education to help my dad's business."

Another buzz: "PO Box 946. Baileys Harbor. 54202."

"Thx." She texts Chris. She fills in the address, blows out a breath, and watches a squirrel climb and circle a narrow tree trunk.

"I think I would be a very good nurse. I have been a waitress for many years and am very good with people. I like to help people. I think I am very patient and have the right temperament to be a nurse," she writes, sounding out *temperament*.

Another buzz: "No prob," from Chris. She shuts her phone.

"I am very interested in learning more about how bodies work and helping people fix what is wrong and help them to be comfortable," she writes. "I know I'll be a good student for you. Thank you." Good enough. She sets that application aside, pulls out the next one, and starts filling in the blanks.

Another buzz: "Can I visit? As friends. Nothing weird."

The knot tightens. What would Ashley think? How long would Ryan stay? Where would he sleep?

Neon catches her eyes. Jacob, Courtney, and another guide, windswept and glistening in either sweat or lake water, haul kayaks out of the water onto a grassy knoll beside the marina. They wear neon t-shirts that say, "Kayak the County."

"Oh, no," Emily whispers, sliding her sunglasses on, hunching over the forms. She continues writing. Maybe Jacob won't notice her, but Courtney does.

"Hey!" Courtney shouts, approaching Emily.

"Hi." Emily plasters on a smile.

"You're Bridget's roommate, right?"

"Yeah, I am. Good morning."

"It's almost noon," says Jacob, coming from behind Courtney. He's smiling, too, and Emily feels guilty she never responded to his text.

"Oh, my gosh. Is it?" She looks at her phone. 11:41 a.m. Almost an hour has passed since she sat down. And there's so much left. Jacob scoots in beside her, and Courtney sits across from her, setting down their Nalgene bottles. They smell like algae.

The other man, squat and muscular with silver Oakley sunglasses on, pulls a wallet from a Ziploc bag. "I'll get the sandwiches. Turkey for you," he points to Courtney, who nods. "Ham for you," he points to Jacob.

"Yes, please."

"You want something?" he asks Emily. "I'm Tyler, by the way."

"Emily," she says, noticing the slight pangs of hunger in her belly, realizing there isn't an easy way out of this situation. "Umm, yeah," she reaches for her purse.

"Nah, it's on the company card," he says.

"Turkey, then. Awesome. Thanks."

"This looks fun," says Courtney sarcastically, taking in the disarray of forms and applications on the table, pulling out her ponytail and releasing giant brown curls that tumble down her shoulders.

Jacob picks up an application. "Holy crap. So, you're sticking around?"

"Maybe. Just applying. We'll see."

"That's great! You want some help? Got an extra pen?"

She considers for a moment. She doesn't want to impose or bore them. She feels awkward after not responding to his text. But there's so much left. She lets out a dramatic exhale. "Yes. Thank you."

She finds a couple more pens at the bottom of her purse. "The perks of being a waitress," she says, handing them off. "Pens everywhere."

Jacob and Courtney use the application she filled out as a reference and scribble in the other forms' blanks word by word—even the essay.

"Thanks so much, you guys," she says. "My brain's all scrambled up right now."

"This is good for me," says Courtney. "I don't think I've written a single thing since I got here."

"Is the essay okay?" asks Emily.

Jacob skims the paper. "It's perfect."

"You're too nice."

He shakes his head with a small smile and continues writing.

"All the ladies like him," says Courtney. "There was this teenager who suddenly decided she pulled a muscle, like, such a liar, so Jacob would have to tow her. It was so obvious."

Emily interlocks her fingers and stretches her arms out in front of her, studying Jacob's forearms and biceps as he writes.

"You've gotten more muscular," she says.

"What?"

"Since I met you." She squeezes his arm. He's blushing. She's flirting. She should have replied to his text. She should apologize, but she doesn't want to embarrass him in front of Courtney.

"From towing in all the pretty ladies," jokes Courtney. Emily laughs. She likes Courtney and recognizes the same sense of humor and bluntness as Bridget. "And then when I tell them he's a musician, they freak out. He has a decent fan base, thanks to me. I don't tell them he's taken. That might affect our tips." Emily's pen skids on the paper. Her spine goes stiff. Something inside her deflates, then aches.

"Just a couple dates." Jacob looks at Emily and reaches for his water bottle.

"Cecelia?" Emily tries to sound as light and breezy as the gust slipping over them.

He nods. "Took your advice."

She wants to know everything—where, when, and did he pay? Of course he paid.

She doesn't want to know anything.

"So, Courtney, Bridget told me you just graduated?" Emily asks, changing the subject. That's about all she could get Bridget to tell her about Courtney.

"I did. Biology, bitches. Cum laude."

"What's next?" Emily asks.

"I don't know. A bunch of people here spend winters in Colorado. I was thinking about that. But I hate skiing. Like, I hate it. My family and I went to Breckenridge once, and I'm an outdoorsy gal, but I mean, you're from Wisconsin, right? We're used to baby hills."

Emily and Jacob laugh, pausing their writing to listen. Courtney takes a drink of water.

"It takes forever to get up those mountains. You can't see the bottom," she continues. "My family are all magically great skiers, and I'm going as slow as humanly possible, singing 'You Are My Sunshine' to keep calm."

Tyler returns with the sandwiches and four tall cans of Arizona iced teas.

"Abby is wondering if we want to go sailing later, after our next tour," says Tyler, sitting down beside Courtney. "You should come too, Emily."

"I gotta run all this to Sturgeon Bay," says Emily, disappointed and relieved at the same time.

"You got lots of time," says Courtney. "Bring Bridget."

"Yeah, come," says Jacob. "We'll celebrate."

"Celebrate what?" Emily asks, cracking open her iced tea.

"You. Pursuing your dream."

....

Emily climbs in her truck and sets the stack of filled-out forms on the passenger seat. She opens the windows, blasts the AC, and turns down the radio. She closes her eyes. Jacob and Cecelia. She blew it. No, she didn't stand a chance. It's better this way.

"Focus on you," she mumbles to herself. "Focus on you."

She texts Ryan, "Cool! I'll check w/ roomies." Ashley can deal with whatever.

She rolls her neck. She should call Dad. She holds her phone in her palm, heavy and sinister, like a big black beetle she wants to fling out the window.

No. Emily will call him after she drops off the applications so she doesn't lose her nerve. And then she'll go sailing. Something to look forward to. She'll sail, maybe swim and drink and celebrate, like Jacob said.

She texts Bridget: "Wanna go sailing w/ me & Courtney later?"

She drops her phone in her purse and puts the truck in drive.

...

Emily drives down the highway toward the cabin to grab her swimsuit and pick up Bridget. "Hello." Dad answers on the first ring. Even in two syllables, she feels the tensity in his voice. She focuses on the Illinois license plate in front of her. "Land of Lincoln."

"Dad?"

She felt brave moments ago, after dropping off the forms and applications, smiling at the woman who said, "Very good! We're cutting it short, but I'm confident there's a few openings in some gen eds. Keep your phone close by." Now she feels she's done something wrong, like a criminal about to confess.

"So, you didn't forget about me," Dad says bitterly.

"How are you?" she asks, stalling, the bravery drying up like a raindrop on asphalt.

"Me? Oh, well. Thank you for asking. Not good, Emily. Things aren't good around here," he says quickly, loudly. A fist squeezes her heart. "We miss you. We need you. Tell me you're on your way home."

"Dad," she says gently, cautiously. "I'm gonna stay, Dad."

"So, I'll start cleaning out your room then? Tell everyone you up and left? They don't matter to you anymore. I don't matter."

Tears blur her vision. She's losing control of the conversation. She's losing her nerve, her anger. Why isn't she going home?

"I didn't expect this from you, Emily. Listen, I'm on my knees here. I need you. Fourth of July is coming. Doug's gonna pull his boat for the parade. You and your friends can ride in it, like always."

"Dad, all those friends are gone. You and Larry and Jack can be in the parade, be cowboys or something."

"Well, I ain't seeing much of Larry these days."

"What happened?"

"He thinks he knows how to run my business better than me, and I got tired of the unsolicited bullshit."

Emily can imagine the scene. She'd witnessed Larry and Dad a dozen times before arguing over the town's new light posts, the best brand of motorcycles, who a woman they both slept with thought was a better lay.

"It doesn't matter," Emily would say when petty arguments started heating up. Both stubborn. Both temperamental. If she had been there, she could have smoothed the situation over.

"Well, maybe you could use a bit of business advice," she says, finding her nerve.

"So, you're doing real good up there then. Realized you don't need your dad? Well, I need you."

"Why can't you be happy for me or worried about me, like other parents?" She's exasperated, wiping tears.

"I guess I'm not perfect."

"No." She sniffles, spiraling into anger. "Because other parents don't steal their kid's money." That's why she's not going back, she remembers. And she's an adult.

She's sailing today. She's celebrating. "Do you have my money?"

"We're partners, Emily."

She shakes her head. "And other parents would have kicked Phil out," she says, without realizing it was there, interlaced in the spiral, "told him to never come back."

"That shit again? He didn't rape you. He didn't hurt you."

"But it scared—"

"You just want me to feel bad. You know, I do feel bad. I'm wondering where I went wrong with you."

"Dad," she pleads.

"Like, did I do something in a past life to deserve this?"

"Dad," she says again.

"You're my girl. I mean it, Emily." His voice shakes. "I'm in a bad way. I'm—I'm not sure how to see through this right now."

CHAPTER TWENTY-ONE

Welcome aboard!" says Abby, sun-bleached hair pulled back beneath a costume captain's hat. Emily grips her strong, narrow hand as she steps tentatively on the hull.

"I don't know anything about sailboats," she says nervously, unsure how to navigate around the silver poles, hovering pulleys, thick ropes, and canvas sails. "They look less complicated from far away." Maybe this was a bad idea.

"Here, sit by me," says Jacob. She offers a grateful smile and sits on the bench beside him.

"Don't worry about a thing," says Abby. "Just enjoy."

Tyler unwinds the ropes from the dock. Cecelia rests her hand on Jacob's knee, purple nail polish glinting in the sunshine. Bridget lathers thick white sunblock on her chest and forearms.

"You're all so lucky," she says. "I'm either super pale or super burned; there's no in-between." Courtney rubs the lotion on the back of Bridget's neck and shoulders.

As they cruise to the open water, the passengers slip beer cans in Koozies and talk about their days, their shifts, and their customers. Except Emily. She's distracted, studying the bluffs in the distance, the gnarled gray roots of cedar trees clutching the layers of limestone like arthritic fingers. She's replaying the conversation with Dad. She's worried about him.

"I forgot a man's third Coors Light, and he wanted fifty percent off his bill," says Bridget, taking a drink. "Like that was the obvious answer for me forgetting his beer."

"These poor parents spent half the afternoon tour reassuring their kid there weren't any sharks in the water," says Tyler.

"And piranhas," adds Jacob, laughing. "He was very fixated on piranhas. I hung back with him and convinced him we were totally safe. That there's only small fish that don't bite."

"You're too nice," says Cecelia, crossing her legs toward him.

"Everyone keeps telling me that."

"This lady at the farmers' market yesterday asked if our bees were vegan," says Tyler. "I was like, 'Yep, they are. Sure.' She was thrilled and bought candles, soap, and honey. Cha-ching."

"You keep bees?" asks Bridget.

"My mom does. She's into it all. I help. And my dad has a tree-cutting service, so I help with that too." Guilt sinks to the pit of Emily's stomach like a stone. Tyler helps *his* family.

216

"All that stuff isn't vegan, right?" asks Courtney with a bemused smile. "Like, honey is made from an animal, so it's an animal product. Right?"

"Maybe she was wondering if the bees were vegan themselves," adds Bridget, laughing. "Such a weird question."

"I knew what she wanted me to say, so I said it," says Tyler, laughing, defending himself with a satisfied smirk. They all laugh, except Emily, taking in the gray-blue of the water surrounding them, a pod of pelicans soaring overhead. Maybe she should go back, start school next spring. Maybe she can convince Dad to downgrade his motorcycle or sell some of his memorabilia to repay her. Convince him to ban Phil. A fresh start.

"I cleaned an already spotless house today," says Abby, waving at a passing pontoon boat. "This lady has me come three times a week, and it's her and her husband in this six-bedroom mansion. So pointless, but the money's good."

"Cecelia was in housekeeping," says Jacob, a light-hearted prompt. "Tell them why that ended."

"Oh, my God. They don't want to hear this," Cecelia says, laughing. "They'll never want to stay at a hotel again."

Emily feels another heavy stone plummet into her stomach—jealousy. She should have texted Jacob back. Her gaze falls to the stark tan line on his thigh.

"What?" asks Tyler. "What happened?"

"Okay." Cecelia takes a drink and gives Jacob a small shove. "I told you that in confidence."

"It's such a good story."

"It was my first ever job here. I'm not proud of this, but I had a ton of rooms to clean and was hungover, and this bed really looked like it hadn't been slept in. So, I didn't change the sheets and made it up real nice."

"Ugh, yuck," says Abby, steering them toward the open horizon.

"Then that night, the next guest slipped into bed and must have felt something. And they pulled out a pair of tighty-whities!"

Everyone but Emily erupts in laughter. A small laugh escapes her lips, but she wishes she skipped out, was in bed, or speaking to Nora, calming and wise.

"Ew, ew, ew," says Courtney. Bridget reaches across the boat and taps her foam Koozie against Cecelia's.

"So, I was fired."

Emily envisions Dad alone at The Honky Tonk, listening to lonely old songs on the jukebox. He sounded so raw, so vulnerable. "I need you," he said. "I'm in a bad way."

"You okay?" Jacob whispers to Emily. He's wiping spray from his sunglasses, his face inches from hers.

She studies his kind eyes.

"Yeah. Good," she says, aware she hasn't said a word since they've left the dock. She leans forward. "Where do you work, Cecelia?" she asks, pushing through the discomfort, the feeling that she doesn't belong here anymore, trying to participate.

"Sips and Drips. It's a make-and-take art studio. Really cool. We serve coffee and wine too."

"Cool," says Emily, leaning back. Jacob slips a beer into a blaze orange Koozie and hands it off to Emily.

"I heard you're going to the tech college in Sturg," says Cecelia, leaning forward, looking at Emily. "That's awesome."

"Yeah." Emily takes a drink of her beer—tasteless. "I don't know. I'm having second thoughts."

"Why?" asks Courtney.

"What?" asks Jacob.

"I talked to my dad," she begins, looking from Tyler to Courtney to Bridget to Abby to Cecelia to Jacob. "And, well, his business back home isn't doing good. He's not doing good." She can see herself reflected in their sunglasses, small and distorted, holding the orange Koozie to her chest.

"Don't you dare go back," Cecelia says adamantly before anyone else can react. She rubs her sooty black hair from her face as if she wants nothing between her words and Emily's ears. "No. He's a big boy. Don't do it."

"This is the guy that stole from you, right?" asks Bridget curtly. Emily regrets saying anything, so she offers a nonverbal response, a nod, and wishes to pass the attention on to someone else, but the boat's occupants remain laser-focused on her, and she has nowhere to run.

"Yikes," says Tyler.

"Yeah, you gotta stay," says Jacob. "You got friends up here. You got a life." She considers this. She does, doesn't she? For now. Until the fall, until they all scatter like her friends after high school.

"I'm telling you, Emily," says Cecelia, reaching across Jacob and squeezing Emily's thigh too tight, like it might pop the idea right out of her body like pus from a pimple. "I'm telling you, do not go back to make him happy or try to fix it for him."

"I feel so guilty," Emily lets out, biting her fingernails.

"I do, too, sometimes," says Jacob. "My mom calls almost every day. If I don't answer she leaves voicemails where she reads scripture or prays for me, my safe return, like I'm the prodigal son."

Bridget and Courtney grimace. Abby shakes her head.

"Yikes," Tyler says again, taking a long drink of beer.

"But I keep telling myself, 'It's my life,'" Jacob adds.

"You can't go, Emily," says Bridget. "You can't."

"I just met you and I second that," says Abby. "You gotta stay."

"Here, here," says Cecelia, raising her drink. "You're staying."

Emily smiles despite the misgivings still knotted up inside. But there's such relief as well, to share, expose, the conviction in their voices. It is *her* life. This is *her* life. She's living it.

She wants to stay.

"Cheers," she says.

"Now, let's sail," says Abby. "You're in Door County, and it's a beautiful day." She turns off the engine and switches on some tunes. "My yacht rock mix," she calls it as she and Tyler wind cranks and pull ropes, saying things like "jib," "boom," and "sheets." A piano solo plays a little melody as the wind billows and expands, the tall white sails rising. The boat propels forward, like receiving a big two-handed push on a swing or sled—rough, quick, and exhilarating.

"Hold on," says Abby, as the boat cuts through the water like a fin. Emily feels like she'll tip over. A rush of adrenaline fills her chest and floods her brain as her body counters the lean of the boat. She smiles. The passengers whoop and holler.

Tyler sings along to "Come Sail Away" by Styx in a high, nasally voice. Cecelia joins, her voice as pure and clear as the drops of water landing on their skin. Emily finds her balance and realizes she's clinging to the hem of Jacob's board shorts.

"Sorry." She releases her grip, embarrassed. "I was scared I was gonna fall in."

"I wouldn't let you," he says, reaching for her hand.

CHAPTER TWENTY-TWO

The Schooner staff gathers beneath the restaurant's awning at eight in the morning on July 4 for a pep talk and annual group photo Chris insists upon before they begin the busiest day of the year. They still need to wrap brats and hamburgers in foil, haul buckets of Bloody Mary mix downtown, portion ranch and tartar sauce, and finish decorating a float. Everyone dons tie-dyed t-shirts that Nora made with the help of Javier.

"There is nothing patriotic *or* nautical about these things," says Chris, laughing, looking down at the spirals and splashes of pink, purple, and blue on his belly.

"I didn't use enough red dye," says Nora, laughing. "Too bad. You have to wear them. I spent ages on these stupid shirts."

Chris laughs along, shaking his head. "Okay. I just want to thank everyone for being a part of the team today. I know there are a hundred other places you could be working up here, so thanks. That's it."

The guilt Emily felt upon waking from a fitful sleep, embarking on her first Fourth away from The Honky Tonk, slowly dissipates like the thin fog rolling off Lake Michigan, evaporating in the sunshine. She feels a part of something familial, especially when they huddle together, Nora on one side, Bridget on the other, their arms over her shoulders, hers around their waists, and they say, "Cheese!"

They convinced her again and again she was meant to stay and that she was doing the right thing—over eggs and chorizo Javier made for them, while sunning and swimming at the beach, and while smoking weed and watching *Up* at the drive-in theater. They told Emily that Ryan could sleep on the couch, at Javier's the nights he stayed with Nora, or in Bridget's bed the nights she stayed at the kayak house.

"Or with you," said Bridget. "Didn't you already sleep with him?"

"Next to him," corrected Emily. "I think that was a one-time thing."

Ryan said he'd come next week or the week after. He said Ashley was ignoring him too.

"She knows nothing happened," he texted. "Just a stick up her ass." Emily knows Ryan's visit won't help the situation, but oh well. It's *her* life.

"This is what we've trained for," jokes Shawn before the staff fans out to their respective places. "This is our 'Nam, brother." He pats Javier on the back as they return to the kitchen.

"See you on the flip side, everybody," says Bridget, tightening the laces of her tennis shoes.

Emily begins the day serving Bloody Marys and screwdrivers with Ingrid and Nora beneath a red canopy tent at a corner of Baileys Harbor. Nora and Emily fill a folding table with cocktails as the crowd seeps into the little town like a red, white, and blue mudslide. Revelers lean against mailboxes and light posts and porta-potties. Emily and Nora have a few seconds to chat before a line forms.

"That was nice Javier made us breakfast again this morning," says Emily with a smile, pouring the vodka. "You think that's the last thing he'd want to do when he does it all day."

"I know." Nora smiles back. "He's so sweet, isn't he?"

"So, you two officially back together?"

"I don't know," Nora says. She fiddles with the jagged amethyst stone on her necklace. "Then what happens in the fall?"

Ingrid hands over drinks and exchanges money until locals join the queue and ask about the new baby. Nora and Emily swoop in to keep the line moving. "She's so good. Frida. Seven pounds, eleven ounces," Emily hears Ingrid say over and over. "Labor went well. Karin is a great big sister. We are so happy. Oh, thanks. I was worried I wouldn't be able to lose the weight with the second one."

It feels strange to Emily to be uninterrupted as she works a Fourth of July shift. No former classmates or their parents, teachers or coaches. No customers of The Honky Tonk, people she's known her whole life, greeting her and asking about her plans, The Honky Tonk, her future. She wonders if they're asking Dad and what he's saying.

She texted him the morning after sailing to quell any doubt or hope.

"Decided 2 stay. Sorry."

He hasn't responded.

Ingrid finally takes a drink from her own Bloody Mary. "I'm such a liar," she tells Nora and Emily as they hand over cocktails and thank customers for adding a dollar or two or five to the tip jar. "My boobs hurt. I'm tired. I was changing Frida's diaper this morning, and Karin came over with a stuffed goat and pretended I was the thing's hill or mountain. I chucked it across the room," she tells them, taking another long drink. "I'm not proud of it. She started crying. I started crying. That British guy showed up last night. I'm so stressed. God. Oh, this Bloody is good. Pumping and dumping today."

A couple hours later, Emily tosses Mardi Gras beads, drink tokens, and Dum Dums from a trailered wooden ship into the red, white, and blue sea of people of all ages on either side of the highway. She smells exhaust and sunscreen. Colin, Alicia, and Molly are on board as well. They're dancing to Katy Perry, barely audible over the firetruck sirens a few vehicles ahead and a high school marching band a few vehicles behind.

Emily takes in the scene around her—the stars and stripes; Uncle Sam hats and Lady Liberty headbands; t-shirts that say Obama/Biden or McCain/Palin or Bush/Cheney; t-shirts with eagles soaring, fireworks exploding, flags waving; spotless military uniforms and crisp camouflage fatigues; children dashing for Tootsie Rolls and Smarties; an elderly man and a toddler waving at Emily like they know her, like she's back in Deer Valley. She loses her breath for a moment, thinking of home.

"There's Tim," says Alicia, her Mardi Gras beads bouncing as she jumps up and down waving to the tall man smiling back.

"He's so cute," says Molly. "And smart too. Right?"

"Because of him, I know there are insect-eating plants up here," says Alicia, laughing. "So, I'm learning and getting some."

"Win, win," says Colin. "Happy birthday, America!" he shouts, winding up and throwing a fistful of Dum Dums like a baseball pitcher.

"Thank you for your service," yells Molly, tossing a handful of drink tokens toward three men in Navy uniforms.

After the parade, Emily works in the restaurant, serving burgers, beers, and cheese curds to jovial customers who smile and say, "Thank you" when she drops off their orders and rushes to the next task. A few unhappy customers groan with displeasure when she reports they're out of iced tea or their appetizer got backed up behind the endless stream of tickets.

"Finally," a man grunts when she delivers his table's onion rings.

And some customers are drunk and have come to The Schooner to get more drunk. They slur and tip one way, then the other like sideswiped bowling pins, unable to focus their glassy gaze on Emily. They make her laugh, "I'm here to celebrate 'merica!" and cringe, "Ever heard of a Black man keeping a job for more than four years?" and uncomfortable, creeping their hands on the small of her back like giant tarantulas, "Sweetie, sweetheart, you gotta come to our place tonight. What's your number?"

Emily's apron pocket bulges with a huge wad of cash. She manages to take bites of a cold, soggy BLT over the course of an hour and snag French fries and cheese curds from baskets waiting beneath the heat lamp. She gulps down ice water when she punches in orders at the register. Her feet ache. Her shirt clings to her sweaty back.

When the kitchen finally closes and the crowd grows bigger at the bar, Chris sends the servers on their way.

"We'll clean up tomorrow," he says as they sit around a table, rolling silverware and drinking their post-shift cocktails. Javier comes out of the kitchen, beads of sweat visible along the sides of his face, pooled in the hollow spaces of his collarbone.

"That was insane," he says, falling dramatically to an empty chair. Shawn comes out next, also gleaming with sweat.

"I'm like, so tired, but way too wound up," says Bridget, wisps of her red hair flying away from her taut ponytail like a glowing halo.

"Let's go jump in the lake," says Shawn, taking a chair next to Alicia.

"Tim's at some barn party," says Alicia, looking at her phone, her mascara and eye shadow smudged from the day. "There's a reggae band playing." Shawn stands and walks purposefully toward the bar. The goat-like eyes of his octopus tattoo meet Emily's like a lurking predator.

"Oh, yeah. We're all going," says Javier, wiping his face with the collar of his shirt. "Wasn't that the plan? I told Ingrid I'd bring that British guy she's got living in her backyard. He's supposed to be at the bar waiting." Javier cranes his neck.

"We go every year," says Nora. "Of course, we're going."

"I feel like I should shower," says Molly, lifting her arms away from her body with a grimace.

"No. Everyone will be gross and sweaty," says Bridget.

"I'm in," says Emily, taking a long sip of her gin and tonic. The guilt lingers, hovering around the edges. She doesn't want to climb into bed until two, until she knows The Honky Tonk is closed and the day is officially done. Until then, she'd toss and turn.

...

The barn overflows with light, with the music of Bob Marley, with the rank smell of marijuana and body odor, with twenty-somethings and teenagers wearing tank tops and flip-flops and the uniforms of wherever they just got off work. There are five or six musicians on the rustic stage. The lead singer tosses his long, thick dreadlocks as he sings with a Caribbean accent. Though the barn doors stand open, air barely moves as Emily squirms her body between undulating shoulders and hips, following her friends to the center where they dance, where the British boy, Simon, a friend of a brother of a friend of Ingrid's husband, sticks close to her. They've hardly been introduced, but he's honing in on her as he dances, attempting the robot, wearing a faded t-shirt with an American flag across the chest. Emily isn't sure if he's wearing it to be funny or ironic or to fit in.

"Are there castles where you live?" she shouts in his ear.

"Everywhere."

"Cool."

"Loads of red barns around here. Never seen so many. Thought it was a myth."

Emily keeps her body moving, but her legs ache, and her feet throb. Even her wrist feels weak as she brings a bottle of Miller Lite to her lips. She notices her friends paired off. Maybe that's why Simon's staying close. Nora and Javier grind against one another, his hand around her waist. Alicia's arms encircle Tim's neck, her beer bottle between his shoulder blades. They gaze at one another with blissful smiles. Molly follows Shawn toward the exit. Bridget dances with Courtney and Tyler. Where's Jacob?

"Want to get some air?" Simon asks her.

"Sure."

Simon takes her hand, and she follows as he snakes through the tight pack of bodies, past Jacob and Cecelia at the edge of the crowd, arms around one another like Alicia and Tim. But they're not dancing; they're kissing—slowly, deliberately. Cecelia combs her fingertips through Jacob's hair, and Emily averts her gaze, the heavy stone in her stomach rolling around. She focuses on the hand holding hers.

Simon and Emily wander toward a grassy lawn. Slats of golden light beam between the planks of the barn. The fresh air cools and soothes Emily's skin and lungs. Simon stands close, tucking his shoulder-length hair behind his ears.

"I like your hair," she says, wondering if British people stand closer than Americans.

"Couldn't be bothered to cut it while away," he says, taking her in. "You look knackered." She shivers under the intensity of his gaze.

"What a compliment." She gives him a gentle shove.

"No." He rests his hands on her shoulders, moving closer. "You look good. Knackered, but good." His eyes are the color of the lake when it rains.

"Big day," she says. Heat radiates from him. "Did you have a fun Fourth?"

"A proper Fourth, yeah. I've been dancing in a barn with you lot."

"I like your accent," she says. Like a strange, jagged melody, like he's pushing his vowels from the depth of his throat, letting them linger around quick consonants.

"Cheers. Thanks. I like yours too."

"Why did you come *here*, of all places?"

"Right, I didn't even know where Wisconsin was, to be fair. But, low on funds, I connected with Logan, who said I could stay free in his campervan."

"So, you're traveling around?"

"Yeah. Gap year. You Americans don't really do that, do you?"

"What do you do exactly?"

"Jet off. Explore."

"Where were you before here?"

"New Zealand in January, after the holidays. Then to the east coast of Aussie, up to Thailand, Vietnam, in San Francisco—bloody expensive. I'll show you pictures sometime. And, now here, then New York for a bit before home."

"Back to the castles," Emily says.

"Back to the castles," Simon repeats.

"We don't have anything that cool around here."

"You're here."

Emily laughs shyly. Sticky with sweat, sore, tired, and tense. She doesn't have anything else to ask or say. Her brain longs to turn off. So, she lets the silence settle and feels her body relaxing, her heart slowing when he moves his hands to her sides, when he steps even closer, when he presses his lips against hers. And she lets him. She closes her eyes and rests her hands on his biceps. His lips are pillowy soft. His tongue slips between her lips, and she opens her mouth, inviting him in, for just a moment before she pulls away.

Too fast. Too risky. This is the very thing she's meant to avoid.

"I just met you." She takes a step back.

"I like you."

But she doesn't trust that. He'll find another girl.

"I'm so tired." She lets go of his arms, noticing a strand of her hair caught in his short whiskers.

...

Emily wakes to her phone vibrating on the floor in the pocket of her denim shorts. She climbs down the ladder, afraid to wake Bridget, but she's not there. Emily exhales, runs her fingers through her greasy hair, and yawns as she checks her phone.

A message from Dad: "Do yurself a favor – dont have kids. They break ur heart."

She stares at the message for a moment, rereads it, then shuts the phone. A hot hurt creeps up her throbbing body, from her toes to the top of her head.

"Screw you," she whispers. She drops her phone on the floor, tears escaping as she climbs back up to bed.

CHAPTER TWENTY-THREE

Nora opens a wooden box carved with flowers. She runs her tongue over her teeth as she thoughtfully scans the cubbies of bracelets, earrings, necklaces, and rings. Emily watches and waits in a black Victoria's Secret push-up bra she purchased in high school and a borrowed skirt.

"I mean, it's a date, so I feel like you have to wear a rose quartz," Nora says, unspooling a necklace from its place.

"Why rose quartz?" asks Emily. "What does that mean?"

"It's a love and romance stone," Nora answers with a mischievous smile.

"I don't know if that's a good idea. I don't know if this whole thing is a good idea." Emily wrings her hands.

"It will help you open your heart and create positive energy," says Nora. "And this *is* a good idea."

"But I'm supposed to be focusing on me," Emily argues as Nora fastens the necklace. The gentle weight of the stone rests on her sternum. She never considered packing jewelry when she left in May. She only owned a few cheap silver necklaces and stud earrings she bought at Claire's over the years. She had never considered jewelry could hold so much power when she asked Nora if she might borrow something.

"You *are* focusing on you," says Nora. "You're going to have fun and meet someone new who you might learn from, who might make you see how beautiful and amazing you are. And he's leaving in a few weeks, so no pressure, right?"

Emily nods. Misgivings spun inside her since Ingrid asked if she could pass her number onto Simon.

"He's smitten," said Ingrid, turning on the coffee.

"Well, that's weird. We barely met." Emily laughed, a pleasant charge buzzing up her spine.

"The British guy?" asked Alicia. "You gotta go out with him. Did you hear him say 'urinal'? He was cracking me up."

"Well, you can give him my number," said Emily. "I doubt he'll call."

But Simon did call the next day and asked if she'd go for pizza with him. He wanted to pick her up, like in the movies, like a proper date. And she said, "Sure."

But she's wondering if she should cancel. Her brain is stirring from the morning spent at Lakeside Technical College, meeting her advisor—a woman with smooth black hair and coffee breath—who peered over Emily's shoulder as she signed up for classes, put an order in for textbooks, and left with a student handbook and more than two-thirds of her new checking account gone.

Maybe she should gather as many of her coworkers as

possible and drink beer on the beach. But it's too late. Nora hands Emily a black tank top with lace along the scoop neckline, and an unfamiliar car pulls onto the woodchip driveway.

Nora claps her hands. "Yay! He's here." Emily's stomach flips.

Simon knocks on the screen door and compliments Emily's outfit in that mumbling accent that seems to skip words or pack them tight together, and she can't quite catch them all. But she hears "lovely" and "posh" clearly.

The last time she experienced anything like this scene, a high school friend picked her up for prom at Ashley's house, holding the corsages his mom picked out at the florist. But she didn't feel the flutters in her stomach she feels now, climbing into the borrowed car. Maybe the closest would be those first few meetings with Todd in his pickup truck or the first time she met Jacob. But Simon's intentions seem clearer, unmarred by the fact that he'll be leaving. What more is there to consider than fun?

He smiles, wearing khaki shorts and a buttoned-up collared shirt crumpled with wrinkles, drumming his fingers on the steering wheel to "Be My Baby" on the oldies radio station, the fuzzy static dissipating as he turns on the highway.

"This is mad," he says, laughing. "My foot's looking for the clutch. Feels bonkers on this side of the road."

Emily's nerves calm as she laughs as well. "You want me to drive?"

"No. This is a proper American date."

"Are you homesick?" she asks him, smoothing Nora's indigo linen skirt over her thighs.

"Nah. It'll all be there when I get back."

"Back to the castles."

"So many bloody castles," he says, his smile widening. "Loads. And you lot put a plaque on a log cabin: 'This was built eighty years ago.'"

Emily laughs again.

"My favorite pub, Dirty Bottles, that's three hundred years old. Parts of the castle are eight hundred years old. My whole village came about in, what'd they tell us? 600 AD."

"Super old," Emily agrees. "So, you graduated from college?"

"Uni? Almost."

Emily keeps the questions coming. Safer to listen, the questions like a shield guarding her from saying something wrong or stupid, revealing too much, making him regret asking her out. And she likes to hear him talk.

Simon's almost done with his business degree. His favorite football league is Newcastle United. "Or soccer to you lot. Your football has nothing to do with feet, you know that. It's just wrong." His favorite musicians hail from Iceland. "Real chill and haunting. I like it for hiking, for painting, anything, really. I'll play you some sometime. But this song here makes me feel like an American."

When they arrive at the restaurant, he buys her a beer. They sit side by side on a bench while waiting for a table, the flutters still there. He rests his hand on her knee.

"You're gonna let me kiss you later, right?"

"Maybe." She bites her lower lip.

"Maybe?" He pinches her side. She squirms and laughs, beer sloshing from her glass to the floor.

"We're the Honeydews" comes over the speakers. Emily looks toward the sound across the restaurant and sees Jacob and Cecelia outfitted with guitars and squared up to microphones. A few people clap, but the din of the large, open dining room remains undisturbed as they begin their next song.

"Follow me," says the hostess. The flutters intensify as they're led to a table not far from the music. Jacob raises his eyebrows and nods in greeting, surprise, as Cecelia starts to sing "Jolene." Emily offers a small wave and chooses the seat facing away from him. She feels exposed and guilty for going out with Simon when she never responded to Jacob. But Jacob is with Cecelia. She studies her menu, takes a gulp of her beer, and asks Simon more questions.

"What's Vietnam like?"

"Brilliant," he says. He tells her about canoeing in Ha Long Bay, about a multitude of painters who make their living creating perfect replicas of classic artwork on the street. She keeps the questions coming, and he tells her about the cheap food in Thailand, so many temples and monkeys and drunken backpackers skinny dipping every night. He tells her about learning to surf in Byron Bay, spiders that eat possums and snakes that chase people, about trying his hardest to appreciate the didgeridoo. He tells her about a cave lit up by glowworms in New Zealand, about kayaking between fjords, eating giant crawfish, and peering in the hobbit holes they built for *The Lord of the Rings*.

"So many things," says Emily, biting into her third piece of pizza, lost in all he's described, inspired and intrigued.

"And that's all good, the things." He reaches for his second piece. "But really, it's the people you meet and experience it all with."

"I feel a bit boring after all that," admits Emily, wiping her face with a napkin, wondering how she and this place can compare.

"Ingrid told me you grew up in a bar, like a cowboy country music bar. That's not boring. You got a cowboy hat?"

"You were asking Ingrid about me?" Emily smirks, the flutters traveling up to her chest, into her neck.

"Maybe." He winks.

"So, what are you gonna do when you get home?" she asks.

"No, no. I gotta stop talking. I'm hungry."

She exhales, feeling secure enough to lower the shield when he asks, "Now you. What does Emily want?" He tucks his hair behind his ears and puts both elbows on the table.

"I'm going to be a nurse," she says, trusting herself, believing herself this time. "I went to campus today and registered for classes and paid tuition. So, it's happening."

"Yeah? That's brilliant." He takes his beer and raises it. "Cheers."

"Cheers." She clinks his glass. "And then, who knows? Maybe I'll travel around like you."

"You could go anywhere, especially as a nurse. Smart move." Simon takes a bite of his pizza, and something over Emily's shoulder catches his attention.

"Hey," says Jacob, approaching. Emily hadn't realized the music stopped, that the sun had set, that the restaurant had nearly emptied.

"Hi," says Emily, quickly wiping her hands with her napkin. "Good job."

"Yeah, cool you could be here. We're trying to get a couple little gigs." He turns to Simon and outstretches his hand. "I'm Jacob."

"Oh, sorry," says Emily. "Jacob. This is Simon. Simon. Jacob." The men shake hands, and Emily remembers Jacob's upcoming trip to New Zealand. "Jacob, Simon was in New Zealand."

"No way. Really?" Jacob perches on the chair beside Simon. "Where?"

"All over, mate," Simon says. "Beautiful place. Loads of fun."

"I'm not sure where to start."

"They got these hop on, hop off bus tours that go all over the country," Simon says and goes on as Cecelia takes the seat beside Emily.

"So, you're staying?" Cecelia asks, setting a fresh cocktail on the table.

"I'm staying."

"Good for you. Any journaling yet?"

"Not yet."

"I'm telling you. I bet you got some good poetry in you. Or not, but it'd feel good to get it out."

"Yeah, maybe," says Emily. The only blank paper she owns is the server pad in her apron pocket. And she remembers the last time she faced a blank page and tried to write about herself. She wrote essays about the symbolism of *The Scarlet Letter*, socialism versus capitalism, and Susan B. Anthony without much trouble. But when an English teacher assigned a three-page essay about her earliest childhood memory, she couldn't decide how to proceed. Every time she wrote a sentence, she felt like Dad hovered over her shoulder. She couldn't shake the feeling that what she wrote was wrong or stupid, that this memory might not have even happened. Maybe she fabricated the whole thing: her mother comforting her after a bad dream, singing "Wildflowers," wrapping her in an afghan and holding her until she fell back asleep. Or was it Dad? No. She's sure it was her mother. And she didn't want to be told otherwise.

She wrote the essay and felt cracked open. A wellspring of tears erupted. She was exhausted and satisfied. Then she thought better of it, imagined Dad reading the words, and tore her work to pieces. She started again and wrote about dancing to the jukebox, about donning that blue dress with tiny silver stars Dad liked. She wrote about climbing on The Honky Tonk stage and the patrons taking turns dancing with her, holding her hands, spinning her around and around, Dad watching from behind the bar with a smile, so pleased, so happy.

Dad hung that B+ essay on the fridge. "Good descriptions!" her teacher wrote near the title, "Dancing for Dad."

But maybe now, with Dad farther away, she could try that writing idea.

"So, Jacob and I went to this open poetry thing a couple days ago," says Cecelia, leaning closer to Emily. "I brought like my best, most intimate poems, right? I'm up there going on about this awful breakup and missing my ex's tongue on my body, and my mom passed out all day on the couch. I'm raw and real. Then these old people go up, these retirees, and they've got poems about chickens and plumbing and snowfall." Cecelia scoffs. "I was so embarrassed."

Emily considers this. Maybe they're done taking life so seriously?

"And then Jacob gets up and reads his poem about God," Cecelia says louder, looking toward Jacob from the corner of her eye.

"You talking about me?" Jacob asks, turning his head toward the women with a curious grin.

"That poetry thing," Cecelia says, waving her hand in front of her face as if she's swatting away a mosquito.

"I thought it was cool."

"Well, I felt like this whore with an alcoholic mom, and Jacob's like, 'My mom made me go to church, and they told us to stay virgins, and is God even real?' I'm Cecelia, by the way." Cecelia reaches her hand over the table.

"Simon."

Jacob swirls the beer in his glass like you're supposed to with wine. "We should pack up our stuff," he says. Emily recognizes the strained, polite smile on his face. He sets a hand on her hand as he rises, "See you later?"

"Leave these two lovebirds alone," says Cecelia, grabbing her cocktail.

Simon pays the bill and takes Emily's hand. She follows him out, relieved to leave behind the razor-sharp tension between Cecelia and Jacob. Another reminder why she isn't pursuing something serious, why she's with Simon, who's swept her up in some carefree, sweet, capricious energy that's awoken a corner of herself she's been missing.

"You want to go swimming?" she asks.

CHAPTER TWENTY-FOUR

Emily's behind the bar pouring a trio of whiskey sodas, talking to a couple, late-sixties maybe, who share a basket of cheese curds and sip from their old-fashioneds.

"We got a king-sized bed at our hotel. It's huge! Let me tell you, we need walkie-talkies," says the man, a Hawaiian shirt hanging off his narrow shoulders. "And she's so little," he gestures to the woman sitting beside him. She's nodding in agreement, carefully popping a curd in her mouth, her lips smeared in a pale pink lipstick.

"I can't even reach the footrest on this stool," she admits.

"She's gonna get lost in that bed," says the man, laughing. Emily laughs along, setting the drinks on a tray at the end of the bar and retrieving the next ticket.

She's working the bar shift for Chris. Something about a doctor's appointment with his wife in Green Bay.

"No problem," Emily said when he asked if she'd be interested. It's happy hour, with thirty or so minutes left until she can nap, shower, and meet up with Simon. But she enjoyed working the bar today, flexing the old muscles, shooting the shit with the patrons, staying in her own little bubble with customers a short distance away.

"You two come up to Door County often?" asks Emily, reaching for two pint glasses.

"First time together," says the woman. "We just got engaged." She holds up her left hand, beaming.

"Congratulations," says Emily, smiling, meaning it.

She's exhausted but in the right kind of mood to hear about love, light, and happy ever since that first date with Simon, since they leaped off the Sister Bay dock holding hands in nothing but their underwear. They made out, clinging to the slick silver ladder while waves lapped over their shoulders, splashing into their kisses, until goosebumps sprung up on their bodies and their fingers wrinkled up like raisins. He dropped her off at the cabin that first night. She didn't want to seem too eager, too easy.

A couple of days later, after a round of mini-golf and a six-pack shared while watching the sunset, after comparing and dispelling stereotypes about one another's homelands, after he said, "I want to lay my head next to yours," she went with him to the stuffy camper parked in Ingrid's backyard, a Winnebago with faux wood walls and orange curtains. She let him leave a trail of slow, wet kisses from her lips to her belly. She was sure he could hear her heartbeat, her pulse softly booming between her legs.

She trembled, gripping the edges of the worn mattress, running her fingers through his thick hair as his tongue searched her crevices, his fingertips gently raking up her ribs, gripping her breast.

Then she felt a shadowy presence in the peripheral. Phil looming, watching. She squeezed her eyes shut and stiffened. Simon stopped.

"You good, yeah?" he asked. Maybe it was his accent, the unfamiliar camper, or this county, but when she opened her eyes, Phil faded. Simon was there, hesitant, waiting for her response. She nodded.

"Yeah," she whispered. He smiled.

"Yeah," he repeated, resumed, and Emily felt such desire for him in that moment, in a way she never experienced with Todd. Uninhibited. Hungry.

She rolled him to his back, left her own trail of kisses, put his hard cock in her mouth, and enjoyed it, making him breathe like that, making him whisper her name: "Oh, fuck. Emily. I'm gonna come."

Last night, after Simon came to The Schooner near close, ate French fries he doused in vinegar, then drank Spotted Cows with Emily and her coworkers until two in the morning, they walked along the private beaches of Lake Michigan, tipsy and heedless, stumbling upon a pedalboat.

They pedaled into the vast lake, Simon turning some ethereal, otherworldly music on his iPod—soft piano, a slow drumbeat, a man singing falsetto in a language neither of them understood. They clasped hands. She couldn't tell where the water ended and the sky began, and that thrilled her, existing on the edge of a brilliant emptiness, present and alive. She wordlessly climbed on top of him, straddled him, kissed him along his jaw, then his mouth, deep and hard. Layer by layer they removed their clothes. She slowly lowered herself onto him while he pushed into her.

And they stayed on the boat, drifting and fucking, Emily so lost in Simon that she didn't notice they'd strayed toward the marina until the boat ground into the gray-black boulders.

"Bloody hell," said Simon, laughing. They clung to one another, spent from the pedaling and sex before Emily returned to her seat, and they labored back to shore, a sliver of orange spilling over the horizon, fishing boats motoring toward the nothingness.

Emily studies the engagement ring, a gold band with a single diamond.

"Beautiful," Emily says.

"Now, we dated in high school," the woman says, flicking her finger up and down to produce some sparkle. "Isn't that the best story?"

"You did? Wow."

"We got back together after forty-five years, after my husband passed," the woman goes on, pointing a thumb at her companion. "I never stopped loving this guy."

"So, when's the wedding?" asks Emily, pulling the Pabst Blue Ribbon handle, tilting the filling pint glass to avoid foam.

"We might just live in sin," says the man, winking.

Emily laughs again and sets the beers on a tray to a waiting Molly. "Look how happy you are," Molly says. "It's the dopamine."

"A lot of it in here." Emily points to her skull.

Bridget approaches, holding an empty tray, and stands beside Molly, who grips the two pint glasses. "Be careful," she warns. "When he leaves, it's gonna hurt."

"Shut up, Molly," snaps Bridget. Groaning before she adds, "Why do you have to do that? Like, must we rain on Emily's parade?"

Molly shrinks, her body closing in on itself and her cheeks turning a shade darker. "I'm trying to be helpful," she says, looking at Emily with an innocent, apologetic expression.

"Well, stop trying to be everyone's therapist," says Bridget, setting the empty tray on top of the others. Molly leaves without a word or meeting Bridget's eyes.

"I feel like she's always analyzing me," says Bridget, clenching her jaw, "judging me."

Bridget's been on edge since Shawn casually called her a "dyke" the other day. "Food's up, dyke," he said when Bridget entered the kitchen. Emily forgot to swallow the chicken tender in her mouth and kept chewing as Bridget's body stiffened like she'd been struck in a game of freeze tag.

"Shut up, Shawn," said Nora, dropping the napkins she was stocking and pointing her finger beneath the heat lamp. Javier shook his head, flipping a burger.

"What? Sorry," Shawn said, raising his hands in surrender.

Bridget didn't say a word—no comeback, no joke, no insult, no denying—just took her plates and left the kitchen.

"He's going through a really hard time," Molly defended him later that shift over silverware rolling while Bridget counted her tips at the register.

"That's no excuse," said Nora. "And I'm so pissed at Javier for not saying a thing, you know. Shawn listens to him, and he could have said, 'Not okay.' But he stood there."

"We all know she's gay, though, right?" whispered Alicia.

Emily wasn't sure what to say. She kept rolling, waiting for Simon to text her back, for Ryan to confirm he was coming next Tuesday.

"Does it matter?" asked Nora. "It's up to her to tell us who she is."

Ingrid approaches the bar as Bridget turns to leave.

"Are you gonna make my drinks, Emily?" Ingrid asks, pointing toward the receipt waiting at the printer.

"Oh, crap. Sorry."

"I can tell you're in la-la land. I'm a little matchmaker, aren't I? Do you know what he was doing when I left today?"

"What?" asks Emily, pulling the receipt.

"Mowing my lawn in a cowboy hat."

Emily laughs. "Such a weirdo."

"I was so anxious about him coming to stay, but then the other morning he was having a tea party with Karin.

Isn't that the sweetest? He calmed the accent down 'cause the poor girl couldn't understand a word, but she was loving it."

That lightness wraps around Emily once more as she pours Ingrid's drinks. Her phone buzzes and vibrates in her back pocket; she's certain it's Simon. She finishes the cocktails, sets them on the tray, and reaches for her phone. A message from Ashley: "Ryan's coming 2 c u? WTF?"

Emily shuts the phone. A sticky combination of guilt and rage run down the back of her throat. She's not sure how to respond: "You can come too," "It was his idea," or "I'm sorry." She wants to tell Ashley about The Schooner, Door County, Simon, Lakeside College. She longs for their relationship to be as it was.

How could their friendship derail and unravel so quickly? Maybe the change wasn't so swift. Ever since Ashley left, the distance between them took on a life of its own and expanded like a balloon with misunderstanding and resentment.

Emily rubs her eyes. She needs a break and longs for a nap.

"Can I have a second?" she asks Brandon, talking to a patron about the best place to find smoked fish.

She steps into the summer heat, perches on the cement backsteps edged with mildew and examines the terracotta pot packed with smushed and crooked cigarette stubs. She opens her phone.

"Ryan asked 2 come," she types. "U can come 2. Or call if u want 2 talk." She sends the text and wishes she smoked, that she had something to occupy her hands, something to watch disappear when she exhaled. She studies the grime and ketchup stains on her tennis shoes, then hears two voices conversing near the dumpsters, a deep, pleading whine followed by a soft, higher-pitched apologetic mumble.

"I remember the first thing you said to me," Emily hears Shawn say as she approaches the conversation. "'Where are the lemons? I need some lemons.'"

"I'm sorry," says Alicia. "Really."

"I could be so good to you." Shawn scoffs. "You don't know what you're missing."

"Well, I just don't see us—"

"Too good for me?"

Emily's skin prickles as she moves closer.

"No."

"You picked the wrong guy."

"Hey," Emily calls, warning them that she is coming, halting the conversation for Alicia's sake.

A quick, sharp grumble from Shawn. He stands like a guard at the gate of the chain-link fence surrounding the overflowing dumpsters, installed to deny coyotes and raccoons an opportunity. One of his hands claws the metal lattice while Alicia hugs her arms to her chest, as if to keep warm, beside a black bag of garbage hanging over the lip of a giant green bin, leaking filth at her feet.

"Hey, Emily," says Alicia. She unwraps her arms. "These bags are so heavy."

"Little stroll by the dumpsters?" Shawn asks Emily.

Emily nods. "I think you got a table, Alicia."

"Great, thanks." Alicia makes her way past Shawn. "That was so fun last night, wasn't it?" she says to Emily quickly, breathlessly, as they walk toward the backdoor. Shawn follows. "Did you hear how Simon says 'aluminum'? You'll bring him to my party, right?"

"For sure," Emily says, anxious to fill the silence. "It's okay if I bring my friend Ryan?"

"Who's this guy now?" asks Shawn. "Am I invited?"

"Of course," says Alicia. "Everyone is."

Emily holds the door open for Alicia, who's wiping her hands on her apron, and Shawn, who stares straight ahead. She lingers a moment, holding the door, silently berating herself for not scolding Shawn, wondering what— if anything—she stopped from happening or being said. But Alicia seems fine. Bridget will be okay. Nora will forgive Javier. Ashley will get over it. Dad will let go.

Her phone vibrates.

Simon: "Bowling tonight?"

She smiles. Everything's fine.

CHAPTER TWENTY-FIVE

Emily awakes out of breath, naked and chilled. It takes a moment to remember where she is, who's beside her. In her dream, she was trapped inside a dumpster, the space black and gray as she crawled along bulging, stinking bags, slick and slimy. She finally found her footing and attempted to lift the lid above her, but someone, something, was bearing down on the exit, and someone was in the darkness with her. She screamed for help but couldn't find air.

She doesn't want to remember more, the hands on her body, reaching and clasping between the bags.

She presses against the naked man beside her and tugs the thin blanket over her shoulder. Simon snores, unaware. She shivers, trying to steady her breath, rubbing her palm over the fine hair on his chest until he stirs, until he turns toward her onto his side and holds her tight against him. Finally, her breath matches his, and she's comforted by his fingers fluttering on the soft, vulnerable space between her ribs and hips as he dreams.

They went to *Macbeth* earlier that night and watched a man betray his king and murder a family. Colin delivered his few lines with a seriousness so unlike him. Emily smiled to herself, so proud of her friend. They went to dinner before that, like a real couple, to a restaurant with cloth napkins and whipped butter for the fluffy free bread. Emily wore another borrowed dress and the rose quartz necklace. They ordered the cheapest bottle of red wine and shared the cheapest appetizer—bacon-wrapped dates—and a slice of three-tiered chocolate cake. They talked about Simon's artwork, the notebooks full of drawings and paintings in his backpack.

Emily spoke of her motorcycle adventures with her dad, her high school basketball career, her grandma's vain attempts to turn Emily into a homemaker. "I know the bare minimum of so many things," she told him. "I hope I don't blow it as a nurse."

"You won't," Simon answered quickly, confidently, plunging his fork into the cake.

A few days before that, they had smoked weed and swung in a deserted park. "I'm so high," Emily said as she pumped her legs, feeling so clever, so light as Simon laughed and the wind rustled her hair. They wandered to a nearby meadow. He lay on his back, Emily straddling him, singing bits of old honky-tonk songs with that twang while he put his arms behind his head, smiling among the Queen Anne's lace and black-eyed Susans.

"You singing me country songs," he said. "A proper American fantasy come true. You're bliss." She stuck out her tongue and shook her head. "You are," he said, pinching and tickling her ribs until she was giggling beside him in the long grass. He started kissing her neck and slid his hand under her tank top.

"And you got the best tits. You know that, right?" he said as he unclasped her bra. She smiled, dizzy from all his kind words, unzipping his fly as he peeled off his shirt. Her breath was quick and sharp as he maneuvered his way on top of her, holding her hands flat to the ground, her body writhing in pleasure beneath him as he kissed her collarbone.

She feels such acute, unabashed happiness when she's with Simon she thinks it could crystalize and turn into something tangible, like a pearl or a diamond, something she could tuck in her pocket or wear around her neck like a talisman.

And the happiness forms a bubble around her. She's only vaguely aware or concerned that Javier hasn't been to the cabin in a while, that Bridget won't acknowledge Shawn or what he called her, that Alicia seems somewhat wary, that Molly hasn't volunteered any advice or observations since Bridget snapped at her. The shifts have been so busy and exhausting that they hardly have time to converse between tables like they once did. When they roll silverware and drink their post-shift cocktails, they don't talk about themselves anymore. They vent about unreasonable, complaining customers who leave crap tips, how limp the onion rings have been coming out, how slow Chris has been mixing drinks, and how Diego seems to be slacking on rinsing the silverware before he runs them through the dishwasher.

"There's bits of food on this!" says Bridget, examining a fork in the dim dining room light.

And the manilla envelope that came in the mail from Lakeside College sits unopened on the dresser in Emily's room. She needs to sort through whatever is inside. She has orientation coming up and a class schedule to share with Chris so he can plan her shifts.

She needs to find a place to live for the winter.

Ryan is coming.

And she worries about Dad, alone in The Honky Tonk surrounded by booze and sad songs.

And these awful dreams.

But she doesn't want to think about these things, anything.

She rests her hand on top of Simon's, then grazes her fingers over his bony knuckles and smooth nails. She exhales, then nestles even closer against his warm skin, brings her lips to his neck, brushing her fingers along his jawline, the short whiskers, until he stirs and moans and kisses her in return. They kiss slowly, their tongues meeting and moving. He tastes like sour cigarettes and stale mint.

Simon props himself up and leans over her, a curtain of hair surrounding her face, tickling her cheeks and ears. She kisses his lips then holds him against her tight, taking in the ceiling stained with rainwater, the cool breeze, and the earliest notes of birdsong coming from the open window.

She's tempted to tell him about the dream but doesn't want to spread that taint and filth into this space. She's afraid to ruin the beautiful image he seems to have of her.

He shifts from her embrace. His lips move to her collarbone, her breasts, and she can feel his erection on her leg.

"Emily," he whispers. "What do you want me to do to you?"

The question catches her off guard, this offer new and seemingly generous. She considers while searching into the blue of his eyes.

She wants her waking body to escape from this world, with this man, for just a moment. And she's going to show him how.

She takes his hand and leads it to the space between her legs. She keeps her hand over his, guiding his fingertips like she's teaching him to play an instrument, to play her. When the rhythm and pressure are just right, tingles gather and grow. She leans back into the bed and lets him continue, kissing her neck, playing her like she's a song.

She doesn't move to please him, but in reaction to his gentle and persistent and patient touch. She feels an electric current begin to vibrate through the marrow of her bones, concentrating in her center. The sounds of pleasure she makes surprise her until she can't think of the sounds or his soft, urgent kisses on her collarbone, her neck, her ear. He keeps the pressure and rhythm, the current intensifying as he slips a finger inside her.

MUDDLED CHERRIES

She moves and moans and savors each sensation until the electricity overtakes her. She feels every bit of her body at once, her toes and eyelashes and elbows.

Emily's out of breath and opens her eyes to Simon.

He's smiling, sleep in the corners of his eyes. "Yeah?"

She nods, the aftershocks of the orgasm still pulsating inside her, a pleasant hum throughout her body, fading fainter and fainter.

CHAPTER TWENTY-SIX

Hugging Ryan feels like holding a bit of home. His t-shirt smells like warm syrup and childhood. His breath smells like sunflower seeds. He stretches his arms to the sky after they embrace. He's paler than anyone should be coming in late July.

"Long drive?" Emily asks.

"Not too bad," he smiles, and any misgivings she had about him coming evaporate like dew. It's just Ryan. Nothing weird.

"Look at this place," he says, gesturing around him, his head swiveling as he takes in the surroundings. "Look at this cabin and these woods and that fucking lake over there. Look what you've done for yourself." Emily wants to hug him again, to sink into that homey smell. She leads him in the cabin instead, shows him where to drop his duffel bag, and says, "Let's get you to the beach."

"Heck yes," he replies. "Oh, wait. Here, this is from Mom." He pulls an envelope from his bag.

"Such a sweetie." Emily rips the envelope. A check slips from a card with a Vincent van Gogh sunflower painting. Five hundred dollars. "She didn't have to do that! That's too much."

"Consider it babysitting money." Ryan laughs. "I'm sure the card talks about me, so I'll go change." He grabs his board shorts. Emily opens the card.

> *Dear Emily,*
>
> *We are thinking of you every day! Thank you for letting Ryan come visit you. We think it will be good for him to get away. (But if he becomes too much trouble, please call.) I know you're aware he's been having a hard time since leaving the service.*
>
> *And I don't want to intrude, but I know you and Ashley are experiencing a challenging season of your friendship. Change and growth are difficult, but I'm sure you two will see through this.*
>
> *You mean so much to our family, Emily. And we're very proud of you.*
>
> *Love,*
>
> *Diane and John*

Emily sniffles and wipes her watering eyes with the back of her hand when Ryan exits the bathroom.

"Your mom," she says, shaking her head.

"She's been driving me crazy lately, but yeah. She loves you."

Their feet sink into the fine, hot sand of Whitefish Dunes as they make their way toward the water. "Look at that horizon," says Ryan as they fan out their beach towels and settle in. Emily delights in his enrapture of the place. The beach is busy and breezy. Children play in the shallows, tossing inflatable balls with bright water wings on their arms, building sandcastles, and chasing the squawking seagulls that strut toward anyone with a chip or cracker or sandwich in hand. Adults sunbathe in lawn chairs and some swim toward the depths. Kayakers paddle beyond a white buoy warning of the riptide.

Emily opens the small cooler she packed with a few beers, cheese and beef sticks, apples, and a water bottle. Chips poke out from her beach bag. She offers Ryan a beer.

"Nah, taking a break from drinking." He lathers sunscreen on his chest and belly.

"Oh." She puts the beer back. "Good for you."

"You go ahead, though. Drink yours."

"Are you sure?" she asks, apprehensive. "I don't have to."

"Seriously, you have one. It's just been getting me into a bit of trouble."

"Oh, no," Emily says, handing him a cheese stick, then opening a beer for herself.

"Yeah. I … I got in a fight with a guy at McDougal's. I don't even remember what it was about. I think I overheard him saying stupid shit about the war, the military," he tells her, streaks of sunscreen on his cheeks and shoulders. "Or not. I don't know. But there was shoving involved, and then we were on the floor."

"God, Ryan." Emily scans his body for bruises or scrapes, relieved to find none.

"Well, and another time I showed up at my ex's apartment and apparently proposed. Her fucking boyfriend was there."

Emily cringes and rests a hand on his forearm. "Was he pissed?"

"No. They had me sleep it off on the couch." He lets out a strained laugh. "And then Dad found me passed out on our walkway one night," he continues, biting into the cheese stick, "and said if I wanted to stay in the house, I had to get my shit together. He and Mom made a big show of dumping all the alcohol down the drain. Even Mom's chardonnay, like I was gonna go into that. I felt so fucking stupid."

"Don't feel bad," Emily says. She's witnessed enough drunks throughout her life do stupid things, dangerous things, again and again. Phil wasn't the only one who spent the night at The Honky Tonk because he'd had too much. "At least you didn't get in a car accident or get a DUI, you know."

"I don't even remember driving home the last few times I went out," he admits, closing his eyes and turning his face toward the sun. "I don't think I cared if I lived or died." He exhales. She swallows the bile rising in her throat. He's so vulnerable, sitting shirtless and pale. She smears the remaining streaks of sunblock into his skin.

"So, are you getting your shit together then?" she asks, the pad of her thumb moving back and forth across his cheekbone.

"Yes and no," he says. "I moved into the basement to try to feel a little less like I was living with my parents. Discovered my old drum set. Remember me drumming, that phase?"

"Very much," she says, laughing.

The banging and clanging constant when Emily and Ashley were in middle school, playing Battleship or watching *She's All That* or trying to learn the choreography from a Brittany Spears music video.

"I forgot what a release it is for me," he says, air drumming around the vicinity of his lap. "So, I've been doing that. And got a counselor through the VA, so that helps."

"Good. And still at Blockbuster?"

"Sadly, yes. But I'm looking into going to college, maybe getting a computer science degree," he says quietly, cautiously, "learn how to make video games, maybe." The comment reminds her of admitting to Todd that she wanted to be a nurse, like it was a question.

"That's great, Ryan. Really."

"Yeah. Thanks. But how are you? It's so wild you actually did it. You just did it."

"I did." She scans the vast lake. The gray outline of a container ship appears miniaturized and unmoving in the distance. She tells him about The Schooner, her coworkers, the customers, about the money, and Lakeside College, and bonfires, boat rides, mini-golfing. She opens up like she once would to Ashley. And he listens. He nods.

"Good for you, Emily," he says, digging into the Cool Ranch Doritos, his favorite. "Seriously. Fucking awesome."

"Dad's really upset," she says, a sharp pull in her chest, unsure if she wants to know what Ryan may have heard or seen.

"Don't worry about him," he says, swatting his hand in front of his face. "He'll be fine."

She isn't so sure.

"Have you seen him?" Emily braves, bringing her knees to her chest.

He nods and licks the cheese dust from his fingertips. "I was in with some friends. The vibe's changed; it's different. Maybe I shouldn't tell you that."

"No. It's okay," she says, finally taking a drink of beer. It's lukewarm, unsatisfying. "How does he look?"

"Uh." Ryan takes a long drink of water.

"You can tell me."

"He looks rough. He has a resting bitch face, like you. But it is … bitchier." He smiles. He meant to make her laugh, she can tell, but pangs of nausea reverberate in her gut.

"I feel so guilty." She wonders who Dad rides his motorcycle with if Larry isn't around, if he's keeping an eye on the mouse traps, how many tumblers have collected around the apartment.

"No. Don't. I shouldn't have said anything. He's a grown adult."

"How's Ashley?" she asks, changing the subject, but this one doesn't feel much more pleasant. Ryan burrows his toes in the sand.

"Sounds like she loves her job in Madison, according to Mom. But she's still pissy and short with us all. I don't know what that's about. Like she's too good for home? Don't worry about her either."

But Emily does worry. Ashley never responded to her last text; she never called. She can't gauge what Ashley might be thinking or feeling like she once could.

"Come on." Ryan rises to his feet, his figure a silhouette against the blinding sun behind him. "Let's go swimming."

They wade into the brisk water. Emily can see the bottom, her feet stirring up the even, parallel ripples of sand, creating beige clouds beneath her. Soon her body accepts the coolness surrounding her. She takes a deep breath and lets herself sink, lingering for a moment submerged. She can hear her breath, Ryan's movements, the whir of the water. She rises. Ryan floats on his back, arms hovering at his side, eyes closed.

"This feels fucking amazing," he whispers.

264

CHAPTER TWENTY-SEVEN

T ake your shoes off, please," says Alicia in a sing-song voice as they enter her home. Emily kicks her plastic flip-flops onto a pile of strappy Tevas and worn Birkenstocks. She introduces Ryan.

Black Eyed Peas rap from speakers in the ceiling. An imposing stone fireplace dominates the room, sitting between expansive windows overlooking the bay, showcasing the orange and scarlet sunset. The space smells like Fraser fir potpourri.

The kayak crew sits on the edge of tan leather couches, talking and laughing, then acknowledging and waving at Emily and Ryan. Cecelia holds a cocktail and gazes up at a painting, something abstract and wild with bold maritime colors.

Alicia wears a black tank top with stringy straps, her makeup fresh and thick. She holds Tim's hand, basking in the role of hostess, Emily can tell.

"Help yourself at the bar. My parents are pretty stocked,

so make whatever you want," Alicia says, gesturing toward a corner of the room with a mahogany bar, shelves neatly lined with liquor bottles, where Shawn mixes a drink, his face furrowed and knotted as he plucks a lime wedge from a glazed ceramic bowl. Molly twirls on one of the three barstools, examining the marble coasters.

"And we got pinot noir, cabernet, chardonnay, Corona, Spotted Cow, right, babe?" Tim adjusts the collar of his striped shirt.

"Everything," Alicia says, nodding, rubbing her glossy lips together. "But the top shelf is off-limits. That's my dad's good stuff."

Emily runs her fingertips over the smooth grain of the bar, scoping out the overwhelming number of choices as Molly shakes Ryan's hand.

"Nice to meet you," she says. Emily is grateful to pass him off for a while, thankful for the ease with which this county takes in a newcomer, a stray, a runaway.

But Shawn doesn't say hello or acknowledge Ryan.

"Can you believe this place? Fucking ridiculous," Shawn says with an edge Emily had ignored until wandering toward the dumpsters. Now, it's all she can see—bitterness and anger glowing like hot coals beneath his skin.

But days have passed since that shift, and when Emily asked Alicia about the encounter, she shook her head. "He's a bit stuck on me. He'll get over it."

"This place looks like it could be in a J.Crew catalog," says Molly, adjusting the bobby pin in her hair. "I feel underdressed."

Molly and Ryan sink into conversation, and Emily wonders if she should have warned Ryan about Molly's tendency to analyze and offer unsolicited advice and diagnoses. But he seems content and comfortable, drinking his seltzer with lime, telling Molly about his life in Deer Valley, that he's a veteran.

Emily pours pinot noir into the lightest, most delicate wine glass she's ever held. It feels like the stem might snap in half when she takes a drink.

"Where's your fuck buddy?" Shawn asks, his irises haloed in red, jagged lines of drunkenness.

Emily scoffs.

"What? Sorry. Just a question," Shawn says, shaking his head quick and hard like he's trying to joggle something loose. "Fine. Sam? Steve?"

"It's Simon. I think you know that." She wanders toward an empty spot on the couch beside Courtney, across from Cecelia and Jacob.

Courtney scoots over, crosses her legs toward Emily, and asks the same question, only with concern and no cussing. "Where's Simon?"

"Logan was looking forward to a guys' night," Emily says, resting a palm on the leather beneath her, fingering what she wonders might be a scar or stretch mark on the animal's hide. "Simon's bummed to miss out."

She initially felt disappointed when Simon explained how excited Ingrid's husband was for a guys' night, to introduce him to friends, play poker, and drink black and tans. But relief followed. She's been spending too much time flying and needs to practice walking on land again, being without him.

"When's he leaving for good?" asks Courtney, also holding her wine glass like it might break.

"Eight, seven days now," Emily says, cringing, her heart thick and heavy in her chest as she says it out loud.

"That sucks," Courtney says.

"Yeah," Emily agrees. "But you know, he's constantly saying like ridiculously nice things to me, and I'm starting to wonder if that's healthy." She notices Jacob listening, leaning in while Cecelia says something about Milwaukee and gigs.

"Soak it up. Is Bridget coming tonight? I texted, but she hasn't responded," Courtney asks Emily.

"I heard a guy in a popped collar call us lame," Cecelia huffs.

"They're not our target audience anyway," Jacob answers, holding the neck of his beer bottle with two hands.

"They're all closing up the restaurant," Emily says to Courtney. "It's been so busy. She'll be here soon." She feels like she's reassuring Courtney of something when she hears Cecelia say, "Nashville, L.A."

A glass of wine later, the house pulses with a crowd of bodies—more of The Schooner gang, Tim's Coast Guard buddies, friends of friends that Emily recognizes from bonfires, dancing at The Sunny Seagull, the laundromat, and grocery store. The music beats louder, and the corner bar is packed.

Nora takes in a gray stone seemingly sliced in half, exposing a pale blue cluster of crystals propped on the mantel.

"Do you see this geode?" she asks Emily and Ingrid. "That's worth like four or five thousand dollars."

"Do you think it would fit in my purse?" asks Ingrid, grinning, darting her eyes back and forth. "Are there cameras in here?"

"They probably wouldn't notice it was gone," says Emily, taking in a line of mercury vases etched in geometric designs.

Javier approaches with a drink in hand, wearing a flat-brimmed baseball cap. Nora continues studying the tiny cavern of crystals while Ingrid tells Javier about Karin's recent meltdowns over food presentation. "Nothing can touch. And I swear she only eats dinner rolls and buttered noodles and white rice." He nods and laughs politely.

"What does this crystal mean?" Emily asks Nora.

"It's celestite. It's meant to increase understanding and, like mindfulness, I guess, spiritual strength, awareness."

"Huh." Emily swirls the wine around her glass like she knows she is supposed to, moving toward the window. Two figures at the end of Alicia's dock are illuminated by lights along the posts. Bridget and Courtney sit, feet dangling.

Bridget rests her head on Courtney's shoulder. Their dark brown and orange-red ponytails line up, side by side.

"Can we talk about it?" Javier says to Nora. "Why are you so weird?" Emily takes that as her cue to move on.

Ingrid joins a game of Twister. Ryan and Molly sit at one of the couches, still talking, legs touching. Shawn reaches his long arm up for a bottle of liquor on the top shelf. Emily's tempted to scold him or tattle on him, but he's surrounded by men she doesn't know, and she doesn't want to make a scene. Alicia climbs up the stairs. There must be a bathroom up there Emily could escape to. Take a moment. Maybe it's Simon's absence or Ryan's presence, but something feels off.

Jacob approaches and goes in for a hug. He leans so far into her that she feels like she's propping him up, like they might tip over.

"Hey. How are you?" he asks, clearly buzzed, teetering on drunk.

"Good," she answers, feeling very sober. "You?"

"I'm okay," he says in a way Emily knows he'd like her to press for details.

"Oh, yeah?" she offers.

"I just. I don't know what to do, you know?"

"About what?" She's tired of listening, she realizes. Tired after all the sleepless nights with Simon, the day with Ryan. She's tired of the customers who want her to be their visitor guide, therapist, comedian, and entertainer. "You'd look so much prettier if you'd smile," said a man at the bar on her last shift. So she did. She apologized first and then smiled and hasn't stopped berating herself for doing either of those things.

"Cecelia thinks we could really be successful." Jacob bites his bottom lip, searching Emily's eyes. "That if we moved to a bigger city, we could get a following, make money doing gigs."

Emily takes a drink of the sharp wine. It dries her mouth. She's not sure what he wants her to say, but she's annoyed.

"So you're going to give up New Zealand to maybe get a few gigs in shit bars with a girl you've known for like two months?" Emily asks in a monotone, her expression hardened. She thinks of Todd. Of the plans she made for them and how Ashley could peer from the outside in and know it was doomed to fail.

"I don't know. I don't know what to do." He rubs his palm over his face, top to bottom. "New Zealand will always be there. She's like my first real girlfriend. I feel like I don't want to abandon her. Enough people in her life already have."

"So, you're gonna save her?"

"You're looking at me like I'm crazy."

"You're naïve," Emily says, surprised by her anger, unable to stop herself, "and too nice."

"I'm sick of people saying that. Are you mad at me?"

"You're being an idiot." She feels like she's shouting over the club music raining down, the laughter and conversation rolling in like waves. She feels like she's drowning, and she needs to come up for air and spit the water she's already swallowed in Jacob's face. He's an easy target. "It's stupid. Live your own life. Didn't you say that? And she's a big girl. Just because you screwed her a few times and broke your Jesus rules doesn't mean you should follow her across the country."

"Whoa. What the heck?"

She doesn't have anything else to say, and she's done listening. She finishes her wine in one gulp, sets the glass down, and heads toward wherever Alicia disappeared to. She doesn't look back as she stomps up the stairs, focused on the family portrait at the top—mother, daughter, father, son, pristine in their matching white button-downs and faded jeans.

Emily turns right, wanders slowly down the dimly lit hall, and peeks into an office. She's probably not meant to be up here, but Alicia's somewhere, she's sure. She wants to hide in a bathroom for five, ten, twenty minutes and collect herself. Escape the noise and bodies.

"He doesn't love you like I do," Shawn says from around a corner, his voice slurred and whiney.

Alicia offers a soft, rustled, apologetic response, but it's interrupted.

"I just want to touch you," Shawn says desperately.

"Don't," Alicia says. "Shawn, stop!"

Emily feels swept in a hurricane, rattled and breathless. "What the hell?" she shouts before rounding the corner.

There's Shawn's broad back and Alicia cornered against the gray wall.

Emily doesn't see what he did, where or if he touched her, but she heard the fear in Alicia's voice. She recognized it and felt it like an echo in her own throat, in her dreams.

Shawn turns around. "What? We're just talking."

"What the hell?" Emily says again.

Alicia pushes past him and wraps her arms around her chest. "He's wasted."

But that's not enough for Emily. "Is he scaring you?"

"We were talking," Shawn slurs out of the side of his mouth. He's trying to find his footing, square up to Emily, but his torso wobbles.

Alicia inhales to answer, but Shawn says, "I'm not a bad guy."

That phrase. Those words. They ignite a bomb in Emily's chest. Heat explodes from every pore. Her body trembles. The hurricane amplifies.

"Get out, Shawn!" Emily shouts.

He dismisses her outburst with a scornful laugh and raises his hands in mock surrender. "Chill out. Nothing happened."

"You are an asshole," Emily says, pointing her finger in his face. Her body has gone from rippling with tremors to rigid as stone as she enunciates every word. "Get. The. Fuck. Out."

He grips her finger in his meaty hand.

"Fuck you." A mist of saliva on her face. It smells like bourbon and bile. "Nothing happened."

Alicia grips Emily's other hand and pulls her toward the stairs, making a getaway. But Shawn doesn't release his clutch. She might split in two.

"Nora. Tim!" Alicia calls as she pulls.

"Shut up. Shut up," says Shawn, letting go. "Shut up." He presses both palms against his skull as Alicia tugs Emily's arm, and they make for the stairs.

Alicia's hair bounces with each step. Heads turn toward the commotion. Emily trembles once more, her voice shaking, barely rising over the thump of the bass, as she meets Nora's eyes.

"Shawn needs to go. He's scaring Alicia. He's scary."

Javier puts a hand on Emily's shoulder, a confused expression on his face as he leans his ear toward her mouth.

"Shawn needs to leave!" she shouts this time, pointing back at the red-faced figure tottering down the stairs.

"Nothing happened," Shawn says, the fight gone from his voice. Now it's casual, calm, a front.

Alicia buries her head in Nora's shoulder. Molly stands beside her, Ryan behind her. Ingrid and Courtney, windblown and flushed, close by as well.

"Go back to the party, everyone," says Shawn, a line of drool running down his chin. Javier doesn't hesitate. He meets Shawn at the bottom of the stairs and puts a hand on his upper arm, steering him away from Alicia and Emily.

"Nothing happened," he booms.

"He was about to do something when I came up there," Emily says to those around her, tears pressing against the back of her eyes when she realizes they don't doubt her.

"Emily's a fucking liar," Shawn says, reluctantly following the pressure of Javier's grip.

Now Tim seems aware, the men at the bar, bodies untangle from the Twister mat, and those seated on the couches rise to watch Shawn escorted out.

"What the fuck?" he says. "I didn't fucking rape her. Nothing happened."

Bridget presses her hand on Emily's back. "That asshole," she grinds out of her mouth as a mass of bodies adds more pressure to Shawn's exit. The front door opens then shuts.

Alicia pulls back from Nora's embrace and turns to those around her, to Tim approaching from across the room.

"I didn't want to ruin everyone's night," she says, her face crumpling.

CHAPTER TWENTY-EIGHT

Emily's body aches like she's coming down with a sickness. With every breath, everything that touches her—the tank top she's wearing, her cotton shorts, the thin blanket over her shoulders—sets off pinpricks of pain. Standing on the precipice of sleep, she hears the distant waves of Lake Michigan, Ryan snoring, cedar trees rustling, and the oscillating fan humming. But she never falls in, never stumbles into a dream, stuck in the gray space between sleeping and awake. The same place when she felt Phil's hand on her cheek, passing over her hair, heard him whispering her name.

She only focuses on *that* hand. All her brain could process or acknowledge, or maybe she was confused. Maybe it didn't happen.

But her body remembers.

Her body reminds her.

His other hand under her grandmother's quilt.

His other hand brushing over her breast, faintly, purposefully as she entered the gray.

His other hand moving over her belly, under the elastic of her underwear. The gray dissipating as his grip on her hair tightened, holding her head against the pillow.

The palm of his other hand cupping, smothering the crest of her pubic mound, frantic as his bitter breath, his fingers parting and searching her. A dull prodding, a breach of thick, hungry worms, deep and quick—a couple of seconds, perhaps not even one—until her body reflexed into a flailing fight. Her limbs windmilling, legs kicking, and arms shoving.

He didn't rape her either. Or did he?

Assaulted? Molested? Groped? Grabbed? She isn't sure where the definitions stop and start; no one explained the parameters.

But he entered a space he didn't belong; he wasn't invited.

And he's taken up residence in a corner of her mind, one her dreams keep pulling to the forefront.

She tugs the covers over her head, hoping to create a cocoon of safety, but shudders, feeling exposed, frightened. She doesn't know what to do but cry.

...

The light around Emily slowly shifts from a moonlit gray to a sunrise white. She hears stirring in the living room, the squeak of door hinges, and makes eye contact with Nora.

"Are you awake?" Nora asks needlessly. She appears on a mission, armed with a smudge stick, that ashy bowl.

"Yes." The sides of Emily's face are stiff from the dried salt of tears.

"We're going to Alicia's. And I called Chris. Ryan volunteered to work Shawn's shifts for a while."

"What?" Emily notices the empty bottom bunk. She didn't hear Ryan leave the room. Maybe she did fall asleep for a time. "But he's on vacation."

Ryan sits on the edge of the couch. "Morning."

"Ryan, you don't have to work while you're here."

"I want to. I want to help. Go with your girlfriends. I got this." He gives a military salute.

...

The sight of Alicia's puffy eyelids and hunched, defeated shoulders send Emily back to the consuming rage she felt hours ago. But the house feels different now, with sunlight flooding every corner.

"That doesn't have marijuana in it, does it, Nora?" Alicia asks, pointing to the smudge stick.

"No." Nora laughs lightly. The laugh travels through the house and meets Emily like a gentle nudge. Molly and Bridget sit side by side on one of the couches. On the bar, a box of donuts dusted in glittery sugar is open next to a pot of brewed coffee. Two empty mugs wait for Emily and Nora.

"Good," Alicia laughs a little as well. "I don't want the house to smell like drugs. My parents would kill me."

"Nora wouldn't waste weed like that," teases Bridget.

"It's so clean in here," Emily notes, pouring her coffee.

"Molly stayed last night, and Tim and half his friends," Alicia explains.

"Hey, I helped too," says Bridget. And Emily feels a pang of guilt as she sinks into the couch, remembering how she took Ryan's hand and asked him to drive them back to the cabin within moments of Shawn leaving. She wanted to get away.

Nora adds her cream, then settles between Alicia and Emily and relays the news she shared with Emily. Chris informed. Shawn fired. Ryan volunteered to step in.

"Yes," says Bridget like a cheer, raising her fist in the air. "Momma Nora saves the day."

"Did anyone talk to Javier?" asks Molly. "I wonder how that ride went."

They all look to Nora. "He texted when he dropped him off. I said thanks."

"Did anyone hear from Shawn?" asks Emily.

"He texted me, 'Never talk to me again,'" says Alicia. "Then he texted he was sorry. And then he tried to call. And then he texted that I was a monster. I finally blocked his number."

"Yuck," says Nora, resting a hand on Alicia's knee.

"I feel really bad." Alicia looks down at her coffee.

"Why?" asks Bridget. "He's a creep. He did this to himself."

Alicia meets the eyes around her, patient and concerned. "So, he asked me not to tell anyone this. But a couple weeks ago, he texted me in the middle of the night, saying he wanted to kill himself."

"Oh, my God," says Nora, shaking her head.

"And we went back and forth, and I was like, 'No, Shawn. You're a great guy.' And he was like, 'Yeah. I'm drunk. I just really like you. Please don't tell anyone.' I didn't know what to do. Like should I have called the police? Then he did it again and again, and he'd apologize the next day and hug me at work, and I was like, 'Okay, he's good.' But then he started following me to the dumpsters or the prep room or in the freezer 'to talk,'" Alicia says, holding up two fingers in air quotes. "And it got out of control, I guess."

The women shake their heads with whole, unbitten donuts in hand, a chorus of sympathy, empathy.

"So, he manipulated you into feeling sorry for him, making you feel like if you didn't give him what he wanted, he'd off himself," says Molly, half question, half statement.

"I guess," Alicia says slowly.

"And told you to be quiet," adds Bridget. Alicia nods.

"I hate that," says Emily louder than she means to, as she recalls Phil's casual command. "I hate that silence part, how they try to control the story."

"Silence is where like the shit festers, you know. Like where shame and trauma grow and get worse," says Molly, appearing stricken. "And I was like trying to be there for him, therapize him, I guess. I didn't know, Alicia."

"It's okay," Alicia says.

"Did you tell anyone? Your parents? Tim?" Nora asks.

"No," Alicia says, gripping the mug with both hands. "I just wanted to have fun and not let him wreck my summer. I wanted to prove to my parents that I could handle myself and do this on my own. I felt like I brought it on myself, like I was too flirty and nice with Shawn and led him on or something. This kind of thing happened to me in high school, remember. And they had to step in. And Tim, I didn't want to bring that grossness into it. I thought Shawn would get over it."

There's a pause as the women process.

"I feel embarrassed and stupid and freaked out."

"Don't feel embarrassed, Alicia," says Nora.

"Well, has anything like this happened to you guys?"

"Like, creepy, scary shit?" asks Bridget. "Yeah."

"Do you want us to share?" asks Molly gently. And Emily feels like she's entering new terrain, like she's on *The Oprah Winfrey Show* or a Barbara Walters special. She shifts with discomfort.

"I'll go," says Bridget. "Umm, well. An uncle, not blood-related, thank God, but still, he taught me how to French kiss when I was maybe six years old." The room feels airless. Emily sets her coffee down, trying to absorb the bluntness of Bridget's confession. "And then, junior year, the assistant track coach slept with one of my teammates. And then they realized he'd installed cameras in the girls' locker room. So, that was fun." Bridget gives a tight smile before biting into her donut, sugar sticking to her lips as she chews.

"I'm so sorry," says Molly. They all do. They repeat the phrase, shaking their heads.

"Who's next?" asks Bridget, leaning against the backrest of the couch.

Molly recalls the dad of children she was babysitting, who came home tipsy from a wedding, rested his hand on her ass, and asked if she was dominant or submissive in bed while the wife was searching for the checkbook in another room. "I was fifteen. I didn't even know what that meant."

"Fuck creepy men," says Alicia.

Emily can see Alicia's feeling lighter, validated, because she feels the same.

Alicia tells of another dad, this time of a high school friend, who told her and a few others at his daughter's birthday party that he wanted to see them naked. "He kept saying, 'Let's play strip poker.' It was awful."

Emily starts talking before she realizes it, piling her story on top of the rest. The words tumble out: "One night, a drunk guy, a regular at my dad's bar, snuck up to my room when I was sleeping. So I woke up to him feeling me up," her voice cracks, "a hand down my underwear." She studies the chipped red polish on her toenails. She receives her own chorus of horrified apologies.

"I'm so sorry, Emily," says Molly.

"That's just gross," says Bridget, shaking her head. "So gross."

Emily said it. She said it out loud. And they're still listening, so she continues, "He never really admitted what he did, but he apologized. He brought in a Bible. He said God was teaching him a lesson. The devil made him do it. He told me not to tell anyone. And my dad didn't want to ban him from the bar because he spent a lot of money and brought in business."

282

"Bullshit," says Nora. "And like, we put up with all this, you know. It's normal, and they all should be in jail or in some kind of trouble. Their wives should at least know, or maybe they do. It pisses me off."

The women share about peeping Toms and creepy neighbors, being followed from movie theaters and late-night study groups, handsy and inappropriate dentists and professors and farmhands and customers of The Schooner.

They tell of friends who were molested by relatives, stalked and threatened by ex-boyfriends or men they rejected, raped in dorm shower rooms and country music festivals.

"So yeah, Alicia. Don't feel embarrassed," Bridget reassures her. "Or feel bad. Everything we all said, that's like barely scratching the surface, you know."

Nora exhales loudly. "You've all been vulnerable, and it's inspiring. So, I feel like I should share something too."

"You don't have to," says Molly.

"No. I'll be mad at myself if I don't," Nora says, setting her coffee down and fingering her dangling earrings. "Okay. I'm classic. My husband hit me. And he forced himself on me—I guess rape. I don't know. Just once or twice toward the end. I think he knew I was checked out. We got married young, and I was super insecure, and yeah, he started hitting me."

"Seriously?" whispers Bridget. Molly has a hand over her mouth. Emily rests her palm on Nora's knee.

Again, they all say, "I'm so sorry."

"It's not like he sucker-punched me, you know. He would slap me on the face, and it was always quick, and he'd hate himself and cry and feel awful, but it would happen again. So I have a hard time trusting men, I guess. And I know they aren't all bad, you know."

Emily nods in agreement. She's thinking of the men who have treated her kind and decent: Jacob and Simon, Chris and Colin and Javier, Ryan and John, and a few of her high school friends, some of the men who frequented The Honky Tonk.

She thinks of her grandpa, bringing her to the kitties.

She thinks of her dad, caring for her, raising her in his own way, and installing that deadbolt like it would fix her fears, like that was enough.

"Now let's smudge the shit out of this place," says Nora.

...

"Hi, Eileen," Emily types from the computer in Chris's office, her knee bobbing up and down. She found the email address on their church directory webpage: "It's Emily from The Honky Tonk. I thought you should know something about Phil. It's been eating away at me. He asked me not to tell, but after Thanksgiving, he was drunk at the bar, and I woke up to him touching me. It was really scary and awful. I thought you should know. Sorry, Emily."

She clicks send before she has time to second-guess her decision.

"Silence is where shit festers," said Molly.

"Their wives should know," said Nora.

MUDDLED CHERRIES

Emily rises from the computer, jittery from the morning's coffee, the morning's conversations, last night's events, last night's sleeplessness, and from what she just did. She told.

CHAPTER TWENTY-NINE

Emily and Simon navigate an uneven causeway of large stones bathed in moonlight. She feels like she's playing a kind of hopscotch, trying to find something solid that won't wobble or flip with each step.

"It's so bright we don't even need a torch," Simon says a couple of steps behind her.

"A torch?" Emily laughs, never tiring of his foreignness. Sometimes, after they've been together for hours, she'll think in that lilting, mumbling accent of his. She'll miss that. "You mean a flashlight?"

"No, love." He gently slaps her ass. "I mean a torch."

She'll miss that too. The way he calls her "love," the way it enters her ear like sweet honey. The way he lingers on the "o."

The waves of Lake Michigan swash in on either side. The sound seems part of the song Simon chose from his iPod—another haunting melody, another Icelandic tune she doesn't understand, something to do with jumping in puddles, he told her. He hums along, his arms outstretched like wings as he tries to maintain balance as well.

Simon texted Emily the day after the Shawn incident, days ago now, during that grueling double shift: "Heard u had a shit nite & ur a champion. Proud. x"

After watching Ryan struggle to perfect the art of frying, consistently overcooking or undercooking fries and curds and tenders; thanking Chris for his understanding, for letting her use his computer; and trying to set aside the prior night's events, the morning's conversation, and focus on the customers; she finally took the rickety metal step to Simon's camper.

She silently hugged him, glancing at a couple of paintings he'd taped to dry. One was of Karin's wild-haired, half-naked Barbies on the gravel driveway, smudged with mud. Another was of a plate on a picnic table with a brat lined with ketchup and sprinkled with raw onion, brown beans, potato salad, and wild strawberries.

He led her to the bed, but she didn't want to have sex that night, to be naked and vulnerable. She wanted to be clothed and held. She wanted to sleep peacefully and safely. So she nestled in his nook, and he turned a show on his iPad, something he discovered in New Zealand, *Flight of the Conchords*. Then he recalled getting so high with some backpackers: a guy from India, another from Germany, a couple of Irish girls.

"We watched these birds flying around, and I figured out how they worked, yeah," he said. "How they fit into the world."

"That makes no sense," she said, envying his assuredness.

"But it did then. I can't describe it."

She opened her mouth to speak. Phil. She wanted to tell him too. But stopped herself. She didn't know where to begin or how to explain. What if he didn't understand like the women? What if he asked the questions she couldn't answer: Why didn't you call the police? Why did you stay? Are you sure that's what happened?

And he was leaving. Sharing that part of her might mar everything, like saying 'I love you' to Todd. Too much. He'd never think of her the same.

"Want to talk about Shawn? Dodgy prick."

She shuddered and shook her head. "No." No. She decided to cast those thoughts aside and let Simon's hand cupping her elbow be enough.

They step onto a gravel path once they reach the island, swing their legs over a limp chain, wander past a wooden shack with entry fees listed on the side of a shuttered window, and down the path bordered by giant pines that seem to sway to Simon's song as well. Emily doesn't remember whose idea it was to hike to this tiny island in the middle of the night toward the tall white lighthouse Emily's only ever seen pictures of and told tourists about—this place of refuge and safety surrounded by shipwrecks.

A beam of light sweeps over them. The beacon blinds Emily for a moment, like a flash photo, before moving on, lighting the surrounding trees and bouncing off the distant waves, illuminating the brick outbuildings and grassy meadow.

"So was this built like twenty years ago, then? And you lot need to turn it into a monument?" Simon teases, gazing up at the tower. "Our oldest lighthouse is Roman, yeah. Two thousand years old, I reckon."

"Oh, I'm from England, and everything's older and more important," Emily teases back in a mocking British accent. He laughs and pinches the fleshy part of her hips.

"Would you like a cuppa tea?" she manages to say between fits of giggles.

"It's just 'cuppa,'" he says playfully, hugging her, gently bringing her to the soft, dewy ground.

These last five days, Emily packed in all the fun and sex with Simon as she could while trying to look out for Ryan, who's working at least one shift a day, and told Chris to keep him on the schedule for the time being.

"I really like it here, Ems," Ryan told her while mopping the kitchen floor, his face slick with sweat, his cheeks rosy from the heat of the fryers, his arms tan from all the sunshine he's soaked in since he arrived. "Nora and I did yoga this morning. I'm going kayaking with Courtney and Bridget tomorrow. Javier's so cool and patient. Chris is awesome. Molly's fucking cute and nice. Is that okay?"

"That's cool with me. Don't know what Ashley's gonna think about that."

"She'll get over it."

Emily and Simon joined the kayaking venture down an estuary where they paddled through swathes of lily pads, past purple irises, spotting blue herons and white egrets, where Courtney and Bridget finally admitted they were a couple.

"Well, Courtney said I had to start telling people, or she'd never talk to me again," said Bridget, her chest falling with a long exhale. "So, there you go. Happy, Courtney?"

"Yay," said Molly, setting down her paddle to clap her hands. Emily was sure she saw the air around Bridget thin and brighten. Simon and Ryan clapped as well.

"Was it a secret?" asked Ryan.

Courtney laughed. "Yes and no, but now it's not."

Simon and Emily went to the drive-in with Tim and Alicia, sitting in a line on the bed of Emily's truck, legs dangling off the edge, the latest *Transformers* movie on the giant screen while they shared Red Vines and popcorn and a hoppy beer Tim brought along.

They got high on the beach with Nora and Javier and built a small bonfire. Javier shared plans to detail his car with Calaveras and orange marigolds. Nora tried to explain what chakra meant. Simon described the beetles he ate in Thailand. Emily taught them a simple line dance while they passed around the joint, scooting and brushing and kicking up the sand.

Simon wore his cowboy hat and practiced his line dancing at The Sunny Seagull, to the amusement of the crowd, to a smiling Jacob and much less amused Cecelia, who played a set before The Midnight Campers came on. Emily approached Jacob as he unplugged and wound up cords.

"I should have been a better friend," she said, cringing, holding her hands tight against her belly. "I hope you do what feels right."

"TBD," he said, hugging her. "I feel bad about what happened that night, and I unloaded all that on you."

"No, I was the shit friend."

"I know you're busy and Simon is leaving soon, but after that, you want to hang out?"

"Go kayaking?"

"Let's do it."

Emily and Simon ate Swedish pancakes and drove up the winding road to the very tip of the peninsula. And while she basked in him, in her friends, in the beauty and joy the county has rained down on her like the golden leaves of autumn, which are coming too soon, she's avoided her email, ignored three missed calls from Dad, deleted the voicemail he left, minimized a text he sent that began "Not even here and ur causing …"

She would deal with all that soon enough.

Emily and Simon lie on their backs. Blades of grass tickle her bare legs as she watches the lighthouse's yellow beam spinning above them. She connects the stars of the big dipper and searches for the cloudy blanket of the Milky Way, but the full moon blots it out, peering down on them with a knowing smile.

"Two days," Simon says, finding her fingers in the grass.

"Two days," she repeats, keeping her gaze upward. "This kinda sucks, you know." But she stops short of saying I'll miss you. She wants to skip this conversation, not acknowledge the impending goodbye.

"Yeah." He turns on his side toward her and drums his fingertips on her shoulder. "You know, I have these wild thoughts about you."

"Hmm," she responds, still looking skyward.

"Like I'm gonna run into you in five years at an airport or something. I'll be engaged, and you're gonna ruin it for me, yeah." She wishes he wouldn't say things like that. She's known all along that she can't keep him and doesn't want any maybes or what-ifs floating around like clouds in her brain once he's gone. She wants sunshine.

"That won't happen." She shakes her head, not meeting his eyes. "You'll leave and that's that."

He doesn't disagree. "It's nice, eh? None of the messy bits."

"Yeah." She finally turns her gaze toward him. No fights. No disappointments. No unmet expectations. No broken promises. No discovering the other person isn't all that wonderful. No rejection.

But she also wonders if that might make the parting easier because she's realizing Molly's right; this is gonna hurt.

He inhales like he's about to say more, but she sets her fingertips over his lips.

"Just look at the stars with me," she says.

But he doesn't. He kisses the tops of her fingers, sucks, and softly bites down. She's surprised by how quickly he turns her on. She'll miss that too. The way he knows what to do now, kissing her lips and neck, moving his hand down her ribs, unbuttoning her denim shorts, sliding his fingers between her legs, finding her, sending electric currents off through her blood and bones and brain.

She'll miss this.

And his thick hair in her hands as she comes, falling around her face, making everything else disappear.

CHAPTER THIRTY

mily stands in a loose, uneven line of others around her age, most accompanied by mothers and a few fathers. It's orientation day at Lakeside Technical College. The high, open space of the cafeteria is cluttered with rows of empty chairs, long tables dotted with placards and brochures, free pencils, keychains, and stress balls. The place smells like high school—cleaning spray and textbooks, an unpleasant mix of musky cologne and sweet perfume. She holds a print-out of the day's schedule to her chest, overwhelmed by what awaits her: Welcome & Resources, Campus Tour, Instructor Introduction, Library & Tech 101, Textbook Pickup.

Emily is riddled with anxiety, apprehension, and goosebumps. The air conditioning moves like a strong current undeterred between the bodies. Emily feels exposed beneath the equally intense fluorescent lights above, like those around her can see she doesn't belong. And she feels fiercely alone, insignificant, watching the mother in front of her smooth her daughter's caramel-colored highlights and center the necklace on her sternum. Maybe she should have asked Nora or Molly to come along, but they're both working. Everyone's busy, and then they'll leave too, like Simon and Ashley and her own mother, like everyone. Like she left Dad.

"Let me see your teeth, hon," says the mother.

The daughter bites together and shows her teeth. The mother tilts her head and squints her thickly mascaraed eyelids like she's peering through bifocals. "Good."

"Next," says someone Emily can't see, and the line moves forward.

A familiar longing for her mom, a mom of her very own, grips her heart like a vice on occasions like this. Not borrowed or substituted, like Diane, but someone to take her prom dress shopping, straighten her cap on graduation day, and stand next to her with a carnation in hand on parents' night during basketball season.

"Give one to your dad," joked a teammate when they were all plucking school color carnations from a bucket in the locker room. "That would be hilarious."

Emily laughed as genuinely as she could and passed the bucket empty-handed, that vise tightening when she remembered that her mother had known exactly where to find her all these years. She was right where she left her. And she never came.

Dad snuck out after the pre-game ceremony to get back to the bar. She was grateful he took time away from the Friday night fish fry to stand beside her for a few moments. But she played terribly—dropped passes, missed shots, botched rebounds. Her friends' parents scolded her from the stands, "Come on, Emily!" while voices in her head said, *You're not good enough. You're easy to leave. You're forgettable. Unlovable.*

Those voices have been swelling since Simon left a few mornings ago, after a long, hard kiss in the musty camper, after Ingrid's husband tapped his knuckles on the door.

"One minute, mate," Simon called. They untangled their limbs. Emily dressed and tried to treat the morning like any other. But the confidence and calm his presence gave began eroding as she left the bed.

"That was fun, yeah?" Simon asked. She wasn't sure if he meant last night's drunken sex after an evening spent partying at The Schooner with almost everyone Simon had met in the county or the whole of their time together.

"Yeah," she agreed, buttoning her shorts and watching him stuff stray clothes in his oversized backpack. Her head throbbed. Her stomach ached. It still does.

"Next," the voice calls. Emily can see the source now; she's next. A plump woman, no-nonsense by the look of concentration etched in her wrinkles. "Name?"

"Emily. Emily Schmidt."

"Schmidt, Emily," the woman runs her finger down a list. She crosses out Emily's name and thumbs through a stack of manilla folders. "Here you are. Schedule. Financial stuff. List of resources. Mary will take your picture." She points to a gray backdrop off to the side, where another middle-aged woman holds a camera.

"Stand here." She points to the masking tape x on the floor.

Emily stands and looks up toward the sea of faces, making eye contact with a few. She sees disinterest, nervousness, and maybe a few second-guessing this decision like herself.

"Smile," says the woman, snapping the picture with forced enthusiasm.

Emily strains to activate the muscles required, but her lips barely move. She was able to function after Simon left, smile and laugh with her coworkers and customers, push through the discomfort of his absence, swat away Molly's attempts to crack her open.

"Really, though. Are you okay?"

"I'm fine," Emily said, stocking the straws.

"'Cause I feel like you might have abandonment issues, you know, like insecurity stuff," Molly said cautiously, sliding clean coffee mugs into the cupboard. "So, it's gotta be hard, right?"

"It was a summer fling." Emily shook her head, wishing Bridget was nearby so she'd have someone to roll her eyes at. "Done. Over."

But now all this change, these new faces, those bright lights, that awful vise around her heart. Molly's right. She is insecure, abandoned over and over and over again, and soon, this little community she's found will abandon her as well. She'll be left behind. Alone.

"You can have a seat," says the picture-taker. "You'll get your ID when you pick up your textbooks."

"Okay." Emily considers asking for a retake but feels the pressure of the line growing behind her. She picks a seat in the back corner. Her future classmates and their parents spread out. She catches bits of conversation. "Your car needs an oil change." "I wish they'd tell us if it's a boy or a girl." "I got chicken thawing for dinner. We'll do pizza tomorrow." A young man scratches his patchy reddish-brown beard. A young woman redoes her ponytail again and again. A few others hunch over their flip phones.

Emily decides against that distraction. Her phone feels like a hot ember in her purse, growing hotter as she continues to ignore Dad's calls and texts. She needs to deal with that. And check her email. She wonders if a reply from Eileen waits. She's been too afraid to check. She feels so afraid all over again. The certainty she felt pointing her finger in Shawn's face, typing that email, leaving her father, applying for college, withering away. Did she do the right thing? Is she doing the right thing? She can't keep up anymore.

Emily rests the folder on her thighs, takes a deep breath, and runs the pad of a pointer finger over the edges of the crisp papers. The sharp and stingy sensation occupies her mind for a moment.

"I thought this was a good idea," says a woman. Emily turns toward the voice and sees a smile punctuated by high dimples, eyes shadowed by bangs so tightly curled like the woman forgot to remove the roller. She's leaning over a couple of empty chairs toward Emily, who finds her smile as well.

"Same here." The vise loosens. "I'm nervous."

"I'm petrified," admits the woman, and Emily's smile widens in recognition. "I haven't been in school since, God, twenty-six years now."

"Are you going for nursing?"

"I am. And you?"

"That's the plan."

"We'll get through this together then." The woman scoots beside Emily. She offers her hand. "Leanne."

Emily exhales in relief, realizing, as Leanne talks of raising a family and working on and off at the local bait shop, that in the absence of a mom, a friend, someone usually steps in.

"And my husband, God bless him, said, 'Leanne, it's your turn now. What do you want to do?' Isn't that nice? Some husbands aren't supportive like that, you know."

"That is nice," says Emily.

"But now I'm here, and oh, Lord! Save me from myself. Why did I want to do this?"

"Yeah," Emily agrees. "I've been a waitress all my life, and I'm good at it, you know. I like it, too, most of the time. But I kinda always liked medical stuff or was interested in it. So, I don't know. Here I am."

"What's your favorite medical show?" asks Leanne, a conspiratorial grin on her face.

"*Grey's Anatomy*." Emily grins back.

"*ER*." Leanne winks. "You're probably too young for that one. George Clooney in his prime. Dr. Ross. Yum."

Emily laughs and lets her body absorb the safety she feels sitting next to this woman. "I love George Clooney."

"Welcome, everyone!" a voice calls from the podium.

"Here we go," whispers Leanne.

Emily feels like a hand holds hers as they sit through the addresses of the president and dean and campus manager, an academic advisor, a financial advisor, a tutoring coordinator, someone who organizes ice cream socials, bean bag tournaments, and visits with therapy dogs. With Leanne by her side, Emily finds herself able to take in the information and leaf through the contents of her folder with clarity. She can do this. As long as Chris can help her find some reasonable off-season housing, as long as The Schooner keeps putting a bit of money in her pocket over the winter, as long as she eats most of her meals there, she should be fine until the tourists return next summer.

As she tours the campus, never straying far from Leanne, she tingles with excitement while taking in the neatly arranged desks and gleaming whiteboards, high lab countertops with microscopes, and beds occupied by manikins in hospital gowns. She finds herself smiling back at the two instructors greeting her and a group of students in one of the nursing classrooms.

"I am a fan of anyone who would choose to pursue nursing," says Mrs. Stadler, a forty-something with graying brunette hair and a necklace of a stethoscope shaped like a heart. "This is a super difficult field, but so rewarding. You'll have so many options open to you. Keep that in mind when you feel overwhelmed. There will be a right fit for you. Chin up, work hard, help each other out, take care of yourself."

The other instructor, Mr. Thomas, "Call me Tom, everyone else does," wears a collared shirt buttoned up to his razor-burned Adam's apple. He offers short, practical advice: "Don't get behind. Find a study group." Leanne elbows Emily.

In the computer lab, Emily feels energized and bolstered as the librarian helps them open their school emails, navigate the library webpage, and find reliable sources. She feels safe enough to open a new tab and log in to her email with everyone around her so unaware of her personal life, so focused on the librarian's instructions, Leanne softly repeating what the librarian says, "'Wikipedia is not reliable. Click the peer-reviewed tab in the upper left corner.' Where the hell is the peer-reviewed tab?"

There they are. An email from Phil, no subject line, an email from his wife, subject: "RE: something you should know."

Emily's pulse quickens as she clicks Phil's name.

"I don't understand. Why are you trying to hurt me and my family? Yes, my wife showed me the email you sent. I'm baffled. Why would you take something I apologized for, a misunderstanding, and turn it into something bigger?"

There's more. But Emily stops and finds the X of the email as her eyes catch "your dad," "no proof." Her stomach twists and turns in knots that travel up her esophagus, constricting her throat. She wonders how red her cheeks burn as she tries to turn her attention back to the librarian.

"Some of you will use MLA to cite sources, others APA, but I'll be visiting classrooms when that time comes," the librarian says.

Emily opens Eileen's email:

> *Dear Emily,*
>
> *I feel such sorrow for you, for the life you've led and the circumstances that might have influenced you to accuse a decent man of such a thing.*
>
> *Phil went to The Honky Tonk to minister to you all. He wanted to share his love of Christ in a place where sin, drunkenness, and ungodliness are all around. I can't imagine what it was like for you growing up in that world, especially without a mother. I know you started turning to alcohol at an early age, and Phil has always worried for you and the path you're heading down— alcohol, drugs, men.*

"That was overwhelming," says Leanne, rising from her chair and gathering her folder and purse. Everyone rises to leave, making their way toward the exit. "Me and computers don't mix."

Emily swallows. It's difficult and sets off a shooting pain in her neck. She might cry.

"Ready to go?" asks Leanne.

"You go ahead," she manages. "Checking my email quick."

"Well, if I don't catch ya, I'll see ya on the first day," Leanne smiles and pats Emily's shoulder. "Enjoy the rest of your summer."

"You too. Thanks," says Emily.

She turns back to the screen:

> I forgive you for this, as I know Phil forgives you as well. We're praying for you, Emily, and wonder if this is a cry for help. If you ever need someone to talk to or shepherd you into a relationship with God, we're here for you.
>
> In Christ, Eileen

Below the message are instructions for accepting Jesus Christ into your life.

She reads the email again, and once more. Her shoulders hunch hard and heavy as she falls into herself, bites her bottom lip, holds her breath, and stares at the keyboard. The placement of each letter appears so strange. They aren't in order. Shouldn't they be in order? It makes no sense.

...

Emily has no time to show the emails to her coworkers before the dinner shift begins. The restaurant is half-full, the bar packed. Nora delivers drinks, Alicia clears plates, Bridget jots down a table's order, and Molly refills the salad dressings. Emily ties her apron around her back, desperate for someone to tell her she isn't crazy or wrong, that she didn't lure him up there, that it *was* a big deal. She even tried calling Ashley while driving back to the cabin, but she didn't answer. And customers are waiting.

Chris approaches, appearing frantic. "You're working behind the bar tonight," he says, tugging on his black whiskers.

That's the last place she wants to be. No chance to hide, to avoid conversations she doesn't want to have right now about the weather and the cherries, where she's from and where they're from, and all those watching, needing eyes.

"Yeah. Whatever," she says, unable to suppress her annoyance.

"It's just been so busy back there. And I gotta step out from like seven to eight—worst time."

"Sure." She feels numb, dirty. She wants to tell Nora what she read, to ask Molly, "Why doesn't he get consequences? Why do I feel like I did something wrong?" She wants to hear Bridget call Phil an asshole or creep. She wants Alicia to embrace her with empathy. She wants the option to hide in the freezer and cry.

"See, me and my wife are starting these fertility treatments," Chris explains. "My wife needs a shot in her stomach, another in her ass. I promised I'd do 'em. We'll do it in the parking lot. This is a terrible time to start all this, but what are you gonna do?"

"Oh, to have kids?" Emily's eyes burn. She's got to get outside her head, herself. "'Cause you want to have kids."

He nods, a small smile.

"Yeah. Sure. Of course."

After sneaking a shot of rail whiskey in the cellar and dropping fives, tens, and a couple of twenties in the tip bucket, Emily eases into autopilot behind the bar. Customers come and go, talking about their sailboats and new knees, swine flu, and the death of Michael Jackson. They talk about their grandkids' T-ball games and cancer treatments and how bright the stars are here. Words and phrases from Phil's and Eileen's emails bounce unwelcome in her brain as she serves people who've come for food, a drink, and some conversation. All these customers, they're nice people, Emily realizes. They're nice to her, for the most part. "Sorrow for you," "alcohol, drugs, men." She wishes she could zap the thoughts like those electric bug traps that electrocute mosquitoes, flies, and gnats with a satisfying hiss and sizzle.

Is it such a bad world, this world that raised her? Is it that much different from any other place people gather? Are these people so bad?

"How was orientation?" asks Nora while picking up a tray of cocktails.

"Good," answers Emily, relieved to see her friend's smile, her open, caring expression. "Good and bad."

"We'll talk," says Nora, winking, spinning around with the tray.

Emily carries that promise as the hours tick on, as customers talk about their pickle recipes and Faith Hill's new hairstyle and ask Emily to send their compliments to the chef. "The best perch in the county." She wonders what they've wept over, what heartbreaks and hurts and traumas and regrets they harbor inside.

Fuck Phil. Fuck him and fuck his wife, Emily decides. They're no better than anyone at this bar. In fact, they're worse. And if she ever sees them again, she'll tell them just that.

"I feel sorrow for you," she'll tell Eileen, "for living with a creep."

"And fuck you, Phil," she'll say to him. "You know exactly what you did, and if God is real, he does too."

That's what she'll tell them, she decides as she refills a pint of beer.

Chris disappears to try to make a baby. Brandon spends too much time giving book recommendations to a man from the East Coast who's curious about life in Wisconsin.

"*Population: 485*, man," says Brandon. "It's all in there."

Alicia and Molly laugh while rolling silverware at a corner table. Nora tells an older couple something with an easy smile on her face, and they're nodding and smiling back.

Bridget starts singing "Happy Birthday" as she sets a slice of cherry pie à la mode in front of a sixty-something so embarrassed and gleeful that the whole of his bald head blushes. He's surrounded by family and friends. Other customers chime in, and soon the whole restaurant boisterously sings along, "Happy birthday, dear … Stan! Happy birthday to you!"

This is her home right now, her world, and it's not a bad one.

CHAPTER THIRTY-ONE

Emily cuts her paddle in the clear water, glinting in the August sun. She can see the bottom of Lake Michigan a few feet below—the fine sand and small jagged rocks mingling as currents pulsate over them. The gentle waves pass her, eventually slapping onto the shore's golden bluffs or slipping into the smooth, shallow caves. Jacob leads the way toward a shipwreck visible from the surface.

"The SS *Australasia*," he tells her, pointing a tanned arm toward the openness. "So, it burned. That's why it sank. The crew got off safely, and fun fact: the guys sent to save the ship saw full meals in the galley. So, they ate dinner before trying to put out the fire, I guess, or tow it in."

"You're making that up," Emily teases. A pelican dives open-mouthed for its breakfast.

"I swear." Jacob laughs, the curly wisps of his hair fluttering like moth wings. "On my life. Scout's honor. I know what I'm talking about now."

Emily dips a hand in the water and lets cool droplets fall from her fingertips to her forearm.

"And to add to the fun fact," he continues, "when the crew of the *Australasia* found out the would-be rescuers ate their meal, a fight broke out on a tugboat."

"That sounds like a kid's book." She tries to splash Jacob with the paddle, but it's awkward for her novice arms, though she manages to send a light spray his way.

"Hey!" He responds by expertly slicing his paddle in the lake and sending a sheet of water her way. She's doused and loses her breath in the shock of cold. When her lungs find oxygen again, she laughs.

"Holy smokes," he says, doubling over himself in laughter. "Sorry, Emily."

"I'm gonna sink your little boat," she teases, wiping the water from beneath her eyes, relieved she applied waterproof mascara. "You bully." But the water feels refreshing on her skin, tickling down her skull and bare shoulders. A breeze sends shivers and goosebumps up her arms and legs, but the sun's rays soon smooth them away. She closes her eyes, turning her face to the warm beams.

She feels content, she realizes, safe in the nest of the yellow kayak, paddling along with Jacob. She feels like some loose thread in her mind has been sewn in by taking him up on his offer. And she's working on hemming in a few more since her friends provided all the reassurance, comfort, and validation she hoped last week after they paused their silverware rolling and huddled into Chris's office. Emily opened the emails for them to read. She listened to them mumble the sentences softly, scoffing and huffing now and then until Bridget said, "What a dick," lingering on each syllable.

"She's delusional," added Nora, shaking her head.

"I mean, I guess I don't know what I was expecting," said Emily. "But not this."

"They're sick. Like, I'm not surprised," said Molly. "Husbands can hurt their children, like molest them and stuff, and some wives will defend them."

"You did the right thing," said Alicia, putting a hand on Emily's shoulder.

Emily tried to harness their words like a pack of wolves, tying them firmly in her brain to ward off the messages, the memory, the feeling that she'd done something wrong. She was relieved when the conversation moved on. They returned to rolling silverware and sipping cocktails, and Alicia announced a redo party before the season ended. Nora shared that she and Javier were officially official after he gave her an ultimatum. The women clapped and cheered.

"That makes me happy," Bridget said. Emily felt inspired by the news, like maybe some things do work out and fall into place. Maybe they just need a push.

She decided to give Dad an ultimatum herself, sitting on the edge of Ryan's bunk after another unsettling dream— her dad was searching for her, pounding on a locked door as she hid beneath a bed.

"It's all these calls and texts," she explained to Ryan. "I've ignored him for so long. Now I'm scared and pissed and just want him to say sorry and give me at least some of the money."

"You know that might not happen, though," he said, rubbing her back with one hand, yawning into the other.

She blew out a breath and typed out the text she'd composed earlier as dawn slowly crept in, as she waited for an appropriate time to wake Ryan and ask him if what she planned was warranted. He knew Dad better than anyone.

"Don't know where 2 start w/ these messages from u. Im hurt & overwhelmed. Im blocking ur # til I get some $: Schooner, PO Box 946, Baileys Harbor 54202."

"Is that okay?" She cringed and held the glow of her phone to his sleepy eyes.

"Yes." Ryan softly slapped her knee. "Boundaries. Putting yourself first."

"I can tell you've been hanging out with Molly. Okay. Here I go." She pressed "Send," and Ryan gripped her knee. As she exhaled, tears flooded her eyes.

They paddle on. Jacob continues to share tidbits he's learned about the coral reef fossils archaeologists found, the Oneota tribe that called the dunes home for centuries, and the salamanders he and Tyler caught last week. "Thanks for coming out with me," he finishes.

"I'm surprised you'd want to after doing it all day, every day."

"I like it out here, don't you? Like, there's nothing you can do about anything." He takes a drink from his Nalgene. His freckles so solid and dark, his hair lightened. He's a different man than the one she met in May. "And it's so beautiful."

"You'll miss it then, when you go?"

"I will, and the people. Such awesome people up here."

Emily agrees and then asks the question that's been on the tip of her tongue since they met on the shore. "So where are you going this winter?"

"New Zealand." He smiles.

"Yay! Good! I think that's a good idea." Emily is giddy for him, the adventure ahead. "Is Cecelia okay with that?"

"You didn't hear?"

"What?"

"Cecelia left."

"She left?" Emily doesn't understand. They performed at The Sunny Seagull days ago, singing into the same microphone. And then another slammed weekend at The Schooner. She didn't hear.

"She up and left. Friday. One of her musician friends in Milwaukee needed a singer, so she's gone." His sunglasses obscure his expression. She only sees the reflection of water, the sky, herself. "The Honeydews are on a permanent hiatus, I guess. So, I'll be playing solo this week."

"Did she ask you to come with?" Emily still doesn't believe it's that simple, then remembers that she once left abruptly too.

"No. She sent me a text," he says: "'Sorry, I realized we're on very different roads. Can't pass this up. It was fun.' Blah, blah, blah. Feel kind of stupid, you know."

"Don't feel stupid." Emily's surprised she doesn't feel more satisfied with the news. A corner of her heart celebrates, but really, she feels sadness for Jacob, for this time of their lives, all these friendships and romances, coming and going. It feels impossible to hold on to anything or anyone with the end of summer approaching. "She's nuts, Jacob. You're so nice and cool. Seriously, don't feel stupid."

"She told me I was too nice."

Emily cringes, remembering she said the same. But he doesn't linger on that thought. He scratches his head and says, "I think I thought I could save her from herself or something. That I was what she needed. I could make her happy."

"No offense. I don't think she needed or wanted saving." Emily remembers Cecelia's steely spirit. "Like, she knew who she was."

"Yeah." Jacob nods like he's realizing something. "Yeah. You're right. But I know she thought I was too sheltered and boring. I always felt small to her. I don't know. Really, I'm the messed up one. I'm still figuring it out and then wonder why I'm trying to figure it out when she could be done with me so quick and easy." He shakes his head, the words stumbling out like gravel from a shoe after a long hike. "I'm pathetic."

"Everyone is messed up." Emily steers her kayak alongside his and rests the paddle across her lap. "Don't you also feel relieved? Like, you're free. You don't have to worry about her anymore. She made that decision for you. You can go to New Zealand and have an amazing time, single."

Jacob laughs and she's pleased to hear it echoing in her ear, to be comforting him, someone, and not the other way around.

"Do you miss Simon?" Jacob takes off his sunglasses, wiping them with his shirt. She reads his expression now, something pained and questioning behind his eyes. Maybe he's seeking reassurance that the longing and confusion dulls and fades to nothing.

"Yeah," she admits. She does. A lingering ache for Simon remains, his easy way of being, the compliments and sex and escape, amplified when she woke to a text he'd sent in the middle of the night. "Even in NYC I'm missing ur tits. x"

"Pure poetry," Nora teased between sips of coffee after Emily shared the text, laughing, making her way to the bathroom. But once she drew the shower's flimsy curtain and tilted her forehead toward the water's spray and sibilance, she cried.

Sometimes she wished Simon hadn't bathed her in such a bright, enchanting light only to cut the beam and leave her. But as the days passed and her friends filled the sharp corners of his absence, she was beginning to feel less and less like he took something away and more and more like he'd given her something.

"You'll miss her for a while," says Emily. "And then not so much." She thinks of Todd, how she doesn't think of him much anymore.

"Yeah, you know, she distracted me from my shit. It was this rebellious thing. And I couldn't analyze too much with her. She got annoyed when I brought up church or God, and like, that's been my whole life. So, I didn't share much and focused on her, and now I feel all the stuff I was trying to bury or run away from resurfacing, you know?"

She nods in recognition. "Oh, yeah. I think you can't really, truly run away from your shit."

"Yeah." His jaw tenses as he rubs his lips together.

"You want to tell *me*?" Emily braves. "What happened."

He hesitates and scans the horizon—vast empty water, thin clouds toward the east, brilliant blue sky above. Seagulls squawk. A dog barks from the beach.

"I'm scared you won't understand."

"Try me." She grips the edge of his kayak.

"My sister. Beth. I caught her with another girl in the church pantry, like, doing stuff. And, how I grew up, that's not okay, you know. We're all supposed to be straight. We're all supposed to stay pure, virgins. They gave us rings inscribed with 'True Love Waits.' We made pledges, and so, it's a big deal." He sets his sunglasses on his lap and puts his palms to his face, over his eyes like he doesn't want to see the memory he's sharing aloud, and Emily's trying to place herself in a world so unlike her own. "She asked me not to, but I told my youth pastor, who told my parents, who told our pastor. Dad found her journal and read it out loud. 'Treasure trove of sin,' he called it."

314

He removes his hands from his face and looks at Emily. She's sure he's gauging her reaction, and she fights to appear unfazed. She's his friend and a bartender, after all, but rage sets the back of her throat aflame.

"She'd done stuff with other people too."

"That's none of your business, though. Or your dad's or your mom's. Like, it's her body."

"Yeah." Jacob bites his bottom lip. "None of it felt right. She looked happy in that pantry, you know. How is that bad? It sounds so stupid to you, I bet. It sounds stupid when I say it out loud, but in the place I was in, it's like she bought a one-way ticket to hell."

"It's not bad." Emily swats at the water.

"Exactly. Thank you! Yes."

"So did she get out?"

"Yeah." Jacob smiles. "She went to the counselor and this camp thing, and Dad made her burn the journal in our backyard like a frickin' ritual. But then she couldn't do it anymore and moved to Minneapolis. 'To live in secular sin.'" He raises two fingers in air quotes and blows out a long exhale.

"What's she like?" Emily wants to hug this woman, made to feel ashamed for feeling good.

"She's awesome. She's funny. She loves those *Funniest Home Video* shows. Like people falling down cracks her up. And she's smart, like, takes things apart and tries to see how they work—the toaster, Mom's hairdryer, her Easy Bake Oven. And she's brave."

"Sounds like it. I'm confused why your parents and these people care so much that she wants to mess around with people. Aren't there worse things?"

"You want a snapshot of my high school dating life? I held hands with a girl in my youth group when we all saw *Batman* at the movie theater. Word got around, and we had to sit down with our parents to discuss 'our intentions.'"

"Seriously? My dad was like, 'Don't get pregnant.'"

"And you're awesome. Everyone up here is awesome. The friends I've met. They've all had sex and been drunk and seem to be living these genuine lives, right? Living and not judging or trying to change and save everybody. And my mom and dad would think they're all lost souls. They're not. You're not. Beth's not. And I want to believe in God; I do. There's a version of God I think is awesome, right? But, like, it's all blown up in my face."

Jacob hangs his head, and Emily feels dizzy from all he's said, like he's spun her around and around and around. "It seems like you're figuring things out," she offers. A weak smile lights his gloomy face. "I thought you'd lived a sheltered life, too, to be fair. I didn't realize church people could be so screwed up until recently." She thinks of Phil and Eileen.

"Me too," he says, a strained laugh coming from his throat. "My now thirty-four-year-old youth pastor I thought was the coolest, like he got me into music and was a huge part of my life, proposed to a teenager last year. And he was all obsessed with Beth's purity."

"Have you talked to Beth? Said sorry?"

"Yes," he says, that familiar energy creeping back into him. "Me moving up here and trying to live a regular life opened her up to talking to me again. We've had a couple huge heart-to-hearts. She sounds more like herself and wants to see me before I go to New Zealand."

"That's awesome, Jacob." But she feels unsettled by what he's shared, compelled to share as well, to meet his honesty. "So, remember when I told you on the beach about that creepy guy?"

"Yeah."

She fixes her gaze on the horizon and tells him. She tells him about waking to Phil. The rubbing, prodding. He listens. He holds the edge of her kayak. She tells him about the Bible in Phil's hands.

"I'm sorry," he says, a pained expression on his face. "Bringing in the Bible like that, to justify what he did. I'm so sorry, Emily."

"It's not your fault," she says, smiling. There's relief, saying it out loud once more to kind and sympathetic ears. But the feeling is bittersweet. She also wonders if she's less attractive to him now.

"And your dad knows?"

"Not details, but yeah," she struggles to answer. "He knows. He was there, downstairs." A rush of regret swims through her veins. She's marked herself, defined herself. Victim. Shared too much. Exposed. She remembers why she didn't tell Simon. "I don't know why I told you all that. It's not the same thing."

"I'm glad you told me."

"Yeah, anyway." She dips the paddle and works to angle her kayak from his, propels herself toward the open water. "Let's get to that shipwreck."

CHAPTER THIRTY-TWO

O ver the summer, many of Bridget's belongings migrated from the cabin to Courtney's bedroom in the kayak house. Recently, her suitcase relocated from under the bunk (now Ryan and Emily's) to the corner of the living room. It's open like a yawning mouth, with t-shirts, jeans, the makeup she never wears, and pairs of running shoes strewn about. Soon, it will zip shut, disappear, and take Bridget with it. She'll be the first to go. Her cross-country team is expected to be on campus a week before classes start and meets begin.

"What are you going to do all week?" asks Alicia, sipping coffee while they prepare the dining room for the day.

"Weightlift and team building exercises and run, run, run," Bridget answers, her eyes downcast as she lowers one chair after another to the floor with fluid movements.

"That sucks." Alicia throws the coffee grounds away. She'll be leaving a week after Bridget. The redo party date is set, "but none of the hot Coast Guard guys will be there this time, ladies. Sorry," she apologizes and turns on the iced tea machine.

"Why? What happened?" asks Nora, wiping a table with a damp rag and blowing the hair from her eyes.

"I told Tim I didn't want to do long distance, then he said it's too hard to keep hanging out with me." Alicia makes a pouty face. "Kinda sweet, huh? Like, his eyes were watering."

"That's too bad," says Emily, grabbing a fistful of napkins from the cabinet. "I liked him."

"And they say girls are clingy," says Molly. She writes the specials on the board: BLT with a fried egg and fries, $7.99. She'll leave a day or two after Alicia and move back into the dorms.

Emily loses focus, a simmering sadness and panic bubbling inside at the thought of all the impending goodbyes, of losing what she's gained.

"What was I doing?" she asks, holding up the napkins. "Where was I going with these?"

But not everyone plans on leaving. While they stroll along the shore of Lake Michigan after a yoga session, Nora asks Emily if she'd join her and Javier in finding winter housing.

"Really? I don't want to be a third wheel," Emily says, ecstatic with gratefulness.

"Not at all. Be real—it would save us all some money. And I hate the idea of you living alone your first winter up here. It'd be my first too. We'll make chili and snowshoe."

Emily wraps her arms around her. Nora laughs and smiles and, after a few moments, says, "And I'm not ready to live alone with a boy again."

Ryan wonders if he might get in on the arrangement as well. "I can't move back in with my parents. And I like it up here," he says while they watch a staticky episode of *Everybody Loves Raymond* he managed to find with a homemade antenna cobbled together with wood, nails, and a wire hanger.

"But you know it will be totally different, right?" asks Emily, concerned. "Half our friends will be gone. I'll be in school. I think it's like night and day."

"People still live up here, you know. How different can it be from anywhere else in Wisconsin? Honestly? I need to get home eventually to get some more clothes, my PlayStation."

While Emily sees, hears, and feels each one of her friends preparing for the next phase of their lives, she also feels a collective urgency to make the most of their final stretches of time together, the final warmth of summer.

She partakes in a croquet tournament with the kayak crew, a few more bonfires with impromptu jam sessions, and plenty of weed, mini-golf, and night swims. Molly invites everyone over to her family's house one morning for pancakes and a tour of the dairy farm.

"These udders *are* quite impressive," teases Bridget with a wink when Molly's dad leads them through the cow barn.

After a lunch shift, Emily enters the cabin to Terry teaching Nora how to make jewelry out of her crystals, stones, and lake glass. He brought a tiny drill, twine and leather cords, silver and gold wire, and a tacklebox full of organized beads, shells, and clasps. They invite her to join, and as Emily winds silver wire as thin as thread around a pink quartz, Terry says, "Very good. Very good."

Another evening, she joins the charter fishing guys who frequent The Schooner on a fishing trip, and Alicia, Bridget, and Ryan come along. Ryan studies the lures and the radars, drinking his can of Coke while Alicia blares the horn and quizzes the captain on his knowledge of Morse code. Bridget and Emily work together to reel in the first salmon, taking turns cranking and pulling, cranking and pulling. When it's in the net, they high-five and hug until one of the guys starts clubbing the slick, shimmering fish in the head with a metal bat. They scream and leap onto the cushions, groaning and clinging to one another.

"It's humane," laughs one of the fishermen, shaking his head.

"One of the eyeballs popped out," says Emily, pointing. "It's over there." Another casually kneels and picks up the eyeball like it's a marble, laughs, and then tosses it into the lake.

One morning, Emily goes on a hike with Alicia and Colin, and Alicia admits she doesn't like sleeping in that big house without Tim. She doesn't want Shawn to know she's single. She's scared he'll show up drunk and angry.

"To hell with him," says Colin.

"He hasn't done anything since that night," says Alicia, running her fingers through her hair. "I saw him at the beach the other day, and he wouldn't even look at me. I get this icky feeling when I'm alone, you know."

A sick sensation radiates from Emily's gut. She doesn't know what to say except, "I'm so sorry."

Colin puts a hand on Alicia's shoulder. "Not only have I taken self-defense classes, but I'm pretty much an expert in stage combat." Emily and Alicia spend the next hour learning to utilize their elbows and knees, the effectiveness of scratching, gouging, and groin kicks among the aspen trees.

Emily sees Jacob at these various events and at his solo gigs as well. Something always lights up inside her when he smiles. The light flickers when they beat Courtney and Bridget in one out of five games of ping pong, when he plays his Bob Dylan or Bruce Springsteen covers, when they snatch a moment from everyone to talk about tourists and music and nursing school and New Zealand.

At each goodbye, she wonders if he feels that spark too, if he feels as drawn to her as she does to him, if he wants to kiss her. But the moments pass, and they're swept up by their rides or friends or shifts about to begin.

And something feels off in her heart—it's too soon after Cecelia and Simon, too soon before New Zealand and nursing school. It would change everything. Maybe they're better off as friends.

And sometimes, when Emily lies in bed with Ryan snoring softly below her and Javier and Nora a thin wall away, her brain skitters from one dark thought to the next. Even with a county full of friends, with all the goodness in her life, she torments herself, remembering that Ashley hasn't reached out for weeks. She imagines Simon has forgotten her and already found another. She recites phrases from Eileen's email. She wonders what The Honky Tonk regulars think of her now. Why did she tell Todd that she loved him? Was she too harsh on Shawn? Is it her fault Alicia is frightened? Should she have handled that situation differently?

And sometimes she feels Phil's heavy hands on her body, the dull prodding of his fingers like a waking nightmare, a phantom pain. She squishes her eyelids tight, wraps herself in a ball, deep breathes, and whispers, "You're okay. You're okay. You're okay."

Most of all, she thinks of Dad. She worries about him. She misses him and their banter on the good days; the sound of him half singing, half mumbling along to the jukebox; the smell of Irish Spring and cigarettes on him; their motorcycle rides; cribbage games; his smile when she made him laugh.

She wonders how much he's drinking. She wonders who's stopping into the bar these days. Who's looking out for him? She wonders if she went too far leaving him like she did.

She wishes things were different. She wishes he was happy for her. She wishes they were planning that trip to

MUDDLED CHERRIES

Nashville and the Smoky Mountains. She wishes he'd send a check and apologize. Isn't she worth that much to him? Or is he calling the relationship quits, like her mom?

CHAPTER THIRTY-THREE

Emily's ears reverberate with the cacophony of patrons talking and laughing, glasses clinking, and the TVs buzzing above her head. Chris turns up the volume of the radio as they transition from "dinner mode" to "drinking mode," as he puts it. It's Bridget's last shift, the night of Alicia's party. They've both gone to prepare for the event—RSVP'd by the kayak crew, Colin's theater friends, the charter fishermen, the baristas of the coffee shop Alicia frequents, and the housekeeping staff of the Cherryland Hotel whom Alicia met sunbathing the day before yesterday, among others. The night should be winding down, but a handful of last-minute diners sit in the dining room while a slew of customers pack the bar.

"You'll be first cut," promises Chris, catching Emily's glance at the clock. "I owe you."

"No problem," she says, trying to suppress her anxiousness.

"I'm telling you," he says, pouring a draft of Stella. "I'm so good at giving shots now—measuring and flicking the bubbles out and sticking that needle in. When you get to that chapter in school, I'll help you out. Then we'll be even."

"Is there a trick?" she asks, curious, pulling a drink ticket from the receipt printer.

"Don't let them see how freaked out you are, or they get really mad."

"Your poor wife," Emily shakes her head, smiling back.

Chris sets the beer on the bar. "She's a saint."

Emily scans the drink ticket in hand—2 Summer Shandy, 1 Tanqueray and tonic—and takes a drink from her water cup.

"My baby girl!" shouts a familiar voice. Emily looks up, startled, frightened even, like someone shook her by the shoulders.

There he is, approaching the bar. She almost spits the water from her mouth but forces herself to swallow before choking on the word, "Dad?"

Her heart accelerates and beats like a drum in her chest. *Da-dum. Da-dum.* There he is. Just like that. A small part of her soars. He came. He cares. Until he comes closer, until she sees that Ryan was right. He looks terrible, gaunt like this version approaching has been hewn from the father she once knew. And he's drunk, she can tell. The kind of drunk where each of his expressions and moods is one of extremes: furious, despairing, jovial. His shoulders are loose, his eyes uneven in their attempt to find focus, to stay open, like they have enough energy for one at a time.

"My baby girl!" he says again, this time in a loud singsong. He slides clumsily onto a bar stool.

"Dad. Wow. What are you doing here?"

"Well, you won't answer me," he slurs, then slaps his palms on the bar and looks around. "What's good here?" He rubs his hands together and meets Bob's eyes.

Bob lifts his cocktail, unfazed, unquestioning. "She makes a damn fine old-fashioned."

"Is that so?" Lighting bolts of red veins flood her dad's eyes. Emily's skin burns hot beneath her polo, the collar too tight around her neck.

"When did you get to town?" She's wondering how many miles he drove in this condition.

"Just now. The Honky Tonk—shut 'er up. Just decided, 'Hey. What is that girl up to?'" He extends a pointer finger and brings it to his temple. "'I'm gonna go find out.' 'Cause I kept calling and nothing. Blocked. Deleted."

"Hey, Em? You got that one?" Chris files through the drink receipts.

Emily looks at the ticket in her hand. "Oh, yeah. Sorry." She grips a pint glass and turns to the taps. Which one again? She checks the ticket. Her hand is shaking. Two Summer Shandys, a Tanqueray and tonic. She pours the beer.

"Nice place here," Dad says loudly. She nods, strategizing how to handle this. "Boat shit everywhere."

"We come every year," says the man sitting beside him, a seventy-something with wrinkling forearms that sag when he brings his cocktail toward his mouth.

Maybe she should send him to the cabin to sleep this off and sober up? Get him a hotel room somehow? A taxi? No, his truck. If she can get him in his truck and take the keys, he can sleep it off there.

"I own a bar," says Dad to the man and the woman beside him.

"Do you now?" she asks, tightening the pastel sweater tied around her shoulders as the AC blasts frigid air over the bar. But sweat runs down Emily's spine.

"Yep. Old country. I like old singing. Jukebox is full of old songs. You know, good stuff. Hank Williams. Ernest Tubb."

"Oh, real old," says the woman.

"Yeah. The good stuff. Not like today, pfft." He swats his hand at the air. More tickets come up.

A couple takes a seat at the other end of the bar. "Kitchen closed?" the man asks.

"In like two minutes," Emily says, checking the clock again. A dozen sunburned golfers stream in, standing behind the seated patrons with dollar bills in hand. Brandon retrieves food from the kitchen. Chris scoops ice cream into the blender. Emily wants to evaporate.

One drink at a time, she tells herself. Tanqueray and tonic.

"Gotta close 'er up, though," Dad says as she's pouring the gin. "For good."

Her head snaps up.

"I owned the joint since that thing was born," he points a shaking finger at her, and their eyes meet, setting off a

329

bomb of emotions in Emily's brain—at once devastated and angry and nostalgic and fearful, full of so much love and longing. A part of her wants to be a child, sit on his lap with a kiddie cocktail in hand like she used to, plucking the rosy-red cherries and popping them in her mouth while he wrote numbers in a notebook, signed checks, and sang along to Woody Guthrie. And another part wants to point toward the door, tell him to never come back, and burn The Honky Tonk to the ground while he's at it.

The couple nods, taking sips from their skinny straws with mild interest.

"But I can't do it on my own anymore, and the world's against me."

"That's too bad," says the woman.

"The recession? So hard," says the man.

"Yeah, fuckin' right. Recession and war and gas now so expensive. Just expensive."

"Are you really shutting the bar down?" Emily asks, wondering if it's a ploy.

"What do you care?"

She scoffs and rolls her eyes. *He's bluffing*, she decides. The couple wanting food wave from the end of the bar.

"Can I get some service here?" Dad asks.

"One minute, Dad." Emily finishes the cocktail, audibly exhaling, avoiding his eyes as she tucks two menus under one arm, asks a golfer what he wants, opens the small beer fridge at her calves with the other, and clutches a Miller High Life.

She decides he got drunk and thought this was a brilliant strategy to get to her without admitting guilt, apologizing, or giving her a dime. She hands the bottle to the golfer and takes his money. "And a Coors," says one beside him.

"Got it," she sets down the menus and pulls a drink ticket while reaching for the Coors. "Vodka Gimlet, Jim Beam Manhattan – olive, 2 IPAs."

He can't shut down The Honky Tonk. And he can't be here tonight. It's Bridget's last night. Alicia's party.

Chris turns on the blender. Patrons raise their voices above the grinding whirl. She tries to move faster, but her shoes stick to the rubber floor mat.

"Hey, bar wench!" shouts Dad. Emily's face flushes.

"Whoa! Sir. No. Uh-uh," says Chris over the blender.

Most of the customers seem too occupied to notice, but Emily sees a few smirks and furrowed brows.

"Oh, my God," she says between her teeth. The customers closest openly stare. "Can you go sleep this off in your truck? And we'll talk later."

"This service, eh?" he looks to Bob.

"Busy place," Bob answers casually, not looking at Dad.

"Thank you, Bob," says Emily.

"Can I get my drink?"

Emily leans toward him. She lowers her voice and pleads with him. "Please, go sleep in your truck. I'll call you when I am done."

"You call me? Not buying it. I wasn't born yesterday. Here I am. I want an old-fashioned." Dad thumps a fist on the bar.

The drink ticket is plastered to her slick palm. The couple set down their menus. She needs to take their order before the kitchen closes. She's gripping the Coors in her other hand. Brandon finally returns.

"Can you do this one?" Emily hands him the ticket saturated with sweat and passes off the Coors, takes the few crumpled bills.

"Hold on," she says to the rest of the golfers. "Kitchen's about to close," she says under her breath as she approaches the couple. "So, sorry. What can I get you guys?"

"She makes a mean old-fashioned," says Dad. They smile politely.

"Sorry," Emily says again. They order two Hacker-Pschorrs, curds, fried perch. Easy. Thank God. She punches in the order.

"Am I next?" grumbles Dad.

She opens the caps of the Hacker-Pschorrs.

"I can't do this with you right now." She sets the bottles in front of the couple.

"One drink," says Dad, struggling to unfurl his pointer finger. "I came all this way."

"Promise?"

"Cross this heart. Hope to die."

She shakes her head and flips a tumbler. She drops the cherries in the glass. They fall to the bottom with wet slaps. The sugar cube.

"Came to see my girl," he says, with a change of tone, a shift in demeanor. He hunches and furrows his face. He looks like he might cry.

"One drink. And then you need to go to your truck," she says evenly. "This is not a good time." A few shakes of bitters.

"You wouldn't answer a damn phone. So there. Yeah. I'm supposed to do what with that? And no good time for you to desert me. But you know."

Emily shakes her head again. "You know why I had to leave." She should stay silent, but she can't help it. She can't listen to that anymore.

She adds the orange slice and muddles, squishing and squashing, gripping the wooden handle until her palm aches. A scoop of ice.

"Had to?" he asks.

"You took everything," she says between her teeth. This conversation should happen in the morning. She pours the brandy.

"Don't start. No. Partners. We're partners."

She pauses, bringing a hand to her forehead, exhaling, adding the Maker's Mark, the ginger ale.

"No. I'm your daughter," she says, louder now, meeting his eyes. But they're glassy and vacant. He's drunk. No one's home. Her chin quivers. She can't look at him, so she looks away at the golfers staring back expectantly, impatiently. Bob gazes at the TV. Brandon mixes cocktails. Chris finally finishes that grasshopper. Nora and Molly roll silverware in the dining room, unaware.

"I took care of you." Dad leans toward her, using both his palms to steady himself as he nearly tips over.

"Oh, wow. Congratulations, Dad," she says sarcastically. "You did what every parent is supposed to do. *You* should have left my money where it was and let me leave like all my friends." She studies the ice cubes bobbing to the surface.

"I gotta shut the place down because of *you*. High and dry when I needed you. You left me. Then you go after Phil's wife? One of the best customers. Couldn't leave well enough alone, huh? Nail in my coffin."

The words finally force open the door she's been trying to keep closed. It's too late. Her anger gushes out like a toxic flood.

"*You* should have kicked that creep out forever after what he did." Spit slides down her lips. Tears glaze her eyes. "*You* should have defended me. He touched me, Dad."

"Is this guy bothering you?" A gentle hand on Emily's shoulder pulls her from that awful night to the one she's in. Chris stands beside her, calm, straight. Brandon holds a five-dollar bill over the tip jar without letting go. Bar patrons gaze toward the scene.

"This ain't your business." Dad narrows his eyes at Chris. But he has no authority here, though he claims ownership. "This is *my* daughter."

"I'm not giving you this, Dad." Emily grips the nearly finished old-fashioned. "You need to go sleep it off."

"You want him to leave?" asks Chris. Emily nods. "Go sleep it off, Dad."

"Sir," says Chris. "Out."

Dad doesn't move.

"Out," Chris says again.

"I want my drink!" yells Dad.

Without a thought, as if possessed, Emily brings her elbow back then forward.

"Here!" she says. The liquid suspends above the bar, glistening in the hanging lights before meeting Dad's face like a colorful tidal wave. Ice cubes bounce off his chin and cheekbones and crash on the wooden bar. The bourbon and ginger ale and bitters stream down his face and drip down his jaw, staining the collar of his white undershirt a sickly pale orange.

Emily's tears blur her sight for a moment, her ears filling with the reaction of the bar customers—gasps and moans, someone cheers, someone says, "Holy shit."

Dad stands from the stool. A guttural sob erupts from his throat as he examines his chest like he's been shot and searching for the bullet hole.

"Jesus Christ," says Chris, exasperated. "Dude. Out, man." He turns to Emily. "You. That way." A gentle push toward the end of the bar.

Dad claws at a bar rag and pats his face, but the golfers grip his shoulders and elbows and steer him toward the door. Someone grips Emily's hand and tugs her away.

"Let's go." Nora leads her out of the bar.

"Wait. We got to get his keys," Emily says, frantic. "Somebody get his keys!" She squirms her hand free and moves toward the front door, but a wall of bodies blocks her way as the crowd cranes their necks and shifts their shoulders to witness Dad forcibly removed.

"You gotta get his keys," Emily says, elbowing her way through. When she finally feels fresh air and meets the eyes of one of the golfers, she asks, "Did you get his keys?" He shrugs and she shoves past him and the others, scanning the parking lot and spotting two white taillights.

"Shit," she says, rushing toward them. "Shit." She reaches Dad's pickup as he reverses with a quick jerk, the motor revving then humming while she slaps the tailgate. "Dad. Dad! Stop."

"Emily! Move out of the way," says Nora.

"He'll kill himself," she says desperately, turning to Nora. She sees Molly following with an empty food tray, Ryan beside her.

The engine revs again. A quick, heavy shove launches her backward. She feels hot nails ripping along her elbows, forearms, and thighs as she skids to the rough pavement. A red glow floods her sight. Brake lights. Dirt floats around her peripheral as feet scuffle. She hears more palms slapping the truck. Ryan demands the keys from Dad.

"The brake. I hit the brake," Dad defends himself.

The engine cuts off.

Nora and Molly bring Emily to her feet. "Should we call the cops?" Molly asks, looking around her for answers. Ryan grips the keys and calls Dad "a pathetic human being. Fucking pathetic," while Nora brushes gravel from Emily's skin.

"No," says Emily, shaking her head. "No cops."

"You're bleeding," says Nora.

"He just needs to sleep it off," Emily tells them, the pain like a thousand needles pricking her skin when she walks toward Ryan and reaches out a hand. "I'm sorry. I'm so sorry, you guys."

Ryan stares furiously into the cab, where Dad rests his head on the steering wheel. He's heaving with sobs.

"Fucking pathetic," Ryan says again. "The truck reeks of whiskey."

"Give me the keys," Emily says, cringing from the pain, the guilt, the humiliation. Nora and Molly hover beside her. "You guys, go back inside. Seriously. It's fine. I got it." She tries not to walk stiffly or limp or show her pain as she approaches the driver's door.

"Dad, move over," she says.

"I didn't know, Emily," he says between sobs. "How's I 'pose to know? I'll shoot him if I see him again."

"Move over," she says, aware of Ryan, Nora, and Molly lingering beside the truck.

"I'm not a bad father. Am I a bad father?" he asks, dragging to the passenger side. "Did I hurt you? Are you hurt?"

"It's okay," Emily assures her friends. Trembling, she steers the truck to the back of the restaurant, past the dumpsters, and down the woodchip driveway. She turns off the ignition.

"Come home, Emily," he mumbles, pleads. His head bobs from side to side. "Help me. You're all I got." He seems so gray to her, hazy, drained of life. She's seen him like this before, many times, but knows that he can be so vibrant, full of color.

If she went back with him, maybe the color would return.

"You're soaked," she says, setting a hand on his damp shoulder. "I'll get you a dry shirt." She wanders into the empty cabin, picking bits of bloody gravel from her arm as she goes, wiping incoming tears with the back of her hand. She pulls a t-shirt from Ryan's pile of clothes, then returns and helps Dad change out of his shirt like he's a child, his eyelids struggling to remain open. "We'll figure this out," she assures him, pulling down the hem of the shirt. He's pissed himself. He's asleep.

She wipes away more tears, deciding to let him be until morning. He's slept in his piss before.

CHAPTER THIRTY-FOUR

"**M**aybe we could host like an intervention when he wakes up," suggests Molly as Nora opens The Schooner's first aid kit on the kitchen table. Ryan paces the living room, mumbling under his breath, though Emily catches a few expletives from the bathroom. She wipes the mascara from under her eyes.

"We're not doing that." She studies the bloody flecks of gravel strewn in the sink. "You guys, go. Seriously. Don't worry."

"Come here, Emily," says Nora, so calmly and motherly Emily might erupt in tears. "Let us help you."

"There's nothing you can do," Emily protests, gripping the sides of the sink to keep herself in place. "I'm gonna stick around the porch, be ready when he wakes up." She doesn't trust Dad to stay put once he rouses. He might stumble back into the restaurant and cause another scene, or stroll down the highway and get hit by a car, or wander toward the lake and drown himself. And she wants to be alone. She wants space to think this through. She wants Molly, Nora, and Ryan to go to the party and let on everything is fine.

"I'm putting antibiotic cream on those cuts so they don't get infected," Nora says evenly, sliding on latex gloves and gesturing toward the open kitchen chair. "Come here."

"Then will you go to the party?" Emily shuffles toward them, masking the relief she feels to be told what to do, to have some direction and care when the decisions before her feel gigantic. She feels like Dad's life is in her hands. She feels responsible.

"It doesn't seem right to leave you," Molly says. She tugs on the end of Emily's braids, squeezing them like worry stones. "This is all so ... traumatic, Emily."

Nora applies the cream silently. Emily winces as the stinging sensation undulates over her skin.

"What are you going to do when he wakes up?" Molly asks.

Emily doesn't want to share what she's considering: follow Dad back home, ask for a refund on her tuition, convince him to sell some of his memorabilia, maybe his motorcycle, pay off the debts, book better bands, and offer better food. Get customers back in The Honky Tonk. Get him back on his feet.

"I don't know. Wait 'til he's sober. Then talk it out."

"Maybe you two should have a mediator, a therapist," suggests Molly.

"This isn't going to be your first gig, Molly." Emily tries to make a joke. But no one laughs.

"Not me," says Molly, flustered. "No."

"Did Ashley know how bad your dad could get?" Ryan asks from the living room, still pink-cheeked and gleaming with sweat from his shift.

"What do you mean?" asks Emily, defensively. "Drunk? Yeah. He got drunk sometimes."

"No. I knew that. Everyone knows that," he says. "I mean like fucked up, like almost running you over fucked up."

Emily winces again as Nora applies more cream and picks a piece of embedded gravel from her skin. "Well, he never tried to run over Ashley if that's what you're worried about."

"I'm worried about *you*," Ryan says. "No wonder you practically lived at our place. You shouldn't have to deal with that asshole alone."

"He's not an asshole," Emily says, shaking now, almost shouting. "He's my dad."

Ryan throws up his hands, and Emily turns to Nora's sympathetic eyes. "He's not usually this bad."

Nora nods. Emily clenches her fist and, feeling compelled to defend her dad, turns back to Ryan. "And don't act like you're so much better than him, Ryan. You were pulling this kind of shit a couple of months ago."

"I fought in a fucking war," Ryan says, tugging on the collar of his t-shirt. "What's his excuse?"

"It's a disease, Ryan," says Molly gently.

"Shut up! Both of you, shut up!" says Emily, putting her head in her hands.

"Okay. Everyone stop," says Nora, rising from her chair. "Quiet."

Emily's breath comes out as fast as if she were running. She hears the wind through the cedars and the clink and smash of beer bottles as someone empties the recycling behind the restaurant.

"Okay. What do you need, Emily?" asks Nora, putting a finger under Emily's chin and raising her eyes level with hers. "From us? Right now."

"I really, really need you all to go to the party for Bridget and Alicia, please. I'll be fine." But no one appears convinced. Ryan huffs from the couch. Molly's eyebrows knot in concern. Nora's expression fluctuates from compassion to vexation and back again.

"I'm so embarrassed and horrified," Emily continues. "I just want to be alone for a while."

"Okay. I'm going for an hour or two," says Nora, looking from Emily to Molly to Ryan as if she's ensuring it's understood, a shared plan. "Then I will come back and check on you and go to bed, and you will wake me if you need anything, okay?"

Emily nods.

"And then *we* are processing this together in the morning because you're not dealing with this alone anymore," says Nora. "Okay?"

...

Emily heaves the stack of textbooks from Lakeside College to the plastic lawn table on the screened-in porch. A bare bulb buzzes from the ceiling. The wooden planks creak with each step. She sits gingerly on a chair and slides her arms through the sleeves of her hoodie slowly, carefully. The cool breeze off the lake and soft cobwebs tickling her ankles and knees distract her from the pain as she scoots in, aware of Dad's snoring from the truck as she sets his keys on the table. The sound so familiar, even comforting—a sound she waited for on those lonely, sometimes frightening nights at The Honky Tonk when he drank too much, stumbled around downstairs, sometimes shouting incoherently, throwing or dropping a pint glass or beer bottle. Sometimes he wept and turned up the jukebox. When silence fell, she'd follow the sound of his snoring to see where he'd ended up, to ensure he was alright—sometimes on a barstool, the couch, the floor, his bed.

But hearing the sound in this place feels surreal, like déjà vu, like an inescapable reality. Now she needs to face it.

She shuffles through the textbooks, checking between the pages to find random receipts and forms, her class schedule, and resource guide. Then she finds the folder labeled "Finances."

Pen in hand, she turns over her class schedule and starts calculating. She makes a list, some guesstimates. Maybe if she sold her truck, his motorcycle, got on eBay, and put up that signed Ernest Tubb poster, that hat he claims Buck Owens wore, those cowboy boots he says belonged to Lefty Frizzell. Her phone vibrates on the table, rattling the keys and interrupting her thoughts. A text from Bridget: "Where r u? U gotta come." A few moments later, another comes from Alicia, a frowning face.

Emily presses her fingertips to her temple, looking at the truck parked in front of the porch. "What am I doing?"

She doesn't answer the texts but goes inside the cabin and reaches for the bottle of Patrón above the fridge. She forces a shot of the sharp, spicy liquid down and pours another, bringing it back with her to the porch.

"I don't want to leave," she whispers to herself, setting the shot down. She rests a hand on the smooth, glossy surface of the *Microbiology* textbook, then *Anatomy and Physiology*. She flips through the pages, takes in the colorful, microscopic images of bacteria and viruses, the diagrams of hearts and intestines. She reads about the integumentary system and wonders which layer of skin her wounds reach— the epidermis, dermis, or subcutaneous layer.

She doesn't want to choose, to give anything up. She wants it all. She wants Dad to be content and safe—at the very least—on his own, as well as with her. She wants The Honky Tonk to succeed. She wants to take these classes, stay at The Schooner, and see what another summer brings.

She doesn't want more nights like this. She wishes Dad had someone, anyone. Those nights when he wasn't alone in his drunkenness—when a girlfriend or random woman followed him to bed, when Larry or Doug had a few too many and ended up on the couch, or various men from town passed out on a barstool or in their trucks—she felt calmer, more relaxed, safer on those nights, like Dad was looked after, so she could hand off responsibility. She didn't worry so much, and at least he wasn't drinking alone. She slept easier those nights.

And then Phil climbed those stairs.

She doesn't want to go back.

Her phone vibrates. A text from Jacob: "Hoping you'd be here. Hang tomorrow?"

She takes the other shot and drops her head in her hands.

...

Emily hears the roar of Dad's truck. It's in reverse, backing through a maze of trees toward The Honky Tonk, then forward toward Emily and the cabin. White lights. Red lights. There's Ryan, running toward the truck, waving his arms, then Nora and Molly and Chris and Phil. Phil? Dad runs into them all with a single audible *smack*, like a door closing. They fall like dominos. The truck reverses.

Emily's searching for the keys, lifting textbooks and cocktail glasses, one of Simon's paintings, a few of Nora's crystals. She gives up and watches Dad hit The Honky Tonk—it explodes in slow motion. Wooden guitars and cowboy hats and boots fly into the air like they're being sucked up by a tornado. Then another *smack*.

She wonders who or what he hit now when she feels a hand on her shoulder and hears her name.

"Emily?" Ryan says gently. "Emily."

She wakes to Molly and Javier hovering over her, Nora

beside her, and Ryan kneeling at eye level, holding onto the table where she put the keys. They're missing.

"Oh, no." Dad's truck is gone. "Where did he go?"

Nora puts a hand on Emily's back. "Look," she says with a slight smile, nodding at the space in front of Emily. Ryan points to the back of her class schedule, beneath all the lists, dollar signs, numbers, and question marks, to a check for two hundred dollars tucked under the shot glass, then a message scrawled in her black pen.

"I'll send more after sale," she reads. "Go to school. Sorry, Dad."

CHAPTER THIRTY-FIVE

Javier, Ryan, and Molly drink their coffee while Emily sits on the end of the couch, where she's been all night, bleary-eyed, quiet. They take turns trying to reassure her and theorize what happened to Dad.

"He probably feels like shit," says Javier, leaning back on the creaking pegs of a kitchen chair. "I'm sure he's okay. Want me to make you something?" Emily shakes her head.

"This could be part of his game, Ems," says Ryan, setting a hand on Molly's thigh, who wears a pair of his plaid boxers. "Now *you* feel bad. This could be what he wants." Emily bites the nail of her pointer finger until it breaks.

"Really, I think he gave you a gift," says Molly, gripping the top of Ryan's hand. "He saw your work and friends and the textbooks and future ahead of you and was like, 'Oh, my God. I've been so selfish.'" A wayward tear rolls down Emily's cheek. "Maybe he'll go back and get some help," Molly adds gently.

"Okay. Okay. Leave her alone," Nora says. "You two to work." She points to Javier and Ryan. "And Molly."

"I'm leaving," Molly says, rising from the chair. "I got something going on today."

Emily exhales and checks her phone again. Her tailbone aches, and the scabbing wounds prick and pull and sting with every movement. She's exhausted and edgy. It's nine in the morning, and Dad has yet to return her calls and latest string of texts: "Tell me ur ok." The sunshine filtering through the cabin windows and the smell of Nora's second pot of coffee brewing momentarily lifts her brain from the haze of last night's events and her sleeplessness.

Nora brings Emily another cup of coffee and sinks in the cushion beside her with that trillium mug in hand.

"It's gonna rain today," she says, glancing out the window Emily had gazed out most of the night, waiting for word from Dad, contemplating whether she should drive around the peninsula or back home to find him, replaying the scene at The Schooner bar over and over. Humiliation would swell inside her, then rage, then regret, then worry. There were so many thoughts and feelings and memories—light and dark, hot and cold—swirling inside her like the tornados that blew their way across Deer Valley now and then, etching their destruction on the land, pulling trees from their roots, knocking semis on their sides, tossing roofs from homes and barns. Exposed, ripped apart, devastated. But then a soft wave of solace would follow when she thought of the note, the check, the apology.

"I know what you're going to say, but I have to ask," says Emily, pressing the mug to her sternum, the heat radiating into her chest. "Do you think I should go back home and help my dad, like with his business, himself? He's obviously so screwed up, and Molly thinks he's an alcoholic."

Nora's shaking her head before Emily can finish, tendrils of hair gently swaying along her jaw. "No," she says. Simple. But Emily's brain still feels conflicted, like two forces pulling each half with equal intensity.

"So, I don't know much about alcoholics," says Nora, resting her feet against Emily's calf with intention. The gesture feels akin to holding her hand, a comfort. "But I know a bit about thinking you can make someone happy at the expense of your own self. My husband hit me, remember, and I felt for him and knew he was better than that and thought that by not telling anyone and not leaving him, I was being compassionate. I thought it was my fault. If I made him happy and was better ..."

"I'm so sorry." Emily furrows her brows and bites her bottom lip.

"No, no. This isn't about me," says Nora, shaking her head with more vigor this time. "What I'm saying is, your dad almost ran you over with his truck and took all your money, and *you* feel at fault."

"Yeah." Emily runs her fingers through her hair. The boiled-down details seem so stark from the convoluted emotions and memories Emily experiences and recalls when she thinks of Dad.

"Maybe your dad should go to some kind of rehab or AA thing, but you can't make him, and it's not your job to make him happy. You just can't. So, no, you're not moving back." Nora's authority and conviction and certainty slows the swirling mass in Emily's mind.

"'Live and let live,'" Nora says. "I think that's a saying for people who love addicts or messed up people. Live your own life." Emily remembers hearing those words. She's trying to recall from whom when the squeak and slam of the screen door interrupts her thoughts.

"Where is she?" Bridget's raspy voice calls. Emily meets her eyes, red and watery like her own, as she enters the living room. "Holy shit," she comes closer with a pouting lip and sympathetic expression. "I heard what happened." Bridget kneels on the floor and pulls Emily in a hug. Nora's arms encircle them both.

Emily sinks into the comfort, reminded of their first night together, after that overwhelming shift, after she cried in the freezer, after they burned sage. They set intentions.

Emily said she wanted to live her own life.

So much has changed; so much feels the same.

"I'm sorry I couldn't come to the party," Emily says into Bridget's shoulder. "Like, this is it. You're leaving. And I missed it."

Bridget pulls back and shakes her head with a smile. Even though Emily can see she's been crying, she notices Bridget's eyes seem brighter and bigger and more open.

"This isn't it. I'll be in Green Bay. I'm coming back to work Labor Day weekend, to visit. There will be other parties."

"And we're gonna go down and see Bridget," says Nora. The word *we* makes Emily smile. Then her vibrating and dinging phone startles her.

"Home. Tough nite. Sorry. Say sorry to ur boss for me," Emily reads out loud. She blows an exaggerated exhale and feels lighter. "He's back home."

"God, what a nightmare," says Bridget. "Look at your arms. I can't believe you didn't call the police."

"Well, he's my dad," says Emily, cringing. "And you've been crying. I can tell."

Bridget nods. "Yeah, summer's over. I had to say goodbye to Courtney. And I'm not sure if we're ready to make a joke about this yet, but I'm planning on telling my parents about Courtney and me, and I'm pretty sure my dad will want to run me over, too, but like sober."

"Oh, Bridget," says Emily, pulled from her own mess. "Do you want someone with you?"

"Yeah, so Molly is coming with," Bridget explains. "She's gonna help me pack up for school and wait in the car while I tell them. Courtney volunteered, but I feel like that might be too much for the coming out."

"I'm proud of you," says Nora, rubbing Bridget's back.

"Yeah," Bridget says, rolling her eyes. "Blah, it's hard to be who you are."

...

With Bridget sent off with hugs and well wishes and promises to see each other soon and Nora showered and off to work with apron in hand, Emily returns to the porch to retrieve the stack of textbooks and folders. Rain thrums on the roof, the leaves, and her truck in a kind of calming, cleansing song. She picks up one heavy book at a time, aware of the tornado swirling inside, slower, weaker, but there, and comes across a blank notebook, "Lakeside College" embossed on the red plastic cover. She sets the textbooks down and flips through the notebook's white pages lined with faded blue, hearing an echoing remembrance of Cecelia the first day they met at the laundromat after she overheard Emily on the phone with Dad. She said something about journaling, getting that shit out, and with such conviction.

Emily carefully sits and picks up the pen she used to calculate a future she doesn't have to live, the pen Dad used to apologize and sign that check.

"So, I've never really done this before. Just essays at school. But here goes," she writes, self-aware and uncomfortable. "My name is Emily Schmidt, and I grew up in a bar with my dad. My mom left when I was little, and it's still hard to think about sometimes. It's a cool bar— The Honky Tonk—and has lots of old music stuff and an old jukebox. I didn't realize it was weird to grow up in a bar until other kids said so. Some thought it was awesome. Others thought it was bad. I guess it was kind of both."

The pen keeps moving, the self-awareness shedding, her mind processing, sorting, focusing on details, memories of her childhood, her home, Dad.

She writes and writes and writes. She writes in incomplete sentences and run-ons, like her English teacher told her not to. She jumps from one thought to the next, shaking out her cramped palm and fingers again and again.

She writes about instinctively knowing when it was safe to talk to Dad, ask him questions, or make requests and when it wasn't—about outgrowing her shoes or struggling with fractions at school. About wanting a birthday party with her friends (not the regulars) with a Dairy Queen ice cream cake instead of the cheap freezer-burned vanilla ice cream they kept behind the frozen chicken tenders for the grasshoppers no one ever ordered. She knew not to ask about why he didn't want to spend time with his parents, the silent resentments and disappointments lingering over them like second-hand smoke. She knew not to ask about her mother.

Then she writes about acts of love from Dad—bathing her as a child and singing "Splish Splash" and inserting her name in the lyrics, making her French toast on Monday mornings and letting her crack the eggs, and taping up her school artwork on the wood-paneled walls of his bedroom. He only missed two or three parent-teacher conferences. He took Emily and Ashley to a Dixie Chicks concert in Minneapolis. He gave her his old truck when she got her driver's license. "So you can go lollygagging with your friends," he said.

She writes about the freedoms he gave her before many of her peers had them, to wear makeup and date and drink and sleep over at whoever's house whenever. He didn't ask, didn't seem to care or want to know, especially when it came to boyfriends or her body. She wished he did. And coupled with the seeming freedom, there was also this intense obligation to him and The Honky Tonk, like she owed them something.

"There's so many contradictions," she whispers as she writes, sounding out the word.

Woodchips shuffle and snap. Chris wanders to the cabin in a hooded raincoat. His shoulders are tight and hunched, his expression grave and shadowy.

"Hey." Emily stands stiffly. She means to apologize, but her tongue knots in her mouth, her cheeks burn red. She wonders if he's come to fire her.

"Hey," he answers back weakly, entering the porch. "Came to check on you."

"Oh, I'm fine," says Emily, embarrassed, shutting the notebook. "Look, I'm so sorry about last night. My dad said to tell you sorry too. I'm so mortified."

Chris pulls on his whiskers and surveys Emily's arms and legs. "It's not bad," she says quickly, wishing she wasn't wearing shorts and a t-shirt.

He winces. "Nora says your dad's back home?"

"Yeah. It will never happen again."

"It shouldn't have happened at all." He clears his throat as if to make room for the rest of what he has to say. "I should have called the police. You're my employee, and this kind of shit shouldn't happen. My wife was pissed when I told her. I was pissed at myself."

"It's not your fault. I shouldn't have thrown that drink in his face."

"Well, no, I don't know about that. Seems like he had it coming." A small smirk appears behind his beard. "Anyway. No. It's what happened after. I mean, Jesus. It seems complicated. I guess it's none of my business. But are you *okay*? Maybe you need to see a therapist or something? My wife told me to tell you the women's clinic has counseling sessions for like thirty-five dollars a visit."

"Thanks." Emily's surprised he isn't upset with her, that he isn't angry. "I'm journaling now. I think it's helping." She holds up the notebook with a half-smile.

"Whatever works." He digs his hands in his pockets. "Well, I know you start school soon, but if you need a day or two off or some help, let me know."

"You're a good boss, Chris," Emily says, feeling an overwhelming fondness for him. "You'll be a good dad."

"Yeah, well. That's nice to say." He tugs on his whiskers once more. "But you're not working tonight, okay? Let things simmer down a bit."

"Okay."

"And your dad isn't allowed back in for the foreseeable future."

Emily spreads peanut butter on a slice of white bread and brews another pot of coffee, thinking of more things to write down. There's so much left inside, and this act of writing *is* helping, like the pen connects to her brain somehow, a channel for her muddled, messy thoughts. It's cathartic.

She returns to her place on the porch, sips her coffee, takes a bite of the soft bread, and continues.

She writes about high school and Ashley, how lonely and left behind she felt by all her friends. She writes about Todd and the hurt and embarrassment, but the comfort and escape he gave her. She writes about Phil and the fear and shame, the rage and nightmares. She writes about Eileen and her denial and disbelief. She writes about Dad again and the dogged intensity of his anger and self-righteousness, the way she assumed he'd never unleash either on her. She was steady. She was there. His daughter.

Then she writes about The Honky Tonk—all the happiness and laughter, all the hurt and heartache within those drafty old walls.

A scratchy meow sounds through the rainfall. Emily's eyes need to adjust when she scans the gray, wet scene outside the porch. She spots the reflective glow of the cat's eyes. A warm excitement wells up in her, like when her grandpa led her to the cats and kittens in the barn.

"Aww, here, kitty, kitty." Emily opens the screen door. The black and white cat comes closer. It's slender with wet and matted fur. Brown gunk clings to the corners of its eyes like filthy teardrops.

"Here, kitty, kitty." Emily pushes through the pain as she kneels and offers an open palm. The cat rubs its moist head on Emily's knuckles. There's a blue collar around its neck.

"Are you lost? You need some love?" The cat purrs as Emily strokes its wet back. "Let's fix you up."

Emily collects her beach towel and pours a dish of milk. She wipes and dries the cat as it laps up the liquid, continuing to purr. "You stay as long as you like." Emily settles back in the chair, draping the towel over her lap and patting the empty space. The cat leaps onto her thighs and snuggles in.

Emily picks up the pen, soothed by the cat's company. Then she writes about the cat, the little home she's created for herself here in Door County, The Schooner and its staff, and her friends Nora and Bridget, Molly and Alicia, Javier and Colin, and Ingrid, Terry, and Chris. She writes about the kayak crew, the charter fishermen, and Cecelia. She writes about the acceptance, solidarity, and pure fun she's experienced. She writes about the thrill of being unabashedly delighted in by Simon, his sweet words, the orgasms. She writes about Ryan joining her. She writes about nursing school and the anticipation and pride she feels to be pursuing something. She writes about Jacob and how she wouldn't be here without him, how he makes her feel seen and nervous and giddy and calm all at once. She hasn't texted him back.

"You hungry?" Emily hears from the driveway. Nora jogs down the path with a to-go container in one hand and an open umbrella in the other. "I got a second between tables. I brought you a BLT. I knew there wasn't much food here. Well, it was Alicia's idea. She's so worried about you. Everyone is."

"You're the best, Nora." Emily sets aside the piece of bread spread with peanut butter. She'd only taken that one bite. "Tell everyone, 'Thank you.' And I'm glad you came. Look who I found." She tilts her chin toward her lap.

Nora's mouth opens in silent joy as she spots the drowsy cat.

"Luna? She came back?" Nora kneels on the floor and puts her forehead against the purring cat's. She runs a hand over its body, discovering the collar. "You shouldn't put this on an outdoor cat. No. She's meant to wander and explore." Nora unbuckles the collar and lets it drop to the floor. She pouts her lips and says in a high voice, "You don't belong to anyone, do you?"

CHAPTER THIRTY-SIX

Emily's not sure it's real that the name on her ringing phone is "Ashley." She flips it open frantically, panicked it might disappear. "Ashley? Hey!"

"Oh, Emily," Ashley responds, her voice shaking.

"Ashley. Are you okay?"

"Ryan told me what happened. Oh, my God. I feel so awful." Ashley sniffles. The sound of her friend's voice sends shivers of comfort and consolation through Emily's body.

"No. No," Emily says, absentmindedly stroking Luna harder than she means to, gazing at the orange and pink and purple clouds between the tree branches, the rain no longer falling. "You don't have to feel bad."

"No, I do. I'm a bitch. I'm a crap friend. I thought you two were sleeping together, and Ryan moved up there for you, and you two didn't want to tell me, and I felt annoyed with your dad drama." Ashley's voice cracks. "But, like, your dad? I can't believe that happened."

"No. I'm a crap friend. I relied on you too much and was mad at you because I thought you thought you were too good for me going to college and making new friends." Emily repeats what she wrote in her notebook mere hours ago.

"I just, I wanted things to be about me for a while, you know, focus on me. But I felt terrible all summer about ignoring you."

"It's okay, Ashley," Emily says, smiling now.

"No. It's not. You've been my friend forever."

"We're still friends forever."

"I wish I could give you a hug," says Ashley, her voice higher now, the sniffles louder.

"Me too." Emily laughs through tears, and Ashley laughs too. "I miss you so much."

"I miss *you* so much." And the laughter continues. Emily wipes her tears with the back of her hand.

"You should come visit," says Emily once the laughter and crying subside. "It's so nice. We can go to the beach. You can come to The Schooner and meet my friends. I got this cuddly cat on my lap. Come this weekend. My boss said I can take a day or two off."

"I would, but I'm headed home. The art camp is over on Wednesday, and Mom and I are doing a spa thing and back-to-school shopping. She still thinks I'm twelve. *You* should come."

Emily hesitates.

"Your dad wouldn't have to know you're here," Ashley adds in a hopeful tone. But it feels too soon, too complicated. "Do you want to talk about it?"

MUDDLED CHERRIES

"Umm," Emily considers. "Not yet. I want to hear about your summer. How was the art camp? I bet the kids loved you."

CHAPTER THIRTY-SEVEN

Emily sinks into the cool sand, damp with dew that soothes her sore and aching tailbone. "This is nice," she says as Jacob settles beside her.

"Yeah, feels good," he says. She senses his gaze but avoids his eyes and reaches into the white paper bag for the warm cherry scones, wondering if he's nervous as well. If he noticed the way she side-stepped his question after a stiff embrace outside the coffee shop: "Hey. I'm sorry about what happened. Everything okay?"

"Oh, yeah," she answered quickly, breezily, awkwardly. "So stupid. How are you? I heard the party was fun. The scones smell so good!"

She doesn't want to be pitied, especially by him. She feels exhausted and emptied out on the subject after analyzing and processing it with Nora, Javier, Molly, Ryan, Ashley, and her notebook. She wants to talk about something light and normal and safe, like the weather. It's already humid and seventy-three degrees. She wants to take off the long-sleeve shirt she's wearing to cover the road rash, but she's not ready for him to see.

Why did she agree to meet him so soon after the incident? He's leaving in a few days. That's why. And he texted again while she was on the phone with Ashley, first with concern: "R u ok?" and then with an invitation to go kayaking or hiking the following morning before her shift. She finally answered the texts after napping on the couch with Luna, watching a couple reruns of *Friends,* and smoking a bowl with Nora, Javier, Ryan, and Alicia on the porch, relaxed and relieved, especially because they left the drama of last night alone. They talked about Nora's aversion to bananas, Alicia's lingering childhood fear of *E.T.*, Ryan's fascination with a frog's life cycle, and Javier's closeted ability to juggle. "I wanted to be a magician when I was little," he admitted, coughing after a hit.

"That's so hot," Nora teased, taking the glass pipe from him. Emily laughed. Then she pulled out her phone and asked Jacob if they could get a coffee to go and sit on a beach. It felt like a brave decision to let him in after the hours spent scribbling in that notebook, like he let her in.

And she craved the peace of the water and woods before the first powerboat revved its engine or beachgoers started blasting Jimmy Buffett, before she faced her coworkers and customers. But the clarity and confidence she felt last night has been replaced by a sour mix of embarrassment and vulnerability.

The anchored sailboats bob in the gentle waves. Birdsong echoes over the harbor. Emily removes her sandals and digs her heels in the sand. "This is exfoliating," she says matter-of-factly, picking a cherry from her scone.

"Is that so?" Jacob slides off his flip-flops and works his heels into the grit as well.

"I talked to my old friend yesterday from Deer Valley," says Emily, chewing on the cherry, "and we got to talking about spa treatments, and she met these big city girls in Madison who get facials with like bird poop or even their own pee in them."

"What?" Jacob asks, disbelieving, laughing, nearly spitting out his coffee.

"They're rubbing this shit into their pores," she continues, laughing as well, feeling the tension crack around them. "Or like they let snails crawl across their faces and leeches suck blood out of their cheeks to tighten them up."

"No. That's sick."

"I know. It's true."

Jacob laughs again and shakes his head. "We're in the wrong business, Emily." He gently nudges her knee. "We should open a spa up here. We'll market it as super natural, no chemical treatments. I'll collect the ingredients, and you can handle the spa thing. Done. We'd make bank. I'm talking fat stacks."

Emily laughs. "It doesn't sound right when you say, 'fat stacks,'" she teases back.

"I'm pretty cool now," he says sarcastically. "I'm not that naive, sheltered boy anymore."

"You're *so* cool," Emily plays along. "People in New Zealand are going to be like, 'Wow. Wisconsin must be the coolest place there is.'"

"That's what I'm expecting."

"Did I tell you the other day this sober guy took a shot of ranch dressing to celebrate his engagement? His friends and fiancée were wasted on shots of bitters, and he wanted to join in."

"Gross. No." Jacob shakes his head. "The thought of that makes me want to gag. I should bring a giant bottle of ranch with me. I'll share it with the people I meet and be like, 'This is part of my culture.'" Emily laughs some more. This is what she needed. She removes the lid of her coffee to dip her scone.

The conversation flits easily from one topic to the next—the Johnny Cash covers Jacob's been working on, Emily's curiosity over what she'll dissect in nursing school, and what Jacob won't miss when he flies across the Pacific: scrubbing the pots caked with Tyler's meal of choice—macaroni and cheese with ketchup and cut-up hot dogs; scraping frost off his windshield; watching Brett Favre quarterback for the Minnesota Vikings; and being home for the holidays.

"I'm still strategizing how to handle that," he says. "Family stuff. I feel like I'm living a double life, rebelling over here and reconnecting with Beth and this other life where I talk to my mom and dad on the phone like I'm still the old me and taking a weird detour in life."

"Hmm." Emily ruminates over this admission, considering Beth. She grinds her feet deeper in the sand.

"I also won't miss getting accused of stealing people's sunglasses. Twice," he says, holding up two fingers, moving the conversation on. "Twice that happened to me this summer."

"How could anyone think you'd do that? You're like the nicest guy ever."

"So I've been told. The one guy's pair was on his head."

"Douche." Emily takes a long drink of coffee. Her body breaks out in a hot sweat. She pinches the front of her shirt and pulls it from her skin, back and forth like a quick pulse.

"You can take that off," Jacob offers.

"Oh, no. Just took a big gulp. I should have ordered an iced coffee," she says. He's biting his bottom lip and nodding. "I'm fine. So … you playing this week? Last show?"

He runs a hand through his hair, and she feels herself flushing, her temperature rising once more. She's attracted to him, so handsome and kind. She wants to run *her* hands through his hair.

"Last one. Thursday. You coming?"

"Yeah," she says automatically. But she's pulled back to her conversation with Ashley, the invitation to join her and Diane.

"Good."

"Well, I think so," Emily corrects herself. Subconsciously, she realizes she's been leaning toward joining them, strategizing a whole scenario in which she can see Dad and bid farewell to The Honky Tonk, if he really is selling the place, and retrieve a few of her belongings.

"Think so?"

She wants to smooth away the disappointed look on his face and assure him and herself that she'll be there, but there's a tug she can't ignore. "I'm trying to decide something."

"Go on."

She slumps her shoulders in defeat. It's more fun to flirt, joke about bizarre spa treatments and the brilliance of Johnny Cash and June Carter than acknowledge the white elephant she's trying to hide beneath her sleeves.

"My friend, the one I was talking about earlier, is going back home to see her family, who were like a second family to me, Ryan's family, actually. She invited me to come see her, and Chris said I could take a day or two off. So, I'm thinking about it."

"Would you see your dad?"

"I don't know. I was thinking I would. He's supposedly selling the bar, and I feel like I want one last look at the place and grab this quilt my grandma made me and my winter stuff."

"Yeah, that makes sense. But are you ready? Are you sure?"

Emily's chest tightens, maybe in defense or in fear. Maybe she's not ready, but as she says what she's been thinking out loud, she's feeling surer.

"I journaled all day yesterday, your ex's idea, actually. What I wrote was all over the place, but like my life was maybe weird and messed up, and I'm mad at my dad for a lot of things and then so happy about other things, and I feel like he really dropped the ball when I needed him not to and then blew things up further. But parents have done a lot worse to their kids. And I love my dad," she struggles over those true words. They're like a twisted knot in the heart she can't untangle, "and The Honky Tonk, not everything about them, you know. It's complicated." She exhales. He's listening. His expression simultaneously pulls her toward him and pushes her away. "God, it's hot."

"You can take off that shirt," he says gently.

Pulling up the hem of her shirt, Emily realizes how much she wants to remain unblemished for Jacob. The breeze soothes her damp skin, but her body trembles, twitches, and shivers as she crumples her shirt and drops it to the sand.

He surveys her for a few moments, scans her arms, then scoots closer and takes her hand. "This okay?"

"Yeah," she says, her heart pounding as he interlocks his fingers with hers and brings them to his shaven chin. She loses her breath as he locks eyes with her and brings their hands to his lips. He kisses her pointer finger, then her middle finger, index, and pinkie. Then he kisses the soft, tender edge of her palm flecked with scars, scabs, and bits of gravel too small and deep for her tweezers. She can't believe this is happening. It's so intimate, unexpected, especially from him. Emily can see his chest rising and falling with an anxious breath as well. But he kisses her hand steady and calm, his eyes closed now. She's no longer fighting a reflex to pull away. She's hoping his lips will eventually meet hers.

"Hey guys," a voice interrupts. Tim approaches with two other men she recognizes from Alicia's party. They're wearing tight-fitting Coast Guard t-shirts and rubber waders, carrying fishing poles.

"Hi," Emily says back, letting go of Jacob's hand and giving a small wave.

"Good morning," says Jacob, his tone laced with disappointment.

"Any perch out?" Tim sets his sunglasses on top of his head and squints at Emily as he comes closer. "Holy shit. It's true."

"What?" Emily wonders if he's referring to her and Jacob. If their chemistry was so obvious to everyone else as well. For a moment, she's pleased.

"You almost got run over? For throwing a punch at some guy or something." He seems baffled, and the two behind him seem amused.

The bald one cocks his head with a grin while the other snaps his fingers, then bows to her. "That was you?"

She looks down at her arms riddled with wounds and swallows the urge to vomit. She feels she's been yanked from a dream, one she's not meant to be living.

"Hey, guys. Shut up," Jacob says, but too softly.

The bald one talks over him, "Last time I saw you, you were getting into it with that guy we tossed out of the party." Emily reaches for her shirt, knocking over her open cup of coffee. She wants to disappear, and her body scrambles to make that happen.

"That guy *was* a creep," confirms Tim. "Alicia's still freaked out by him. I think."

"As she should be," says Jacob, like he's trying to get a word in.

"Well, you're a legend," says the bald guy.

"Thanks," she says as lightly as she can.

"So did you land your punch?"

"I gotta go to work." Emily feigns disappointment, pulling on her sandals and moving toward her truck, gripping the keys in her pocket, abandoning the spilled coffee and half-eaten scone.

"Hey, would you tell Alicia 'Hi' for me?" asks Tim.

"Sure." She wraps her arms around her chest, aware of Jacob picking up the trash she left behind.

"Emily," he calls. She winces as she turns. Her body longs to escape. Her brain tells her the reasons why: *You cause trouble wherever you go. He's leaving. He's too nice, naïve. It's too soon after Simon. It's too much before nursing school. He's getting too close, and you like him too much. He'll abandon you too.*

"I'm sorry. They're idiots. You don't have to go."

"No. Seriously. I gotta go get ready for work," she tries to reassure him, her body in motion. The moment has passed. This isn't meant to be.

"Can we hang out later?"

Emily opens her truck door and slides in. Her brain flits to Beth.

"You know what your sister wants from you?" she says, gripping the wheel, turning the ignition, not waiting for an answer. "She wants you to defend her. She wants you to choose her and not live a fake life where you try to make everyone comfortable. She wants you to call your parents out."

He runs a hand through his curls, blinking like there's something in his eyes.

"I gotta go," she says again, shutting the truck door.

CHAPTER THIRTY-EIGHT

B y the time Emily clocks in for her shift, she's made up
her mind. She's already texted Ashley: "I'm coming."
She's going home.

"Can you be back for the Friday dinner shift?" asks
Chris, like he's not the one doing her a favor.

"No problem." She pulls on the cuffs of the long-sleeve
shirt she's wearing beneath her polo, aware of the bar
patrons' glances.

"Tell me the truth, Emily," Bob says from his barstool.
"Did you mean to throw that drink in my face?" He
winks and offers a smile. She appreciates his attempt at a
joke to casually rip down the curtain of discomfort and
awkwardness she's trying to navigate through.

"She wouldn't be the only girl to toss one at ya, huh?"
asks Lloyd, the guy next to him, who erupts in a cackling
laugh.

"Can't believe I missed it," says Joe, shaking his head,
truly disappointed it seems.

Then the row of men swaps tales of locals and tourists driving off docks under the influence, knocking down rows of mailboxes, plowing through a herd of cattle. Emily wonders if this is meant to make her feel better or if they're lost down that winding road of barroom conversation.

"Dennis Nelson took out the nativity scene in front of the First Baptist years back," someone says when Ingrid comes beside Emily and rubs a hand between her shoulder blades.

"You okay, sweetie?" she asks.

"I'm okay. Thank you." Emily wishes she could write it on her forehead and get on with the shift. But the questions and comments and advice keep coming—while she pulls food from beneath the heat lamp, ladles ranch dressing, stocks straws and napkins, while she punches in her orders, and fills cups with RC and Squirt. Brandon recommends Sylvia Plath. Maria tells her to pray the rosary. Colin lists Shakespeare plays with dysfunctional families. "*The Taming of the Shrew*, *Romeo and Juliet*, *King Lear*. Dads getting pissed when their daughters won't do what they want. Timeless," he says. Chang wonders if she's heard of qigong. Iona suggests rubbing honey and garlic on Emily's wounds to help them heal faster.

She wishes there was some home remedy to soothe the ache radiating from the depths of her skull, fighting to hang on to the conviction that returning to The Honky Tonk and facing Dad is the right thing to do. Her heart hurts too with a stinging disappointment over the realization that she won't see Jacob before he departs, and though she could reach out after her shift, it doesn't feel meant to be, marred by what Dad did, the awkward interruption of whatever was happening on the beach. Was he going to kiss her for *her*, or was it an act of pity? He said he wanted to save Cecelia. Is she the next best thing?

But he's leaving. There's no point in adding more drama and heartache to her life. Just run away.

"We were so close," she whispers to herself in the pantry, "and he's so sweet."

"How you doing, kid?" asks Terry, wiping down the prep table.

"I'm okay." Emily scans the shelves for a tub of horseradish, feeling her phone vibrate in her back pocket while he tells of an uncle who drank it all away, his money, relationships, health.

"His kids wanted nothing to do with him there at the end," Terry says when Emily finally spots the container and pulls it from the shelf. She turns to Terry, waiting to hear what finally did the uncle in: liver failure, car accident, suicide. She's not naïve. She grew up in a bar.

"That's sad," she says when he finally tells her, meaning it but wishing he hadn't told her any such story. What was the point? Everyone knows someone who fucked it all up. She wonders if she and Dad will one day be an anecdote someone tells to illustrate the dangers of drinking.

"Yeah. My grandma said, 'Drink when you're happy, not when you're sad.'"

374

"That's good advice." Emily forces a smile. If only it were that simple, that easy.

Ryan isn't convinced a visit to Deer Valley is the best idea until Emily reads her latest text from Ashley: "Yay! So excited 2 squeeze the shit out of u. Not literally. Gross," and he remembers he has stuff he'd like brought back as well.

"If I give my mom a list, would you—" he begins.

"No," she answers sarcastically. And he laughs.

Nora's less willing to bestow her blessing along with Alicia and Molly. They tell her so while rolling silverware.

"I'll be staying with my friend. I need some of my stuff. Just like Bridget," she says, changing the subject. "Tell us how that went, Molly."

Molly sets down the silverware and adjusts the bobby pin in her hair. "She didn't need me while she told them. I stayed outside playing with these puppies for like an hour. She didn't say much when I drove her to campus. I knew she was processing. Then she'd randomly blurt out something. She said her dad shook his head a lot and said, 'This is the last thing I need.'"

Nora winces and Alicia bites her nails as if in suspense. Emily is in awe of Bridget's bravery.

"Her mom was worried about what grandparents and church friends would think. Then she told Bridget it was a phase. Her dad blamed it on her spending too much time in girls' locker rooms. And then it ended with him asking where her first cross-country meet was. So, I guess they talked about that, and that was it."

"Huh," says Alicia. "They listened at least. I'm sure it's a lot to take in."

"Sounds like it could be a happy ending," says Emily with a high, hopeful tone, but everyone's expression suggests they aren't sure. "Right?" she asks, trying to elicit some kind of decipherable response.

"Maybe they'll accept it, and all will be well," says Nora, tugging on her earring while meeting Emily's eyes, "or this will be a lifelong struggle. Who knows?"

They drink their cocktails and resume their rolling. Emily focuses on the silver fork and knife, pressing them together, rolling them tight in the paper napkin, wishing this parent-child stuff could be easy. She's wondering what version of Dad she'll deal with in a day or two. He responded with "Free country," when she asked for permission to stop in and pick up some belongings.

"Are you excited you and Ryan get the room all to yourself while Emily's away?" Alicia asks Molly with a smirk. Emily's shoulders relax as she laughs.

Molly's cheeks brighten with color. "No," she says with a wide, shy smile.

And Emily remembers. "Oh, Alicia. Tim says, 'Hi.'"

"Na-uh?" asks Alicia, clearly intrigued. "Really?"

"Yeah. I saw him at the beach this morning, going fishing with these super sexy waders on."

"Like, how did he say it?" asks Alicia. "In a casual afterthought way or a pleading kind of way?"

"Pleading." Emily smiles. "Definitely."

MUDDLED CHERRIES

"Oh, God. Mr. I-Can't-Talk-To-You-Anymore-Because-It-Hurts-Too-Much," Alicia says, exasperated, dropping a handful of rolled silverware into the bin for emphasis. "What a wimp."

CHAPTER THIRTY-NINE

One of Emily's vertebras pops into place when she and Ashley embrace outside the Carr home. There's such familiarity in the hug—a quick, tight compression followed by a gentle hand-rub up and down Emily's back. But Ashley smells different, maybe a new shampoo or perfume, and when they part, Emily notices Ashley's cheekbones seem more defined, or maybe it's the spiral silver earrings she's wearing that makes the shape of her face different. She looks like an adult. Emily wonders if she appears changed as well.

"Thank you for coming," says Ashley with a smile so wide and genuine, lit up by the late morning sunshine.

"Thank you for having me," Emily responds over the sound of clicking cicadas and screeching blue jays, realizing the air around Deer Valley is heavier and thicker than Door County's. "I feel better seeing you." And she does, though her limbs and tailbone ache from the hours spent in the truck, where she sucked the salt off countless sunflower seeds and listened to the Lady Antebellum CD she never returned to the library on repeat. She felt a sense of dread and longing at the thought of returning to The Honky Tonk and seeing Dad, combined with a giddiness and trepidation over reuniting with Ashley, peppered with something like relief and regret over leaving without saying goodbye to Jacob.

"That was weird yesterday," he texted as she passed the county sign. "Sorry. Try again be4 I go?"

She's hoping Ashley will help her compose a response and clear her head of this infatuation. It's a distraction. He's leaving. She needs to sort things out with Dad. She needs to focus on school, money, herself.

Emily spots Diane occasionally peering through the front door window as she and Ashley put the past behind them in a hurried, apologetic exchange interspersed with more hugs and a few tears. "No, I'm sorry," they keep interrupting each other until finally they enter the house, and Diane pulls Emily into a hug.

"It's so nice to have you," she says in a singsong, swaying from side to side, her soft cheek pressed against Emily's.

"So nice to be here," Emily says in a singsong as well, feeling the chill of the AC wrap around her bare legs, noticing the spread of snacks arranged on the kitchen counter—puppy chow dusted with powdered sugar, shiny red grapes plucked from their vines, slices of cheddar cheese neatly lined up along Ritz crackers.

"You didn't have to do all this, Diane," says Emily, relieved it's cool enough to keep her long-sleeve shirt on.

"No. I love it. It's so nostalgic for me to have my two girls here." Diane hands out small plates with faded blue forget-me-nots dotting the rim. Emily's heart expands at the word *my*.

"These snacks make me feel like I'm in kindergarten," Ashley jokes, popping a grape in her mouth. "Just need a little milk carton."

"Ugh, I don't miss those. How they got all soggy around the mouth bit," says Emily.

"'Bit.' I can tell you were hanging out with a British boy," teases Ashley, and Emily gives her a playful shove.

The comment seems lost on Diane. She bites into a slice of cheddar with a wistful expression. "Sometimes I wish I could have one more day when you girls were little," she says.

Emily fills her plate like she has on so many occasions in this house—between playing Barbies or My Little Ponies, jumping on the trampoline or running through the sprinklers, taking the quizzes in Ashley's *Seventeen* magazines or dancing to the Backstreet Boys, watching *The O.C.* or sitting somewhere in the house or backyard—talking and gossiping and planning her future with Ashley.

Emily combs through her memories. "Huh, I'm trying to remember the first time I came over."

"You were reserved when your dad dropped you off," says Diane.

"You remember?" asks Ashley.

"I do," Diane says with a sly smile. "I'll never forget it because once you two got over the initial shyness and started playing, you were giggling nonstop. Having the best time. The sweetest sound ever. I remember saying to John, 'I can't imagine laughing that much. I think I'd be sick.'"

"What were we always giggling about?" asks Emily, remembering she once thought they were so funny together that they could star on that Nickelodeon show *All That*.

"Everything was funny to you girls," Diane says, moving toward the refrigerator. "What do you want to drink, Emily?"

"Sprite?" Emily asks, but she wants to get back to memory lane. "What else do you remember about that first visit?"

"Umm." Diane slides the can across the counter. "You had this Bud Light duffle bag. And I remember giving your dad crap—" she stops herself, eyes wide and focusing on Ashley like she's been caught in a lie. Emily turns to see Ashley swiping a flat hand beneath her chin, a cut-it-out gesture.

"Oh, I'm sorry," Diane says quickly, scratching her head. "Umm, you two were—"

"No. It's okay, you guys." Embarrassment travels down to Emily's toes, the memory tainted by Dad, by what he did. A pain and itchiness radiate from her injuries. But it's not possible or plausible to remove him from her past. "You can mention him. He's not Voldemort." And she doesn't want him eliminated or erased, she realizes.

"He's not my favorite person right now," says Ashley.

"Mine either," says Diane.

"It's fine," says Emily. "It will be fine."

But Diane shakes her head. "When Ashley told me what he did, I was fuming. I was about to drive right down to that bar and say, 'What is the matter with you, Ron Schmidt? Get it together.'"

Emily wonders what stopped her—work, other plans, too worried about what the local gossips might think if she did something like that, too scared, too nice. Emily's disappointed, but that's not Diane's job. She's not her mother.

"I appreciate that," says Emily. "Ryan had some choice words as well. I'm lucky to have you guys." Ashley rubs Emily's back once more, and the silence overwhelms her. She wishes a radio or TV was on, something to derail the trajectory of the conversation.

"Did Ryan send you a list?" Emily asks briskly.

"Mom's already packed it all up," says Ashley.

"We're lucky to have *you*," says Diane, backstepping. "You know what? I think you and that place saved Ryan from himself."

"Oh, gosh. I don't know about that." Emily worries about what Ashley might be thinking or feeling at the remark. "Did he tell you about Molly, the girl he's been kind of seeing?" Emily tries to reinforce the fact that nothing happened or is happening between her and Ryan.

"He doesn't tell me much, you know. He's too cool for school," says Diane. "But reading between the lines, I'd say he's rather smitten."

"Sounds like you found some awesome friends up there," says Ashley. "I'm excited to come visit." Relief washes over Emily.

"Does your mom know about the guy you've been hanging out with?" Emily asks, adjusting the focus to Ashley.

"Oh, I know about Mr. Renaissance," says Diane, eyebrows arched in delight. She winks at Emily.

"What?" Emily asks, laughing.

"Okay, okay. Can you leave now, Mom?" Ashley teases, giggling, turning red.

"Oh, jeez." Diane rises from her stool.

"Wait. No. What? Mr. Renaissance? You just told me his name was Dan, and he liked French-press coffee and Wes Anderson movies," Emily says, recalling other details she won't share in front of Diane: he stutters when he's nervous, tries to sell his hemp jewelry on Madison's street corners, and likes to kiss Ashley's ankles and work his way up.

Ashley giggles then settles into a shy smile before admitting, "So, he loves Renaissance fairs. Like, has a costume and everything." She covers her face with her hands. "He's not employed by the fair. He just loves 'em."

Emily suppresses the urge to make fun. She doesn't want to stifle Ashley's excitement. "I love that," she says.

Ashley uncovers her face and continues while Diane looks on approvingly.

"So, he took me to the one in Madison and was so into it, and it was contagious, like, I was seeing the awesomeness in it. We watched this blacksmith guy forever, and I was like, 'This is an incredible art.' And there's music and food. It was fun."

"And Ashley called after and was the most enamored and happy I've ever heard her about a boy," says Diane.

"Mom!" Ashley admonishes, covering her face once again. "He's probably not like 'The One,' so I don't know. It's stupid. It's probably a waste of time."

"That's okay." Emily shrugs her shoulders. "A good waste of time."

"Don't overthink it, Ashley," Diane interjects. "Honey, you always do that. You self-sabotage."

"Mom. Okay, can you seriously leave us alone now?" Ashley grits her teeth.

"Fine. Okay. I'm out." She gives Emily another wink. "But before I go, let me say one more thing." She doesn't wait for permission. "Please enjoy your singlehood and dating, girls. Is he kind? Do you like being with him?" she asks rhetorically. "That's all you need to know right now. Let it happen, or not happen, you know."

"That's super wise, Mom," says Ashley sarcastically, impatiently. But Emily's turning the words over in her head when Diane excuses herself. "Pedicures in an hour," she says on her way out.

"It's not a waste," Emily says. "I think your mom's right." She thinks of Todd, then Simon, Jacob.

"Yeah, probably." Ashley bites her lip. "Anyway, are you ready to see your dad?"

Emily picks a grape from the pile and rolls it between two fingers. "Yeah," she lies, pressing down until it splits. The gooey pulp and dark seeds spill out. "It'll be fine."

While practicing various speeches and thinking through possible scenarios of how the encounter with Dad might play out, she's tempered her hopes for a heartfelt understanding, even after the note and check he left behind. He might get angry, emotional, mean. He might be drunk and erratic. He might act indifferent. So, she set herself goals while tossing and turning in her bunk last night, driving down Interstate 29: retrieve a few belongings, say goodbye to The Honky Tonk, and ask Dad about his plans, money, drinking, in that order, because she's wondering how far they'll make it through a conversation before it spirals into blame and bullshit. But she doesn't want to explain all that now.

"I don't know what to say to this guy I kind of like," she says instead.

"What guy?" Ashley reaches for a handful of puppy chow.

"This Jacob guy."

After Emily's shared the details of their first meeting at The Honky Tonk, his kindness, their chemistry, Cecelia and Simon, the laughter and conversation, the music and kayaking, the almost-kiss at the beach, his last text, she and Ashley compose a text together.

"Ran home be4 bar sells. Sorry we couldn't meet up. Have fun in NZ. Hope u come back next summer. I'll miss u."

CHAPTER FORTY

s Emily drives toward The Honky Tonk, she envisions Dad hunched over the bar, alone in the shadows, nursing a bourbon with a full ashtray of smoldering cigarettes close by. He's defeated and worn. He only rises from the barstool to repeat the saddest songs on the juke-box, Patsy Cline and Hank Williams, or take a piss, until it's time to flip the "Open" sign at 11:30 a.m.

The roof of The Honky Tonk appears as Emily turns down the cracked county road and maneuvers around potholes while her stomach floats to her chest. Maybe she should have forced some Cheerios down.

It looks the same—barren with a flowerless lawn, flaking paint, and neon signs cluttering the dusty windows. For a moment, it's any other day in her life—after school, after basketball practice, a night at Ashley's, a night at Todd's—driving toward the bar, her home.

Two vehicles she doesn't recognize are parked alongside Dad's truck: a white sedan and a gray SUV dotted with bumper stickers: "Mountains, Please," "Coexist," and "Baby on Board." Her anxiousness calms into curiosity. She cuts the engine and grabs her phone from her purse, noticing no text from Jacob. Now it's her turn to be ignored, she decides. Serves her right. She cringes, recalling what she wrote: "I'll miss u."

"That's so lame," she protested when Ashley insisted she include that last line.

"No. It's true, isn't it? Come on. Who cares? It's sweet."

But now it feels like an overreach, too much, too vulnerable, too real, maybe a little too confusing and unfair. Or maybe she's overthinking it, like Diane warned against.

Emily slips out of the truck and shoves the phone in her back pocket. Laughter and conversation filter through the screen door over the sounds of Faron Young's hard, bouncy voice. She recognizes the song before she starts walking, "Live Fast, Love Hard, Die Young." It's one of Dad's favorites.

"Equipment's top-notch, clean. We kept good care of it. And I wouldn't replace that fryer if I were you. No, sir." She makes out Dad's voice as she steps closer. "It's been seasoned, put in its time, if you know what I mean. The flavor's perfect." He's talking the place up.

"Like my grandma and grandpa's old place. That fryer flavor was legendary," she hears a young woman's light and pleasant voice.

"I think it's the curds that do it. Those cheese juices or something," Dad says, and everyone inside laughs—Dad, the light, pleasant voice, along with a deep, rolling one, and a polite, practiced chuckle Emily recognizes from using one so often herself.

"Hello?" she says as a way of greeting and interruption when she finally enters. Dad leans against the jukebox in a tucked-in black Honky Tonk t-shirt. He's a stark contrast to the dad she left in the pickup a few days ago, the dad she threw a drink at, the dad who nearly ran her over. He's holding a mug of coffee, as is the tall man beside him, wearing the tightest jeans Emily's ever seen on a grown man and a trucker hat so white and clean it distracts her for a moment from the fleshy, freckled woman with a baby wrapped to her chest in a length of cloth. The woman bobs with the beat of the waltzy tune, her flouncy olive-colored dress swaying on the floor.

"Hi," Emily says brightly.

"Who's this?" asks a slight man with thinning hair. He's holding an armful of folders and wearing a maroon sports coat.

"My daughter, Emily," Dad says. He clears his throat like saying her name plugged it up somehow.

"Hi," she says, unable to read Dad's emotions as he introduces Allen Halverson, a realtor, and Grant and Amanda Reimer, who are a few signatures away from owning the place. The couple talks over each other to tell Emily their plans: turn it into a brewery, add a playground and tire swing, picnic tables, plant trees and a garden they can utilize along with local farmers they'll get to know to bring fresh, real food with a Wisconsin twist to customers.

"Like German-type stuff," says Grant. "Brats and pretzels but like with gourmet coleslaw and stuff."

They want to host live music, inside and outside, open mic nights, craft fairs, and yoga once a week.

"Wow," says Emily, looking around the place, wondering where all this newness will go. "That sounds really cool." She means it. She's enraptured and energized by the plans, but defensiveness grips her around the shoulders. What will Larry and Doug think? The baseball leagues? Is it not good enough the way it is?

No, she answers her own silent question. *It's not.*

"And this is Suzie," Amanda says, rubbing the downy hair of the baby's head. It looks like dandelion fuzz, like it could blow away. "So, I guess she'd grow up here. Like you."

"Well, that sounds pretty neat," says Allen, like he's trying to get the conversation where it was before Emily walked in. "How do you like that?"

"Hey, Suzie," Emily says, coming closer to the bulge wrapped tight, safe, and cozy against her mother.

"Emily's moved to Door County, that thumb part of the state, you know," says Dad. "She's gonna be a nurse." Emily turns from the baby to him when she wonders if it's pride, acceptance she hears in his voice, or if he's playacting the doting father and wants her to act along.

"Door County. Oh, yeah. Real nice," says Allen quickly, still trying to move the conversation along, it seems. "My wife and I have been. Real pretty sunsets."

"We've never been," says Amanda, looking to Grant. He scratches his meager beard. "We're both from Minnesota."

"And we usually go to Colorado when we can get away," adds Grant.

"He's got a hard-on for the Rocky Mountains." Amanda rolls her eyes. Emily laughs at the remark, deciding Amanda will make a good bartender. The locals will take to her. But the young couple seems too easygoing, naïve. Do they know what they're getting into with this place?

"Mandy. Jeez. Let's be grown-ups, babe," Grant says, shaking his head with a grin.

"Well, you do." Suzie lets out a weak cry. Amanda pats her baby's rump softly. "Shh, shh, shh," she blows between her teeth.

"Me and Emily here have the Smoky Mountains on our bucket list," Dad adds, meeting Emily's eyes timidly. He didn't forget.

"Oh yeah. I've been," says Grant. "You gotta go in the fall. And get some sweet tea, barbeque, moonshine."

"Well, that sounds peachy," says Allen, setting a folder on one of the dining tables and flipping it open. "So, the inspection went well."

Emily excuses herself, pulls a black garbage bag from the cupboard beneath the register, and sneaks upstairs to complete the first item on her to-do list while Dad's occupied, while they're talking about offers and terms and the antique appraiser who will create an itemized list of the memorabilia's worth.

"Then you can decide what stays and what goes," she hears Allen say as she steps into her bedroom.

It's all the same—the faux-wood walls, teal dresser, sheer yellow curtains stained from rainwater. But she's not the same, she realizes, taking in the patchwork quilt spread over the twin mattress, the framed photo of her and Ashley at senior prom on her nightstand, the scraps of the horse calendar she tore to bits after Todd broke it off with her littering the floor.

This place was meant to be a part of her life forever, she thinks, a wellspring of emotions rising from her gut. She sniffles, fingering the thick stitches on the quilt, realizing she's not who she was when her grandmother gifted it to her; when she took that photo with Ashley, tipsy on Arbor Mist and Goldschläger; when Todd handed her the calendar and it felt like some kind of validation, some great prize and promise.

An innocence has been lost, a carefreeness, along with an ignorance and sense of powerlessness she's begun to recognize.

She removes the phone from her pocket, sets it on the nightstand, and sits on the edge of the bed. She faces the deadbolt on the door. She wants to cry, remembering why it's there and how contaminated and unsafe the space felt after Phil did what he did.

But the creak of the stairs stops her tears.

"Hey, is it okay if I nurse her up here?" asks Amanda, breathless from the climb, unwinding the length of cloth to release the squirming body practically fused to her.

"Oh, yeah. Sure." Emily rises from the bed.

"No. Sit. Hang out with me." Amanda tugs down a strap of her dress, revealing a full, round breast and dark red nipple, the color of dried blood. "You don't mind, right?"

"Not at all." Emily sits beside Amanda. Suzie's little pink mouth roots out her mother with a cry and whine before she latches on. The baby closes her eyes and feeds, content.

"Good. Because as much as I'd love to do it in front of old Allen there, I had a feeling you'd be better company." Amanda snakes a finger through Suzie's petite fist, who grips tight in response. "It can get long and boring, you know. Doing this every frickin' four hours."

"I can't imagine." Emily winces. "That's a lot."

"Yeah, but, like, as much as it drives me crazy sometimes, I miss her when I'm not with her." Amanda looks down on her daughter. "Yes, I do," she says in a high, pouty voice. "I miss you, you stinker."

Emily thinks of her mother then, talking to her in baby talk, offering her finger for Emily to hold like her life depended on it, missing her. She can hardly imagine, not anymore anyway. But she catches herself wanting desperately to believe they shared something similar.

Amanda hums and Emily feels a surge of sympathy and empathy for this woman who can't be much older than herself, maybe five or six years.

"What made you want to buy this place?" Emily pulls on the hem of her denim shorts, aware of the scars they hide. She's searching for an opportunity to warn Amanda that this place is likely cursed.

"So, I grew up in my grandparents' diner." Amanda's eyes meet Emily's—warm and sharp, the golden brown of whiskey. Amanda remembers pouring countless cups of coffee to people who became like family, who watched her grow, celebrated with her, and grieved with her. "It was like a homey, welcoming place. I loved it. They loved it. Grandma made *the* best pies in the whole world."

Emily relates in many ways but says, "Coffee is a lot different than liquor, you know, like what it does to people."

"Yeah. Grant's a bartender. That's how I met him. He's so good at it. But, he's got some stories."

"I bet."

"After college we got married, and I started working for this accounting firm, but I hated it. I hate it. Then Suzie here comes along, and I was like, 'I can't go back there. It's too much.' I felt stifled and claustrophobic, probably some post-partum shit. I wanted to be back in the country, have space, and something we could do together as a family. I feel like we're always chasing something or looking to the future like, 'It will be better at such and such time,' and I was like, 'I don't want to work all day, and then you work all night, and we're working toward what? Let's bring the good stuff to us, you know. Create a place people gather.'"

Emily nods, taking this in.

"Do you think we're crazy to take this place on?" Amanda bites her lower lip, a vulnerable expression on her face.

"No," Emily says immediately, caught in Amanda's dream and expectations, before remembering herself and backtracking. "Well. I mean, I don't want to lie to you. It's not been doing the best."

"Yeah. Your dad told us."

"He did?"

"We came here a month or so ago to get out of the house, take a drive. I was going crazy. We found this place and were like falling in love with it and your dad's behind the bar going on and on about how awful it is, how bad it's doing." Amanda lets out a chuckle. "The recession, Obama," she begins to list.

"His daughter left him," Emily adds on.

Amanda cringes and nods. "Something like that."

Emily laughs and raises a hand. "That would be me."

"As you should. 'Cause you're a grown-up."

"Yeah." Emily nods. But she doesn't want to talk about Dad and her. She wants Amanda to know what might be coming—drunken brawls and creepy men, maybe a divorce, bankruptcy, a daughter who resents them both. "So, you asked to buy it?"

"Kind of, yeah," Amanda remembers. "Grant and a few of his buddies have been scheming to open a brewery for ages, and this is so what I dreamed of. It feels like I gotta give it a shot. And, if it falls apart, I'll go back to accounting."

"That's awesome." Emily scans her room, imagining the space becoming Suzie's, then spots the deadbolt. She isn't satisfied. She needs Amanda to understand. "But are you sure? Like, is it safe enough for a daughter?"

"What do you mean?"

Emily points to the lock with a shaking finger. "That's to keep drunk men out." A silence falls over the women. Amanda shakes her head, and Emily wonders if she's derailed everything—the deal, the dream. *Dad will be so upset*, she thinks.

"Sick," Amanda finally says, letting the 'ck' crack hard in her mouth.

"I thought you should know. It was just this one guy," Emily explains, her insides roiling as she remembers. "This real religious guy. He said the devil made him do it."

"Oh, yeah. The devil," Amanda says sarcastically. "Like this is frickin' Narnia or Middle Earth. Bullshit."

And Emily latches on to the anger seething from Amanda. Her sternum heaves as she recalls the incident, the fear and shame and nightmares, the emails. "Why do men do shit like that?" she asks. "Why do they have to ruin everything, you know?"

"Power? Entitlement?" Amanda huffs. "You know, when Suzie was born, I realized I was like devastated to have a girl because I'm so sad and scared for everything she's gonna have to face and go through in life *because* she's a girl. And how can I protect her from all of that everything?"

"All that everything," Emily starts, speaking the thoughts as they come to her. "I'm realizing what I was taught to believe and accept as not being a big deal, or being partially my fault, like I asked for it somehow, are big deals, and they aren't my fault, you know."

Amanda nods. "Yeah, I know." And even without offering specifics, Emily understands Amanda experienced some shit too. Maybe every woman has. "What's his name?"

"Phil Karlsen," Emily says, her sternum relaxing as the name leaves her lips.

"Phil Karlsen," Amanda repeats. "Snake. I bet he's got a tiny dick too. Well, he's not ever coming in here again, that's for sure."

Emily lets out a laugh. "So, you're gonna stay?"

"Heck, yeah." Amanda looks down on Suzie. "We're not gonna live in fear."

Emily smiles, feeling the air soften, the light brighten, feeling pleased this will be one of her last memories in the room.

...

Emily lugs the heavy bulging garbage bag filled with clothes, the quilt, her winter boots and coat down the stairs. She feels dizzy and lightheaded from all the emotions, the events of the last few days, and hunger. She craves a grilled cheese sandwich with a side of salty fries and a couple maraschino cherries. But there's another conversation yet to have. And she wonders where it will go or if it's worth having when she notices Dad behind the bar, pouring Maker's Mark in a glass.

"So, the prodigal daughter returns." He rubs his shaven jaw. "I only got a minute. I gotta get to the bank before opening here."

"Okay." Emily feels small, unsure. "I thought you'd want to talk, maybe."

"I got a few minutes. Say what you got to say." He looks up and around at the wall, the blank TVs, and rows of liquor bottles. Any direction but Emily's. She searches her brain, running over the litany of topics she meant to cover, her palms sweating, stomach growling. He cuts the silence. "I guess there's not much point in opening. It's all over." His eyes meet Emily's for a moment, like he's gauging her. Does he want her to feel sorry for him? "Just get rid of as much food and booze as I can and call it a night."

She doesn't respond. He's given her nothing to respond to. No greeting. No questions. No apologies. No concern. She drags the bag toward the door, biting her tongue, her lip, anything to hold in the hurt and anger at the edge of her throat, about to burst through.

"What do you want me to do with the rest of your stuff?" He eases onto a barstool. The mask he wore for Allen, Grant, and Amanda dropped. *There's the defeated man*, Emily thinks, yanking the bag through the door frame.

"Burn it!" she yells over her shoulder. The fresh air does nothing but fuel her rage.

"Whiney drunken bastard," she says between her teeth as she heaves her belongings into the bed of the truck. She's tempted to forget the whole thing, drive back to Ashley's, then Door County, and be done—return to the safety of the cabin, to Nora and Luna, Javier and Ryan, The Schooner, nursing school, and the promise of another summer with Bridget and Molly and Alicia.

SALLY COLLINS

What's the point? She kicks the gravel and takes a slow spin around as she considers her next move.

She realizes she has left her phone inside.

She realizes she did not come all this way to cower and turn around with her tail between her legs.

She realizes Dad is still her dad, and dammit, there's this primal urge to stay in his life.

She thinks of her friends, the conversations, advice, validation, empathy, and love. And like they're some kind of gods or angels or saints, she closes her eyes and prays for guidance, asking whatever is up there or out there to let her draw from the same well of strength Nora drank from when she left her husband, when Bridget came out to her parents. And somewhere inside, she pulls threads of peace and focus, determination and self-righteous anger, weaves them tight together, and wraps them around her like armor. There's not much more he can do or say to hurt her now.

She marches back inside, letting the screen door slam. Dad starts at the clap of wood on wood.

"What the hell?" he mumbles. "You know better."

She proceeds silently behind the bar, grips the tumbler in Dad's hand, pulls it away, and as calmly as her body allows, tosses the ice and liquid into the sink. It splatters and clangs against the silver basin flecked with rust.

"You got to be kidding me," he says, shaking his head with an incredulous grin. "You're turning into your grandma."

398

"No." She shakes her head as well. "No. I'm not doing this with you while you're drinking. What the hell, Dad?"

"Jesus. In my own house. At least you didn't throw it in my face," he says like he's trying to make a joke. "Honky Tonk days are over. What more do you want from me?"

"How about a 'Nice to see you, Emily. Thank you for coming, Emily. Sorry I caused a humiliating scene in front of your friends and almost ran you over, Emily.'" She glares at him, but he avoids her eyes, running his palm flat against the bar like he's stroking it. "What happened to the guy who was just in here with those people—all nice and polite?"

He shrugs, reaches for a bar rag, and begins winding it around itself.

"It's like you don't know how to talk to me without being a jerk, well, no, like an asshole. Always acting like some poor, pitiful victim."

She wipes spit that gathered in the corners of her mouth.

"I'm a bad guy." He blinks rapidly, agitated, cornered. "I'm a bad guy, huh? Can't do anything right. I hurt everybody."

"Oh, God," she interrupts him. "I wouldn't have come back here if that was true, would I?"

He studies the back of his hand, creased with wrinkles.

"I feel awful about what happened. You know that, right?"

"What part? The part where you took all my money?" She feels lit on fire. "Or was it when you made me sit and listen to Phil's dumb excuses with a Bible in his hand so I'd shut my mouth, and he could keep spending money? Or when you nearly murdered me?"

She could go on but decides to stop there, wait, fold her arms, and stare him down. Let him sweat it out. He continues studying his hand, then the walls with posters of faded men in cowboy hats, the PBR clock. His eyebrows furrow and twitch. She wonders if he might cry.

"Why didn't you tell me what Phil really did?" he finally asks.

Emily wrings her hands. "I guess I didn't want to say it out loud. I guess I thought telling you I was scared would be enough," she explains. "But you kind of laughed it off and said, 'Hazard of the trade.'" He grimaces. "I didn't even want to admit to myself what really happened, so I don't know. I was ashamed."

"I'd have killed him if I'd known." Dad makes a fist and clenches his teeth.

"Well, I didn't need you to kill him. I needed you to care and believe me and listen when I said I didn't want him back in here."

"What can I say? Sorry." He shrugs his shoulders. "All I could think about then was keeping this place afloat. And, my brain didn't go there, you know. I thought it was a misunderstanding."

And there are too many misunderstandings, Emily decides, too many silences.

"Why didn't you tell me how bad the bar was doing?" she asks, moving the conversation along. "That you were taking my money?"

He studies his fingernails and bites one, then another. "Thought I could get us out of this mess." Tears pool then skim down his cheeks. He wipes them as fast as they fall. "I needed you to hang on a little longer, Emily."

"I couldn't anymore, Dad. I'm almost twenty-one. I gotta live my own life too."

"It was always me and you, you and me. Even when you were with the Carrs, basketball, your boyfriends. I knew you were in my corner."

"I still am. I don't want to give up on us, Dad. I'm not Mom." Warm tears slide down Emily's cheeks. Dad's chin quivers. He buries his face in the bar rag, sniffling, shuddering.

"I know I hurt you," he says. The words muffled in the worn, tattered cloth. She circles around the bar and sits beside him, rests a hand between his shoulder blades. She lets him cry. "I'm such a fuck-up," he says into the rag. "Fuck-up. I fucked up. I'm a fuck-up."

"What's the plan then ... to un-fuck it up?"

He releases the rag, his face red and wet and questioning.

"What are you gonna do?" she asks. "I want to hear."

"Pay you back?"

"What else?"

"Help Grant and Amanda figure out the place."

"I like them."

"They remind me of me when I bought this heap." He straightens up, gazing around the space with a slight smile.

"What else?"

"Help my brother with harvest this year. Take the motorcycle out with Larry. Go fishing with Doug. Maybe get our trip on the calendar?"

"What else?" She's not satisfied. And she's not sure she ever will be with him.

"Is there something you're trying to get at, Emily?"

"Maybe check in with me and be happy for me and ask me about me and my life and friends and boyfriends." This might be too big of an ask. She doesn't trust him. She's uncertain, teetering on unhopeful. There's too much shit. But it's what she wants, and it feels good to say out loud.

"So, you're gonna be a nurse, huh?" he asks. He's trying.

She's not ready to plan that vacation or invite him to Door County. She's not sure she's ready to forgive. But it's a start.

CHAPTER FORTY-ONE

Emily picks at the greasy grilled cheese in the empty, quiet bar. She takes in the place between sips of a kiddie cocktail. The meal comforts and satisfies her, though she's anxious about encountering a regular, regretting her promise to stay until Dad returns, flip the open sign, serve Larry or Doug, the farmer next door who craves a fried fish sandwich now and then, whoever might find their way to the bar. She's not sure if they'll be happy to see her, if they'll blame her for leaving Dad, or the end of The Honky Tonk.

"Don't hold your breath," Dad said, tapping his pockets, checking for his wallet, keys, and phone. "There's a good chance no one will show."

She felt closer to him after their conversation, like a layer of grime between them was scraped away. But more layers remain.

They talked about nursing school. Emily attempted to

sum up her new friends and a summer of music, mini-golf, swimming, and sailing as concisely as she could, walking a fine line between not wanting to hurt Dad's feelings and wanting him to know her more fully. The conversation felt strange, awkward at times, like they were auditioning for a play called *An Adult Relationship*.

"And a little romance," she admitted. "This British guy."

"Well, there you go." Dad cracked a smile. He seemed naked without a glass of something in hand. "Nothing wrong with that."

They exchanged a brief hug before Dad picked up a pile of papers and left her alone.

Emily finishes her sandwich and wipes her fingertips across the front of her shorts; she's used to wearing an apron. She opens the till and slides a few quarters from their cubby, meandering toward the jukebox, over the scuffed, uneven floorboards long worn of wax, stained with bitters, ketchup, probably saturated with beer, where her path has crisscrossed thousands of times. The ceiling fan thrums above, dust bunnies clinging to the whirling blades. The frozen smiles of so many men on the wall watch as she goes. That small stage has been too empty for too long. It's time to say goodbye. A bittersweet sensation comes over her as she slips the coins through the slot, a jingle of silver. F12, B08, E27.

A piano ditty, some fiddle, and then Charline Arthur's brassy voice. She smiles, absorbing the sound, replaying memories until tires crunch the gravel in the parking lot. She forgot to lock the door behind Dad, assuming no one would arrive until the open sign was turned. 11:04 a.m. She tries to soak in as much of the song and solitude as she can before the door swings open.

She turns her head and recognizes the figure immediately. Jacob.

He smiles that genuine smile that makes her feel like the only person in the room. And she is. He's here for her. She steadies herself with the jukebox as surprise and pure joy emanate from every cell inside her.

"I'd like some alcohol." His expression is mischievous, playful. He's pleased with himself at the remark, she can tell.

"What are you doing here?" Emily asks, taking quick, shuffling strides toward him, not waiting for an answer, wrapping her arms tight around his torso. He wraps his arms around her too.

"I decided to leave a couple of days early to spend time with Beth. I hope you don't think I'm a stalker."

Emily shakes her head in the crook of his shoulder. He smells like Old Spice. Her cheeks shiver from the intensity of her smile.

When they pull away, she studies his brown eyes— coffee with a bit of cream—the freckles dotting his tanned skin and mouth stretched into a smile. She licks her lips and runs her fingers through his wispy curls.

Wordlessly, their mouths come together, and her body

trembles with wanting and happiness. He pulls her tighter against him, and their tongues respond to one another. He tastes like sweet soda.

"I've been wanting to do this for so long," he whispers between kisses.

"Me too." She kisses his neck, his collarbone. Charline Arthur's voice fades.

"I'm so glad you're here," he says before meeting her lips with his once more, holding her hands in his, firm and steady.

The jukebox plays Emily's next song.

...

Ashley is the first customer of the day, beckoned by Emily to meet Jacob, have some lunch, and listen to her favorite jukebox tune one last time. Then Bernie comes to start his shift, red-eyed and weepy as he enters. "Your dad didn't tell me you'd be here." He's shaken up by the changes ahead but has been promised a job with Grant and Amanda. "I like the idea of a little girl running around here again."

A few locals pop in for a soda and sandwich, a beer and burger. Then Larry comes, then Doug, then Gladys and Jack. They embrace Emily warmly, asking about Door County, The Schooner, "And isn't that the boy we met in spring?" Jacob rises to greet them all as well.

Soon Dad returns, but the conversation and merriment keep Emily behind the bar, Jacob and Ashley on their stools. Larry talks about a beautiful motorcycle ride to the North Shore, swallowing one too many flies, then skipping a stone the farthest he ever has on the surface of Lake Superior. "It's gotta be some kind of record." Fred's on about taxes, as usual, and Margaret's on about the corrupt justice system. Tammy lists the birds who've been frequenting her feeders and birdbaths.

Doug talks about the northerns and walleyes he reeled in. "Flakiest, fattest fish I've ever had," he brags.

Jack takes up residence at the slot machine while Gladys warns Emily about a career in nursing. "You're gonna see some shit. You know that, right? Deal with some crazy people? A friend of mine in the ER says a guy once came in with a toilet brush up his rectum."

At Emily's request, Jacob retrieves his guitar and plays Johnny Cash and Hank Williams covers on the stage, calling her up to sing June Carter's part of "Jackson." She sings the lyrics with that country twang her choir teacher berated her for.

Word spreads that The Honky Tonk is closing. Emily's in town, one night only.

As dinner approaches, Dad and Bernie throw all that's left in the fryer and on the grill while Emily pours beer and mixes cocktails. Soon, high school friends stream in with their parents, Emily's former teachers and basketball coach. Greg Babski, who used to cut her hair, Diane and John, and even Nicole and Todd, who gives Emily an awkward hug across the bar and says, "The place'll be missed."

They pile curds and fish and tenders and fries on serving platters beside a Bud Light ice bucket for money. "Take whatever you want," Dad says. "Five, ten dollars. I don't care. But you're all paying for your drinks!"

Familiar voices and smells and sensations swirl in Emily's brain like the margaritas she's mixing in the blender. She forgets how old she is more than once until she spots Jacob asking Ashley about her art influences, discussing which muscles kayaking works and strengthens with Mr. Anderson, her old basketball coach, and performing "Sweet Caroline" while the crowd sings along, "Bum, bum, bum!" She's giddy. She's giving Jacob knowing glances, and he responds with that smile, a wink. *He's still here*, she thinks.

Dad comes beside her behind the bar, nodding along to the beat of the song, holding his cocktail, wearing a satisfied grin.

"Hey, Dad," she says. He leans his shoulder into her own with a gentle nudge.

"Thanks," he says. Tiny pools of tears reflecting the light around them dance in his eyes.

EPILOGUE
- MAY 2010 -

Emily hunches over The Schooner bar, over her open *Microbiology* textbook, studying for the last final of the semester. She rereads the same paragraph on phagocytes over and over. "They can ingest and even digest foreign particles," she mumbles to herself. She bites her bottom lip and fights the urge to glance at the front door. "They extend their cytoplasm into—"

"So, will she have to push out the afterbirth too? Is that painful?" Chris interrupts.

"Umm, we didn't really get into the specifics of that in anatomy, but I wouldn't think that part is painful," she answers as honestly as she can, trying to reassure him. "It's not bony like the baby, you know." He nods, face etched with worry, and turns to a spreadsheet on the bar containing the summer server schedule: "Emily," "Nora," "Alicia," "Molly," and "Bridget" are written in scribbly block letters. "Colin" and "Ingrid" appear sporadically as well, along with newbies "Tess," "Josh," and "Casey." Emily looks forward to when the place is busy enough for their shifts to overlap. She's looking forward to the conversations, the catching up, the jokes, the laughter, and the comradery. But for now, she tries to study. One more final to go.

"They surround the foreign particle and form a vacuole," she mumbles.

"How will they know they got it all out?" Chris asks.

Emily can't help chuckling. "They've done this a hundred times. I'm sure everything will go smoothly."

He blows out a breath and tugs on his beard. "Waiting is the worst."

Emily doesn't disagree. She spins her barstool toward the entrance once more. She chews on her thumbnail, resigned. Her brain isn't absorbing another thing today. She can't focus. There's too much distraction, too much happening and changing for her to care about cells and enzymes.

She's struggled to focus ever since the snowbirds returned after a winter in Florida or Arizona to open and air out their second homes, plant marigolds and petunias, ready for the comforts of Wisconsin: a decent old-fashioned, cheese curds, fish fry. The first wave of tourists wasn't far behind, slowing traffic as they took in the blossoming cherry trees as fluffy and white as wedding dresses. The transient workers and college students are almost all in the county as well, with their summer clothes and bicycles and dwindled bank accounts.

The snowbirds and tourists and acquaintances and old friends, Alicia and Courtney and Terry and Tyler, all ask Emily how her winter was.

She tells them about the tres leches cake Maria baked for her birthday, about passing the dark nights with trivia, chili, and movies; tailgating outside of Lambeau Field on an eighteen-degree day, strapped into thick snowmobile boots, eating grilled brats, and sucking down a Bloody Mary while it froze from the outside in; ringing in 2010 at The Schooner with cheap champagne and pickled herring one of the regulars brought in for good luck, clearing the dining room of chairs and tables and dancing to Miley Cyrus and Lady Gaga.

She tells them about living in a borrowed home with a toasty gas fireplace, massive television, and the strongest water pressure she's ever experienced, melting the stress knots in her back. She tells them about visiting Ashley in Madison, eating hunks of raw tuna and salsa dancing with strangers. She tells them about sledding down the hills of a snow-covered golf course with Nora, kicking Ryan's ass in cribbage, and accidentally wiping jalapeño juice in her eye when Javier taught them how to make tamales. "It stung so bad!" She tells them the rest of the time was spent in class, at The Schooner, and studying, studying, studying.

She doesn't tell them about scaling precarious piles of ice shoves to be closer to the greenish wisps of northern lights one January night or accidentally burning dinosaur-shaped chicken nuggets when she was babysitting Ingrid's kids one snow day because she was preoccupied gazing at the camper parked in the snow drifts. She doesn't tell them about the journal she keeps, filled with the nightmares that still come, the hurt she's still processing.

She doesn't tell them about watching Ryan wrestle with more than the urge to drink over the winter months, a struggle even Molly couldn't stave away with regular phone calls and periodic visits. He took long walks into the whiteness with Nora or Javier or Emily, but mostly alone, smoking joints and hurling snowballs at trees, sharing bits of what was playing out in his brain—what he saw in the war, what he did. Until Diane, John, and Ashley visited while Nora and Javier were in Mexico, convinced Ryan to call the VA again, commit to biweekly counseling sessions, tour college campuses, apply, pursue that dream of creating video games. He'll start classes in the fall, after a summer working in The Schooner kitchen.

Emily told Jacob about that and the cribbage and sledding and jalapeño juice. He sent her postcards. They exchanged emails. He'd call her using international calling cards from hostels and payphones. They scribbled and typed and talked about their days spent on either end of the globe, about sperm whale sightings and the 206 bones in the body, about diving for paua shells and feeding chickadees from an open palm.

Emily described a Christmas spent visiting her dad at her uncle's farm, snowmobiling from tavern to tavern as they always had, playing darts and pool, eating buffalo wings dipped in ranch and drinking a few beers, about the way they seemed to avoid certain topics, about the mix of trepidation and anticipation she still feels over committing to a trip with him. Jacob described a Christmas spent apart from his family, the guilt and anger that plagued him on a sunny beach singing "Jingle Bells" with a slew of twenty-somethings from around the world.

"Still a lot to work through," he said.

"Same here."

"I miss you."

"I miss you too."

He asked her if maybe they could be boyfriend and girlfriend when he got back.

"Maybe," she said sweetly, certain he could hear the smile on her voice, even over those thousands of miles.

She can't focus because he'll be here soon.

Summer's about to begin.

ACKNOWLEDGEMENTS

Many thanks to you, dear reader, for choosing to spend time with this story. That means the world to me.

And to the early readers, Dan Powers and Sara Niese, who encouraged me on and asked for more chapters. To Ann Heyse, Paul Elliott, and Allison Vroman for the invaluable feedback and kind critiques, and to Katie Dahl for gifting me Anne Lamott's *Bird by Bird* when I felt daunted.

To the countless friends and family members who cheered me on, especially my book club, the Door County Published Authors Collective, and the team at Write On, Door County.

To the staff of Peninsula Publishing – past and present – for the opportunity to share and hone my writing, especially Dave Eliot, Madeline Harrison, Myles Dannhausen Jr., and Allison Vroman. To the restaurants where I served,

Wilson's, Porta Bella, and especially the Cornerstone Pub, for the long-lasting friendships and profound/funny/heartfelt conversations over silverware-rolling.

To the team at Ten 16 Press, for seeing something special in this story and helping me share it with others, especially Shannon Ishizaki for leading the project with such positive energy. To Shannon Booth, my brilliant editor, for polishing *Muddled Cherries* with a keen eye, making this story cleaner and clearer. And to Kaeley Dunteman, for creating the cover of my dreams.

To my loving and supportive family.

To Luke, for never doubting me.

To Mom, my biggest fan, always.

And to Greta, my everything.

Finally, I want to acknowledge the work of Bessel Van Der Kolk, MD, author of *The Body Keeps the Score*, and Judith L. Herman, MD, author of *Truth and Repair*.

For trauma survivors of every kind, one of the most healing and powerful acts an individual or community can offer is simply a listening ear. To those survivors, you and your story matter.